N. J. Crisp is well-known as a writer for television: *Colditz*, *The Expert*, *The Brothers* and *Secret Army*.

He served in the RAF as a pilot from 1943 to 1947 and then tried various jobs while continuing to fly in the RAFVR, including manager of a radiocab firm, trainee with Marks and Spencer and typewriter salesman. By 1951 he could devote all his time to writing short stories – one of which appeared in the volume *Best Saturday Evening Post Stories of 1959*.

Also by N. J. Crisp:

THE GOTLAND DEAL

THE LONDON DEAL

THE ODD JOB MAN

A FAMILY AFFAIR

N. J. Crisp

# Festival

Futura
Macdonald & Co
London & Sydney

A Futura Book

First published in Great Britain in 1981
by Macdonald & Co (Publishers) Ltd
London & Sydney

First Futura edition 1982

Copyright © N. J. Crisp 1981

This book is sold subject to the condition that it shall not, by way of trade or otherwise, be lent, re-sold, hired out or otherwise circulated without the publisher's prior consent in any form of binding or cover other than that in which it is published and without a similar condition including this condition being imposed on the subsequent purchaser

ISBN 0 7088 2090 5

Reproduced, printed and bound in Great Britain by
Hazell Watson & Viney Ltd, Aylesbury, Bucks

Futura Publications
A Division of
Macdonald & Co (Publishers) Ltd
Holywell House
Worship Street
London EC2A 2EN

# AUTHOR'S NOTE

The central characters in this novel are imaginary, and do not exist, but since a play was needed to which they could refer, I used a stage play of my own which, at the time I began writing this book, had not yet been produced.

By chance, and at short notice, that play was premiered at the delightful Theatre Royal, Windsor, where it was called *Jet Set*, in October 1979.

By then the novel was in its final stages, but, in fairness to the well-known and excellent cast, and the highly efficient management at Windsor, I should perhaps make it plain that my own 'first night' was a happy occasion and, thank heavens, bore no resemblance to the fictional and far less pleasant one portrayed in these pages.

On the other hand, although I suffered no such agonies myself, I am given to understand that similar events are not completely unknown.

N. J. Crisp
London
*January 1980*

# CHAPTER ONE

The Sunday traffic was light. Once past Richmond, he put his foot down. Nicola spoke for the first time since they had left the flat.

'Why the sudden rush?'

'You said it started at twelve,' he said.

'We don't want to be the first ones there.'

He allowed the speedometer needle to fall back, and normal silence was resumed until they reached the M3.

'You take the first turn off,' Nicola said.

He fumbled for the London *A-Z*, and handed it to her. 'You'd better look it up.'

'I told you,' Nicola said with bleak patience, 'Staines Road, past Kempton Park racecourse, and turn right. Maurice said you can't miss it.'

'Have you ever been there?' he enquired rhetorically. 'No. So just look it up, will you please?'

She opened the *A-Z*, and bent her head. He could not hear the sigh, but it was there all right. The turn-off came up. At the bottom of the sliproad was a complicated looking roundabout, governed by traffic lights. The first set turned green, and a Mercedes behind hooted at him with deep-throated imperious impatience.

'Which way now?' he demanded, confused.

'There,' she said, pointing. 'It says Staines.'

He followed the sign, which led to the right. The Mercedes swooped past contemptuously and disappeared. They drove on for what seemed a long time. No racecourse appeared.

'How far is Kempton Park supposed to be?' he asked.

'I don't know.'

'It'll show you on the map.'

'Christ,' Nicola said. She closed the *A-Z*, and threw it

on the back seat. 'Why can't you follow simple directions without having to pore over a map? It's a disease.'

When they reached the outskirts of Staines he pulled into a filling station, bought some petrol he did not need, and asked where Kempton Park racecourse was. The attendant looked at him, amused.

'The other side of the M3, mate. Miles away.'

He paid for his unwanted petrol, climbed back into the car, turned round, and set off in the direction from which they had come.

'Why are you going this way?' Nicola asked.

'Because we've been going the *wrong* way,' he said tightly.

'We can't have been. Maurice distinctly said turn off the M3 on to Staines Road.'

'Staines Road,' he said 'runs between Staines and Kingston. We should have turned left, not right.'

Nicola looked at her watch. 'It'll be all over before we even get there, at this rate.'

'It would help if you could learn to read a map.'

'Don't patronise me because you've cocked things up,' Nicola said dangerously. 'It wasn't me who spent bloody hours on the phone. I was ready and waiting.'

The telephone conversation had lasted no more than a few minutes, but he managed to swallow his resentment of her hyperbole. He knew that the calls irritated her, for some reason. He saw his small son one Sunday in four, at his mother's house, where his former wife delivered the boy before he arrived, and collected him after he had departed. The remaining three Sundays in every month he invariably spoke to James on the telephone. He cherished those brief chats, the sound of the boy's clear, treble voice, but afterwards he always felt sad. Nicola, whom he had only met months after the decree absolute, would usually leave him alone until he came out of it, for which he was grateful. It showed that she understood, to some extent, but other occasions, like today, showed that she did not understand all of it by a long way.

Regrets were one thing. They were natural enough, time would take care of most of them, and when chance had led to him meeting Nicola, so different, so warm, so frank, so honest, those which remained should have vanished. Most had. But not about James.

The child constantly recurred in his thoughts. The boy would grow up without him, monitored only at four-weekly intervals, and then only for three or four hours. Most of his son's life he would never know about. He felt as though part of his very being had been amputated. He could not help that feeling, but neither had he ever been able satisfactorily to explain it to Nicola.

Maurice opened the door, holding a bottle of red wine and a corkscrew. He was wearing black trousers, a black silk shirt, and a pendant on a gold chain round his neck.

'Hello, darling,' he said. 'We'd given you up. Glad you could come, Harry.'

'We got lost,' Harry said. 'My fault.' He had met Maurice once before, at a pub in Derby, a few weeks before.

'No it wasn't,' Nicola said. 'I've been giving him a bad time.' Her whole manner had changed, instantaneously, as it often could. She gave Maurice the warm, delightful smile which transformed her face, and hugged him affectionately. 'How's everything?'

'Fine,' Maurice said. He closed the door. 'What have you done to your hair?'

'Had it lightened,' Nicola said. 'I felt like a change.'

'You daft tart,' Maurice said. 'They're all in there. Well, those who could get here. Some can't make it.' He indicated the room from which a babble of conversation and laughter was coming.

'I brought this,' Harry said. He handed over the bottle of Beaujolais he was clutching.

'Oh thanks,' Maurice said. 'Stick it on the table with the Spanish-type plonk. What's yours? Red or white?'

'Red, please,' Harry said.

He carried his glass of wine into the room. The floor boards were bare, and it was either sparsely furnished or had been cleared for the occasion. He recognised none of the people there, and felt like an outsider. He was an outsider. He even looked like an outsider. He was the only man present who was wearing a tie, much less a suit.

Nicola was in a good mood now, laughing and happy among her own kind. She was talking to a stocky, dark, good-looking man in the far corner. A silent girl held his arm timidly.

'. . . what a night. Everything went wrong. Do you remember? Oh, no, you'd left before then.'

'Got the elbow, you mean.'

'Get off. You were jolly good.'

'I could have been, I think. Never seemed to get the chance, somehow.'

'We were all the same,' Nicola said. 'The great undiscovered discoveries.'

'Sir's henchman invited me for a drink. I knew that was it, either a lead at last, or the elbow. "Leonard," he said, "you have a splendid talent which I much admire." Well, he had to say that, since he'd been instrumental in having me taken on in the first place. "However," he went on, "the plans we have in mind for the forthcoming year do not appear to offer you the opportunities you so richly deserve." So I knew Sir's henchman was playing hatchet man and it was the elbow.'

'That's what I got,' Nicola said. 'He must have a set speech.'

'Saves him learning a new one, I suppose. How did you find it after you left?'

'Awful,' Nicola said. 'I was out of work for nearly a year.'

'Ah, well, at least Maurice remembered us.'

'Yes, thank God for Maurice.'

Harry lit a cigarette and stopped listening. They were like people reminiscing about the old school. Well, he supposed it was like that.

Maurice was talking to someone else nearby.

'Bernard couldn't make it.'

'What about Marcia? Is she coming?'

'She's at Leatherhead, and Lewis is at Colchester or

Cambridge, I forget which, and there's some complication about who's looking after Randolph, some relation who's developed hives or leprosy or something. I gave up, it all got far too complicated.'

'Fancy calling a little boy Randolph. He's going to be Randy from the time he finds out what it's for.'

'Unless he grows up to be queer.'

Harry gave that up too, mystified. No one offered to introduce him to anybody. He wandered back into the hall and refilled his glass.

'Thank heavens someone brought something decent,' a deep, velvet voice said over his shoulder.

Harry looked up at a tall, handsome man, who picked up the bottle of Beaujolais.

'Me,' Harry said.

'Then drink it, I implore you,' the man said. 'For the sake of your liver.'

'It's all right,' Harry said. 'I don't mind Spanish.'

'Well, I do,' the man said, 'so with your permission . . .'

'Help yourself,' Harry said.

'I will. In fact, why don't we take it with us, to guard against the urgent pangs of thirst?'

He's pissed out of his mind, Harry thought.

'As you may shrewdly suspect,' the man said, 'I am well-nigh pissed out of my mind, a condition I intend to cling to for the remainder of the day. Not a bad do, is it? Apart from the rotgut.'

'Very pleasant,' Harry said.

'Yes. Hospitable bloke, Maurice. Ah, darling,' he said. 'Allow me to introduce . . . I beg your pardon, sir, but I didn't catch your name.'

'Harry,' Harry said. 'Harry Belmont.'

'How do you do.' She was a slim, attractive woman in her late thirties.

'This is Harry Belmont,' the man said, 'to whom I was just remarking . . . on second thoughts, I shall remark later. Excuse me. Nature calls.'

He wondered out of sight, carrying the bottle. Harry cleared his throat, and offered his packet of cigarettes.

'Do you smoke?'

'No, thank you.'

Harry lit a cigarette for himself. He was acutely conscious that everyone was chattering amiably to everybody else, except him and this unknown woman. Moments dragged by. It seemed like five minutes.

'I'm terribly sorry,' he said uneasily. She wore a wedding ring, but that was no guide. 'The gentleman who introduced us . . . I don't actually know who . . . that is . . .'

She smiled. 'Ben Stamford. My husband. I'm Veronica. Not to worry. He's like that.'

'Ben Stamford. Of course. I thought I knew his face,' Harry said, untruthfully. They smiled brightly at each other. Harry sought desperately for inspiration.

'Have you come far?' she asked eventually, with deep interest.

'Shepherds Bush,' Harry said. 'You?'

'Kilburn.'

'Ah, yes.' Harry tried to think of something intelligent to say about Kilburn, and failed. 'Quite enjoyable, driving this morning, quiet roads and so on, wasn't it?'

'We haven't got a car,' Veronica said. 'Ben lost his licence last year.'

There seemed no need to enquire why Ben had lost his licence last year. 'Don't you drive?'

'Yes,' Veronica said, 'but we were flat broke anyway, at the time, so we sold the car.'

One thing about these people, Harry thought, in his limited experience anyway, they often shamed conventional social prevaricators like himself with their unexpected frankness.

He said, 'It wasn't an enjoyable drive, it was hell. We were late starting out, we lost our way, and ended up spitting and snarling like cat and dog.'

Veronica laughed then, and he thought she was probably a rather nice, if shy woman.

'Who's the other half of the "we"?'she asked.

'Nicola Feary.'

'Oh, are you with Nicola?'

'Yes.' His status, apparently, was far from being common knowledge.

'I'm very fond of Nicola. She's a lovely girl.'

'Yes.' Yes, she was, he thought. Everyone said she was. He knew she was. So why, increasingly of late, was she nothing of the kind?

Maurice was clinking a spoon against his glass.

'Can we have a bit of hush, please?' He had a light, soft voice, and no one took much notice. He raised the pitch an octave. 'Will you lot kindly belt up for a minute?'

'Silence for our revered lord and master!' Ben Stamford bellowed from the doorway, his summons from nature attended to. There were a few cries of encouragement, but after that they all turned towards Maurice, expectantly.

'Thank you,' Maurice said. He rotated a smile at his captive audience. There was something curiously feline about his well-ordered, regular features. 'I thought I'd better say a few words before you all get completely smashed.'

'Too late, squire,' Ben Stamford remarked. The bottle of Beaujolais in his strong right hand was empty, Harry noted.

'To all of you,' Maurice went on, 'thank you for coming, and a special welcome to those you've brought with you, girlfriends, boyfriends, lovers, and even a few wives and husbands, I notice. It's good to have you here, all of you, but if the guests will forgive me, I'd just like to address a few remarks to those whom it will be my pleasure to work with for the next six months,'

'Oh, don't start cracking the whip already,' Leonard groaned.

'Any more cheek from you, and I'll send you back to Birmingham,' Maurice said.

'Not that!' Leonard threw up his hands, as if warding off a curse. 'Anything but that.'

There was a general laugh. Harry smiled politely. He had not the faintest idea what they were laughing at.

'Leonard did six episodes of that dreadful soap opera,' Veronica Stamford whispered into his ear.

'Oh, I see,' Harry whispered back, 'thank you.' Either she was a perceptive lady, or his expression had conveyed utter ignorance instead of amusement. Both, probably.

'Speaking of Birmingham reminds me,' Ben Stamford reminisced, 'of the time I met Uncle Lew, or Lord Grade as he is sometimes affectionately called by his intimates. Well, not always affectionately, come to think of it . . .'

'Shut up, Ben, there's a good chap,' Maurice said. 'You can hold forth later. Just now, it's my turn.'

'Sorry,' Ben said, contritely. 'Sorry.' His expressive hands mimed the action of sewing his lips closed.

'Before I agreed to do this season,' Maurice said, 'I insisted on a completely free hand. The unquestioned freedom to choose the plays I want, and the people I want. Well, I got my free hand. That's why you're all here. I'm not interested in second choices. Only the best, and that's what I've got. Most of you have worked with me before, and I know you're all good, but let me tell you this. You're going to be better than you've ever been. I know exactly what I'm after, and together we're going to achieve it. What? Simple. The finest season there's ever been, or ever will be, at Treganwy.'

There was a silence. Harry was no part of any of it, but even he was impressed. He studied Maurice Gardiner. Despite the man's normal relaxed, informal jokiness, there was no doubt about it – when he chose, he could inspire something close to awe, or even adulation from this hand-picked group of very different individuals. He thought back to that pub in Derby. Perhaps it had been there too, at least in Nicola's attitude, even though he had not noticed it at the time.

'Is that how you pronounce it?' Leonard wondered. 'Treganwy?'

'So the Professor tells me,' Maurice said.

'What's he like? Supposed to be a bit of an autocrat, isn't he?'

'He'll walk all over you if you let him,' Maurice said, tolerantly, 'but provided you stand up to him he's all right. He's like most people accustomed to having their own way, he needs a firm hand. As for what he's like – a typical establishment figure, I suppose. Wealthy land-owning family, manor house, Justice of the Peace, local bigwig, practically hats off and forelock-pulling stuff.'

'With a name like David Griffiths,' Ben said, 'there's got to be a touch of the look-you's.'

'Not a bit of it,' Maurice said. 'Completely anglicised. I think they were a border family originally, and what with Harrow and Cambridge, the Guards during the war, and being Professor of Eng. Lit. back at his old college, until his father died and he took over the estate, I doubt if he pronounces Treganwy correctly anyway.'

'You seem to know a lot about him,' Leonard said curiously.

'He talks a lot,' Maurice said, 'about himself and the theatre which he tends to regard as one and the same thing, although I'm weaning him away from that idea. Just the same, you have to give the man credit. I mean, who in their right mind, twenty years ago, would have dreamed of a summer theatre at Treganwy, which was no more than a somewhat shabby would-be genteel spa in its heyday, and that must have been before Methuselah was born. A place with a few quietly dying hotels, whose principal claim to fame was that you could see Snowdon on a clear day, if you were lucky? But he did it, single-handed at first, just a makeshift, temporary building in the early days, then bullied and cajoled the money from God knows where for the present theatre, wonderful sight lines, flexible stage, all the facilities, beautifully equipped. Twenty years ago, nothing. Today, a tourist attraction, the hotels refurbished, full all through the season. O.K., it's a centre for Snowdonia as well, but mostly it's the theatre pulls them there, not only a repertoire of plays audiences enjoy seeing, but a prestigious place for people like us to work. O.K., nowadays it's run on Arts Council grants, and County Council grants, and District Council grants, and trust funds, and Lord knows what else, but it was the Prof who drummed up all the loot in the first place. You have to give him that, and at least not yawn in his face when he carries on as though the theatre was his own personal property. I reckon he's owed that much.'

'A friend of mine worked there two or three years ago,' Nicola said, 'and she told me he used to invite the cast to a reception after the first night of each play, and then go round telling all of them what he thought of their performances. I don't mean the usual rubbish, how lovely, you were marvellous. Criticising. Making suggestions.'

'There'll be no crap like that,' Maurice said firmly. 'There'll be no interference from the Prof, and that's a promise. There's only one boss this season, and that's me. He understands that. I know exactly what I'm after, and I'm going to get it. They've had some good seasons at Treganwy, but nothing like this one's going to be. We're going to set the standard for the future. In the year 2000 old men will be telling their grandchildren how lucky they were to see the plays we're putting on at Treganwy this year. Now, since even I can't follow that, I suggest you all go and have something to eat. There's still plenty of wine left, and you'll need something to mop it up.'

The quiches and pâtés, the salads and French bread and cheese were laid out attractively in the small dining room. Harry stood his ground in the friendly elbowing for position, found a plate eventually, and helped himself. He found Nicola beside him for the first time since they had arrived. Someone must have worked hard to produce such a tempting array.

'Did Maurice do all this?' he asked.

'No,' Nicola said. 'Stage management. Linda and Alan, and I think Marion made the quiches.'

'Oh.' He supposed the names belonged to some of the younger faces present, but he had no idea which. He forked a piece of quiche from his plate. Someone jogged his elbow, and he nearly speared his palate. He choked quietly for a few seconds.

'There's a chair over there,' Nicola said patiently. 'Balance it on your knee.'

Harry sat down next to a small, pretty girl who looked about nineteen. They nodded and smiled at each other politely.

'You've met Leonard's girlfriend, Sue, haven't you,' Nicola said.

'No,' Harry said. 'Hullo, Sue.'

'Hullo,' Sue said. She dealt efficiently with her salad. She was a tidy eater. 'Which plays are you going to be in?'

'None of them,' Harry said. 'I'm not involved in all this carry-on.' For some reason, he thought she might not be either. Still, best to be cautious. 'Are you in the business?'

'No. I'm a receptionist. What do you do?'

'Well, on my passport, it says I'm a banker,' Harry said.

'God, that sounds grand,' Sue said, impressed. 'What do you do? Invest in plays or something?'

'I'd be hard pressed to back a Punch and Judy Show,' Harry said. 'And it would be a pretty eccentric banker who risked money in the theatre, anyway. In any case, all I really am is Foreign Clerk in a small merchant bank. Just one of the ants who swarm into the City every day.'

'Oh. I see,' Sue said. She placed her knife and fork neatly on her empty plate. 'Will you be able to go to Treganwy to see any of the plays?'

'The odd weekend, with any luck,' Harry said. 'Although it's not all that easy to get to. And I'll probably spend my holiday there during the summer. Will you be going?'

'I don't know,' Sue said. 'I only met Leonard last week. Would you like me to bring you some trifle?'

'No thanks,' Harry said. 'But I'll fetch some for you.'

'No, really,' Sue said. 'I think I'll see what's happened to Leonard anyway.' She got up and smiled at him. 'See you later.'

Harry turned round to talk to Nicola, and found that she had disappeared in the meantime. He looked at his watch, and concentrated on his food. He wondered what time Nicola would be ready to go.

There had been a cold, continuous drizzle, all the way from London to Derby, when he had driven up the M1 that Saturday. It was Nicola's last night. She had been appearing there for six weeks, and he had arranged to drive her back to London.

The weather seemed to have kept the local citizens at home, and the Playhouse was half empty. Harry collected his complimentary ticket from the the box office and sat through the final performance. The play was Alan Ayckbourn's *Relatively Speaking*, and Harry thought it was very funny. He also thought, as usual, that Nicola was exceptionally good. Not that, he gathered from Nicola, he was qualified to judge such matters. Sometimes, when he passed a favourable comment on a performance in a television play or series episode, she would look at him, astounded, as though some apparently intelligent person had suddenly revealed himself as the village idiot. 'How can you possibly be so blind?' she would wonder. 'She was way over the top. She didn't feel any of it. It was all tricks, trembling lips, and wide eyes into the camera. There was nothing good about it. It was pure, unadulterated crap.' And Harry would shrug, and keep his peace. She was probably right. He was not equipped to distinguish between the true and the false in an actor's performance. What he knew about was foreign exchange. Just the same, he thought Nicola was good that night. He thought he was right about that.

Afterwards he met her at the stage door, carried her suitcases to his car, and stowed them in the boot.

'I said I'd see the others for a drink before we leave,' Nicola said. 'Do you mind?'

'No, of course not.'

The pub the company used was in a side street. There was a juke box in the Lounge Bar, and the landlord was calling time as they walked in.

'Too late,' Harry said.

'We use the little bar at the back,' Nicola said. She led him through. 'They know us here. We shan't be thrown out.'

So it proved. She introduced him casually to the people there.

'This is Harry. Elaine, Frank, Deborah, Victor, and this is our director, Malcolm.'

'Hullo . . . how do you do . . . hullo . . .' Harry made polite noises, promptly forgot which name belonged to which face, covered his ignorance by buying a round of drinks, and sat at a small table with Nicola.

A man of about thirty-five, with an oddly feline cast of feature, came in and propped himself on the bar, talking to the director. He waved at Nicola, and smiled. 'Hullo, darling.'

'Hullo, Maurice,' Nicola said, smiling back.

'Who's that?' Harry asked, in an undertone.

'Maurice Gardiner,' Nicola said. 'He was a director at the National when I was there. He was in tonight. Come up to see Malcolm, I suppose. They're old mates.'

Harry glanced at his watch. 'We ought to be going fairly soon,' he said. 'So if you want to talk to your friends . . .'

'I thought you were splendid, darling,' the light voice with the neutral accent said. Maurice Gardiner had come over to their table, a glass of scotch in his hand.

'Thank you,' Nicola said. 'This is . . .'

'Hopelessly miscast, of course,' Maurice went on. 'I've just been telling Malcolm so. Not your sort of part at all, he should have known better, but you sailed in all guns blazing, and pulled it off just the same.' He appeared to be ready to continue his analysis, but Nicola managed to cut in and effect the introductions. Harry knew that she did not like her work discussed in front of him, and could see that she was embarrassed.

'Hullo, Harry,' Maurice said. 'Let me get you two a drink. What would you like? Same again?'

'As a matter of fact,' Nicola said, 'we were just going.'

'You can't do that,' Maurice said firmly. 'Not when I've come all this way to see you.'

'We don't have to go yet,' Harry said. 'Let me buy you one. Scotch and water, isn't it?'

He went to the bar, bought the drinks, and came back again.

Maurice was saying '. . . so I shall be running the Festival at Treganwy, this year.'

'How marvellous,' Nicola said.

'Thanks.' Maurice took his drink. 'Your good health.' Harry lit a cigarette, and sat in silence.

'Not a bad programme, although I say so myself,' Maurice said. 'Which it should be, since I chose it. Well, with the exception of the obligatory genuflection in the direction of Welsh nationalism in the form of a rubbishy play by some pseudo who's supposed to be the Welsh George Bernard Shaw, which he most certainly is not. Still, I can't get out of that one. Must have something local to keep the county grants rolling in. It concerns an unspeakably boring family of English intellectuals who arrive in Wales, and meet an old shepherd with an allegedly silver tongue. It's all as multi-syllabically pretentious as you'd expect, but Bernard Fyfield can do the Welsh bit as the shepherd, so we'll just about get away with it.'

'Oh, will Bernard be there?'

'I know he's an old fart,' Maurice said, 'but he can be very good, if he's directed properly.'

Nicola made a non-committal noise, and sipped her drink.

'Apart from Bernard,' Maurice said, 'I'm taking Robin Haslem, Leonard Sherwen, Ben Stamford . . .'

'All the old crowd from the National days,' Nicola said affectionately.

'That's right,' Maurice said. 'Good people who haven't yet had the recognition they deserve. I wondered if you'd like to come aboard.'

'Me?' Nicola was genuinely surprised. She was touchingly modest sometimes, Harry thought. He stubbed out his cigarette and smothered a yawn.

'Unless you've got something coming up,' Maurice said.

'After tonight, I'm out of work,' Nicola said. 'My agent thinks I should stay in London, and try and get back into telly.'

'Well, up to you entirely,' Maurice said. 'We'll be doing *The Importance of being Earnest*. I thought you might like to play Gwendolen.'

'I've already done that on tour,' Nicola said doubtfully.

'I know,' Maurice said. 'I saw you in it. That's what made me think of you. Then there'll be the *Dream*, played Elizabethan style, none of your circus ring shit, for which I shall need a Helena.'

'That takes me back to the days when I got the Best Student award at drama school,' Nicola said.

'They're good parts,' Maurice said signficantly.

'Oh, I know,' Nicola said. 'And I'm sure you'll make them seem different, but . . . what else is in the repertoire?'

'Apart from the Welsh rubbish,' Maurice said, 'which wouldn't concern you, that's cast already, I'll be putting on a sort of entertainment, singing, dancing, a light-hearted thing I've written myself.'

'Well, that settles it,' Nicola said. 'I can't sing.'

'It's not a bloody opera,' Maurice said patiently. 'You'd only have a couple of solos, and you'd be coached for those.'

'I don't know,' Nicola said. 'Singing scares the knickers off me, it really does. I appreciate you thinking of me, Maurice, honestly, but . . .'

'Well, that's the repertoire,' Maurice said. 'Except for *Uncle Vanya*.'

'*Uncle Vanya?*' A far-away, covetous look came into Nicola's eyes. 'That's one part I've always wanted to play,' she said, dreamily. 'Yeliena.'

'Yeliena? That's very interesting,' Maurice said. The pause was only momentary, but Harry, watching his face with detached interest, was certain that the man was making lightning-fast calculations and adjustments in his head. 'Yes,' he went on. 'That could fit in very nicely. So if you can play Yeliena, you don't mind having a bash at a bit of warbling.'

'To do Yeliena,' Nicola said, 'I'd strip off twice nightly.'

'You don't have to go that far,' Maurice said. 'At least, not for my benefit. That's agreed then. Gwendolen, Helena, Yeliena, and a few pranks in my entertainment. I'll get on to your agent on Monday.'

'When do we start?'

'Rehearse in London end of February, beginning of March. Travel to Treganwy, more rehearsals there, open in April. The Festival finishes second week in September, but we may do a short tour after that. I'll let you have all the dates.'

Harry drove out of Derby, and gained the motorway. His headlights cut an advancing swathe of light in front of the car, and he cruised at a comfortable sixty miles an hour. Nicola said nothing, and he thought she might have gone to sleep, but when he glanced quickly at her, sideways, her eyes were wide open.

'You'll be away all summer,' he said. Already he could feel the sad ache of the approaching separation.

'It's six months' work,' Nicola said. 'Besides, Treganwy's a marvellous place to be, especially with someone like Maurice directing.' Her fingers squeezed his knee briefly. 'I shall find a lovely little cottage,' she said, entering into one of her day-dreams with which he was familiar. 'And you can come and stay whenever you can get away for the weekend, and there'll be bank holidays, and if you take all of your holiday at once, you could spend August there. I shan't be rehearsing any more then, we'll have the days to ourselves, and we can climb Snowdon, and apparently there are wonderful beaches within a couple of hours' drive . . . I can't wait. It'll be fantastic.'

Harry smiled affectionately, but said nothing. He thought it more likely that she would end up sharing cramped digs with two or three others, and that access to any beaches would be highly theoretical in view of the climate. Wales was not exactly the Costa del Sol. It would probably rain most of the time. But she enjoyed her fantasies, and hated it when his common sense punctured them. He had learned not to do that, except by accident, or from extreme irritation.

'I wonder how much my agent will get for me?' Nicola wondered aloud, the practical side of her nature reasserting itself.

She found out a few days later, during the course of a querulous telephone conversation.

'I told him that eighty pounds a week was ridiculous for an actress of your standing,' her agent said. 'No one goes to a place like Treganwy for less than a hundred a week any more, but Maurice says that eighty a week is as much as he can manage. Claims there just isn't the money available, and that only two people in the entire company are getting a hundred or just over, and most of them have settled for less. I think you should turn it down.'

'At least I'd be working, Clive,' Nicola said.

'By the time you've found somewhere to live and kept yourself,' Clive's voice said metallically in her ear, 'you'd be working for practically nothing. The allowances are appalling, as well. I don't know why Equity let them get away with it. So I'll tell him you don't want to do it, O.K.?'

'No, wait a minute,' Nicola said. 'If I don't take this, what else is there coming up?'

'I've put you up for several parts in television recently . . .'

'Yes, but nothing's happened,' Nicola said. 'I haven't even had an interview.'

'They didn't feel you were right,' Clive said, 'but they were all very interested in you, and promised to bear you in mind for the future.'

'I don't want to be out of work for bloody months again,' Nicola said.

'You'd be better off staying in London, and keeping yourself available,' Clive said. 'Queening it in Treganwy just isn't worth it, not at eighty a week. If you cut yourself off for six months, people forget you.'

'Something could come of it,' Nicola argued. 'Treganwy's always reviewed in the posh papers, and Maurice is a marvellous director . . .'

'Darling,' Clive said acidly, 'I don't care how talented he is, he's fizzled out like a roman candle in the past, and he'll fizzle out again at Treganwy. The man's either an egomaniac or half potty. Why do you suppose he didn't get anywhere when he was at the National? Because he's always got on the wrong side of the people who matter, and he always will.'

'I don't give a fuck about the people who matter,' Nicola said, her face flushed with anger. 'I like working for Maurice, he's offered me a part no one else has ever let me play, and I'd rather spend six months in Treganwy than sign on at the labour exchange every week, and sit around waiting for the bloody phone to ring.'

'Well, it's up to you,' Clive said coldly. 'My advice is to turn it down, but you're perfectly entitled to disregard my advice if you feel you know better. I'll ring Maurice now, and tell him you'll accept eighty a week.'

Nicola hung up, and looked at Harry. Her hands were shaky, and apprehension was setting in.

'I think my agent's going to give me the sack,' she said.

The red wine had run out. Harry sampled the white, but it was sharp and bitter, and he abandoned it. In the kitchen two girls and a young man, whom he assumed were stage management, were cheerfully washing up. One of the girls made a cup of instant coffee for him and he carried it back to the living room, perched himself on the window sill, and lit a cigarette, which tasted harsh and disagreeable. He was smoking too much, but there was nothing else to do.

The talk was more boisterous now, voices were pitched higher under the influence of the Spanish wine which might be inferior but still possessed an effective alcohol content, and a noisy argument had developed.

Harry had missed the beginning of it, but Maurice Gardiner was holding forth excitedly.

'. . . jealousy is the most destructive emotion in the human catalogue of idiocy. What's more, it's silly, and utterly demeaning.'

'Surely the point is, the way Othello is manipulated by an evil man, himself jealous of Othello's essential goodness.' The speaker was a tall, thin man with a beaked nose.

'No, Robin, that is not the point,' Maurice asserted impatiently. The man with the nose must be Robin Haslem, Harry supposed, adding one more to his limited cross-index of names and faces. Perhaps the rather beautiful red-haired woman beside him was his wife? 'What difference does it make if Desdemona *had* been screwing around a bit on side?'

'I should have thought it made a lot of difference,' Leonard Sherwen said.

'Why?' Maurice demanded. 'Sex is a natural function, no more than a means of reproduction which happens to be briefly enjoyable as well. The whole idea of so-called faithfulness is to do with property, not morality. Men wanted to be certain that their heirs came from their own cocks and not someone else's. Surely the pill's finally killed off such a stupid by-product of bourgeois capitalism. If a woman feels better for an affair with someone else, why not? Why shouldn't she? It's always been O.K. for men. I'll bet Othello had the odd bash when he was away fighting all those wars.'

'Well, if I were married,' Leonard said, 'I should take exception if my wife started having it off with someone else.' His newly acquired girlfriend looked pleased, and somewhat hopeful.

'In that case, you'd be treating your wife like a piece of property, not a human being,' Maurice said. 'That's no more than possessiveness, pride, hurt feelings, yes, and in a way, the worst kind of avarice.'

The sudden shrill of a telephone ringing from, it seemed, some point under Harry's feet, made him start. He looked down. The ringing telephone was on the floor.

'Someone tell whoever it is to ring back tomorrow,' Maurice commanded, and went on developing his theme.

Harry supposed he was the appointed someone, crouched down, and lifted the receiver. He could not hear what the caller was saying in the hubbub.

'Sorry,' Harry said. 'Could you call back tomorrow?'

'No, I could not', the voice said, sharper and louder. 'This is Professor Griffiths. Who is that?'

'Hold on,' Harry said. He covered the phone. 'Maurice,' he called. 'It's your Professor. I think he wants to talk to you.'

'Oh, really,' Maurice said, with an exaggerated sigh. 'That man's incapable of dealing with the smallest thing without referring to me first. Still, I suppose I should be thankful it's not midnight, which is not unknown.' He crossed to Harry, and took the phone. 'Hullo . . . a get-together for some of the cast . . . well, yes . . . when? . . .' Conversation had stopped. Harry could hear the sharp squawk from the earpiece but not what the Professor was saying. 'Where are you? . . . oh, I see . . . could we make it the morning? . . . why, what's happened? . . . well, I suppose I'll have to . . . yes, but I'm not a member . . . yes.'

Maurice hung up. They were all looking at him with curiosity.

'The Professor's in London,' he said, 'and he feels we should meet and discuss final arrangements. He's got a meeting with the Arts Council tomorrow, so I'm afraid I shall have to humour the old boy, and leave fairly soon. There's still plenty of wine left, well white anyway, Ben's knocked off all the red, so you lot can carry on in my absence.'

'As a matter of fact, it's time we were going anyway,' Veronica Stamford said.

'I'll give you a lift,' Leonard said.

'Nonsense,' Maurice said. 'Stay as long as you like. No need to break up the party just because the Prof wants me to hold his hand.'

'No. Our children have gone to some friends, but we must pick them up soon,' Veronica said.

'Same with us,' Carol Haslem said. 'I promised my mother we wouldn't be late.'

The exodus began, and the party ended in a flurry of thanks and good wishes.

'I enjoyed that,' Nicola said. 'Do you know the way back home?'

'Yes,' Harry said. 'We join the M3 at the next roundabout.' He drove carefully. Given the food, he thought he was inside the limit, but he did not wish to test his assumption by being breathalysed. 'Why was Maurice so heated about *Othello*?'

'It was nothing to do with *Othello*,' Nicola said. 'He was being defensive. His live-in girlfriend's a model. She works abroad a lot, and she's been having it off with someone. Or at least, he thinks she is. She probably is.

She was having a ding-dong with a fellow when Maurice was at the National. It's a pretty peculiar relationship.'

'Maurice strikes me as a pretty peculiar chap all round,' Harry said.

'He's talented, he knows what he wants, and he thinks I'm good,' Nicola said. 'That's all I care about.'

Maurice parked his car on a yellow line and walked into the Garrick Club. He had changed into a suit, and was wearing a tie, which always irked him. An attendant asked for his name, agreed that he was expected, and showed him upstairs to a bar.

Professor Griffiths was talking to someone who looked like a judge. He caught Maurice's eye and nodded briefly. The Professor was an austere-looking man, tall, with thinning white hair, who smiled only rarely, probably because he had no discernible sense of humour.

Maurice stood where he was, shifting from one foot to another, until the Professor left his companion and gestured Maurice to join him. Maurice was developing a headache, and he asked for an orange juice. The Professor ordered champagne for himself, and led the way to a quiet table.

'We can talk here without being overheard,' he said. 'I can't give you more than half an hour, I'm afraid. I'm dining with Judge Wilby. Have you completed your casting?'

'Yes,' Maurice said. 'I signed Nicola Feary last week. She'll play Gwendolen, Helena and Yeliena.'

Professor Griffiths frowned. 'I don't quite understand you,' he said frostily. 'We agreed on Sally Warran for Yeliena, not Miss Feary.'

'Sally turned it down flat,' Maurice said. 'If we could pay decent money, we might have got her, but . . .'

'We pay what we can afford,' the Professor said. 'In any case, I authorised you to offer her a hundred a week.'

'She laughed in my face,' Maurice said. 'Anyway, Nicola settled for eighty, so we're saving twenty quid a week.'

'I wish you'd consulted me about this,' the Professor said. 'I'm sure there must be better people available than Miss Feary.'

'I can't spend my life on the phone clearing everything with you, Professor,' Maurice said tightly. 'Nor do I intend to. I'm the Director of Productions, time was running short, Nicola was free, I had to take a decision and I did.'

'I think you made a mistake, not a decision, Mr Gardiner,' the Professor said. 'I prefer to see artistes of better standing than Miss Feary appearing at my Festival.'

'Nicola's a good actress,' Maurice said. 'I can only assume you don't know her work.'

'I've seen her on several occasions,' Professor Griffiths said, 'and I disagree with your assessment of her.'

'Well, that's too bad,' Maurice said. 'Nicola's what you've got.' The familiar bubble of black anger was rising inside him, threatening to burst. He tried to control it. He had to remain on at least reasonable terms with this irritating individual for the next six months, and for preference something better than that. It had gone wrong too many times in the past. This Festival was his chance to get back, to mend his fences with the National, or impress the Royal Shakespeare, or interest West End managements. It was vital not to blow this one. He tried to inject a conciliatory tone into his voice. 'Keep an open mind, Professor, that's all I ask. I know how to get the best out of Nicola. I think she may surprise you as Yeliena.'

One of the Professor's rare smiles, or at least a look of inner self-satisfaction, flitted briefly across his features. 'As it happens, we shall never know whether you're right about that or not,' he said, 'although I very much doubt it. Miss Feary will not be playing Yeliena.'

'There's no other way,' Maurice said, trying to suppress his impatience. Was the man incapable of comprehending the complications of casting five productions in repertoire? 'When I couldn't get Sally, I had to switch some of the parts around. Marcia's too old, Linda hasn't got enough experience, Fiona's in four productions already, she can't possibly do five . . .'

'I'm not referring to your permutations, Mr Gardiner,' the Professor said. 'Miss Feary will not play Yeliena because the entire repertoire will have to be revised. You will be kind enough to let me have a draft of the new dates within a few days. Fortunately the programmes and publicity material have not yet gone to the printers.'

'Revised? Why?' Maurice asked, confused and baffled. What the hell was the idiot on about? 'You've agreed all the dates already.'

'There has been a new development of great significance,' Professor Griffiths said, 'as a result of which we shall not be doing *Uncle Vanya* as planned.'

'You mean you don't want to open with it? But *Vanya's* the key production.'

'I mean the play is to be dropped completely,' the Professor said. 'We shall not be presenting *Uncle Vanya* after all.'

'Look,' Maurice said, close to despair at the man's ignorant myopia, 'the entire Festival's geared to four plays and the entertainment. We've contracted cast, stage management, everybody, on that basis. You can't drop one of them just like that. It doesn't work any more. The whole thing falls to pieces.'

'There will still be four plays,' Professor Griffiths said, 'but the key play will no longer be *Uncle Vanya.* It will be another one. That is why I required you to come and see me. So that I could inform you of that decision. Also of something most exciting, which will make this year's Festival utterly unique.' He gestured, and a deferential waiter approached at once. 'Another glass of champagne, and an orange juice for my companion, if you please,' the Professor said.

# CHAPTER TWO

Maurice was trying to give up smoking, but he lit a cigarette now. He needed it. The Professor's eyes, usually as flat and dull as pebbles, were sparkling. He was positively basking in self-approval.

'I see. John Cramer,' Maurice repeated flatly.

The Professor nodded. 'Confirmed last night,' he said. 'I've been trying to get John to appear at the Festival for years. He's finally agreed.'

The mad dreams of a mad Professor, Maurice thought resignedly. He had heard this kind of crazy euphoric nonsense before. He remembered the self-styled impresario who wheeled and dealed a living by mounting tatty tours of provincial theatres, using scenery and wardrobe which looked second-hand and were, and for whom Maurice had once directed a couple of plays when he was particularly hard up. That 'impresario' had assured Maurice that Anne Bancroft, it was known, was looking for just such a play as Maurice was to be contracted for, and that a copy of the script was, at that very moment, winging its way across the Atlantic, where a friend of a friend of a friend who happened to be a neighbour of Miss Bancroft's would press it into her hand personally, thus jumping the queue, twenty-four hours after which Miss Bancroft would be on the phone.

It was not flam. The man genuinely believed it. He really had persuaded himself that Anne Bancroft would fly to England and tour Eastbourne, Brighton, Plymouth, Wolverhampton, Hatfield, Norwich, Bromley and Richmond. After which, inevitably, with Anne Bancroft playing the lead, the play would transfer to the West End, and six months later would open on Broadway.

Maurice had sat through a bibulous lunch listening to

all this nonsense, nodding politely because he needed the job very badly at the time, while the 'impresario', eyes gleaming with the stratospheric ambition of the truly small-time operator, pointed out what this happy prospect would mean for Maurice in terms of his director's royalties, since he would certainly take the play into the West End and, given Anne Bancroft's approval, there was no reason why he should not direct it on Broadway as well. Unspoken was the other aspect, which was that, given the kind of small print the 'impresario' was wont to insert in struggling playwrights' contracts, the 'impresario' could anticipate something of a fortune for himself, since the movie companies would be bidding against each other for the film rights of such a runaway success.

Needless to say, there was never any word from Miss Bancroft. A telly person out of *Crossroads* played the part. The play opened in Eastbourne, staggered through Brighton and Plymouth, and closed prematurely in Wolverhampton. Two weeks later Miss Bancroft's agent returned the script with a stereotyped letter of thanks, but no thanks. The 'impresario' blamed Maurice for the play's failure, and cancelled his contract for the second production. There was small print in Maurice's contract too.

Then there was the independent television producer who wasted Maurice's time discussing a TV movie to be shot on location in Yorkshire, for which, he asserted, Robert Shaw was about to sign at any moment. This was after *Jaws* but before that fine actor's sad death. Maurice doubted if Robert Shaw ever knew anything about it. Anyway, for whatever reason, the project was quietly dropped, and Maurice's opportunity to direct his first film went away.

There were endless other examples which Maurice had heard about. Gregory Peck, who was going to appear in a British TV series about a lawyer, because he liked playing lawyers . . . Michael Caine, so impressed by a first novel set in London that he was about to return from Hollywood to make the film version . . . Jane Fonda, so taken with the convoluted ideology of an amazingly wordy first play by some confused sociologist that she would appear in it at the Edinburgh Festival . . . Jack Nicholson flying over to do this . . . Dustin Hoffman to do that . . .

None of these breathlessly, if briefly, anticipated events had ever happened, all were almost certainly the products of fevered imaginations.

What was it that made apparently intelligent people fall victims to such dotty hallucinations? Now Professor Griffiths had joined the loonies. John Cramer. God Almighty. Why not Lord Olivier for Treganwy? In some ways, the idea of Larry going there would be marginally more credible. At least he was resident in the United Kingdom, and did not, to the best of Maurice's knowledge, command something over a million dollars a picture.

It was true that, a few years ago, Richard Burton had played on the stage at Oxford one summer before returning to the States to star in the film of *Equus* the following year, but there were special, personal reasons for that appearance. That was the exception which proved the rule, and the rule was that it did not happen, except in the fantasies of otherwise sane men.

Now David Griffiths, JP, was at it, one-time Professor of Eng. Lit. One would think the fathead would know about logic.

'Professor,' Maurice began, patiently, 'John Cramer lives in Spain . . .'

'He did live in Spain,' Professor Griffiths corrected him. 'He sold up before Christmas, and moved to a rented villa near Cannes. After appearing at the Festival he's flying to America, where he intends to buy a house on the West Coast.'

'He's still a tax exile,' Maurice argued. 'He daren't come back to the UK, or those thieving bloodhounds at the Inland Revenue'd take him to the cleaners.'

'It is true that he can only spend a limited period here,' the Professor agreed. 'That is why he'll only be appearing at the Festival for three weeks. Hence the re-scheduling which is necessary. I've noted the dates he'll be available, if you care to glance at them . . .'

He handed over some scrawled notes from his briefcase. Maurice took them without looking at them.

'He's due to start shooting a Civil War picture in May,' Maurice said tiredly. 'I saw that in *Variety*. There was a copy lying around my agent's office. He's playing General Lee, or Stonewall Jackson, I forget which.'

'You're out of date,' the Professor said. 'Shooting has been postponed for a year. After he's set up home on the West Coast he's returning to New York where he opens on Broadway in the autumn in the transfer from London of *Last Rites for Beresford*.'

'I thought Paul Newman was going to play Beresford, and then make the movie in Canada.'

'That was the original intention, but Newman found that he had other commitments,' the Professor said. 'John Cramer has taken his place. He'll play for six months on Broadway, make the Civil War picture, and then go on to make the film of *Last Rites for Beresford*. Happily, that leaves him free to appear at the Festival.'

Jesus, the fool was obstinate. As hooked on his daydream as any addict on his next fix.

'Assuming you're right,' Maurice said, 'that means he'll earn somewhere around three or four million dollars in the next two years. Professor,' he continued, pleading for sanity, 'Treganwy's a marvellous festival. Bags of prestige. Great. But in twenty years, you've never had one star name, because you can't afford them. If we can't even pay Sally Warran more than a hundred a week . . .'

'Oh, we can run to more than that for John Cramer,' Professor Griffiths assured him. 'He'll receive a hundred and twenty a week, the same as Ben Stamford and Bernard Fyfield.'

'Ben and Bernard need it,' Maurice snapped, his nerves stretched to snapping point. 'John Cramer stopped thinking in terms of anything less than how many hundred grand five years ago when he became what the money men call a bankable name. Honestly, Professor,' he said plaintively, 'I'm sure you've tried to get him and all that, and perhaps his agent's given you the polite run-around, and you've read too much into it, but there's simply no reason why he should do it. Not one.'

'There is in fact just one,' Professor Griffiths said, bathed in sly pleasure. 'Me. He's doing it for me.'

'Oh, really,' Maurice groaned. 'With all possible respect for the way you built up Treganwy . . .'

'You apparently are not aware,' Professor Griffiths said, his professorial manner toppling over into the downright pompous, as though correcting some backward student, 'and indeed there is no reason why you should be, that I knew John well when he was an undergraduate at Cambridge. True, he left after a year, having decided to go to RADA, rather than take his degree. A pity in many ways, I've always felt. He has a good intellect, as those novels of his demonstrate, but an academic discipline might have given him a formidable mind indeed.' The arid old intellectual snob, Maurice thought, who had been born in Ramsgate, the son of a bus driver, and whose first job, which had lasted three weeks, had been as an apprentice salesman in a shoe shop. 'However, I digress,' the Professor said blandly to his pupil. 'I have kept in touch with John intermittently over the years. I nearly persuaded him to appear at the Festival in 1968, but at that time he obtained a film role in Hollywood, and was obliged to disappoint me. However, finally, this year, he will be able to manage it. I note a certain scepticism in your expression,' the Professor went on. 'Perhaps you'd care to glance at this. We have spoken on the telephone since, of course.'

Maurice took the engraved sheet of notepaper. The brief letter was typed and came from an address near Cannes.

> Dear Professor Griffiths,
>
> John asks me to apologise for the delay, and to say that he hopes to speak to you concerning the Treganwy Festival in the near future. In the meantime, perhaps you would be kind enough to forward the script you mentioned.

The letter was signed 'Valerie Foster, Secretary to John Cramer.'

Maurice caressed his temples. 'What script?' he asked. His headache was getting worse.

'I have only one copy,' the Professor said, handing over a foolscap-sized envelope. 'You'll have to get the requisite number run off as quickly as possible.'

'Who wrote it?'

'It's by a television writer,' the Professor said. 'His first stage play, I believe. I forget his name. Personally, I never watch television. It happened to arrive on my desk at the right time. John didn't want to do a classic, and this is a modern piece. He'll play the part of Stephen.'

'If it's one of those disjointed things, where people are supposed to pop up like disembodied genii in all corners of the stage, I don't think that's what the theatre should be doing,' Maurice said mutinously. Television writers were apt to imagine, fondly, that their latest cherished telly offering would transfer to the stage with no more adjustment than the ingenious use of lighting and blackouts as an optimistic substitute for the original six or eight sets, filmed exterior inserts, and electronic editing facilities. Maurice had witnessed such productions at places like Hampstead and the Open Space. To his mind, they merely demonstrated, forcibly, what a bastard medium television was in the first place.

'All the action takes place in one set,' the Professor assured him. 'A patio alongside a large house on some sub-tropical island somewhere. When you talk to the designer, bear in mind that I'd like some money spent on this setting. It must look stunning, and reek of wealth. The sound effects are also important. You can find the necessary cash by trimming your scenic budget for the *Dream*, which I always felt was much too extravagant.'

Maurice was deeply wedded to his concept of *Midsummer Night's Dream,* in every detail. He had no intention of mounting just another production of the *Dream.* There were too many comparisons which the critics would make.

'Just hold it there,' he said. 'I'm sorry, but first of all you talk about shuffling a carefully worked-out schedule, and now you want to screw up my conceptions by slashing budgets.'

Professor Griffiths was not listening. He was looking at his watch.

'Kindly read the play I've given you,' he said, 'and telephone me at my hotel before midnight. I'm afraid you'll have to excuse me now. It's time I joined Judge Wilby.'

'Judge whats-it can bloody wait,' Maurice said harshly. 'We haven't finished yet. You walk out now, and you've got no Director of Productions. If you imagine you can send for me, issue a few orders which wreck all my ideas, and toddle off to rabbit on about hanging and flogging to some geriatric, you'd better think again. I'm not a waiter you can crook your finger at.'

'I beg your pardon?' From the Professor's chilly expression, the words were not meant to be taken literally.

Oh, God, please stop that black bubble from bursting. Please. Take a deep breath. Not another screaming match. Another idiotic, hysterical gesture, another abdication born of pride. Not another varnished version for Anna's benefit, and the expression of silent contempt on her face. Not another summer mooching around the house, moodily decorating, gardening, putting up shelves to fill the time, making phone calls, at first jocular ones about happening to be free unexpectedly, finally practically pleading . . . Not that feeling of helpless humiliation as Anna discovered the pile of unpaid bills and sat down without a word, but with a glance which said more than any words, to write the cheques on her own account, disdainfully leaving him to address the envelopes. Not that. No. Never again.

He essayed a smile, which felt wrong, and therefore presumably looked wrong as well.

'Professor,' he said, 'I don't mean to be rude, but . . .' Where were the words? God damn it, where were they? He, who could be so fluent and articulate, who could always strike the right chord with an actor, and, even with the most difficult, temperamental ones, invariably find a way to control them, to use that very temperament to bring out the facet in an interpretation which he was seeking – why could he not find the right words now to defend himself against this pompous pedant's autocratic behaviour, when, for all the Professor's academic pretensions, he was in truth a man of inferior intellect, whom Maurice ought to be able to bend to his will? But then he had a head start with actors. They respected him, and this idiot did not. Why was it that it was always the pseudos and the phonies, the men with little original talent or none, who landed up in positions of power? Treganwy Festival might be financed by the taxpayer, in one way or another, because of its excellence due to the ill-paid hard work of a generation of numberless creative and artistic people, but somehow Professor Griffiths, who was neither creative nor artistic, made no financial contribution himself, and never had done, somehow he managed to retain the power from the beginning, and held it still. Where were the words? 'The first time we met we agreed that, if I took on Director of Productions, there'd be no interference on the artistic side . . '

'I'm not interfering,' the Professor said curtly. 'Persuading John Cramer to appear is hardly interfering. It is a major contribution to the success of this year's Festival, one which, I am bound to add, you were quite incapable of making yourself.'

'All these changes you've been talking about,' Maurice said, 'are based on the assumption that Cramer will actually appear. Frankly, I don't believe it. In the end, he won't agree, but even if he did . . .'

'I'll see that you have a copy of his signed contract within the week,' the Professor said. 'I presume that will satisfy you on that score.'

'Even if he did,' Maurice repeated, 'what you're suggesting would upset the balance of the entire Festival. We've already got one first play, that terrible Welsh thing.' The Professor's eyes were dull pebbles again. It was he who had christened the embryo playwright the Welsh Bernard Shaw. 'I'm sorry,' Maurice said stubbornly. 'I know you think it has merit, but honestly, it's not very good. It has literary pretensions, but it lacks real content, and the structure's adolescent. Don't misunderstand me. We'll paper over the cracks, and make it look good, which is more than it deserves, but now you want to shove in another first play as well. Treganwy Festival has a reputation, and surely you don't want to see that damaged. We're already committed to one dog. Why risk making it two? If Cramer really is interested in appearing at Treganwy, why can't he play Voinitsky or Astrov?'

'I've already made that plain,' the Professor said. 'He doesn't want to.'

'Well, I don't want to drop *Uncle Vanya,'* Maurice said, 'and see the *Dream* turned into just another production by skimping on scenery, especially when you haven't even thought fit to so much as consult me. If you'd discussed this with me earlier, when there was still time, I might have been able to come up with some suggestions which would have retained the balance I want to see at the Festival, instead of which . . .'

'I see no purpose in continuing this discussion,' the Professor said. He rose to his feet. 'I've already kept Judge Wilby waiting long enough. You have certain misgivings about my intentions. If you are unable to come to terms with them, I can only suggest that you withdraw from the Festival. Despite the inconvenience, I am prepared to release you from your contract. I shall not find it difficult to replace you, Mr Gardiner. There are many good directors only too anxious to work at Treganwy. Be so kind as to let me have your decision when you telephone me later tonight.'

Professor Griffiths turned and left the bar with measured dignity. There was still some orange juice left in Maurice's glass, but he needed something stronger than that. He gestured to a passing waiter.

'A large whisky, please.'

'I'm sorry, sir,' the waiter said, eyeing him up and down, 'but I don't believe you're a member, are you? Only members are allowed to buy drinks, here, sir.'

Harry Belmont finished cleaning his teeth and inspected the result in the mirror. They were white enough, but somewhat uneven. Nicola had urged him to have them capped at one time but he was reluctant, and she seemed to have forgotten about it. In any case, she had not mentioned it for some months.

His mouth felt fresher now, which was a relief, but he swallowed a couple of Panadol. Opening another bottle of wine during the evening had been a mistake, as he had realised after one glass. Still, Nicola seemed to be ready for it, and steadily drank most of the remainder while they sat watching television, saying little to each other. He was relieved when she got up and said she thought she would have an early night. It seemed to have been a long day, and the wine at lunchtime and during the afternoon had induced a dull lethargy.

He went into the living room and took the empty bottle and glasses into the small kitchen, which was no more than a few steps. The one-bedroom flat was the kind which a cautious estate agent would have described as 'compact'. It was hardly large enough for two, and there were times when tempers frayed just because of the sheer lack of space. On such occasions Nicola would announce that she was going out for a walk, or Harry would decide to go outside and wash his car.

Just the same, London property prices being what they were, and the once-unfashionable Shepherd's Bush now being described by haughty estate agents as a 'high price area', it was all Harry could afford, given his other commitments. Fortunately service charges were not high, and Nicola bought all the food, so they managed comfortably enough.

He went into the bedroom and started to undress. Nicola was propped up in bed, reading from her Penguin copy of Chekhov plays, murmuring quietly aloud as she did so.

'. . . everyone blames my husband, everyone looks at me with compassion: an unfortunate woman – she's got an old husband! This sympathy for me – oh, how well I understand it! As Astrov said just now . . .'

Harry placed his suit on a hanger. The fitted wardrobe was not very large, and he had bought a second-hand additional wardrobe when Nicola moved in which took up most of what little available space there was in the room. Even so, Nicola's clothes always overflowed from what was theoretically her wardrobe into his, and he was obliged to force the hanging clothes sideways to make just enough room for his suit. He sighed quietly, climbed into bed, and picked up the *Observer* which he had not had time to read properly yet.

'. . . you senselessly ruin human beings, and soon,' Nicola murmured 'thanks to you, there will be no loyalty, no integrity, no, no capacity for self sacrifice left . . .'

Harry turned to the leading article.

'Can't you fold a newspaper quietly?' Nicola enquired. 'I can't concentrate if you're going to do that all the time.'

'Sorry,' Harry said. He creased the paper with infinite caution.

'. . . that doctor is right – there's a devil of destruction in every one of you. You spare neither woods, nor birds, nor women, nor one another.'

She seemed to have paused, momentarily, and Harry took the opportunity to shake out the final fold to his satisfaction. Nicola breathed out heavily and put her book down.

'That's the last crackle,' Harry said. 'Complete hush from now on.'

Nicola shook her head. 'I don't feel like doing any more, anyway.'

'Would you like me to hear your lines?' He often did this when she was learning a part.

'I haven't started learning it yet. I'm reading it through, that's all.' She still sat propped up on her pillows, staring, apparently, at a particular fold in the curtains.

'Oh, well . . .' Harry dropped the newspaper on the floor, and reached for the bedside light. 'Ready?'

'Not yet. Give me a cigarette, will you?'

Harry got out of bed again, more or less patiently, and fetched his cigarettes and lighter from his jacket in the wardrobe.

'I don't know how you can bear to smoke after you've cleaned your teeth,' he said.

'You are a predictable man,' she said. 'You always say that.'

'Well, that's some slight improvement,' he said, smiling. 'You usually say "boringly predictable".' He sat on the edge of the bed, gave her a cigarette, and lit it for her. 'Now, I suppose you want a cup of coffee.'

'No,' Nicola said. 'I want to talk to you.'

He knew what that meant, and groaned inwardly with apprehension. 'Why is it you always decide to talk to me when I want to go to sleep? We could have talked all evening. There was nothing worth watching on television.'

'I didn't feel like it then. I feel like it now,' Nicola said. She drew on her cigarette and puffed out smoke. Harry could not understand why she smoked at all, since she never inhaled. 'When I go to Treganwy, I shall move out all my things,' she said.

'Well, of course,' Harry said. 'You'll be there for six months, you'll need nearly all your clothes. I shall be able to hang all my suits up properly for a change.'

She did not return his smile. 'No, I mean everything. When the Festival's over, I shan't come back. Not here.'

'Oh. I see.' It was not entirely unexpected. Something of the sort had been brooding on the horizon for months now, like a tiny but threatening storm cloud, but he had chosen to ignore it, hoping that it would change direction and go away. It was still a shock to find that it had arrived.

'I've been thinking about it for a long time,' Nicola said. 'You must have realised that. It's never going to work out, I know that.'

'I don't agree,' he said steadily.

'I must consider myself,' Nicola said. 'I'm knocking on – nearly thirty. I must do something soon, something positive, not just go on drifting, and since I'll be going away for six months anyway . . . well it's the right time.'

'To find someone else?'

'I don't know,' Nicola said. 'But if I do . . . I don't want to have to think about you.'

'When you first got the job, you were talking about renting a cottage, and me coming for weekends.'

'That was then,' Nicola said. 'I thought, well, perhaps I should settle for what I've got, second best, but I can't.' She reached out quickly, took his hand, and squeezed it. 'I don't mean that unkindly.'

'I don't know how you call anyone second best kindly,' Harry said.

'I suppose the truth is, I'm immature,' Nicola said. 'I've been living with you, and there've been other men who were important to me . . . I've told you all about them . . . and you're the nicest and the best, you are really. But even now, at my age, I'm still hoping for a knight on a white charger. Everything simple, straightforward, no hang-ups, no obstacles. Quite likely it won't happen, and one day I'll look back, and be sorry. Most people seem to settle for what they can get. But I don't want to make that kind of compromise, Harry . . . or I can't . . . not yet, anyway.' She squeezed his fingers again tightly. 'I'm sorry.'

'So am I,' Harry said.

Maurice dialled the Paris hotel. 'I'd like to speak to Miss Bowley, please,' he said.

'One moment.' There was a long pause. Maurice sipped his glass of whisky, and waited. 'I'm sorry, but there is no reply,' the pleasantly accented voice said. 'Do you wish to leave a message?'

'No thank you,' Maurice said. 'No message.'

He hung up, ripped open the brown manila envelope, and took out the script. 'Paula' it said on the title page. He glanced at the cast list. Oh, great. Trust Professor Griffiths to overlook a minor detail like that, the stupid old bat. Glumly, he began to read.

They lay in bed side by side, their bodies almost touching, but between them was a gulf which it seemed impossible to bridge.

'I know this sardine tin of a flat isn't exactly gracious living,' Harry said, 'but I'm due for a salary review soon, and I could sell this place then, and find something bigger, perhaps at Ealing.'

'It's not about money,' Nicola said. 'And I don't want to live at Ealing.'

'You liked it here at first,' Harry said, mourning the past. 'You insisted on making new curtains, made me get rid of that Indian rug, chose the occasional table you wanted . . .'

'I suppose I was doing the home-making bit,' Nicola said. 'Changing the nest around.'

'If we move, you could have everything the way you wanted. Do it from scratch.'

'That's not what I want,' Nicola said. 'Not now.'

'I always thought we'd get married, eventually.'

'Eventually took too long,' Nicola said. 'Besides, I'm an actress, and what's more, I'm good, I'm better than most.'

'I know that . . .'

'When I came out of drama school, clutching my silly award, I thought I'd be acclaimed – the new rising star. Instead of which, it took six months to find an ASM's job at Chesterfield. When I joined the National I thought that was it, I'd got my chance. That didn't happen either. I went abroad with them, and had some fun, but I didn't get one decent part all the time I was there. But I'll make it one day, I'll be able to pick and choose, people are going to know who Nicola Feary is all right. I know I've got it inside me, it's there, and that's the most important thing in my life, and always will be. The fact that I'm an actress.'

'I've never argued about that,' Harry said. 'I know how much it matters to you. I've never tried to stop you when you had to go away to work, have I? I know that banking bores you, and that whereas you naturally feel at home with your own kind, like that party today, I don't really fit in. I can't help that. It's no use pretending I feel at ease with them, because I don't.'

'That doesn't matter,' Nicola said. 'You're very good about sitting in a corner, and waiting patiently until I want to go home. And the time's always come when I have wanted to go home.'

'So what's the point? Where's the connection?'

'I don't know,' Nicola said. 'But there is one.' She stretched for the ashtray and carefully stubbed out her cigarette.

'There's no reason why we shouldn't get married now,' Harry said. 'There's nothing to stop us.'

'Yes, there is,' Nicola said. 'Or I wouldn't be talking about not coming back.'

'I think that's what you wanted at one time.'

'For quite a long time,' Nicola said, 'but not any more. I couldn't live with that guilt of yours.'

'I don't have any guilt,' Harry said.

'Oh, you do,' Nicola said. 'There's nothing for you to feel guilty about, but you do. Sometimes I think you cherish it, and if it ever starts to grow dim, you keep blowing on it to keep the flame alive. I suppose you must enjoy punishing yourself in some twisted sort of way. I don't know why. That's your problem. It's not one that I'm going to take on. There's no reason why I should.'

'You always lose me,' Harry said helplessly. 'Your conversation's like a pianola gone mad. Nothing relates, there's no sequence, no reason, no link between one thing and another.'

'Well, I know what I mean,' Nicola said. She turned her head on the pillow and looked at him. 'Don't hate me though, if you can help it.'

'Always before, you've been coming back, there've been some of your things lying around,' Harry said. 'I just can't imagine it as it was before I met you. Not now. No bottles all over the bathroom, no hairpins in the drawers, no shopping lists stuck on the wall, everything tidy again.' He shook his head. 'No hoovering when I want to watch the news, even.'

'You'll have to get a cleaner,' Nicola said. 'Oh, no. Your mother can come and clean for you. She'd enjoy that. She'll be pleased anyway, when she knows I'm not coming back. She never did like you being mixed up with some tart of an actress.'

'Now then,' he said. 'No digs. You've no right . . . not now.'

'Make love to me,' Nicola said.

He did so, at first with a kind of sad affection, and even though the climax was as breathless and passionate as always there was a kind of melancholy even about that. As if, even though she would not be leaving yet, the act were the final one, the last goodbye.

The Professor's voice down the phone was irritable. 'I requested you to ring me before midnight.'

'I've only just finished,' Maurice said. He had only just finished that scotch left over from Christmas as well, he thought, staring at the empty half-bottle, but the contents had done singularly little good.

'Well? As briefly as possible, please. I wish to get some rest, and I never sleep well in hotels.'

'You do realise,' Maurice said heavily, 'that *Paula* only has a cast of five, whereas *Uncle Vanya* has nine?' The silence from the other end led him to believe that the Professor had realised nothing of the kind. 'Actors are already contracted on that basis,' Maurice reminded him.

'I don't quite see your difficulty,' Professor Griffiths said. 'They're all in other productions. Four of them will be paid for doing rather less than anticipated, that's all.'

'Fine,' Maurice said. 'I'm glad to hear that money isn't as tight as all that. I imagined from the way you were talking at the beginning that we had to watch every penny.'

'Anything else?' the Professor enquired brusquely, ignoring that.

'Oh, yes,' Maurice said. 'There is indeed.' He studied his sheet of handwritten notes, and discovered that he could hardly read them. To hell with it. He remembered most of them. 'I take it you also realise from the title of the play that the leading part is Paula and not Stephen? Also that Marcia Hambridge is the only actress in the company who could conceivably play Paula, which will be about as bizarre a piece of casting as has ever been witnessed on any stage in the history of the theatre?'

'You exaggerate as usual,' Professor Griffiths said coldly. 'If we were starting from scratch, I might choose someone else, but she'll be perfectly adequate. She's an experienced actress. I'm sure she'll be able to cope with the role.'

'She hasn't worked since she gave birth,' Maurice remarked. 'And that was five years ago. Can you really see Marcia making her first entrance in a bikini?' Marcia's beam and legs were of Edwardian proportions.

'For heaven's sake,' the Professor snapped, 'the text isn't sacrosanct. She can enter in a beachrobe or something. A long one,' he added. 'Besides, none of this is important. No one's going to be looking at Marcia when John Cramer's on the stage.'

'Ah, yes, funny you should mention that,' Maurice said. 'I'm sure it's a tiny detail, but there are thirty consecutive pages when he's not even on stage at all, much less uttering.'

There was another silence, a longer one this time. Apparently that small point had eluded the Professor as well.

'That will certainly have to be dealt with,' he said eventually.

'Yes, I reckon,' Maurice said. He was one up at last, and it cheered him slightly. 'I don't see much point in importing one of your actual film stars to play what's only a second lead, and then keeping him out of sight for over half an hour to boot.'

'The author will have to be spoken to,' Professor Griffiths said. 'Whether by you or by your successor, I shall now be glad to learn.'

'Well, on the assumption that Cramer actually turns up,' Maurice said, 'I wouldn't mind trying to make this effort come off. Nothing is impossible, as they say, and if Cramer's willing to risk it, why shouldn't I? It would certainly be a challenge. Like climbing Everest in plimsolls and a string vest.'

'Cramer will appear,' the Professor said, unamused.

'O.K., but if he doesn't, we drop *Paula* and put back *Uncle Vanya*. On that condition, I'll have a shot at it. And if the miracle does happen, I must say, I'd quite like the chance to direct John Cramer.'

'You shall have your wish,' the Professor said. 'Good night.'

Maurice hung up. He considered opening the playscript again, and tinkering with it now, but decided against it. He was tired and somewhat blurred around the edges. Leave it until the morning. He dialled the Paris hotel again.

'I'm sorry, but she still doesn't seem to be in her room,' the pleasantly accented voice said.

'Thank you,' Maurice said. No, in someone else's room, he thought, the whoring cow.

By chance, the London rehearsals were to take place in hired premises, a boys' club off Goldhawk Road. It was within easy walking distance for Nicola and she enjoyed it, despite the cold wind which chilled the air. She ignored the motorists, stalled in the traffic, who eyed her long, booted legs with reflex lust, but she was agreeably conscious of the reaction she evoked.

Inside, they were all there, the familiar faces, and some she did not know. Coffee was being brewed, and sipped thankfully, and there was a hubbub of cheerful conversation.

'Where have you been keeping yourself? I haven't seen you since that disaster in Nottingham . . .'

'On the dole, mostly . . .'

'Bloody cold in here, isn't it . . . ?'

'Darling, I rang you last month, but you were up in Granadaland . . .'

'That was a year ago . . .'

'I could have sworn it wasn't that long. Doesn't time fly . . . ?'

'It must be below freezing in here. We shall all get frostbite . . .'

'Oh, the glamour of show business. Grotty rooms, dirty floors, and no heat . . .'

'Apparently the boiler's packed up . . .'

'Any self-respecting factory worker'd walk out on the spot . . .'

'Yes, let's all go home . . .'

'Anyone know what accommodation's like in Treganwy . . . ?'

'I'm told there are caravans in the theatre grounds . . .'

'I'm not living in a lousy caravan for six months . . .'

'What's he like to work with? Victor whats-it? I've seen his stuff on the box, of course . . .'

'Like most television directors. No idea of working with actors. All he cares about is where his rotten cameras are . . .'

'Where's Maurice? Seeing about the boiler . . . ?'

'God, I hope so . . .'

'I thought you were very good. Have you done anything since . . . ?'

'Not on the telly. Went to Farnham on the strength of it though. God's gift to young male actors, *Secret Army* was. A pity it finished . . .'

'No hope of more than one episode though. Everyone escaped . . .'

'Half of them got killed, as far as I could see. You got shot, didn't you . . .'

'Yes, and I died beautifully too, on film, but it came out over length, and the bastards cut it . . .'

'Not much money though . . .'

'Well, that's the BBC, tight fisted lot. ITV's much better . . .'

Nicola loved it all. It was this which made it all worthwhile, cancelled out the wretched periods out of work, signing on at the Labour Exchange every Wednesday, taking odd jobs to buy a dress or a pair of shoes, leaving lists of phone numbers where she could be reached in case her agent called. This first day was like emerging into the sunlight, knowing that they were really launched. For six long months these were the people she would be with, work with, drink with, eat with. On this day, she loved everybody. She knew that would not last, but today, just for a few hours, she did. She even smiled warmly at Bernard Fyfield, whom she knew slightly, but he pointedly ignored her. That was no special badge of honour. Bernard ignored pretty well everybody.

She was introduced to Marcia Hambridge. Marcia laid claim to be forty-one, which since she had a five-year-old son was presumably moderately accurate, but in her sweater and jeans, which she really ought not to wear, no make-up, and a scarf tied round her hair, she looked a good fifty.

Marcia eyed her closely, with something less than immediate liking, and devoted a brief monologue to her return to the theatre in which she referred to herself several times, pointedly, as the leading lady of the company.

Silly old cow, Nicola thought, nodding and smiling brightly, and turned away to speak to Robin Haslem.

'I've only just found out you're playing Yeliena,' he said. 'I think that's great. You'll be super.'

'I hope so,' Nicola said. 'No, damn it, I'm going to be. I can't wait to get started. I've been dying to play Yeliena before it's too late, and I've got to be good. For one thing, Maurice said that some of the good agents might be coming to see it.'

'Why? Are you pissed off with yours?'

'He's pissed off with me,' Nicola said. 'Anyway, he's not right for me.'

Although Maurice made an unobtrusive entrance somehow they all sensed that he had arrived. The conversation did not come to a sudden stop, but it quietened sufficiently for him to be heard without being obliged to raise his voice.

'I have one or two announcements to make before we begin,' he said, 'so we may as well all sit down and make ourselves comfortable.'

The folding wooden chairs were unstacked and passed from hand to hand, clattering as they were set up on the floor.

'There aren't enough to go round,' Ben Stamford said.

'Alan is just off to find some more,' Maurice said.

Alan Cakin, a classically handsome young ASM, nodded, went out, and came back later with armfuls of chairs. Maurice did not wait for him to return.

'First of all, my apologies about the temperature,' he said. 'I've already complained, and the caretaker's trying to get the boiler going. In the meantime, keep your coats on, and gloves and mufflers too, I suggest, if you have them. If there's no heat an hour from now, we'll pack it in, and go home.'

'Or possibly the pub,' Ben suggested to his neighbour.

'That said, I have to announce certain changes,' Maurice said. 'The first one I think you'll find very exciting, as it concerns an addition to the company. Someone who will join us for the first few weeks of the Festival. He will only appear in one play, since after that he has to leave for America, but that will be enough to make this the most fantastic season Treganwy's ever seen.'

'Herman the talking dog,' Ben suggested.

'Shut up, Ben,' Maurice said automatically. 'You're not going to believe who it is when I tell you,' he went on. 'I didn't believe it myself, but it's true.' They all looked at him. Maurice well knew the value of a pause, and he let this one spin out. 'John Cramer,' he said eventually.

There was more than one variety of silence, he thought. Any audience demonstrated that. This particular silence had turned from anticipation into frank disbelief.

'Jolly good, Maurice,' Ben Stamford said at last. 'Now pull the other one. Who else have you signed? Jane Fonda and Warren Beatty?'

'No,' Maurice said. 'Just John Cramer.'

He took a document from his breast pocket and held it up. 'His contract,' he said. 'Also I've spoken to him on the phone. He'll be joining us in Treganwy, where he'll rehearse for, and take part in, the opening production.'

'Well, I'm buggered,' Ben Stamford said.

'Is this kosher, Maurice?' Leonard Sherwen asked. 'You're not having us on?'

'Straight up,' Maurice said. 'On my grandmother's grave, poor old soul. So we can guarantee the "Full House" signs'll be out for the first few weeks all right.'

''Well, that's what it's all about,' Robin said. 'Bums on seats.'

'Who'll be dropping out of *Uncle Vanya* for the first month then?' Ben Stamford asked. 'Me?'

'That brings me to my second announcement,' Maurice said. 'We shan't be opening with *Uncle Vanya,* in fact it will be removed from the repertoire entirely.' Nicola looked up sharply. 'In its place will be a new play called *Paula*. Marcia, you'll play the title role.' Marcia looked gratified. 'John Cramer will be Stephen, the man you're secretly in love with.' Smug delight of infinite purity glowed in Marcia's face. 'Ben, you'll rehearse for the part of Stephen as well, because you'll take over for the rest of the season when Cramer leaves.'

'O.K.,' Ben said. Marcia glanced at him, and pursed her lips doubtfully.

'Nicola, you'll play Mary, who is Marcia's secretary.' Marcia nodded approvingly. Nicola's stomach turned to lead. She stubbed out her cigarette angrily. 'Bernard, you're Willem, a wealthy Dutchman who is Marcia's husband, and Leonard, you'll be Peter, Marcia's son.'

'Just a moment,' Marcia said. 'I think I got that wrong. Who's supposed to be my son?' Every trace of delight and gratification had disappeared like magic.

'Leonard,' Maurice said, pointing. 'Him.'

'I'm afraid I don't see how that can possibly work at all,' Marcia said coldly. 'How old am I supposed to be, for God's sake?'

'About forty-five,' Maurice said.

'I never mind playing older than I really am, should the part call for it,' Marcia said. Oh, shut up, you hypocritical old bag, Nicola thought. 'But I fail to see how I can possibly be supposed to have a son of thirty. It would be utterly unreal.'

'Leonard won't be playing his real age,' Maurice said patiently. 'You were married young, and he's supposed to be twenty-four. The distance the stage is from the auditorium at Treganwy, we can get away with that all right.'

'Why can't Alan play my son?' Marcia demanded,

indicating the handsome young ASM. 'He'd be much more suitable.'

'Look, darling, leave the casting to me, all right?' Maurice requested, keeping his patience, just about. 'It'll be O.K., I promise you. In any case, I really don't want to get bogged down in any discussions now. Linda's got copies of the scripts for you all, let's read it first, and talk later.'

Linda began to hand round copies of the play to the actors concerned. She was a small, pleasantly pretty girl of twenty-two, and this was her first job since leaving drama school.

'So, moving on . . .' Maurice began.

'Before you do,' Robin Haslem said, 'how about me? I was playing Astrov in *Uncle Vanya*, and if we're not doing it, and I'm not in the new one . . .'

'You'll have more time off, that's all,' Maurice said. 'That applies, of course, to the others I haven't mentioned as well.'

'Right,' Robin said. 'No complaints about that.'

'There are no race tracks near Treganwy, old son,' Ben Stamford said.

Maurice continued with his announcements. Nicola switched off. She took her copy of *Paula* from Linda, and started to skim through it rapidly.

'. . . and I'm sorry there have been so many changes,' Maurice concluded. 'But it can't be helped. It's not as bad as it sounds. You'll all receive new schedules, and I think you'll find everything fits in. Alan, go and see if that idiot caretaker's gone to sleep, will you?' Alan went off obediently. Nicola approached Maurice.

'Can I have a word, please?'

'Not just now, darling,' Maurice said. 'Where the hell's the wardrobe mistress got to?'

'I don't want to do this play,' Nicola blurted out.

'Let's go and have another coffee,' Maurice said. 'Come on.' He led the way into the tiny kitchen, and closed the door. 'Black with no sugar, isn't it?'

'Never mind the coffee,' Nicola said. 'I'm sorry, Maurice, I'd love to work with you again, but you know the only part I was really keen on was Yeliena, and if you're not doing *Uncle Vanya* after all . . .'

'I had no choice,' Maurice said soberly. 'John Cramer wouldn't do *Vanya*. Don't ask me why. For some reason he's willing to play Stephen, and that's all there is to it. There's nothing else I can do, and let's face it, it's a hell of a feather in our caps to get Cramer to Treganwy.'

'I can see all that,' Nicola said. 'But instead of a great part, suddenly, I'm Marcia's dogsbody, running around fixing drinks . . .'

'You haven't had time to read it properly. There's more to it than that.'

'I think you'd better recast,' Nicola said. She wanted to cry. 'You won't have any trouble. God knows there are enough actresses out of work.'

'I don't want to recast,' Maurice said. 'Mary's not a bad little part. It needs a few things doing to it, admittedly, but we'll sort that out.'

'It's crap compared with Yeliena, and you know it,' Nicola said. 'That kind of role for a woman gets written about once every hundred years.'

'I'd like you to think this over very carefully,' Maurice said. 'I could recast, of course, but think of your career. You'll be playing with John Cramer. Where else are you going to get that kind of opportunity? This could be a once-in-a-lifetime chance for you, Nicola. Your character doesn't just fix drinks, you know. She's also having a ding-dong with the Cramer character.' Nicola was unconvinced, which must have shown on her face. Maurice assumed his little-boy air, and his voice took on a pleading note. 'I'll be honest, darling. I can do without any more problems just now. I've got quite enough already, trying to handle our pedantic Professor, who's a right pain in the arse. I've got exactly the team I want, and you're part of it. I'd hate to see it broken up at this stage of the game. You're needed more than you realise. Why don't we see how it goes? Once you get involved in the part, you'll enjoy it, I'm sure you will. So stick with it, eh? Just for me.'

Nicola knew exactly what he was doing, and also that it

was all bull. Maurice simply did not want the hassle of finding someone else now that rehearsals were starting.

The door burst open, and Ben Stamford came in, a script of *Paula* in his hand. He was hiccuping with laughter.

'I've been reading this . . .' He waved the script, hardly able to get his breath. 'Marcia's described as . . . oh God . . . the most desirable woman in the world!'

He fell into a chair, hooting helplessly.

'Marcia . . . the most desirable . . . and John Cramer can't make it with her . . . Cramer! . . . can you believe it? . . . can't you imagine Marcia queening it all over Treganwy? . . . she'll be impossible . . . oh, God, I can't wait . . .'

'You wait until you have to take over from Cramer,' Nicola said, laughing with him. She could not help it.

'Oh, no. I'd forgotten about that . . . me, finding Marcia so maddeningly sexy that . . . it's too much . . . I deserve a knighthood if I bring that off . . .' Tears were streaming down his cheeks. 'I think I'm going to wet myself,' he moaned.

Maurice smiled thinly and walked back into the rehearsal room. Marcia had obviously been waiting for him.

'Oh, there you are,' she said. 'I'm a little bit worried about my first entrance.'

'You'll be wearing a beach robe,' Maurice told her. 'We don't think a skimpy bikini would be in good taste, not at Treganwy.'

'Yes, I think that would be much better,' Marcia said, relieved. 'That's what I thought – it might offend the tourists.'

'I think the heat's coming on,' Leonard said.

'Thank God for that,' Maurice said. 'All right,' he called. 'We'll read through the first act of *The Importance of Being Earnest,* and then break for lunch.'

They took their places around a long table, their books in front of them. The read-through began. Nicola sat staring at the pages sightlessly.

'Good afternoon, dear Algernon. I hope you are behaving very well.'

'I'm feeling very well, Aunt Augusta.'

'That's not quite the same thing. In fact the two things rarely go together.'

'Dear me, you are smart!'

Nicola vaguely noticed that the dialogue had stopped for some reason.

'Come on, Nicola,' Maurice said.

'Oh, is it me?' Nicola hurriedly turned a page.

'Do try and stay awake,' Maurice said.

'I'm always smart!' Nicola read. 'Am I not Mr Worthing?'

'You're quite perfect, Miss Fairfax.'

'Oh! I hope I am not that,' Nicola read. 'It would leave no room for developments, and I intend to develop in many directions.'

That was my intention, too, Gwendolen dear, Nicola thought, as Lady Bracknell launched into her longish speech, but that's gone up the spout in no time flat. Why on earth would someone like John Cramer want to appear in a play like *Paula* at a place like Treganwy? It made no sense. None at all.

'Won't you come and sit here, Gwendolen?' Lady Bracknell said.

'Thanks mamma,' Nicola read. 'I'm quite comfortable where I am.'

If only she had been reading Yeliena. She ached to play Yeliena. She supposed that this was something like the way women felt when they miscarried, and lost the baby they had been looking forward to for years.

# CHAPTER THREE

There was a trunk, a large battered suitcase, and several overflowing carrier bags. Harry carried them downstairs. The trunk went in the boot with two carrier bags, the suitcase and the remaining carrier bags on the back seat.

Harry went back upstairs. Nicola was in the bathroom. Harry tapped on the door.

'Come on. Time to go.'

'Shan't be a minute. I'm just having a pee.'

Harry checked the flat for the last time, but none of her possessions were left. Even the steak knives she had bought once had gone. The flat looked bare and unfriendly without her possessions lying around.

Nicola came out of the bathroom. 'You go and get in the car,' she said.

He looked at her and nodded. 'All right.'

She walked round the small rooms, the kitchen, the living room, the bedroom. She stood looking at the double bed in silence for a full minute.

'Oh, shit,' she said aloud, went into the hall, and slammed the front door behind her.

The company were travelling by special coach. Maurice had gone ahead in his own car with the advance party. Harry drove to the pick-up point, unloaded Nicola's luggage, and watched as the driver stowed it into the luggage compartment.

There were others there seeing wives or husbands or lovers (or ex-lovers he thought) off, and he nodded and smiled at those he recognised. Some of the cast remembered him, and greeted him cordially as they climbed aboard.

Robin Haslem and his wife, the rather beautiful red-haired girl, were talking to each other in low voices. They seemed to be having an argument. Finally Robin gestured impatiently and handed something to her.

Nicola and Harry stood uneasily beside the coach.

'I suppose there's nothing to say except goodbye,' Harry said.

'Don't look so sad,' Nicola said. 'Smile at me.' Harry did his best. 'How's that?'

'Terrible,' Nicola said. 'You'd never make an actor.'

'Will it be all right if I write to you?'

'Yes, of course. Anyway, I expect I'll give you a ring. Let you know how things are going.'

'All right,' Harry said. 'I'd like to know what John Cramer's like, anyway.'

'Well, there's no reason why you shouldn't come and see him in the play, if you can spare the time. That's if you feel like it.'

'I can spare the time,' Harry said. The driver climbed aboard and started the engine.

'Take care,' Nicola said. She hugged him briefly. 'And thanks for the bottle of wine.'

'God bless,' Harry said. 'I hope it works out for you.'

He watched as she got on to the coach and sat down in the back seat. He stood with the other people, waving. Nicola turned her head once, and lifted her hand, and then the coach turned a corner and went out of sight.

Harry found himself beside Mrs Haslem as he walked towards his car.

'I'm going to Shepherds Bush,' he said. 'Can I give you a lift?'

'No thanks. Wrong way. Will you be able to go and see Nicola?'

'I may go to the Cramer play,' Harry said evasively. 'I suppose you'll be there pretty often.'

'I doubt it,' Mrs Haslem said. 'Fares to Treganwy are expensive. Goodbye.'

She walked on. Harry got into his car. He did not want to drive home. He supposed he could go and see his mother. She would be glad to see him. No. He had to face that empty flat some time. He had to get used to it.

He started the engine. Pretend it's any other Saturday.

But any other Saturday, for a long time now, Nicola would have been there. Or, if she had been working away, he would be on his way to see her.

The coach left London, gained the motorway, and settled down to a steady monotonous growl. There was little to look at except passing traffic, and the weather. The latter mostly consisted of low cloud and mist, with an intermittent drizzle of rain, and was not worth looking at. Nicola unloaded the carrier bag she had brought on board.

'French bread, cheese and pâté,' she said. 'And Harry gave me a bottle of Riesling.'

'Lager,' Leonard said, unveiling his cans. 'And a pork pie from the deli.'

'Ham sandwiches,' Robin said. 'I was a bit hung over this morning, so I wasn't thinking about booze.'

'I wasn't thinking about food for the same reason,' Ben said. 'But I did manage to filch enough from my nearest and dearest's meagre housekeeping money for half a bottle of scotch.'

They were all sitting on the long back seat. Below them, the rear wheels swished on wet concrete.

'A mixed bag,' Ben said, 'but sufficient to render the journey moderately tolerable. Scotch anyone?'

'Let's start with the wine,' Nicola said. 'It'll give us an appetite.'

'It might if there were any means of getting the cork out,' Ben said.

'I've got one,' Nicola said. 'A folding thing. I always carry it around with me.'

'In case of emergency,' Ben supposed. 'Very wise.' He watched Nicola rummaging among the contents of her huge shoulder bag. 'Like digging for a lost thimble in a rubbish tip,' he remarked.

'I know it's here somewhere,' Nicola said. She started to go round again. 'Where is the sodding thing?'

'Forget it, darling. You need a team of men and a bulldozer.'

'Got it,' Nicola said, triumphant. She handed the object

to Ben. 'You can do the necessary. I've got some plastic cups.'

'What else can you achieve with this device?' Ben asked, examining it. 'Remove stones from Boy Scouts?'

'Quite likely. I've never tried. It gets corks out of bottles, that's all I know.'

'You're right,' Ben said. He poured wine into the plastic cups and distributed them. 'Nicola . . . Robin. . . .'

'I'd better pass, since I'm not contributing anything,' Robin said.

'Nonsense,' Ben said. 'All for one, and one for all on this seat, and ignore the envy of the peasants up front. Besides, if hunger does set in later, I shall have one of your filthy ham sandwiches. Anyway, you'll owe us a round of drinks or possibly two, that's all.'

'I'm flat broke until pay day,' Robin said. He took the cup. 'Not a sausage.'

'My dear chap,' Ben said, 'join the club. I think I have one solitary pound note in my wallet, which I shall probably preserve as a souvenir.'

'You could cash a cheque,' Nicola said.

'Cash a cheque!' Ben laughed. 'What a sweet, simple, unworldly girl you are to be sure. My bank hasn't cashed a cheque in living memory. They write nasty letters ordering me to do nothing of the kind. That's why I never see any telly. The set was repossessed six months ago.'

'Well, here's to us,' Nicola said. 'And the Festival.'

'May we all receive the fame and fortune we deserve,' Ben said. 'No, better revise that, on second thoughts. We may have achieved that already.'

'No, we haven't,' Nicola said. 'I haven't, and nor have you. None of us have. We need the kind of luck John Cramer had, that's all. He's very forceful, but I don't think he's all that brilliant any more. You're just as good an actor as he is, if not better.'

'It's not a question of how good,' Ben said seriously. 'It's more than that. Cramer only has to stand there, and glower from under those protruding eyebrows, and you're looking at him when he's on the screen. No one else. I have to work my socks off to make people look at me. Still, let's take a chance and drink to the original toast. The fame and fortune we deserve.' They drank.

'Not bad,' Ben said. 'Not bad at all. Your fellow has good taste. I liked him at Maurice's party. Seemed to be a very nice chap.'

'Yes, he is,' Nicola said. She considered making it clear that Harry was not her fellow any more, but it was too soon. She would have to work it out inside her, genuinely come to terms with it herself before she could adopt the necessary casual, throwaway tone. She fumbled for a cigarette, lit it, and looked out of the window. A lorry thundered past, throwing up a cloud of spray.

Ben's bright eyes studied her for a moment but he said no more about Harry. He was a much more deeply sensitive man than his conversation sometimes indicated. That was a front, and Nicola knew it.

'Come on Robin,' he said. 'Cheer up. Pay day's only just around the corner.'

'Oh, it's not just that,' Robin said. 'Carol's been giving me a lot of stick lately, that's all.'

'Wives are like that,' Ben said philosophically. 'They worry about trifles like tax demands and paying the rent, and getting pregnant, or not getting pregnant. Unless she's caught you being a naughty boy again? Is that it?'

'You name it, and that's what's wrong,' Robin said. 'I don't know if I can take much more of it.'

'I thought I perceived a certain lack of ardour when your better half bade you adieu,' Ben admitted.

'She made me give her my Access card,' Robin said, aggrieved. 'Said we were already in hock up to our necks, and she didn't want me using it to get money, and buy clothes I didn't need.'

'What low suspicious minds these women have,' Ben sighed.

Robin grinned wryly. 'Justified in this case,' he said. 'I wouldn't have minded so much if we'd talked it over, if she'd asked. But it was "I'll take that. You're not to be trusted with it."'

'There's a sergeant-major in all of them,' Ben said. 'Me, I surrendered my Barclaycard years ago. The idea of being able to acquire things on the spot by waving a silly little piece of plastic . . . I'm not temperamentally equipped to deal with it. I can get into quite enough trouble without that.'

'I was relying on it to see me through,' Robin said glumly.

'I can lend you a fiver, if you like,' Nicola said.

'Don't do it,' Ben advised. 'You'll never see it again.'

The coach droned hypnotically on. They finished the wine and started on the lagers, with whisky chasers. The conversation became fragmented, with long periods of silence.

'You've hardly said a word,' Ben said to Leonard. 'What's wrong? Girlfriend trouble?'

'She is not my girlfriend,' Leonard said. 'And yes, that is the trouble.'

'Ah, I see. You lust after the little lady, and she's spurned you.'

'She thought we had something going,' Leonard said, baffled, 'which was news to me. She was just someone to take to the cinema and parties, nice company, but that's all. Last night, she started making plans about coming to Treganwy and staying with me, and when it emerged that I didn't visualise anything of the kind, there was a scene. Tears, the whole bit. In the end, I had to push her through her front door and run.'

'You must have given her some reason to think you were interested,' Nicola said.

'I didn't,' Leonard said. 'Honestly. I mean, she's a nice girl, but she didn't turn me on, not in that way.' He brooded at the rain-streaked windows. 'It's always the same,' he said. 'If I'm a bit friendly, girls start getting ideas. I don't know why.'

'It must be your fatal charm,' Ben said. 'Which totally eludes me, to be brutally frank.'

Nicola closed her eyes. She was pleasantly drowsy. She felt secure and protected with these three men. She did not fancy any of them. Men who aroused her were few and far between, and the feeling was always allied with something deeper, which was why splitting up with Harry was so hard, but they were her friends, her own kind, and she experienced a kind of love for them, a sense of peace in their company.

It did not occur to Nicola to wonder why that feeling was reciprocated, why these men chose to sit with her, when there were plenty of young, good-looking women on board the coach. Nicola was analytical about her work, and her appearance, since that partly governed the roles she played, but while she could often be introspective, that did not extend to self-analysis.

She accepted it as a fact of life that those people whom she liked nearly always responded in kind. Without any conceit, she took it for granted. She would have been taken aback, and inclined to scoff, if someone had told her that many, women as well as men, found instinctive re-assurance in her very presence, her composure; that the sense of peace she found she also gave, with her warmth, her gentleness, her inner integrity. Because she offered trust it was returned in full measure, and justifiably so. Nicola could be relied upon, come the crunch, to be steadfast and true.

Nicola was consciously aware of none of this. All she knew was that she needed these men, her friends, she needed the six-month-long engagement away from London, before she could face the necessary break with Harry. She had needed these circumstances to do it.

It was done too, she thought dreamily, if sadly. She had left nothing behind. Not a trace of her remained in that flat. There was no reason for her ever to go back there again. She would have to find somewhere to live in the autumn, when the Festival was over. She supposed she would be obliged to share a flat with two or three other girls. Six months before she need worry about that. Plenty of time. No point in thinking about it yet. Think about the Festival. About playing with John Cramer. She might attract the attention she needed that way . . . all kinds of people were bound to come and see him . . . and would therefore see her as well . . . but was there enough in Mary to make an impression? . . . it was only a supporting part . . . could she inject that vital something in it to stand out?

. . . or would she simply be on stage, yet virtually invisible, while all eyes were fixed on John Cramer . . . perhaps she should have followed her first instinct, and pulled out . . . perhaps it was a mistake . . . but there was the necessity to end with Harry . . . that had come into it too. . . .

Perhaps it had been another mistake to make that impulsive suggestion that he should come and see the play . . . but he might not, he had not said he would . . . and even if he did, they could be just friendly . . . weeks would pass before they opened, and by then it would be nice to see him again for a day or two . . . there was no reason why they could not remain friends. . . .

The last thing she remembered before she fell asleep was Ben's voice, apparently in the far distance.

'I hope this hotel Maurice has booked us into has got a bar.'

Harry hoovered the flat, which did not take long, although he disliked doing it. He tried polishing the table and chest of drawers, but gave that up. Nicola managed to make it look effortless and easy. He merely seemed to be making a mess.

He could go shopping, or read a book, or watch television. None of them appealed much.

He would have to arrange for someone to come in regularly, and before he told his mother about Nicola, or she would take over like a dose of salts, fixing up twice-weekly sessions, and, it suddenly occurred to him, arriving to cook for him three weekends out of four. He would have to wriggle out of that somehow. How to manage that without hurting her feelings was another matter. His mother's feelings bruised easily when it suited her, which was when she wanted something.

The sheer silence in the flat was weighty and oppressive. He turned on the radio, but that was even worse, and he switched it off again. Nicola liked the radio on when she was at home during the day. The cheery jingles of the Capital programmes only emphasised that she was not there.

He supposed he could telephone, even if it was Saturday and not Sunday. Why not? Perhaps it was wrong to have a routine. Perhaps his calls should be pleasurably unexpected.

He sat down and dialled. That was different too. Just deciding, and doing it. Usually he hummed and ha'ed, and looked pointedly at his watch, hoping that Nicola would prompt him. She never did. Finally he would remark casually that he supposed he ought to phone, and she would decide to go and have a bath, or make coffee in the kitchen, or go and lie on the bed and read the Sunday newspapers. She never remained in the room, although since the small conversion was a shoddy one she could almost certainly hear what he was saying, unless the bath water was running.

'Hullo,' he said into the phone. 'It's me.'

'Oh, hullo.' The voice, like his own, was as neutral as ever, but also contained a note of surprise. 'Is something wrong?'

'No. Why?'

'You always phone on Sundays.'

'I wasn't aware that any rules had been laid down,' he said, which was unfair, since he had made his own rules. 'How's James?'

'Fine. Over his cold.'

'Good. Can I speak to him?'

'He's not here. He's gone to a birthday party.'

'Oh, I see,' Harry said.

'I suppose I could fetch him if you like,' the voice said, doubtfully. 'It's only across the road.'

'No, no, leave him. Let him enjoy his party.'

'Yes, it might be best if you spoke to him tomorrow, as usual. I'll tell him you called though.'

That sounded like a prelude to the "Well, I've got something in the oven," or the "Sorry, there's someone at the door," goodbye announcement, and Harry spoke hurriedly.

'As a matter of fact, I was wondering if I could see him tomorrow.'

'Tomorrow? It's not his Sunday to go to your mother's.'

'I know,' Harry said. 'I mean spend the day with me. I'd pick him up of course. Give him lunch and so on.'

'I'm afraid I've made other arrangements,' the voice said.

'Nicola's not here. She's working away.'

'That's beside the point. I've arranged a day out for him. Some friends are taking us to Whipsnade Zoo.'

He could hardly call her a liar. It might even be true.

'Oh, well,' he said, 'another time perhaps. I'll talk to him tomorrow morning, and see him at mother's next week.'

'Yes. You'll have to excuse me. I've just got out of the bath, and I've only got a towel wrapped round me.'

'Then how were you going to fetch James from across the road?' Harry enquired, but she had already hung up.

He replaced the receiver. He wondered if there was anything worth seeing at the cinema, and decided that it did not matter if there was anything worth seeing or not. He had to get out of this damned flat.

Nicola came awake as the coach began its descent of Treganwy's long main street, with its rows of small shops, and occasional neo-Georgian hotels, set back behind spacious lawns.

At the bottom of the hill the coach changed gear and began its ascent as the road climbed the other side of the gentle valley. The clouds were higher now, and patchy. The setting sun found a break somewhere miles ahead, and for a few fleeting seconds picked out Snowdon.

Nicola gazed at the spectacle through the windscreen of the coach, awed. There was snow on the summit of the mountain, which seemed to be sitting in towering majesty at the end of the main street, as if the coach were about to drive straight into it.

Thickening cloud cut off the sun, ending the brief optical illusion, and the mountain receded out of sight behind a veil of mist as if a curtain had been slowly drawn, but Nicola found it an unforgettable sight.

She was to find that it was not one which was often seen

from Treganwy. Most of the time the mountain was invisible, or a mere looming, distant, shapeless mass. But it was at that moment that she became determined, one day, to climb Snowdon.

There was no sign of the mountain the following morning when Nicola got out of bed and looked hopefully out of the window. There was no sign of anything very much. The tourists had not yet arrived to disturb the somnolent inactivity of Treganwy's Welsh Sunday.

Nicola was sharing a room with Linda. The hotel was at the lower price end of Treganwy's limited range, although comfortable enough, tucked away in a side street on the edge of the town. The company had their accommodation paid for a week. After that, they were on their own.

Like most of the others Nicola and Linda explored Treganwy after breakfast; this was neither terribly time-consuming, nor exhausting. Apart from the hotels, the shops, all closed, looked unexciting, but at least provided one of everything. The few prices which were visible on the traditional Welsh furniture in the antique shop were as alarming as any in London, indicating, presumably, that at least some of the anticipated visitors would have a lot of money to spend.

There were two small cinemas, two churches, several chapels, a sports field with a football pitch, and what they took to be a lake, which proved to be a reservoir.

It was a grey town, because of the stone out of which most of the buildings were constructed. Not ugly, just a little monotonous, but the air was brisk and pure, even if its hint of dampness accurately foretold more approaching rain.

At the far end of the town there was a sign pointing towards the Palace Hotel, and at the entrance to the drive a board promised bars, haute cuisine, games room, tennis, and private swimming pool, and told them that the AA had given it four stars.

They could just see the windows of what looked like

the dining room through the trees, half way up the hill, but just then the rain materialised and they turned back.

The few locals who were around glanced at them neutrally, noting their presence, but showed no great interest. The locals had seen companies of actors come and go every year for twenty years, and took them for granted when they did not ignore them. The actors were useful enough in attracting the visitors, but experience had taught the inhabitants that actors, while agreeable enough people, would unlike the tourists provide no great source of revenue.

The rest of Sunday was a lazy day, spent in desultory talk and reading the newspapers. Nicola borrowed the housekeeper's room, and pressed the clothes she would be wearing that week.

Work started at 10 am on Monday in a hall belonging to the town council, which they would use for rehearsals. *The Importance of Being Earnest* had reached a fairly advanced stage in London, but they had done little more than block *Midsummer Night's Dream,* and concentrated on that. Maurice issued the script of his 'Entertainment' which, at first glance, threatened to run something less than an hour, but he promised them lots of fun improvising the remainder. He had decided not to start on *Paula* until John Cramer arrived.

Nicola walked to the theatre at lunch time to have a look at it, and was pleasantly surprised. Despite a certain air of improvisation where bits and pieces had been added on the theatre itself was spacious and modern, larger than she had anticipated, with an agreeable bar and a cafeteria. The facilities were good, and the dressing rooms uncommonly light and airy. The stage was semi-apron style, wide and deep, and the curtain, if used, would not conceal the apron. That could create some problems with *Paula,* she thought, which was written for a proscenium stage.

Outside the stage door, in one corner of the car park, were three caravans. Nicola eyed the ungainly things, sitting at angles on the asphalt, and determined that she was not going to spend six months in one of those. Most of the other actors seemed to feel the same. In any case, the property master and the master carpenter had taken over one of them, and the wardrobe supervisor one of the others, which was full of clothes and from which came the busy sound of machining.

Nicola took the opportunity to go in and talk about her wardrobe for Gwendolen. She managed to steer the supervisor towards the dress which had caught her eye. She tried it on, they both inspected the result, the supervisor pinned it where it was too full around the waist, and promised to make the necessary alterations.

Maurice was flexible about time off from rehearsals to find accommodation, and gradually they began to get themselves fixed up. Maurice himself was staying in a self-contained flat at The Hall, which was Professor Griffiths' residence. Maurice had worked hard repairing the damage done by his outburst at the Garrick Club, and the Professor had, if not quite melted, at least begun to exhibit a stiff cordiality. In any case, it was traditional that the director of productions should stay at The Hall during the Festival, and the Professor was a great one for tradition.

'It's easier for me to jump on any daft ideas he gets, if I'm on the spot,' Maurice explained to the company.

Several of the cast, including Bernard Fyfield, took tiny flats in a row of converted cottages. Marcia settled for a bed and breakfast place for the time being, and would later look for a house for the month of August only, when her husband and little boy were to join her. Robin Haslem and Ben Stamford agreed to share a bungalow which was sparsely, not to say inadequately furnished. There would be room for their wives and children at a pinch, provided both families did not arrive together. Leonard Sherwen met a local family who took to him, and offered him a large room with its own kitchen. In the end, it was the ASMs and DSMs, even more impecunious than the rest, who moved into the caravans. Alan Cakin shared one with two DSMs, and Linda managed to squeeze herself in, improbably, with the wardrobe supervisor.

And Nicola found her cottage.

There was no bell. She hammered on the knocker. A small, birdlike, middle-aged woman opened the door, and peered at her cautiously.

'Mrs Roberts?' Nicola asked. 'I saw your card in the newsagent's window. It said you had a cottage to let.'

'Come in,' Mrs Roberts said.

A coal fire burned brightly in the living room. Mr Roberts was not much taller than his wife, which made his paunch look bigger than it really was.

'Well, I expect you'd like to look round,' Mrs Roberts said. She sounded doubtful for some reason.

Originally a tiny workman's cottage, all the accommodation was on the ground floor except the attic, which was unused, for the very good reason that it was full of junk. A double bedroom led directly off the living room, there was a small dining room, also with an open fireplace, the other side of the cupboard-like hall, and an extension built on to provide a kitchen and bathroom.

And that was it. But Nicola was enchanted. The furniture, if old-fashioned, was solid and well-built. The kitchen was decently fitted, with an electric stove and a refrigerator, and the bathroom, although cramped, was adequate.

At the side of the cottage was a small lawn of coarse meadow grass, surrounded by what she supposed were meant to be flower beds, in which weeds were already thriving vigorously. Nearly two miles outside Treganwy, the cottage was one of a small cluster perched half-way up a hill, beyond which, somewhere in the distance, was Snowdon.

In all her fantasies, which were fairly rich and frequent, Nicola had never dreamed of anything which would suit her so well. It was perfect. She could see it all now . . . waking in the big double bed to the birds and the rising sun . . . the well-stocked refrigerator . . . a cosy fire to keep her company when she was not at the theatre . . . having Leonard, and Ben and Robin to dinner . . . relaxing on the lawn on warm summer afternoons . . . and she would give a party one day for all the cast in this, her very own cottage . . . she could hardly believe her luck.

'I was afraid it might have gone,' she said.

'Well, we've had lots of people interested,' Mrs Roberts said. 'But we've been running the Merion Arms, you see.' Nicola had noticed the Merion Arms on the way, a small, undistinguished place which offered bed and breakfast. 'But my brother, who owns a hotel near London, he's not in the best of health, poor soul, and we're taking over his place for six months, while he recuperates, and we want someone to take it on for the full period.'

Nicola's interest in Mrs Roberts' brother was zero, but she grasped the important point.

'Well, that's just right,' she said. It occurred to her that in the face of someone's illness she should blend her delight with some degree of sympathy. 'That is, I'm sorry about your brother, and I hope he makes a full recovery, but I need somewhere to live for just the six months.'

'You'll be one of the actors, I expect,' Mrs Roberts said dubiously. She appeared about as impressed by the profession as the residents of Treganwy itself, but Nicola nodded, and gave her a winning smile anyway.

'Do you go to the theatre much, Mrs Roberts?'

'Never been at all,' Mrs Roberts said. 'Have we, Elwyn?' she added, perhaps wishing to check her facts. Mr Roberts pursed his lips, gave the proposition the consideration it deserved, and shook his head firmly.

'The thing is,' Mrs Roberts said, 'we take a pride in our home. Take all the furniture, for instance. It may not be new, but it's good, and we wouldn't want it spoiled . . .'

'I'd look after it as if it were my own,' Nicola promised her. 'Keep everything clean and polished . . .'

'. . . by cigarette ends, and beer stains, and the like,' Mrs Roberts, who had not finished, went on. 'Because I expect you'd be having people here, and giving parties, and so on.'

'That hadn't even crossed my mind,' Nicola lied promptly. 'I shall be working too hard for anything like that.'

Mr Roberts spoke for the first time. 'There's another difficulty, you see,' he announced. 'And that's the garden. Our pride and joy, that garden is. We would't like to think of it being let go.' He shook his head lugubriously. 'Couldn't bear to think of that garden being allowed to get run down, and with you being that busy, and never here . . . well . . .' His voice died away as he contemplated the impending catastrophe.

Nicola glanced through the window at the beds of weeds, and the patchy, unkempt lawn, which clearly had its last contact with anything like a mower in the somewhat distant past.

'Oh, I love gardening,' Nicola said. 'I'd keep the lawn mowed, and look after the flowers, and . . .' She groped for the appropriate words. '. . . do the weeding . . . and prune . . . and graft . . and things like that.' She knew nothing whatever about gardening, but there must be books on the subject. To spend her six months here in this cottage, instead of in a wretched caravan, or some dreary room, she would stand on her head.

'Yes, but I'm afraid the mower needs sharpening,' Mrs Roberts said, dredging up the final, impossible obstacle.

'I'll have it sharpened as soon as I move in,' Nicola said, disposing of that one. She felt there could be no remaining objections.

'We were really thinking of a single gentleman,' Mrs Roberts said. 'Or a *married* couple.' Her eyes flickered to Nicola's third finger, left hand, bare of rings, to Nicola's eyes, to the stringy hedge which flanked the lawn.

Beyond the hedge was the shape of Maurice's car. Beside the car was Maurice Gardiner frowning impatiently, and looking at his watch.

'Oh, that's no one,' Nicola said quickly. 'I mean, he's my director. He very kindly offered to drive me here, but now he'll want to get back to rehearsals. What I'm trying to say is, I shall be here on my own. I shan't be sharing with anyone.'

'What people get up to is their own business. Live and let live is what we say,' Mrs Roberts said. 'But we do have neighbours, and we have to consider them. Besides which, we shall be coming back at the end of summer.'

'Well, I shan't be getting up to anything,' Nicola said. 'I'm here to act for the season, and that's all that matters, as far as I'm concerned. There's no one in my life just now, not even a boyfriend, so you needn't worry about the neighbours. There'll be nothing for them to see.'

'Well . . .' Mrs Roberts said doubtfully. She sought her husband's eyes. Silence reigned. Neither gave any indication one way or the other, as far as Nicola could see, but presumably some form of telepathic communication took place. 'Three months' rent in advance, breakages to be paid for, electricity on top,' she said finally.

Joyfully, Nicola took out her cheque book.

'How much will the rent be?'

'Forty pounds a week,' Mrs Roberts said.

'Forty!' Nicola was appalled. That would be half her salary gone, just to have a roof over her head.

'We could get far more than that during July and August,' Mrs Roberts said.

'Yes, but you said you don't want all the trouble of separate lettings,' Nicola reminded her. 'Surely, at this time of year, you'd have trouble finding anyone at all.'

'Thirty-five a week,' Mrs Roberts said firmly. 'We couldn't possibly drop below that, could we Elwyn?' Mr Roberts, reproducing what seemed to be his main conversational gambit, pursed his lips and shook his head.

Nicola climbed into the car.

'Sorry I've been so long,' she apologised. 'Anyway, it's all fixed up.' She would have to get on to her bank with a damn good sob story, she thought, or that bloody cheque would bounce. She wondered if she had been conned rotten.

'I don't know why you want to live all out here, with no transport,' Maurice said, accelerating downhill along the narrow, winding lane.

'It's only about half an hour's walk,' Nicola said, 'and I like walking.' It suddenly occurred to her that, after an evening performance, she would be slogging up this hill on her own at eleven or twelve o'clock at night, in pitch darkness.

'How much did they sting you?'

'Too much,' Nicola said. 'But I wanted a place I could think of as my own home for six months.'

It would feel like her own home as soon as Mr and Mrs Roberts had gone, she was sure of that.

John Cramer flew into London Airport from Nice, travelling first class on Air France. He received his usual VIP treatment, although this did not quite extend to Immigration, where the officials were respectful, but made certain they were familiar with all the details of his visit, his plans while in the UK, and his proposed date of departure.

There were no reporters or photographers waiting for him at the airport. Cramer wanted minimum publicity on this trip, and had made that plain to the PR firm he employed. Despite the myth to the contrary, sedulously fostered by those who craved attention, anyone, even a film star, could move around the world, let alone London, without being unduly bothered unless he wished to be. Reporters and photographers en masse appeared, by and large, when they were drummed up, and not otherwise. It would be the London show business feature writers he would have to worry about.

The only person waiting for him was Valerie Foster, at the wheel of his blue Rolls Royce Corniche drop-head coupé. She had driven it up from the South of France a few days beforehand, and crossed over on the ferry from Cherbourg to Southampton. She got out, watched the porter as he stowed the luggage in the boot, tipped him generously from the expenses float she always carried and got back into the car, but this time into the front passenger seat. Cramer would drive. Cramer always drove. He disliked being a passenger, particularly with a woman at the wheel.

'Good trip?' she asked.

'Same as usual.'

'No need to hide behind those shades,' she said. 'The press won't bother you until later.' Cramer made no move to take his sunglasses off, despite the dullness of the day, even when the Rolls Royce entered the exit tunnel.

'I didn't get much sleep last night,' he said.

His conversational voice was flat, with a faint, harsh rasp. It enhanced his sheer animal masculinity. Everything about Cramer turned women on. His eyes were a light, piercing blue, of formidable intensity. A slight scar marred his left cheek, and gave his somewhat saturnine face a faint air of menace which, added to those eyes, came in handy when he was playing heavies. He was not a conventionally handsome man and, at forty-five, there were frown lines on his forehead, tiny cracks splayed out from the corners of those eyes as if he were always squinting into the sun; the skin on his face was coarsening prematurely. It all added up, by means of some curious chemistry, to a blatant, urgent sexuality, which was why he was where he was, both in his private and professional life.

Cramer was not tall, but his body was muscular and powerful. He worked hard, in some ways, to keep himself in good shape, or at least to stem the damage imposed by time and other factors.

The Rolls Royce glided imperiously on to the M4 and drifted silently along at seventy miles an hour.

'You said you didn't want the Dorchester or the Savoy,' Valerie said, 'so I've taken the Crown Suite at the River Park Hotel. It's not bad.'

'Fine,' Cramer said, although with little interest. Other people arranged such things. They just happened.

'And at Treganwy,' Valerie said, 'there's only one hotel, the Palace, which claims to have a suite. I haven't been able to check it out, but . . .'

'Yes, all right,' Cramer cut her short, bored. He flashed his headlights at an impudent Mini which was obstructing the Rolls Royce's silent progress. The Mini hurriedly moved out of the way.

'Some of the show business editors have been

on,' Valerie said. 'The *Mail*, the *Express*, the *Mirror* and . . .'

'Who the hell tipped them off?' Cramer growled. 'I told Manny I didn't want anything.'

'It wasn't him,' Valerie said. 'Someone in the hotel, probably, hoping to earn a few pounds. Besides which, your Professor's been broadcasting it. I put them off for the time being, but you'll have to do something. If you make too much of a secret of it, they're going to think they're missing something juicy.'

The elevated section of the M4 at Chiswick was jammed solid because of a broken-down van on the inside lane. Even the Corniche could not penetrate the stationary rows of cars and articulated lorries; Cramer sat staring through the windscreen. His fingers drummed on the steering wheel.

'Who was the one who did a piece on me when we were shooting in Madrid?' he asked, at last.

'Vincent Consel,' Valerie said.

'He played fair,' Cramer said. 'I'll talk to him.'

The Crown Suite was much like any other suite in any other modern hotel, anywhere in the world. Cramer had occupied such suites in many countries in most of the continents. It lacked the grand piano which Claridges might have provided, but Cramer was not musically inclined.

'I need a shower,' Cramer said. 'Then you can get what's-his-name, and give me a drink.'

Cramer came out of the shower, slipped on a white towelling wrap, called to Valerie, lay on the bed, and lifted the bedside telephone.

'You're through to Mr Cramer now,' Valerie's voice said. 'Vincent Consel for you,' she added, tactfully giving Cramer a needed reminder of the newspaperman's name.

'Hullo, Vince,' Cramer said.

'Hullo, Johnnie,' Vincent Consel said. 'Nice of you to remember me.' That was flannel, not irony. Vincent Consel knew them all, and was accustomed to being on first-name terms with those he had written features about, who included Garbo, Dietrich and Brando.

'Listen,' Cramer said, 'I'm going to level with you. This is a private trip, of no interest to anyone but me. It's a personal thing, and I don't want people hanging about for interviews all the time.'

The journalist chuckled into the phone. 'Naturally, I believe you,' he said. 'But some of my more cynical colleagues even now knocking it back in El Vino's wouldn't. If you want a recipe to arouse intense curiosity, you've hit on it in one.'

'I know that,' Cramer rasped. Valerie came into the bedroom and silently handed him a glass of whisky with ice and water. 'Suppose I give you an exclusive,' Cramer went on. 'Just you. What then?'

'The other hacks would lose interest,' Vincent said. 'They're a jealous bunch of bastards.'

'That's what I thought,' Cramer said. Valerie had begun to unpack his cases. He watched her slim, high-heeled legs as she moved efficiently around the bedroom.

'Suits me fine if it suits you,' Vincent said. 'When did you have in mind?'

'Hold on,' Cramer said. He covered the mouthpiece. 'Valerie. Stop doing that.'

She looked at him. 'Why?'

'You know why,' Cramer said.

She knew why, as she looked at him lying on the bed in his white towelling wrap. The ice-blue eyes seemed to bore through her clothes. Her heart began to bump. She swallowed.

'This won't take long,' Cramer said. 'Start now.' He uncovered the mouthpiece. 'I'm going to be tied up for about an hour,' he said. 'But we could kill a bottle of scotch some time after that, if you like.' He gestured to Valerie to come closer to the bed.

With fingers which were not quite steady Valerie undressed, while Cramer talked steadily into the telephone as he watched her. Her clothes lay on the floor where they fell. That man could turn her to fire without laying a finger on her.

Cramer chatted away on the phone, making small talk, until she stood naked in front of him.

'O.K. then, Vince,' he said casually. 'See you then. Look forward to it.'

He returned the receiver to its rest, sat up, and slipped off his white towelling wrap. He held out his hand. Valerie took it. He continued to look at her in silence for half a minute. Then, suddenly, he pulled her on to the bed, and covered her at once.

Valerie caught her breath. Her fingernails scored into his back.

'You bastard,' she groaned.

'Yes,' John Cramer said. He continued to drive into her until she thought she would faint.

# CHAPTER FOUR

Cramer topped up Vincent Consel's glass, which took the whisky bottle below the half-way mark. So far all they had done was chat idly, and reminisce about mutual acquaintances. Cramer told a story about Anthony Quinn which Vincent had heard before, but he laughed noisily anyway. Cramer told it well, effortlessly mimicking Quinn's voice.

Vincent was glad he had decided to send a couple of sandwiches down to his stomach before he arrived. This was going to be one of those evenings. In Madrid, a night's solid drinking with Cramer had ended at three am with Cramer, apparently, completely unaffected. Fortunately Vincent had a good head for drink, and iron self-control in keeping its effects at bay for long enough to get his work done. He had had a lot of practice, being obliged, more often than he could now recall, to keep pace with some of the hardest drinkers, both male and female, in the world of show business.

In Madrid he had forced himself to put the bones of it down on paper before he surrendered, collapsed on to his bed fully dressed, and passed out. The following morning, groaning, he forced himself to get up and catch his early flight back to London. On the plane, still hung over, her peered blearily at his misty, quivering notes, and realised that he had a pretty good feature on Cramer. It was gutsy, it caught the outward characteristics of the man, while not betraying the confidences which Cramer had wanted kept off the record.

And it had paid off. Here he was, back for an exclusive, no trouble at all, merely by making one phone call after a routine tip-off.

Cramer took a deep swallow of whisky and Vincent followed suit. He sometimes felt that it was a tough way to make a living, matching glass for glass with characters like Cramer. However, it was no more than an occupational hazard as far as he was concerned. He could cope with it when he was required to, which was on occasions like this, but except on duty he drank very little. He remembered the story about the dresser to a well-known actor, one of whose duties was to ensure that a virgin bottle of scotch was delivered to the dressing room nightly, before every performance. Vincent was not in that league, thank God, a bottle-a-day lush.

He wondered if Cramer was in that league. It was hard to make the man out. Cramer could certainly put it away, but there was none of the gossip about him which surrounded some of the piss-artists in the business, none of these stories about problems in the studio, or on location. Cramer's reputation was the reverse: highly professional, always on time, ever ready to work late or forgo a day off, he treated the camera as the intimate friend it was to him, and he always knew his lines for the day's shooting even if they bore little resemblance to those in the script.

Cramer was not universally popular with screenplay writers, Vincent knew that. As an actor, Cramer believed that a film evolved as it was being made, that he and the director would find opportunities, and faults, which would never be apparent to a man working on a typewriter months beforehand.

Writers, on the other hand, who might have spent a year or more slaving over the screenplay, did not easily accept that an actor was likely to come up with something better on the spur of the moment, but since Cramer not only exercised script control these days, but also had a considerable reputation as a writer in his own right, there was nothing they could do about it, except complain. Which they did, as the saying went, all the way to the bank.

Ironically though, on the one occasion when Cramer had flatly rejected the draft screenplay lock stock and barrel, and insisted, successfully, that if he were to star in the film he must write the screenplay himself, the script was adhered to word for word. For some reason, that movie had not been one of Cramer's greatest successes.

Vincent Consel knew all these things, and as a well-read man who made a living from words himself he found them of absorbing personal interest. His readers, however, would not. Despite the bums and tits which had begun to infiltrate Vincent's paper his own signed features were still, he liked to think, well-written, and reasonably up-market. Just the same, anything about scripts and writers was 'yawn-and-turn-the-page' time. A surprising number of people still liked to believe that actors made it up as they went along.

As for Cramer's drinking habits, Vincent was content to leave those to the gossip columnists, poor sods, and none of them had yet referred to John Cramer as being tired and emotional. The man probably cut loose in between movies, or when he knew he could sleep it off the next day, one way perhaps of coping with the stress of his artificial, if astoundingly highly paid life.

While Vincent and Cramer chatted and swigged whisky in the sitting room of the suite Valerie Foster came and went at intervals, showing Cramer messages, checking this and that with efficient brevity. Vincent had thought what an attractive girl she was when he met her in Madrid. She still was.

At one point she said to Cramer, 'You were going to speak to Denise tonight.'

Cramer looked at his watch. 'Oh, you do it. Say I'm free this weekend, and arrange something.' Valerie nodded and went. She must be using one of the bedrooms as an office, or perhaps the Crown Suite boasted a study. Vincent had never explored it, although he had been there before once. Was that Aznavour? He had forgotten.

'How is your first wife?' Vincent asked. He had met Denise Cramer once, years ago, at a Cannes Film Festival.

'Fine,' Cramer said. He reached for the whisky bottle.

'You still see her then?'

'Naturally,' Cramer said. 'Whenever I see the children, which is as often as I can.'

'She's not thinking of marrying again?'

'I wish she would,' Cramer said.

Vincent thought there was something concealed behind Cramer's casual reply, and he thought he knew what. He wondered whether to pursue it, glanced at his watch, and decided against it. He must establish the line his feature would take before they started on the second bottle of scotch, and so far he had very little.

Valerie came in, announced that she was going to dinner, and asked what Cramer intended to do about food

'I'll send for something later on, if I feel like it,' Cramer said. He looked at Vincent. 'How about you?'

'I wouldn't mind something,' Vincent said. 'Cold buffet, perhaps.'

'I'll arrange it,' Valerie said.

Vincent wondered if Cramer and that good-looking girl were having it off. Probably. Cramer was the kind of man who needed sex wherever he was, and just now his second wife was in the South of France.

'Will Wendy be joining you at Treganwy?' Vincent asked. John Cramer might not be courting publicity, but Professor Griffiths was. Every paper in Fleet Street had received the press handout, written in the turgid prose which for some reason seemed to afflict academics.

'No,' Cramer said. 'She's preparing for the move to California.'

'Where will that be? Beverly Hills? Coldwater Canyon?'

'No idea,' Cramer said. 'We'll rent somewhere to begin with. Take our time before buying. It's got to be the right place.' The bottle tilted and gurgled over Vincent's glass again.

'If it's all right with you, Johnnie,' Vincent said, 'I'd like to get down to business, before you get me so smashed I can't even talk. What's with this Treganwy thing?'

'Nothing at all,' Cramer said. 'I'm doing a play there, that's all.'

'Come on,' Vincent said. 'Do me a favour. International film stars do not appear in a new play no one's ever heard of in some God-forsaken hole in North Wales.'

'I do,' Cramer said.

'Yes, but why? Off the record, if you like. You know I'll respect anything you say.'

'There's nothing to go off the record about,' Cramer said.

'It doesn't make sense,' Vincent said. 'There's nothing in it for you. There can't be. There's no earthly reason why you should do it.'

'There's a perfectly good reason,' Cramer said. 'David Griffiths was a professor at Cambridge when I was an undergraduate there. He's been after me to appear at Treganwy for years, as a personal favour to him, and I've finally been able to oblige.'

'But you haven't worked in the theatre for . . . how long? Ten or twelve years?' Vincent knew perfectly well how long it was. He had looked it up. He took pains to be briefed about his subjects.

'I'm opening on Broadway in the autumn, precisely because I feel it's time to do some theatre again,' Cramer said.

'Yes, but if the figures I hear being bandied about are right, you're being paid a fortune for that,' Vincent said. 'And anyway, that's just the prelude to the movie. Treganwy never did pay well . . . unless you think this play might turn into a film later on?'

'I'm being paid practically nothing,' Cramer said. 'And I'd be amazed if the play ever became a film.' He was not surprised that this sceptical, worldly, acute journalist had missed the explanation which was under his nose, but he was relieved. It had been a calculated risk talking to Vincent Consel, or any journalist, but he had guessed that none of them would perceive the obvious. The minds of even good newspapermen like Vincent Consel ran on tramlines, sex, fame, money, achievement. It was not much of a gamble to take that Vincent would fail to imagine the horrendous, stomach-knotting fear which afflicted him at nights, and it had come off, as he had expected. Just as well. The truth was bad enough when Cramer was forced to contemplate it, alone, in the small hours of the morning. Cramer knew himself. He could just about wrestle with it, provided no other living person ever knew. For anyone else to know the truth would be utterly unbearable.

'You're not having me on?' Vincent asked. 'That's all there is to it. A personal favour?'

'That's all there is to it,' Cramer said. He stared straight into Vincent's eyes.

Vincent chewed his lip for a moment. He had the feeling that he was missing something, that somewhere there was some chink in this invincible man's armour, some unimaginable human weakness which he could not identify, but which would provide a key to Cramer the man, which, good as that first feature had been, Vincent yet knew he had failed to find. But facing those steady, unblinking, glacial eyes, the half-formed suspicion that this Treganwy business had some deep, unexplained significance wilted and died. He was pretty certain that no man who could stare at you like that, unwinkingly, for so long, had something to hide.

'O.K., let's forget Treganwy,' Vincent said. 'But I've got to have something to pin a feature on. Some angle.'

'Time we cracked the second bottle,' Cramer said. He got up. As soon as his back was turned to Vincent he blinked rapidly, several times, with relief. Early in his career Cramer had learned how the camera loved his pale blue eyes, especially if he held a steady, level gaze with no movement of the eyelids. It was also, he had discovered, pretty effective in certain situations in his private life too. He had practised assiduously and could, if he wished, stare without blinking for long periods, but recently it was becoming more of a strain.

He parked the new bottle on the low table between them and sat down again in the deep armchair.

'My early life,' he suggested. 'Starting with nothing . . .'

'I don't want to do the barefoot, East End boy who made good again,' Vincent said. 'The world's bloody bulging with them.'

'I was born in Hounslow,' Cramer said. 'Which is about as far from the East End as you can get.'

'It's still the same story,' Vincent said. 'Workman's

cottage, two up two down, no bath, and a bog out the back. Your father was a fireman during the blitz on London, came home one day to find your house had been bombed, your mother was dead, and you, a small boy, trying to dig her out with your bare hands. That was how you got that scar on your cheek.' Now, as previously, Vincent was not convinced that Cramer's scar had really been caused by the explosion of a German bomb. Football studs could tear a boy's face like that, and Cramer had played a lot of football when he was young. Still, a star was entitled to put a certain gloss on his stories, and there was no percentage in nit-picking if you were trying to get a man to tell you something interesting. 'After that, the conventional heavy stepmother, trouble at home, you ran away a couple of times, but still managed to sail through grammar school, passing every examination in sight, and finally collected a prestigious scholarship to Cambridge. By now you had the acting bug, you auditioned at RADA, got a place, and quit Cambridge after a year.'

'You could write my biography,' Cramer said, smiling.

'I couldn't,' Vincent said. 'I only know the public image, not the private man.'

'I'm an actor,' Cramer said. 'The image is what people want to see.'

'Correction,' Vincent said. 'You *were* an actor. Now you're a star. That makes it a different ball game.'

'So I drop my trousers and shit like anyone else,' Cramer said. 'Big deal.'

Vincent smothered a burp which contained a trace of bile. He was not sure which one of them was rambling, himself or Cramer.

'You picked on me,' he said. 'Come and do a feature, Vince, exclusive. Well, you know what they say about bricks without straw, Johnnie. So come on, give with some straw, and I'll make a brick. If you want some kind of snow job, you've got the wrong man. I'm not here to do a re-hash of old press handouts.' Vincent had the momentary illusion that he was sitting somewhere outside his own head, looking at himself. The snarl in his own voice made himself, as observer, curl up. One glass too many.

He always became aggressive, for no reason, when he had had too much. God, what a lost day tomorrow was going to be. He must control himself, at least until he walked out of this suite, on unnaturally stiff legs, so that he did not betray himself by staggering. Vincent was not the kind to apologise but he managed an affable smile, in the hope that would take the sting out of his offensiveness. The scar on Cramer's cheek was more visible than usual, but if that betrayed anger his voice did not.

'O.K., Vince, fair comment,' Cramer said pleasantly. 'Now I know what you're after, let's start again.'

Fortuitously, a cold buffet on a trolley was wheeled in at that point. The process of selection, before the waiter was dismissed, gave Vincent the opportunity to pull himself together. Then the business of eating provided an excuse to leave his brimming glass of scotch untouched.

Cramer merely nibbled at cheese and biscuits, having got into the habit, he explained, of eating dinner very late.

'All right,' Cramer said, sipping his whisky as Vincent ate. 'Let's look for something that'll suit you. How about my last film? You probably know I directed it myself. That was a first. I've never done that before.'

'I heard that it ran four weeks over schedule,' Vincent said. 'And enough over budget to give the money men ulcers.'

'I happen to think the result will be worth it,' Cramer said. 'There were also quite interesting reasons for the overrun. Whether you'd find them interesting, I don't know.'

'I probably would,' Vincent said. 'The trouble is, it's too soon for a feature to appear like tomorrow, which is what you seem to have in mind.'

'Well, in the fairly near future,' Cramer said. 'The whole idea is so that I'll be left alone while I'm in Treganwy.'

'That movie's not scheduled for release in London until late summer, is it,' Vincent said. 'That'll be the time to tie in that kind of thing.'

'Fine. We'll talk again about that,' Cramer said. 'There's my next novel. Anything there?'

'The one you were working on when we talked in Madrid? Have you finished it?'

'Due for simultaneous publication in New York and London in the autumn,' Cramer said.

'I'm not sure mine's the right paper,' Vincent said. 'I mean, I think your books are bloody good, and I'll be glad to give it a puff come publication day, but we're not the *Guardian*, which is basically read by people who might buy books, hence its minuscule circulation. We're mass circulation, basically read by people who don't buy books, except TV spin-offs or the latest soft porn in paperback, which isn't your scene.'

'No, it isn't,' Cramer said, with feeling.

'You see, in one sense, your novels have been one hell of an achievement,' Vincent said. 'The reviewers paid you the ultimate compliment. They treated you as a serious novelist, bandied comparisons with Graham Greene about, and so forth. Great. Terrific. That took some doing, considering that actors aren't supposed to have any brains, and film stars even less.' Cramer smiled thinly, the same smile, it occurred to Vincent, which Cramer had used in the small part as a pathological killer in the early movie which had made his name. 'But although your books have sold respectably, gone into paperback, translated, and all that, they haven't been the runaway bestsellers one might have expected, despite your name on the covers.'

Cramer gestured dismissively. 'I wasn't trying to write bestsellers.'

'You mean you were writing for the critics?'

'No, I don't,' Cramer said tartly. He was finding his irritation with Vincent hard to conceal. 'I was writing for myself.'

'Whether that might be regarded as wanking or not,' Vincent said, 'is an argument I'd enjoy, but my readers wouldn't know what the hell we were on about.'

Cramer sighed, and sipped his whisky again. He had slowed down, Vincent observed, which was probably just as well.

'We'll have that argument some other time, when we

meet socially,' Cramer said. 'But thanks for the back-handed compliment anyway. It's true, I do want to be regarded as a serious writer. In fact in a perfect world I think I'd pack in the acting business, and stick to writing.'

'Why not?' Vincent enquired. 'What's stopping you?'

'Money,' Cramer said briefly. He smiled sardonically. 'As you pointed out earlier, my books may sell well, but they're not smash hits.'

'I could also point out,' Vincent said, 'that what you might regard as a modest success would have most writers moving to Ireland to avoid tax. You probably earn more from your books in one year than most professional novelists in this country do in ten. Mind you, they don't expect to run Rolls Royces.'

'Everything's relative,' Cramer said. 'Things happen more or less by accident. Many years ago, when I was with the Royal Shakespeare on twenty quid a week, I thought I was rich. Now I not only support two wives, and their children, I prop up a whole empire, agents, lawyers, managers, publicity men, business advisers, accountants, and God knows what else besides. It's a great big inverted pyramid, with me holding it up. It's Catch-22. Unless my earnings go on increasing, not just stay as they are, but increase, the whole bloody lot collapses. And remember, I'm the one underneath. I'm the one who stands to get crushed. In the insane world of the movie business I can keep that pyramid in the air. But I'm only as good as my last picture. If the time ever comes when I flop, or make a fool of myself, stop being a bankable name, I'm finished. Wiped out.'

'The heart bleeds,' Vincent said unsympathetically. 'I think you should make up your mind what you are, and stop trying to have it all ways. There are actors. There are writers. There are a few actors who write. I can't say I know of any writers who act.'

'A Jack of all trades? I've never seen why a man can't be master of all.'

'He's more likely to land up making his money from one, and a dilettante at the rest,' Vincent said. 'This pyramid of yours . . . I remember being at some literary do.

There was an academic, wrote brilliant novels, about one every five years. The critics loved him. He was a household name, at least in the households of those who read the *New Statesman* and the *Spectator*. Spoke at literary lunches, reviewed books himself for the *Observer*, gave talks on Radio Four, a regular guest on television book programmes, that sort of bloke. He was laying down the law about why writing should be a part-time occupation, guff about how he needed time for his art, with no commercial pressures, the virtues of being able to lay a book aside, nourishing his roots in real life. Real life! His college, book reviewing, radio and television! Anyway, you know the kind of crap. Now that merchant didn't know it, or perhaps he did, but what he really meant was that he was shit-scared of putting his talent to the ultimate test without the security of his lecturer's salary coming in nice and regular. He was frightened of being a freelance, of making that final commitment, living on his ability. Because deep down, he knew he didn't have the ability. He was a dilettante. So he needed his own pyramid, which he couldn't get out from under, a far cry from yours, admittedly, a Ford instead of a Rolls Royce, the cottage in the country he was buying, school fees at Bedales for his only son, the urgent necessity for his annual pilgrimage to Greece . . . what the hell was I leading up to?' Vincent wondered. 'Oh, yes, I know. The best writing is done by professionals because writing is a profession, and like any other it needs constant practice, the guts to rely on it for a living, which implies the courage to risk failing, and a lifetime's experience is no bad thing.'

Vincent realised that, unconsciously, the glass was at his lips again. He leaned over and put it down.

In doing so he failed to notice the bunching of Cramer's fist. Cramer breathed deeply, and deliberately relaxed his clenched fingers.

It would have been a pleasure to knock Vincent Consel spinning from his chair, but not one he could indulge. He smiled grimly to himself. That would have given the man the basis for a feature, all right. But he needed this journalist. He must not show how often his remarks – perhaps random from booze, perhaps shrewdly perceptive, it was impossible to say – were inflaming raw nerves.

'I always assumed you received a hefty salary yourself, and even heftier expenses,' Cramer said, with a smile any witness would have sworn was genuinely friendly. 'I take it you intend to resign tomorrow, and join the ranks of the freelances.'

'Christ, no,' Vincent said cheerfully. 'I'm a newspaperman, not a writer. There's a difference. But I respect the bastards who can do it, because I know they've got something I haven't. Oh, yes, I've the traditional half-finished novel at home, but it's been around too long. Even if I do finish the fucking thing some time, and it gets published, and it's a wow, that won't turn me into a writer. I've managed to face that particular uncomfortable fact. It might mean I was a good amateur, but there's a hell of a difference between the amateur and the pro. Every bugger thinks he can write because he learned the alphabet. Why, God knows. Most people can run at a pinch, but that doesn't give them the delusion they're Olympic milers.'

Cramer judged that the time was ripe. It would probably lead to some more needling barbs from Vincent Consel, but what the hell. Why should he, John Cramer, take any notice of a half-drunken hack?

'I've never written anything for the stage yet,' Cramer said reflectively. 'There's an American producer who wants to commission a play from me. Try it out off Broadway.'

'You're the sort of bloke who really turns me up, do you know that?' Vincent groaned, although his reaction was cordial, not hostile. 'Is there any damn thing you can't turn your hand to?'

'The problem is, finding the right subject,' Cramer said. 'The producer did put one to me, it happened to a friend of his, but I'm not sure. Do you mind if I try it out on you? See what you think?'

'The night is young,' Vincent said. He caught sight of his watch. 'Well, not all that young, but still . . . go ahead.'

'This man,' Cramer said, 'lived in New York. He'd been married for a long time to an English woman. They had two sons. The play begins when the wife flies home to see her parents, who are getting on. She's to stay for three months, and come home on a liner – the second half of a round-the-world cruise. A sort of holiday for her. Well, the man has been dying to have an affair. . . .'

'Why?' Vincent interjected.

'Someone he knew,' Cramer said. 'He'd never done anything about it, much though he wanted to. It seemed to him that an affair was the only way to get this woman out of his system. So while his wife was abroad, he did, but it wasn't like an affair. It was wonderful. It was glorious. Far from getting her out of his system, it was the reverse. He knew that he couldn't live without her. He knew that he had to tell his wife as soon as she came back from England.'

Something seemed to have attracted Vincent Consel's interest and he was listening with close attention. Cramer thought that he had got it right. Not too oblique, just sufficient to arouse the journalist's instincts, to make him speculate, wonder, and want to hear more.

'He met the boat,' Cramer went on, 'and drove his wife to their home. She seemed in a strange mood. He assumed she was tired. He gave her a couple of drinks to calm her, and he was just about to lead up to telling her about the other woman when, to his astonishment, she suddenly burst into floods of tears. He tried to console her, without knowing what was wrong, but that only seemed to make her feel worse. She kept on crying, and sobbing things like "It didn't mean anything . . . honestly . . . you must believe that . . . if only I'd flown straight home instead of coming on that damn boat . . . it was only because I missed you so much . . . I was thinking about you all the time. . . ."'

'That'll make a good scene,' Vincent remarked.

'That's what I thought,' Cramer said. 'Anyway, the man started comforting her, and before he knew where he was, he was in bed with her.'

'Sexy bastard, isn't he,' Vincent said.

'Well, this was really only from compassion,' Cramer said.

'Oh, I see,' Vincent said.

'Just the same,' Cramer said, 'he lay in bed afterwards and thought, "Oh, my God, what have I done?" He couldn't very well tell his wife he wanted to marry another woman when he'd just made love to her, after all.'

'It could be a bit dodgy,' Vincent said. 'I can see that.'

'So he thought he'd better leave it for a month or two, and lead up to it gradually.'

'Sound thinking,' Vincent said.

'But before he got around to telling her,' Cramer said, 'she announced, all smiles, that she was pregnant.'

'The plot thickens,' Vincent said.

'So now he was in a hell of a quandary,' Cramer said.

'He would be,' Vincent said.

'He couldn't very well divorce a pregnant woman,' Cramer said. 'But . . . he had no way of knowing whether the child was his or not.'

'Gripping stuff,' Vincent said. 'What happens in the end?'

'I haven't quite worked that out yet,' Cramer said.

'No, I mean in real life,' Vincent said.

'Oh,' Cramer said, 'I think she had a daughter.'

'Was it his?'

'She looked a little bit like him. But of course, he could never be certain, short of blood tests.'

'Did he have blood tests done?'

'He wasn't that sort of man,' Cramer said.

'A gentleman to the end,' Vincent said. 'Did he ever marry this other lady, his own true love?'

'I think there was a divorce later on,' Cramer said. 'As far as I know, they're still married. Do you think it would make a play?'

'I can see it all,' Vincent said. 'With you in the lead.'

'It's not my sort of part,' Cramer said.

'You surprise me,' Vincent said. 'You say this all happened to a friend of this American producer?'

'That's right,' Cramer said.

'Amazing,' Vincent said. He looked at his watch again. 'Well, I shall finish this glass and then be on my way.'

'We haven't come up with anything for your exclusive article yet.'

'Maybe not, Johnnie, but you've done your best,' Vincent said. 'And a nod is as good as a wink to a blind horse, as they say.'

'You've lost me,' Cramer said. 'Although I don't think you're a blind horse.'

'True,' Vincent said. 'Nor am I a great believer in coincidence.'

'What kind of coincidence?'

'As you well know, Johnnie,' Vincent said, 'much more circulates around Fleet Street than ever gets into the papers. What kind of coincidence? Well, let's have a look. Your first wife, Denise, was an Australian girl, wasn't she?'

'Yes. What about it?'

'I vaguely remember,' Vincent said, 'that having given you two sons, she spent six months in Australia seeing her parents. You may not recall it too clearly yourself. You were no star then. You were the ex-toast of the Royal Shakespeare turned telly actor for the money. But you were well enough known for people to notice when you were seen around with a lissom young lady called Wendy. Whether your wife came home on a cruise ship, I don't know. . . .'

'She did, as a matter of fact,' Cramer said.

'There you see? Another coincidence,' Vincent said. 'I do know that, nine months after your wife returned home, she gave birth to a daughter. Also that you were divorced a year later, and married Wendy, and gave her a couple of kids. You're a one for procreation, aren't you.'

'I like children,' Cramer said.

'A suspicious chap might imagine,' Vincent said, 'that you were telling me something juicy concerning your first wife, under the guise of an anecdote about some friend of a friend, which might become the plot for a play.'

'I can't answer for other people's suspicions,' Cramer said. 'But I'd have thought the man doesn't come out of it too well, either.'

'He sounds like a right bastard to me,' Vincent said. 'But it's a funny thing – if he were a star, for example, the public'd lap it up. They wouldn't blame him then. The old Hollywood myths are long dead. These days, they like their stars to have warts off-screen. Within limits, of course, but I reckon this'd be well inside. No, they'd blame the wife. If it were the bloke next door he'd be a bastard, but no one lives next door to stars, do they. He might even get some sympathy, waiting until this daughter was born, who might not be his, and then taking all the blame at the time of the divorce. He could come out of it smelling of roses.'

'I suppose, with that sort of thing, it depends how it's handled,' Cramer said.

'A few hints,' Vincent said. 'Veiled implications, nothing definite, but everyone gets the message.'

'You know your own business better than I do,' Cramer said.

'There's still a law of libel in this country,' Vincent said.

'If these suspicions were justified,' Cramer said, 'I don't quite see who's going to sue. If anyone was lunatic enough to go into court, the whole thing would be dragged out into the open, other parties would have to give evidence, the whole truth would come out, and the case would be in all the headlines. Who in their right mind would want that?'

'That's an interesting question,' Vincent said. 'Why are you trying to plant this story, Johnnie? What's Denise done to you?'

'Nothing,' Cramer said.

'Well,' Vincent said, 'thanks for the scotch, Johnnie. I think I shall go home now, and sleep it off.'

He stood up, straightened his tie, located the door, and marched towards it steadily on unnaturally stiff legs.

'Have you got what you want, Vince?' Cramer asked.

'Nothing I can use,' Vincent said. He managed a

dignified turn, and stared at Cramer. 'Not for me, Johnnie.'

'I want to be quite certain,' Cramer said. 'If you're not interested, I shall have to speak to someone else.'

'You will,' Vincent said. 'No sweat. They're around. Do you know something? I owe you a vote of thanks. I never thought that I worked for an up-market newspaper, but we're a bit above what you want, at least while I'm there.'

'O.K. Vince,' Cramer said. 'Up to you. Sorry to have wasted your time. I thought we could talk to each other, but I was wrong. I hope you won't mind being left behind in the future though. I need to have confidence in the press men I deal with. You won't expect much co-operation from now on, will you. Nothing I have anything to do with, anyway.'

'Johnnie, boy,' Vincent said, 'you are undoubtedly the biggest shit I've ever come across. That's saying something in my line of work, believe me.'

Valerie Foster was drinking coffee in the foyer, where she could see the lifts. She watched Vincent Consel emerge. He crossed the foyer, eyed the revolving doors suspiciously, waited his chance, and made it with scarcely a stumble. Outside, he spoke to a top-hatted doorman. The doorman raised one hand imperiously and a taxi drew up. The doorman held the cab door open, palmed a tip from Vincent, who climbed in, and the taxi drove off.

Valerie rode a lift up to the top floor, walked silently along the carpeted corridor, and entered the suite. She could hear Cramer's voice coming from the main bedroom, and even though the door was closed and she could not distinguish the words she knew, from his tone, who he was talking to.

She opened the curtains, and stood staring sightlessly out over the lights of London until she heard the receiver being banged on to its rest. Then she went in.

'Would you like anything?' she asked. Cramer shook his

head and started to undress, pitching his clothes carelessly, anywhere, 'Was the interview all right?'

'Useless,' Cramer said. 'You'll have to set up someone else. I'll tell you which one in the morning.'

'All right,' Valerie said.

'Oh, and call Denise too. Cancel this weekend. Make it the following weekend.'

'You're due at Treganwy then,' Valerie reminded him.

'I do know that,' Cramer said. 'Which means you also call Treganwy, and say I'll be a day or two late.' He got into the big double bed and propped himself up on the pillows. 'Is there a gymnasium in this hotel?'

'No, but there's a good one quite near. I've arranged for you to use that.'

'Twice daily work-outs?'

'It's open house,' Valerie said. 'You can live there, if you want to.'

'I must keep in good shape,' Cramer said.

'Was that Wendy you were talking to?'

'Yes,' Cramer said.

'How was she?'

'Hysterical,' Cramer said.

'Why don't you let her fly over and stay with you at Treganwy? She needn't bring the children. They could stay with their nanny.'

'Dear God,' Cramer said. 'I like to be with my children whenever I can. Don't you know me any better than that?'

'Well, all right. The children could come too.'

'I don't want Wendy at Treganwy,' Cramer said. 'I don't want the children. I don't even want you any more than necessary. I want to be on my own. That's the whole point.'

'On your own? Working with a company of other actors?'

'They don't count,' Cramer said.

Valerie sat on the edge of the bed and studied him curiously. 'Why is Treganwy so important to you, John?' she asked. 'Why won't you tell me?'

'It's not important,' Cramer said. 'I'm doing a pompous old idiot a favour, that's all.'

'That doesn't sound much like you,' Valerie said, smiling. 'I never did understand why you even considered it, much less accepted.'

'All right, I'll tell you the truth,' Cramer said. 'It's my way of taking a complete break. Perfect relaxation. No pressures, everything off my back. Including personal relationships. Nothing to do but play an undemanding part, in an unimportant play, in front of uncritical audiences, with actors who'll be no competition. My idea of pure bliss. The ideal method of unwinding. Is that so hard to understand?'

'No, I suppose not,' Valerie said.

'Get into bed,' Cramer said. 'I'm tired. I need some sleep after last night.'

'Was Wendy hysterical then, as well as tonight?'

'She was gearing up,' Cramer said.

'For the same reason?'

'There's only one reason,' Cramer said. 'I can't stand women who try and use moral blackmail.'

'What kind of moral blackmail?'

'The overdose threat,' Cramer said. 'Either do it, or shut up about it. Trying to use it as a weapon is about as cheap as you can get.'

'She might mean it,' Valerie said.

'People who mean it don't talk about it,' Cramer said.

'If this is the way you talked to her,' Valerie said, 'I'm not surprised she got hysterical. Why don't you try and discuss things with her reasonably?'

'I was perfectly reasonable,' Cramer said. 'I assured her that our marriage was not in danger. I told her that, whatever the relationship between you and me, her security was not endangered in any way, and that I was certainly not contemplating divorce.'

'I see,' Valerie said.

'I don't know what more she wants,' Cramer said.

'I expect she wants you to give me up, or something to that effect,' Valerie said.

'Yes, she used words like that,' Cramer said. 'Naturally I wasn't going to lie about it.'

'Naturally,' Valerie said.

'I was completely honest with her,' Cramer said. 'I told her that much of the time you filled a need, but that did not affect her. That she was still my wife, and would remain so, and the sooner she accepted the situation, the better for all concerned. I think that was absolutely rational.'

'Yes,' Valerie said. 'Very rational.'

'I don't think she'd mind if she didn't know,' Cramer said. 'If I did what most men do, have hole-and-corner affairs, and keep them secret.'

'It's not a question of not knowing,' Valerie said. 'It's a question of having her nose rubbed in it.'

'I'm damned if I'm going to lie,' Cramer said. 'You're a fact in my life, and I'm not going to deny you.'

'Thank you,' Valerie said, 'for whatever that amounts to, but it doesn't make me feel very important.' She stood up. 'I think I'll sleep in the other room if you don't mind.' She met Cramer's ice-blue eyes. 'Good night,' she said.

'Don't you start trying the moral blackmail bit too,' Cramer said. 'It doesn't work with me, you should know that.'

'I'm not,' Valerie said quietly. 'I've got myself into something I can't handle, and I don't know what to do about it, that's all.'

'You knew the position from the beginning,' Cramer said. 'I made it clear enough.'

'Yes, you did,' Valerie said. 'But that was then. It's different now.'

'Nothing's changed,' Cramer said.

'For you, no,' Valerie said. 'Obviously not. Perhaps that's all it was, or ever will be, just animal. You can be so many different people, John. Sometimes I think you're acting a part all the time, off the screen as well as on. You *can* be charming when it suits you. You *can* make a woman feel . . . I don't know . . . wonderful. You did me, anyway. Not that I've seen that side of you much, lately. Not since you signed to play *Last Rites for Beresford* on Broadway, in fact.'

'I don't have to apologise to anyone,' Cramer said. 'I've

been getting the film edited, and those crucial sequences re-shot. There haven't been enough hours in the day.'

'The way things are,' Valerie said, 'I don't think I even like you, much less anything else.'

'No one has ever mentioned anything else to my knowledge,' Cramer said.

'No,' Valerie said. 'But I'm still a human being. I do have feelings of my own. I don't simply exist for your convenience. I'm not one of those plastic female things you can deflate and shove away in a drawer when you don't want to use it.'

'Women are all the same,' Cramer said. 'They don't like the truth. None of them.'

'You're very proud of that, aren't you,' Valerie said. 'Speaking the truth.'

'It's a strident, commercial world,' Cramer said, 'where con men and hucksters flourish, and people use lies and self-delusion like a drug. But all that's for the third-rate, the little people. I believe in not only facing what's true, accepting it, but acknowledging it, and speaking it out loud.'

'It can also be a good excuse to be unkind,' Valerie said. 'Or downright cruel. I wonder if, deep down, you really face what's true about yourself?'

'Oh, I know myself,' Cramer said. 'Make no mistake about it. That's the first rule. But in case you don't know me, I'll tell you something before you retire to your own room. I don't make bargains to sleep with anyone. Nor do I make promises I've no intention of keeping.'

'No. You don't have to,' Valerie said. 'I know that. But what happens when, one day, you need help? Really need it. What happens then?'

'Like everyone else, I was born with a brain, a body, and my own talents,' Cramer said. 'The only difference between me and the rest is I know that's all I need, or ever will.'

'Well, good luck superman,' Valerie said. 'I suppose now I'll have to look for another job.'

'Not on my account,' Cramer said. 'You're an extremely efficient secretary, which is why I employed you. I didn't hire you as a part-time whore. I shall still need a good secretary. It's up to you.'

'I'll find one for you, before I leave,' Valerie said.

'Good night' Cramer said.

Cramer woke up at three o'clock in the morning. His heart was thudding violently and he was drenched in sweat. The remnant of the latest variation of the same recurring nightmare leered its amusement and slipped away into the recesses of his mind, to await another occasion.

It had to be exorcised, Cramer knew that. It must be. Well, that was what he had deliberately set out to do, and he would do it. He despised the weakness, somewhere deep inside himself, which brought the mocking dream into being, but in a few weeks' time he would have overcome it.

He switched the bedside light on, went into the bathroom, and swallowed the pills which the combination of scotch and the scene with Valerie had made him forget to take. He dismissed the fleeting thought of Valerie from his mind. That was not important.

He got back into bed, switched off the light, waited. But it was the fear which came first, before the relaxed and needed oblivion of sleep.

The fear which was so intense that he lay rigid, his body stiff, his stomach cramped into ugly knots.

# CHAPTER FIVE

Cramer drove to his sons' public school to collect them for the weekend. The last few miles after leaving the M4 were particularly pleasant. It was a sunny, warm day for the time of year, and the gentle Wiltshire countryside was pregnant with the onset of spring.

The blue Corniche drop-head was not an especially inconspicuous car, and was the object of nearly as much attention, when he drew up at the school, as Cramer himself.

Paul and Mark were too old now to allow themselves to appear to be waiting anxiously as they used to a few years before, running eagerly to meet him with broad, beaming grins. Today they detached themselves from groups of other boys and strolled towards him, as befitted young men, but their eyes were still as bright with pleasure, and the smiles they gave him warmed Cramer's heart.

He embraced them both, hugging them fiercely, as he still did, even though Paul was now as tall as he was and Mark only a couple of inches shorter. He loved the feel of their strong, muscular young bodies, the still-growing fruit of his own seed.

Cramer spent a few minutes shaking hands with their friends, whose names he made a point of remembering from one visit to the next, chatting to them, laughing at their relaxed adolescent humour. These contemporaries of his sons were now rather above anything so childish as asking for his autograph, but some of the new, younger boys were not, and shyly offered him their books, awed by his very presence. Cramer signed them all, asking them questions first, joking with them, ruffling their hair, taking pains to ensure that each autograph book carried some personal message as well as his flowing signature.

These days, Cramer normally refused to give autographs and treated his 'fans' brusquely if he was accosted, but this was different. This was for the sake of his sons, not out of self-gratification.

In point of fact, Paul and Mark stood by looking faintly bored, disdaining such displays of juvenilia, but Cramer knew that they enjoyed his fame, even though they now considered themselves too mature to show it, and were secretly pleased by the attention he attracted from their schoolmates. It was their pleasure which gave him pleasure.

After a decent interval Paul's housemaster appeared and invited Cramer to join him for a glass of sherry. This was the same invitation which Cramer always received, and he accepted cordially as usual. It was, he thought, like a scene in a well-loved play, familiar, but always enjoyable.

He sat in the housemaster's agreeably spacious study, sipping his glass of sherry decorously, listening to the thin greying man's comments on school activities and his sons' studies, smiling at the housemaster's drily humorous summary, which he always managed to vary, but which always told much the same story. Paul's work was, as ever, of single-minded excellence, Mark's much more erratic, sometimes brilliant, sometimes slapdash, often in the same subject. Even were Mark to adopt his chosen career in due course, a reasonable degree of academic achievement would be no bad thing, the housemaster suggested. After all, despite some evidence to the contrary close at hand, the housemaster smiled, it was, for most people, an extremely hazardous profession . . .

Outside the mullioned windows birds sang and the sky was blue. The wing of the school which Cramer could see was pleasing and gracious, its grey stone bathed in the soft sunshine. Beyond stretched the playing fields, surrounded by trees. There was nothing in sight to spoil it, nothing ugly or cheap, and Cramer felt wonderfully at peace, as he always did when sitting in this room, listening to this pleasant, civilised man.

It was all a far cry from the grimy, stark, London

grammar school which Cramer had attended, a product of late Victorian bad taste which had worn badly, with its cramped square of asphalt playground surrounded by mean streets of terraced houses, its playing field, shared with other schools, two miles away.

Including all the extras it cost Cramer over eight thousand pounds a year to send his sons to this place, with its ancient and honourable traditions, and the fees rose inexorably every year as inflation took its toll. It was no longer a significant amount of money to Cramer, although it had been in the beginning, but even then he had not begrudged a penny of it. This was what he had wanted for his sons from the day they were born.

Cramer's political views were strongly to the left. He did not agree with Vanessa, although he respected her sincerity, but he supposed they differed about methods rather than ideals. He preferred to keep his work and his politics in separate compartments, although if he could find a challenging radical subject which would also be successful box office, so much the better. He made no secret of his radical views, had lent his name to campaigns against racism, approved of militancy on behalf of the under-privileged, and was active in the anti-nuclear lobby.

Cramer had no difficulty in reconciling the provision of private education for his sons with his political support for a socialist philosophy which would bring about the abolition of public schools. The present system was, until it was changed, a fact of life. A lousy system it might be, and he would offer his support to changing it, but until then he would beat 'them' at their own game. Had Bernard Shaw not adopted much the same attitude?

The housemaster had moved on from Mark's shortcomings to a discussion of Cramer's novels, which were, of course, in the school library. According, it seemed, to a friend of the housemaster's who was concerned with such matters, it was distinctly possible that Cramer's first novel might become a set book in the 'O' level syllabus. Not this year, the mills of academe grind exceeding slow, perhaps not next year, but it could very well come about one day, the housemaster believed . . .

Cramer smiled a wry acknowledgement. He supposed that would be premature immortality of a kind, to join the 'moderns' like William Golding and Harold Pinter, a subject for school children to perspire over in examination rooms.

It would be about the only kind, too. Cramer did not believe in personal immortality. The only purpose of life was life itself. The only reason for living was to live.

His duty sherry consumed, Cramer shook hands with the housemaster and said goodbye until the next time. He joined his sons and drove back to London, to the house in Highgate which had been his home until the divorce, and which was still home for Denise and the children.

The house was set in a quiet avenue. It was big and rambling with a large garden, mostly lawns, but with a few trees and flower beds.

Some of the furniture and carpets dated back to the early days of their marriage and had a comfortable, well-used look, which would have given the place a nostalgic feel had Cramer been a nostalgic man, which he was not.

Denise gave him a bright, if somewhat artificial smile. She had now entered her forties but she looked much younger, as trim, poised, and attractive as ever, although somehow her good looks had a curious, enclosed detachment. She would age well, Cramer thought. He kissed her lightly on the cheek, enquired after her health, picked up his ten-year-old daughter, Ann, and swung her in the air while she squealed with delighted laughter.

Cramer took it for granted that it was incumbent on him to make sure that there was no 'atmosphere', no awkwardness, when he came to see the children by his first marriage, and he did so now as always. After all, there was no reason why it should not be an easy, natural occasion. In other times – or even today – a father who was a seaman, or in the forces, might only see his children at intervals of months, or even a year or more. Absence did not mean any lack of love and devotion, and Cramer always showed an abundance of both.

These occasions were for them, and he gave himself to them absolutely. On Saturday afternoon he took Paul and Mark to watch Arsenal play at Highbury – and Ann, who cared nothing about football, insisted on going too because she wanted to be with her Daddy.

They sat in the stand, cheered the Gunners on, hooted disapproval of their opponents' every foul, booed the referee when he awarded a penalty against Arsenal, groaned when the visiting team scored, and carried out an inquest on Arsenal's defeat all the way home, finally deciding to lay the blame at the door of the manager.

In the evening, this time with Denise as well, they went to a musical, chosen for Ann's benefit, and afterwards had a late supper at the Connaught, where Cramer was well known and received the kind of service which he took for granted. Denise was doubtful about this, and thought that perhaps she should take Ann home.

'It'll be terribly late before she gets to bed. She is only a little girl, after all.'

'Oh, come on,' Cramer said. 'It won't do her any harm to stay up late for once.'

'She'll be so tired,' Denise said.

'I'm not tired,' Ann said. 'Not a bit. I could stay up all night.'

'No, you won't,' Cramer said. 'Home at midnight, O.K.? Like Cinderella.'

On Sunday they lunched in the Thames Valley and went on to Whipsnade Zoo. This was mostly a treat for Ann, and she ran excitedly from one enclosure to the next until the previous night began to catch up on her.

'My legs are tired,' she said.

'We'll come another time,' Cramer said. 'Paul and Mummy'll take you back to the car. Mark and I won't be long.'

He strolled along with Mark, thinking. Paul was no problem. He was nearly eighteen, due to take his 'A' levels in the summer, after which he intended to go to medical school and eventually become a surgeon. All of which he would achieve, Cramer had no doubt about that. It was Mark. . .

'I'm told you made an impression in the school play,' Cramer said.

Mark grinned. 'It wasn't a very big part,' he said, 'but I had one good scene. I knew I could steal the show, and I did.'

'I wish I could have seen it,' Cramer said. 'I was going to be there, it was all arranged, but we were on location, ten days behind schedule. . .'

'It's all right, Dad,' Mark said. 'I know what it's like.'

'Well, that's the point,' Cramer said. 'You don't know what it's like. Actors can't work unless someone employs them. Writers and painters, at least they can write and paint, even if no one buys what they do. They can keep working, they can live on hope. But you can't act on your own. All you can do is sit and wait, write letters, pester people. Wait for a chance. And when the chance comes it may be a terrible part, not worth doing. It's not all first nights in the West End, and deciding which leading part you're going to play in which film. That's given to very few people. For many, if not most, it's heartbreak, unfulfilled ambition, false hopes, and eventual disillusion. It's a tough business.' Mark was listening with obvious patience. 'I know I've said all this before,' Cramer went on, 'but you're sixteen years old now. Old enough to understand the reality and face what it really means.'

'I do,' Mark said. 'You've said before, no one should become an actor unless that's what they want so much that there's nothing else in the world they can do. Literally nothing. Well, that's how I feel.'

Cramer sighed. 'O.K., if you still want to go to drama school when the time comes, I shan't stop you, even if I could. But there's something else you should think about, which I haven't mentioned until now, because you weren't old enough to know what I was talking about. Perhaps you're still not. I don't know. It's this. The worst thing that can happen to an actor. And it's not being out of work. Nor is it not making enough money. An actor can be rich, but if he doesn't respect what he's doing, what he is, he's more poverty-stricken than any beggar. It only happens to a few perhaps, those who have set their sights high, who believe that the performing arts mean just that. A performance can be art. And if a man realises, no matter how much in demand he is, no matter how well he's being paid, that in fact, in truth, judged by whoever holds the scales, he really isn't very good, *that* is the bitterest thing an actor can ever be obliged to face. That is the ultimate tragedy for him.' He smiled at Mark. 'Too airy fairy for you? Too high-flown?'

'No,' Mark said. 'But surely all you're saying is, don't get self-satisfied. Don't ever believe that you can't get better.'

'No,' Cramer said. 'I'm saying that some realise they're never going to get any better, that, never mind their status, their real stature is never going to measure up to their private dreams of themselves.'

'All right,' Mark said. 'I expect there have been thousands of failed Rembrandts. But there'd never have been one Rembrandt if he was so afraid of failing that he decided to be a cobbler instead.'

'Ah well, I didn't expect to get through to you,' Cramer said. 'Every young actor, against all the statistical evidence, believes he's going to set the world alight. Sensible warnings, like there are fifteen thousand members of Equity in Great Britain alone, and eighty per cent of them are out of work at any one time, simply bore the pants off him. Each one of them thinks it won't happen to him. He's the chosen one who's going to be better than Olivier.'

'That's not my ambition,' Mark said. 'I want to be better than my father. That's my target.'

He smiled at Cramer and Cramer smiled back, touched by the boy's frank admiration which his cheeky remark implied, and curiously moved by the uncritical nature of his adolescent ambition. Cramer hoped the boy would never lose it. No, more than that, he determined fiercely, he would make certain his son never lost it, no matter what.

'Thank you for the compliment,' Cramer said. 'Now let's get down to cases. Drama school, yes, agreed. But I want you to be fit to do something else, and that means getting a degree in something or other.' Mark made a face. 'I don't care what,' Cramer said. 'Call it insurance. It'll make me feel better, even if not you. But I hear your work's erratic, you're not fulfilling your potential. That's got to change from this day on.'

'You didn't take your degree,' Mark said, 'and you've done all right.'

'You're about to learn a harsh fact of life,' Cramer said. 'You do as I say, not as I do. You can be a big wheel in school plays so long as it doesn't interfere with your work. You go to university first, and *then* you go to drama school. That's the deal, and you don't argue about it, because you don't get a choice.' He looked at his watch. 'Time to go.'

They turned and walked back towards the car park. Deer suddenly scuttled across a neighbouring enclosure for no apparent reason.

'I wouldn't say no to an American university though,' Cramer said, 'if that idea happened to appeal to you.'

'How do you mean?' Mark frowned in youthful puzzlement.

'I'm moving to the States for good,' Cramer said. 'Buying a house on the West Coast. You know that. It'll be a big place. Room for everyone. I shall make sure there is.'

'I see.' Mark studied the ground as he walked along, thinking. 'When you say everyone. . .'

'You and Paul at the moment,' Cramer said. 'Ann's too young as yet. You'd live your own lives, of course, but it would be good to have you. That goes for Wendy too, and I know you get on with her.' In truth, the meetings between Cramer's second wife and his elder sons had been brief, but they would all get on, he was positive of that. He would make certain of it. 'And the little boys won't get in your hair.'

'Have you talked to Paul about this?'

'Last night,' Cramer said. 'After you'd gone to bed.'

'What did he say?'

'I gathered that an American medical school had a

certain attraction,' Cramer said, 'but he's going to think it over. I'd like you to do the same.'

'What about Mum?'

'I'm thinking of your best interests,' Cramer said. 'You and Paul. When I discuss it with her I shall expect her to do the same. Anyway, I'm not looking for instant answers. I shall see you again when I've finished at Treganwy, and we'll talk about it then. You know about the Broadway play. During that, I shall rent an apartment in New York. You could fly over and stay with me, see how you like that, generally play it by ear. Kick the idea around in your head, that's all I ask.'

'Yes, I will,' Mark said. They were approaching the car park. The blue Rolls Royce glittered in the sun. Mark's imagination had already soared far ahead. 'If I came to live with you in America, you could get me parts in films,' he said.

'That's not beyond the bounds of possibility,' Cramer agreed. 'Provided you get a degree first.'

'Degrees are easier to get in the States than here,' Mark reflected. 'MA's are two a penny over there.'

'Don't push your luck,' Cramer said. 'Or I shall stipulate a Ph.D first.'

Cramer drove to Wiltshire. Ann, exhausted, slept soundly in the back, and did not wake up even when her brothers were dropped off. Cramer embraced his sons again, they kissed their mother goodbye, and from then on, until the Rolls Royce drifted to a stop in Highgate, conversation came to an end. Denise stared fixedly through the windscreen, apparently deep in thought, and only stirred when Cramer switched the engine off outside her home, seemingly surprised to find herself there. Ann mumbled something incomprehensibly without opening her eyes, and Cramer smiled.

'Bed for that one,' he said.

'Do you have to get back to the hotel?' Denise asked. 'Or can you have a meal here?'

'I'll have dinner with you, and stop over,' Cramer said. 'I'd like to take Ann to school in the morning.'

Denise did not drink, but either her friends did or she

kept scotch in the house against Cramer's infrequent visits. He did not enquire which. That was her business. Once Ann was in bed he poured himself a glass, declined her offer of wine with the meal, and stuck to whisky while they ate.

The big house belonged to Denise. Cramer had made it over to her at the time of the divorce. Subsequently he had chosen not to abide rigidly by the terms of the agreed settlement, but increased her alimony in line with his own improved fortunes. It was important to him that she did not want for money and although she spent little enough on herself she was able to afford live-in help, which she needed to run a home of that size. The Italian girl who fulfilled this function at the moment was off for the weekend and they had the house to themselves.

Cramer complimented Denise on the meal, but otherwise he did not try to make conversation. He was content to wait.

A gas log fire flickered cheerfully in the dining room, and Denise looked even younger by the light of the candles burning on the table, but there was a tightness around her mouth which hinted at inner strain.

'Coffee?' she asked.

'Not just yet,' Cramer said. 'Later perhaps.' The neck of the whisky bottle clinked against his glass.

'Shall we go into the living room?'

'I'm quite comfortable here,' Cramer said.

It was a comfortable room. He had always liked this dining room. Denise was, perhaps, better at creating a sense of home than Wendy, but then, since their marriage, he and Wendy had never been in one place for very long. They would create a real home in California, a good home for all his children.

The silence between them spun out until it was a lowering, oppressive presence in its own right. Denise fiddled uneasily with her serviette. Cramer calmly watched the gas flames licking the ceramic logs.

'Well, you're obviously not going to say anything,' Denise said at last. 'I assume you're waiting for me.'

'I'm at your disposal, if there's anything you want to say.'

'Paul tells me that you've suggested he should go and live with you in America,' Denise said.

'And Mark,' Cramer said. 'I talked to him about it this afternoon.'

'Will you be wanting to take Ann away from me as well?' Denise asked bitterly.

'The boys are old enough to know their own minds,' Cramer said. 'Ann isn't.'

'Old enough to be tempted by the kind of bribes you can offer, I think you mean,' Denise said.

'You're still a beautiful woman,' Cramer said calmly. He was in control of this situation, and he thought Denise knew it as well as he did. He had no intention of participating in a shouting match. 'You had your admirers in the past.' Denise winced. 'I imagine you still have. When are you going to get married again? You wouldn't lose financially. The present arrangements would continue. I've always made that plain.'

'If I met a man, and fell in love with him,' Denise said, 'someone who could be a father to my children, then I expect I'd marry him. So far, I haven't.'

'The children already have a father,' Cramer said.

'Only biologically,' Denise snapped. 'No more. You descend on them and play the part for a few hours, twice a year, when you can spare the time to fit the role into all your other commitments. Oh, it's a good performance, I'll grant you that. Well acted. We get for free what you're usually paid for doing, and you're no cheap skate. You put all your talent into the charity show, and it's very convincing. At least it convinces the children, but they don't know you as I do. You're acting a part all the time, John, father, lover, husband, ex-husband, tough guy, radical, actor – yes, you even act the part of great actor. I've come to believe that's because, unless you're acting, there's nothing there. You're a hollow man. As a human being you're non-existent. You're nothing but a walking, talking charade.'

Cramer smiled at her from the far end of the refectory

table, the weary, patient smile she had once seen him employ as Beckett. The smile was not reflected in the polar ice of his eyes, but the faint scar on his cheek was no more prominent than usual and she knew that he was unmoved. The man was invulnerable, she thought despairingly. Her outburst had not been rehearsed, but it was the product of rebellious and often lonely years, brought to a head like some over ripe boil by the events of this weekend, all the pent-up anger, reflected in the most hurtful things she could throw at him. And it was all to no avail. None of it penetrated, not one word. It all bounced off his impermeable armour . . . of what? What was it made this man so impregnable, so unafraid, so incapable of revealing any human weakness or the slightest trace of vulnerability? Had he been born with fear lacking from his make-up? Was that it?

'You're not being very logical, Denise,' Cramer said levelly. 'The reason I want the boys to come to America is precisely so that I may give them my presence, all the time.'

'And what about my presence?' Denise demanded. 'Haven't I the right to give them that, as much as you? More than you, in fact?'

'If it comes to the pinch,' Cramer said, 'Paul and Mark have the right to choose. I think it would be best to avoid that, for you and me to reach agreement. I would rather any steps taken were by mutual consent. I'm thinking of the boys' own welfare, and I suggest you do the same.'

'Oh, yes,' Denise said. 'You're only thinking of them, not your own selfish wishes, of course not.'

'I wonder why it makes you so angry, if I'm rational about what would be best for them for the next few years of their lives,' Cramer said. 'If it's because – and don't fly off the handle again, I emphasise *if* – *if* it's because you still have some sneaking hope that you and I might get together again some day, and you see the children as honey in the pot which might attract me, you're dealing in fantasy. Wendy is my wife now, and will continue to be so. She has given me two sons . . .' he smiled ironically

'. . . who need a father. My marriage to you ended years ago. It's over. It's dead.'

Denise sighed. 'You can be so clever,' she said, 'so perceptive, which is what makes it so strange that you're also unfeeling, that you lack even elementary compassion. Yes, it's true, for quite a long time I did harbour that fantasy, as you call it. It seemed to me that our marriage had ended without any real reason. You blamed me for something which I'd done, yes, and yet at that time I loved you so much. I thought I'd hurt you in a way your pride couldn't take, driven you away, when that was the last thing I wanted to do. It all seemed to be a dreadful misunderstanding which one day we'd sort out. I used to sit here at nights listening for the slam of your car door. Sometimes, I heard it . . . or persuaded myself I heard it. I'd draw the curtains and look out of the window, hoping it would be you. But of course it never was your car.'

'That was never on the cards,' Cramer said. 'You should have known that.'

'It took time, but I did realise it in the end,' Denise said. 'It also dawned on me, quite slowly, that you didn't leave me because I'd had one stupid, silly, transitory affair, meet Wendy and marry her, the whirlwind romance of the newspapers. Wendy was in your life before, probably long before I went away. I'd given you the excuse you needed, and you seized it, the chance to walk away playing the injured hero, and lay the blame at my door. When I did finally work that out, I knew I'd been the biggest fool ever born, begging you not to go, sitting here dreaming you might come back, blaming myself for the whole thing. That was when the fantasy died, John. And if ever I had any doubt that, not only was it dead, but the worms had eaten every scrap of it, this would have settled it.' Denise leaned over and took a tabloid newspaper from underneath a chair cushion. She held it up. It was open at the show business page. 'I assume you've read this?'

'I glanced at it,' Cramer said.

'What did you think you were doing?' Denise breathed. 'Don't you care who you hurt?'

'There are no direct quotes from me,' Cramer said.

'And if you analyse it carefully, it doesn't really say anything.'

'Not directly, perhaps,' Denise said. 'It's all slimy innuendo. At first I was so angry with the reporter I could have killed him, but then I realised you must have fed it to him. Suppose Paul or Mark saw this? Or Ann?'

'They don't take newspapers like that at school,' Cramer said. 'And Ann wouldn't understand it. I'm surprised you saw it,' he added disingenuously. Had she not, it was pretty certain that some well-meaning or non-comprehending friend would have shown it to her. The paper's lawyers must have vetted it, he thought. The insinuations were so veiled as to be almost totally obscure, except to the quick-witted, or those directly concerned. He supposed he owed that journalist another bottle of scotch some time.

'Maria reads it,' Denise said. Maria was the au pair. 'She showed it to me. Fortunately her English isn't all that good. She didn't grasp what it meant.'

'What would you like me to do?' Cramer asked. 'Issue a formal denial?'

'That would only draw attention to it, as you well know,' Denise said savagely. 'If you took the trouble to deny it, everyone would assume it was true.'

'Would it help if I saw to it that there's never again anything like that in the press which could be misinterpreted?'

'Is that the bargain?' Denise asked, her voice high. 'No more stories like that if Paul and Mark go to America with you? And if I won't agree, the next one's more explicit, so that Ann's friends understand it? Is that the price you're exacting?'

'I want all my sons with me,' Cramer said. 'I always have. Up to now I've considered your feelings, you've had Paul and Mark. Now I want them, and one way or another I'm going to have them. Whether it's easy or whether it's difficult, that's up to you, but it won't make any difference in the long run.'

Denise stared at him. Unconsciously she had been running her fingers through her long hair and it hung over her face like a curtain. Behind the falling strands her eyes glittered from helpless fury, or tears, or both. Suddenly she hurled the folded newspaper at him violently. It fell short, skidded along the table, and knocked the glass of whisky into Cramer's lap. He picked up the glass and set it back on the table. The liquid soaked through his trousers. Denise stood motionless. Her fingers clawed her hair, helplessly.

'Ann is your child, John,' she whispered at last. He could hardly hear her.

'I don't think I've ever treated her as if she were not,' Cramer said.

Denise shook her head. 'I don't want you to stay the night,' she said. 'I don't want you to take Ann to school in the morning. Leave her alone from now on. Let her forget you. At least let me have Ann. Don't try and take her away from me as well.'

'I'll go,' Cramer said. He stood up. 'But for Ann's sake. If you're likely to behave hysterically like this in the morning I'd rather she didn't see it.'

'For Ann's sake . . . ?' But Denise did not go on. She had no words left. She turned blindly towards the door.

'Denise!' Cramer commanded. Automatically, his ex-wife stopped dead in her tracks. Cramer came round the table, moved close to her, stretched out his hand, and tilted her chin towards him. She resisted him, her jaw was rigid, but he forced her to look at him.

'In theory, according to doctors, it is possible,' Cramer said quietly and gently, 'that Ann is my child. But I have four other children, by two different women. All sons. As far as I'm concerned, the odds are against it.'

Flakes of snow began to drift against the windscreen as they approached Treganwy. The wipers silently flicked the offending obstacles dismissively aside, but thin patches were beginning to lie on the roof-tops of houses.

'Snow in April,' Cramer grumbled. 'Bloody ridiculous.' He turned the heat up.

'Not in North Wales,' Valerie said. 'This is mountain country.'

'Thank you for the geography lesson, Miss Foster,' Cramer said.

Valerie chose not to reply. When Cramer was in an ill humour she had learned that he was best left alone, and he had been touchy to the point of surliness since the weekend. She wondered if something had happened when he saw Denise and the children, or if he was angry about that piece in the tabloid, or if it was because of her own defiant rejection of him. No, not the last, she thought wryly. What she had given him was easily replaceable. There would be no shortage of willing volunteers for the service Valerie Foster had provided off duty.

Cramer saw the sign indicating the Palace Hotel and turned into the drive.

'When I've checked in,' he said, 'you can see if there are any messages you ought to deal with, and then take this car back to London.'

Valerie stared at him surprised. 'Why?'

'I'm going to be working with a bunch of no-hopers who are just about scratching a living,' Cramer said. 'I don't want to rub it in.'

'But you'll need transport,' Valerie said. 'God knows where the theatre is, and if the weather's like this . . .'

'If I want a car I'll hire one locally,' Cramer said. 'I can't turn up for rehearsals in a place like this in a bloody great Rolls. That'd be putting the poor bastards down before I even start.'

'Whatever you say,' Valerie said. She puzzled for a few moments, as the Rolls wound its way up the curling drive towards the hotel, over the uncharacteristic sensitivity towards his fellow artists which Cramer was displaying. She supposed that, despite the contemptuous way he spoke of them, he could still identify with them. They might be unknown by his standards, but they were still actors like him, they followed a common trade, and long ago Cramer must have played in places like this. Still, it was not like him, Valerie thought, but she was rather touched at this insight into his intentions. He meant to be one of them, just another actor for the brief duration of the play, working and living the way they did. Except, of course, for his suite at the Palace Hotel . . .

Cramer checked in while young porters eagerly doubled to and fro, bringing in his luggage. The blonde receptionist tried to behave as if the Palace Hotel, with its four stars and haute cuisine, were accustomed to receiving guests like John Cramer, but she did not quite make it. Knights, viscounts, minor business tycoons, and the occasional lord she took in her stride. The slight quiver in her voice and the shining interest in her eyes dented her effort at matter-of-factness as Cramer signed his name, and smiled at her.

'Thank you, Mr Cramer,' she said. 'We have several urgent messages for you, and some overseas cables.'

'Miss Foster will deal with all that,' Cramer said pleasantly, and turned away. He had been vaguely aware of a man with a somewhat feline face who had been among those watching him with interest as he stood at reception. The man was now walking towards him, hand outstretched.

'Mr Cramer? I'm Maurice Gardiner.'

'Yes. How do you do,' Cramer said absently. He turned towards Valerie, which took him away from the proffered hand. 'Let's check through that stuff upstairs, Val.'

'I have the advantage of you,' Maurice said drily. 'I know both your face and your name.'

'Well, it's been good to meet you,' Cramer said. 'We must have a chat some time.'

'That'd be nice,' Maurice agreed. He winked at the attractive girl, referred to as Val, who was smiling at him with ironic amusement and whom he guessed was paid to remember details.

'Mr Gardiner will be directing your play,' Valerie told Cramer.

'Oh, Christ.' Cramer swung round and pumped Maurice's hand penitently. 'I'm sorry . . . I should have remembered . . .'

'Forget it,' Maurice said. 'My fault for not introducing myself properly.'

'I was thinking about something else, but that's no

excuse,' Cramer said. 'I do know about you. I looked you up. You've done some good work.'

'I thought I'd meet you and say hullo,' Maurice said, 'but if you're busy just now . . .'

'No, of course not,' Cramer said. 'Come and have a drink.'

The suite was on the top floor of the hotel. It was less spacious than Cramer was accustomed to, but the outlook over the valley was agreeable, the rooms were spotlessly clean, spring flowers in vases lent freshness and colour, and there was a personal note of welcome from the hotel manager. There was no bar in the suite, and no refrigerator, but there was a cluster of bottles on a trolley and a breathless maid brought in a bucket of ice. They were trying hard at least.

The bustling porters carried in the luggage. The hotel manager arrived to offer his personal greetings and assurances of instant service. Cramer got rid of him as quickly as he decently could and poured whiskies for himself and Maurice, but the telephone kept ringing insistently.

'Look, tell them no more phone calls,' Cramer said. 'Sorry, Maurice . . .'

'You'd better look at these cables,' Valerie said. She dealt them into his hand. 'The studio want to take out another ten minutes before they release your film, Fred's not happy with the draft screenplay for *Beresford*, and Burton's turned down the part of Smithers.'

'This'll only take a few minutes, I promise you,' Cramer told Maurice.

'It's O.K.,' Maurice said. 'It's a whole new world. Fascinating.'

'The trouble with the movie business,' Cramer said, 'is that there are too many people sitting on their bums in big offices with nothing to do but talk and interfere. If there were fewer cables, meetings, and transatlantic phone calls, we'd get more films made.'

Maurice sipped his scotch and watched Cramer and Valerie as they sat conversing in undertones. Finally Cramer stood up, rolled the papers into a ball and threw them into the waste-paper basket.

'O.K. then,' he said. 'Stall the studio. I want to be there for any cuts. It can wait a few weeks. Tell Fred I agree about the screenplay. He can bring in that writer we were considering in the first place. And Richard was never going to play Smithers. That was cloud cuckoo land. A good supporting actor, that's all we need. Send him the list of my suggestions. And that's it, until I've finished here at Treganwy.'

'I'll do my best,' Valerie said.

'I mean it,' Cramer said. 'I don't want to hear from anyone except you, and then only if the world stops turning. From now on, I'm in purdah. I'm Maurice's man for the next few weeks, and no one else's.'

Maurice smiled faintly. He had had no need to look Cramer up. He knew the man's work – and his reputation. He shook hands with Valerie, hoped that she would be able to come and see the play, and watched her slim legs with appreciation as she walked towards the door.

Cramer sighed as he topped up Maurice's glass, which did not need it, and his own, which did.

'Now let's talk about important things,' he said.

'Bread and butter matters first,' Maurice suggested. 'I expect you'd like to meet the rest of the cast as soon as possible. How would you like to play that?'

'How would you like to, more to the point,' Cramer said.

'On their home ground, if you don't mind,' Maurice. 'Something casual, like drinks in the theatre bar.'

'Not the whole lot at one fell swoop, I hope.'

'Just those you'll be working with,' Maurice said. 'You'll get to know the rest as you go along.'

'Fine.'

'Professor Griffiths will be holding a much more formal do at The Hall,' Maurice said. 'The stuffed shirt bit. If he's your mentor and boyhood hero, I'm sorry . . .'

'Far from it,' Cramer said, with the twisted grin which was his genuine one.

'You'll be exhibited to every bigwig within a radius of thirty miles,' Maurice said, 'while the Prof preens himself in public on his triumph in persuading you to appear at Treganwy. Which is fair enough really, because he did.'

'Will the rest of the cast be invited?'

Maurice shook his head. 'Just you and I,' he said.

'He can stuff that,' Cramer said. 'You can tell him that I'll go as one of the cast, but not on my own.'

'I think you'd better tell him that yourself,' Maurice said drily.

'Right. I will,' Cramer said. 'Silly old sod. He should know better.'

So far, Maurice found himself unexpectedly impressed. Cramer was making all the right noises. Perhaps he really did intend to behave as a working actor, instead of the visiting prima donna to which, to be fair, his standing certainly entitled him. Maurice took a copy of the script from his briefcase.

'I think we've got one or two problems with this play,' he said.

'Only one or two?'

'More may emerge,' Maurice allowed. 'The first is that the author isn't available. He's in Rome working on a telefilm. Day and night, by the sound of it. The director's changing all the locations, the lead's got to be American instead of English, he has to fall for a German girl who was originally Scots, and the Italian actors can't say the lines as written. Anyway, the poor devil's rewriting as they go. I need hardly say that the whole potential disaster is a co-production.'

'So I'd imagine,' Cramer said.

'The upshot is, the author can't get back for us,' Maurice said. 'He's very apologetic, delighted the play's going on, but has no alternative but to give us carte blanche.'

'I expect we'll survive his absence,' Cramer said.

'Well, personally, I prefer the author to be around when needed,' Maurice said. 'But he can't be, so that's that. The first problem is length. I've timed the original script and I make it about two hours thirty minutes. That's too long. We need something just under two hours, in my opinion.'

'There are plenty of obvious cuts to be made,' Cramer said.

'I agree,' Maurice said. 'I've done some work on the

script, indicated the stuff I think we could happily lose, loosened up some of the dialogue, especially Peter's and Mary's, and re-jigged Scene Two, Act One, so that it builds, instead of just wandering about haphazardly. I've marked up a script with my suggestions, and perhaps you'd have a look at it and see what you think.' He handed Cramer the marked copy of the script.

'Snap,' Cramer said. 'I've been working on it too. We'll compare notes later.'

'The title,' Maurice said. 'With you in it, it seems perverse to call it *Paula.* I mean, Marcia Hambridge is a good experienced actress, even if she does like to be a bit more grand than she's any right to be, and I've no doubt she'll tell you about her West End experience, but that was ten years ago, and even then she wasn't playing leads. I've got two suggestions for a new title, *Beautiful People* or *Jet Lag,* but if you've got a better one, fine.'

'How do you think this'll go at the box office?' Cramer asked.

'While you're playing Stephen, it'll be a sell-out,' Maurice said. 'No question.'

'In that case, sod the title,' Cramer said. 'Leave it as it stands, as far as I'm concerned. Do you have any plans for this thing after the Festival?'

'Well, there are plans, although we'll see how it stands up after Ben Stamford's taken over from you,' Maurice said cautiously. 'We could well tour it for a while, or perhaps see if we can take it to the Shaw, or Greenwich, and the West End if we're lucky.'

'You worry about the title then,' Cramer said. 'For a few weeks here, I'm not bothered.'

'O.K.,' Maurice said. 'It'll certainly save arguments with the printers. They're getting mildly hysterical already because we've held them up. But I was really thinking about you. Stephen's got some good scenes, but the part's only half the size of Paula's.'

'I did realise that,' Cramer said, 'when I first read the script.'

'Do you especially like this play?' Maurice asked curiously.

Cramer said, 'It might come together when we've worked on it. I don't know.'

'It seems a strange choice to make for your return to the theatre after quite a long time,' Maurice said. 'You could have had your pick, Macbeth, Henry the Fifth, Richard the Third, Hamlet, any of the great roles. The National or the Royal Shakespeare would have rolled out the red carpet.'

'I couldn't commit myself for more than a few weeks,' Cramer said. 'Besides, that wasn't what I wanted.'

'I gathered from the Prof you preferred a contemporary play,' Maurice said. 'But a supporting part in something completely untried – and at Treganwy? It's not even a role for which you'd spring to mind, to be completely honest, if I were casting this play in the perfect world, with someone like Faye Dunaway playing Paula.'

'Perhaps you and I see the part differently,' Cramer said. Maurice wondered if that was the first hint of a storm warning, the initial faint, distant darkening of the sky, long before the thunder and lightning arrived. 'But anyway the play's not the point. Professor Griffiths may be full of inflated self-esteem, but there was a time, during that brief year I spent at Cambridge, when he unlocked doors for me. The use of language as an art form, a tantalising glimpse of words which combined emotion, reason, summed up the depths of the human experience – an insight into poetry, if you like, except that it includes prose as well. I owe him that. So coming here, working with you, doing this play, it's for him – and that really is a kind of genuflection in the direction of a twenty-year-old boy, a quarter of a century ago, and the Professor, who, almost by accident, showed that boy some far horizons which he had not previously realised were even there.'

Maurice was not really listening, although in so far as he took in Cramer's words they seemed to resemble an obscure piece of mathematics which finally produced a doubtful answer. But he was more concerned with immediate and personal worries.

'How do you see Stephen yourself?' Maurice asked casually, if carefully.

'He's a radical who sells out,' Cramer said. 'The typical Social Democrat, who turns his back on what he knows is right for the sake of personal gain.'

'I see,' Maurice said neutrally. 'I thought we might go for all the humour we can get from Stephen. Paula's got some pretty heavy stuff to say, and we need a contrast. Besides, he's her court jester. That's the way it's written. Isn't it?' he added quickly, not wishing to appear dogmatic.

'He can be played as a lightweight, or a heavyweight,' Cramer said. 'But I see no reason why a heavyweight can't have a sense of humour, despite the convention to the contrary. Besides, if you're talking about dialogue, my way's indicated when he talks about having to operate within the lousy system as it is.'

'And is promptly put down by Willem for displaying the hypocrisy of radical chic,' Maurice pointed out.

'He's only put down if it's played that way,' Cramer said. 'I don't think it should be.'

'I'll have another look at the script tonight,' Maurice said. 'I must admit, I haven't seen Stephen as a kind of brooding revolutionary manqué.'

'I think it'll lend the part the depth it needs,' Cramer said. 'But it's also my personal beliefs coming through.'

'What, exactly, are your beliefs?'

'I'm a lifelong socialist,' Cramer stated firmly.

'Really,' Maurice said. 'I watched you drive up to the hotel. How do you reconcile your socialism with a car costing what . . . forty or fifty thousand pounds? I'm guessing. I've no idea.'

'There's nothing to reconcile,' Cramer said patiently. 'I'm a socialist. I also prefer to drive a good car, and the Rolls is the best car in the world. Why the hell shouldn't a socialist drive the best car in the world? Just because of my convictions why should I respectfully stand aside, own something inferior myself, and leave the best to plutocrats, speculators, Arab sheikhs and so on?'

'M'm.' Maurice mused for a few moments. The kink in his lips made him look like a mildly puzzled cat, eager to pounce, but not quite certain if it had actually spotted a mouse or not. 'Come the revolution, "a Rolls in every garage" might be a popular slogan, but with the things doing about ten miles to the gallon, and only enough oil left for a few decades, it doesn't seem to be a particularly practical programme to me.'

'I'm a Marxist,' Cramer said, 'because Marxism seems to me to be the only really scientific explanation of capitalism. But I'm not a revolutionary. I believe in a pluralistic society, provided it's a just one.'

If that was an answer, Maurice thought, Treganwy was the theatre capital of the world. He consulted his watch unnecessarily.

'Well, I must go,' he said. 'I have a meeting with our designer about the set. It's been a pleasure to meet you, and it'll be very interesting to see how this play turns out.'

Maurice walked thoughtfully through melting slush towards the theatre, trying to decide if he was worried or not. Cramer had all the presence and magnetism of a star and had distinguished himself in the most difficult roles there were, in his time. He would certainly knock out the Treganwy audiences even if he merely stood on stage and read the lines. There was no good reason to doubt, given the man's impressive track record in the theatre before he turned to TV and films, that his conception of Stephen – bizarre though it might seem to Maurice – could result in one of those jolting, exciting, exhilarating performances which would lift this play, turn it into something else again, and provide one of those rare theatrical experiences when the auditorium was as full of breathless excitement, pounding hearts and fixed eyes as a bull ring.

The trouble was, Maurice thought that Cramer was a hypocrite. Not the common or garden, straightforward, frankly dishonest kind of hypocrisy which often veiled some nagging insecurity, which it was a director's job to discern and use to his own advantage. No, Cramer was the worst sort, the one who rationalised any inconsistency out of sight if it got in the way, and ended up rock solid, impregnable, and immune.

Maurice wondered if it would matter. Presumably not. On the evidence of his films, he had steadily grown in stature and ability since the days when Maurice, as a schoolboy, had watched, transfixed, at Stratford, when Cramer, with the apparent lack of artifice of pure art, had impaled the audience on the agony of his youthful Hamlet.

Beside that, the part of Stephen presented no challenge whatever, merely a poseur, immensely talented, but emotionally inadequate, hiding his own desperate insecurity behind a barrage of barbed witticisms.

Maurice relaxed as he turned off the main street of Treganwy and walked up the hill towards the theatre.

No, there was nothing to worry about. Cramer was experienced enough, professional enough, and most of all good enough, to perceive that the part risked being a pastiche. It was his intention to add another dimension which would bubble and strain beneath the dialogue and give Stephen a third dimension, or perhaps, as he had miraculously achieved with that Hamlet, even that fourth dimension which no one had spotted before.

Maurice began to whistle cheerfully. He found himself looking forward to rehearsals with keen and pleasurable anticipation, and having thought it through, viewed Cramer through more tolerant and kindly eyes. Perhaps he was less of a hypocrite than Maurice had imagined, or possibly his hypocrisy was less impermeable, which would mean that Cramer was more vulnerable than he seemed.

Maurice liked to know where his actors' weak spots were hidden. This was not usually a very difficult exercise. Most actors carried a mass of visible insecurities around with them.

Maurice wondered if Cramer had any and if so what they were.

He thought about that for a while and then dismissed the question from his mind.

There was nothing, that he could conceive, for John Cramer to feel insecure about.

# CHAPTER SIX

Cramer joined the cast with whom he would be working with no more difficulty or drama than one goldfish swimming across a pool to join a few other goldfish.

Maurice deliberately engineered the encounter so that it was as casual as possible. The theatre bar was opened for the occasion, the cast asked to drop in for a drink after rehearsals, and Maurice made sure they were not kept waiting before he and Cramer arrived together.

Just the same, there was an air of tenseness and apprehension among them before Cramer appeared. They were about to start working with a man hailed by the critics as a young actor already on the verge of greatness as long as twenty years ago, when only Bernard Fyfield was established in the profession, Marcia Hambridge and Ben Stamford were still at drama school, and the remainder were schoolchildren, or, in the case of the ASMs, mere toddlers. A man whose force and vitality always seemed too big for the television screen. A man whose first film role had been tiny and unpromising, but who had invested it with such dynamic vigour that it sparkled like a precious stone among paste fakes in that otherwise mediocre picture, leading to more, and steadily larger parts. A man who was one of the few film stars known all over the world, able to choose his own roles and make the movies which appealed to him – and the queues would form, just because he was in a picture.

Few of the cast had ever worked before with an actor of his standing. None of them had ever appeared with a star of his magnitude.

It was true that all of them, deep in their secret hearts, even the sixty-year-old Bernard Fyfield, believed that given the opportunity they too could be names in the West

End, could succeed in films, could become stars, just as John Cramer had. These beliefs were rarely voiced openly; they belonged to day-dream time in the bath, to the empty days spent surviving until the phone rang again with the offer of a part, private beliefs, or articles of faith, applied as balm to the wound when anticipated, desperately needed work did not materialise because some director thought they were 'not right for the part'. If they ever spoke of these private beliefs to each other it was with a laugh, mockingly, sending themselves up, or in rare, quiet moments of self-revelation, but that was only possible with someone very close and understanding.

But they did believe, just the same, fiercely and implicitly. They believed in their own talent. They had to believe. Without that there was nothing left.

Since they believed, sincerely, that each possessed a potential far beyond actual achievement, there were obvious realities to be accounted for. Why it was such a struggle. Why there were those long, aching weeks out of work. Why they were not starring in the West End. Why they were not in films at all, let alone playing the parts of which they knew they were capable.

But they all knew the reasons. It was a matter of luck, getting the breaks. Being around in the right place at the right time. Knowing the right people. A few lucky ones got the breaks, most did not. They happened to belong to the majority. They were still waiting for fate to offer the right chance. Their turn was yet to come.

So none of them felt inferior to John Cramer. Nor were they especially envious of him. With very few exceptions, actors are generous people. Cramer had made it, and jolly good luck to him. Any of them might have been in his shoes, given the right breaks, but the breaks had gone his way and not theirs. That was the way it went. They had no complaints about that, there was nothing to complain about. The whole profession was an enormous great roulette wheel, and so far their numbers had not come up. But they would one day. One day. . .

'This is Marcia Hambridge,' Maurice said.

'Hullo, Marcia.' If Cramer felt that Marcia did not

much resemble the part she would be playing, of the most desirable woman in the world, his cordial smile, showing his white, even teeth, did not show it. 'I think I was at Stratford with your husband, many years ago.'

'That's right,' Marcia said, gratified. 'He wasn't sure if you'd remember.'

'Yes, of course,' Cramer said. 'He played Octavius, I recall. Please give him my regards, won't you.'

Marcia beamed happily.

'Bernard Fyfield,' Maurice said.

'I saw you at Edinburgh in *The Master Builder*,' Cramer said. 'Must have been ten or twelve years ago. An astonishing performance, I thought.' The ambivalence of the remark was lost on Bernard who was instantly won over.

'Nicola Feary,' Maurice said.

'Nicola.' Cramer's handshake was firm and masculine. His eyes lingered on hers for that fractional moment which all women recognise, and Nicola was no exception.

'Leonard Sherwen. . .' Maurice said. '. . . Ben Stamford.'

'You played the lead in the first telly I ever did,' Ben said. 'I was straight out of drama school. I had ten lines. It was a play, I've forgotten what it was called. We did it at Birmingham.'

'I remember,' Cramer said, smiling. 'The old studios at Gosta Green. Do they still make programmes there?'

'No,' Ben said. 'It's a new mausoleum-type building now called Pebble Mill. Typical BBC. Swarming with bureaucrats who'd be quite happy in their jobs, if it weren't for the few irritating people who actually want to put shows on the air, and they're mostly doing local radio. The network television studio's poked away in a corner as though they'd really much rather pretend it's not there.'

'The technical people work hard enough,' Nicola said. 'I thought the camera crew were smashing.'

'Nicola was in a classic a few years ago recorded at Pebble Mill,' Ben explained.

'Yes, I know,' Cramer said. '*Darien Point.* I saw a few

episodes of it. I usually watch public broadcasting when I'm in the States. Everyone was talking about it in LA.'

'So I gathered,' Nicola said. 'I got lots of letters from America from people who'd liked it. I only wish the size of the royalty cheques matched the appreciation.'

'That's the trouble with PBS sales,' Leonard Sherwen said. 'All prestige and the money's peanuts.'

'That's ridiculous,' Cramer said. He was nursing a glass of red wine, which he hardly touched. 'The only television which intelligent people watch with any real attention in the States is PBS. Things like *I Claudius* and *Anna Karenina* and *Darien Point*. If the money's that bad, why don't Equity do something about it?'

'Why don't Equity do something about a lot of things,' Leonard Sherwen said.

'Treganwy for a start,' Ben Stamford said.

Cramer joined in the general, approving laughter, and Maurice, watching, was satisfied that the major hurdle had been surmounted. The others had embraced Cramer as one who appreciated, if not shared, their scale of worries. None of them by so much as a glance mentally excluded him, even though his car alone, which he had so tactfully sent back to London, represented more capital than any of them would ever acquire in their lifetimes.

That was a credit to them, but also to Cramer for the easy way he had joined in with no side and no pretensions. Good for John Cramer, Maurice thought. He's playing it right.

Cramer continued to do so when some of them adjourned to the nearby pub which the company had adopted as their own. It was Ben who bought the first round.

'I feel like something to remind my liver that life is real and earnest, and no bed of roses,' Ben said. 'To wit, a large scotch. The same for you, John?'

'I'd rather have half of bitter,' Cramer said. 'Wine makes me thirsty.'

Cramer bought his round, when his turn came, but again he stuck to beer. Maurice permitted himself a quiet purr at the way things were going. Cramer could afford to buy drinks all round all night, without even noticing, but that would have been patronising – and disastrous to the relationship which a cast needed among themselves. Maurice's opinion of Cramer was rising by the minute. The man had feeling and discretion.

The conversation meandered away from show business, and Ben complimented Cramer on his novels.

'As a matter of fact,' Ben said, modestly, 'I'm a tyro practitioner myself. Not in your league, I'm afraid, but my first novel was published two years ago. First novel? Who am I kidding. My only novel.'

'Really? What was it called?' Cramer asked.

'Oh, you'll never have heard of it,' Ben said. 'No one has. I got five hundred pounds advance, and it's sold two thousand, six hundred and forty-three copies at the last count. When I want to impress people though, I casually reveal that it's been bought by a film company.'

'I'm impressed,' Cramer said, smiling.

'Don't be,' Ben said. 'The sordid truth is that a Wardour Street barrow boy, a right crook even by the flexible standards prevailing in that sink of iniquity, paid me one hundred pounds for a twelve-month option. I was so carried away with joy that I then allowed him to con me into writing the screenplay on spec.'

'What happened to it?'

'I wouldn't know,' Ben said. 'I haven't heard a dicky bird. And he's not the sort who answers the telephone. Too many people are trying to get money off him. I'm being wise after the event, you understand. I've learned not to trust impressive letter headings since – and too late. I imagine he's racing up and down Wardour Street with the script clutched in his grubby fist, trying to con some sucker into putting up front money on the strength of it, so that he can stop the receiver's men moving in.'

'I'd like to read it,' Cramer said. 'Have you got a copy with you?'

'Look,' Ben said, embarrassed, 'I was just telling a story against myself. I wasn't fishing, honestly.'

'And I'm not biting,' Cramer said. 'But I seem to spend

half my life reading scripts, and I know whether one works or not. I shall have quite a lot of free time for the next few weeks and I might as well look at yours, if you'd like me to. But if you'd rather I didn't, fair enough.'

'I'd rather you did,' Ben said promptly. 'Forget my token resistance. I'm not proud. And by the most amazing coincidence, I do happen to have a spare copy with me. I was going to do some work on it. I need hardly say, I'm sure, that you'll find there's a right juicy part in it, intended for me, but if you'd like it you're very welcome.'

'Thanks very much. I'll bear that in mind,' Cramer said drily. He turned to Maurice. 'That reminds me, I've read your suggested revisions to the play . . .'

'Excuse me. Nature calls,' Ben said diplomatically. He got up and wandered off.

'I'll take a rain check on most of them,' Cramer said. 'I've got some thoughts of my own. But I don't like your insertion into Act Two, scene one. It's very neatly done, and it works, but I don't think we need it.'

'The idea was to bring you back on, and to involve you in that scene,' Maurice said. 'Otherwise, you'll be off-stage for half an hour or more.'

'I got the idea,' Cramer said, 'But that's Willem's scene. We needn't change the play for my benefit.'

'For the audience's benefit as much as yours,' Maurice said. 'Let's face it, you're the one they'll have paid to see.'

'I really don't want to argue about it,' Cramer said. 'I knew the size of the part when I agreed to do it. So let's forget the insertions. O.K.?'

'All right,' Maurice said. 'Whatever you say.'

The feeling returned that there was something odd, something which he could not pinpoint. Maurice was rather pleased with the new bits he had written in for Cramer. He thought they were witty and, moreover, served a dramatic purpose. Why should Cramer be so intent on the original structure, which served to emphasise, as no doubt the playwright had intended, that the play was not about Cramer's character at all?

And Maurice's first, nagging question came back again.

Why was the man doing the play at all? What was the real reason?

The receptionist at the Palace Hotel handed Cramer his key with a shy smile.

'Miss Foster phoned earlier,' she told him. 'She said she'll call back.'

'Thank you,' Cramer said. He summoned up an answering smile from somewhere, although he felt bilious and out of sorts. He disliked beer intensely. 'Can you have some sandwiches sent up please? Beef, turkey, whatever you've got.'

'Yes, of course, Mr Cramer. Right away.'

'Oh, and I'd like a self-drive car delivered here by nine o'clock in the morning. Will you arrange that?' He had decided during the walk back from the pub, as the depression deepened over him, that there were limits to his self-imposed identification with the rest of the cast. He simply could not slog his way round this dreary little town on foot for weeks on end.

The receptionist's smile faltered and she looked distinctly worried.

'I'm terribly sorry, Mr Cramer,' she said, 'but the local people only have Cortinas and Marinas. If you could possibly wait until noon for your car to be delivered, I could arrange for a Volvo or a Mercedes from the firm in . . .'

'A Cortina will do fine,' Cramer said. 'I don't want anything bigger anyway.'

That was not strictly true, but there seemed little point in sending his Rolls Royce away only to reappear with a Mercedes.

In his suite Cramer poured himself a neat whisky, drank it in one swallow, and breathed out deeply. He added ice and water to the second glass, picked up the bottle, carried it across to the most comfortable armchair, sat down, and started looking through the script of the play. After a few moments he took out his pen and began scoring out words and phrases.

One of the porters brought the sandwiches, arranged on a bed of crisp lettuce leaves, and departed. After he had gone Cramer supposed that he should have tipped him. Hell. He was accustomed to having Valerie around to deal with things like that. As if on cue, the telephone rang.

'I'm only calling to reassure you,' Valerie's cool voice said. 'Nothing's come up I can't handle, and I've told everybody you're incommunicado until you've finished at Treganwy.'

'Fine,' Cramer said. 'Keep it that way. I don't want to have to think about anything except this play.' With his free hand he lifted the whisky bottle and topped up his glass. 'Have you done anything about lining up your successor?'

'I didn't think there was any hurry,' Valerie said.

'There isn't,' Cramer said. 'Provided I have someone when I leave for the States, at least as good as you, and preferably better.'

'If you mean as your secretary, that will be arranged,' Valerie said. 'If you mean in bed, you'll have to take pot luck. You can do your own screening in that direction.'

'It'll be a pleasure,' Cramer said. He thought that might be the cue for her to ring off, but she did not do so.

'How's it going?' she asked after a pause.

'All right. Had drinks with the cast today.'

'How did it go?'

'Pleasant enough, in a somewhat boring way,' Cramer said. 'The trouble is, they're all such thoroughly little people.'

'There's a lot of us around,' Valerie said sadly.

'The world is full of them,' Cramer said.

There were plenty of them at the Professor's reception too, Cramer thought, puffed up little people in this case, strutting around, turkey-like, dismally unaware of their own essential puniness under their fatty layers of self-importance. There were civic dignitaries, a few titles, retired admirals, academics, so-called gentry, a rag-bag of non-people, let alone little people, assembled for the

Professor's self-glorification, there to admire not his Utrillos, his Canaletto, his Chippendale furniture which graced his Elizabethan Hall – many of 'them' possessed such things – but the social prize which they could not produce, and Professor Griffiths could. John Cramer.

Cramer had no intention of playing the Professor's game. Compared to this lot, Maurice and some of the actors were giants of integrity. Marcia Hambridge and Bernard Fyfield clearly enjoyed hob-nobbing, but the rest obviously shared his own amused disdain for the proceedings. Cramer accepted glasses of Dom Perignon champagne and canapés from attentive servants, but he refused to be parted from Maurice, Nicola, Ben and Leonard – to the Professor's thinly veiled irritation, as time wore on.

'John, I'd like you to meet Mr and Mrs Geraint Rees,' Professor Griffiths said, trying again for the umpteenth time. 'Geraint is an old friend of mine, and I know he'd like to talk to you about . . .'

'How do you do, Mr and Mrs Geraint Rees,' Cramer said, giving them a charming smile. 'This is Nicola Feary, whom I'm sure you must have seen on television in *Darien Point*, and this is Ben Stamford, who is a novelist as well as an actor. You must meet Leonard as well. Where is he?'

Cramer turned away from the faintly bemused Mr and Mrs Geraint Rees. He heard Mrs Geraint Rees ask politely, if with some disappointment, 'And what part did you play, Miss Feary?'

'Sonia Darien,' Nicola said.

'Really? Wasn't she the one with all the blonde hair?'

'I was wearing a wig,' Nicola explained.

'Oh, I see. Isn't that very uncomfortable, with all the lights they have in studios, and so on?'

'It was bloody murder,' Nicola told her affably.

Professor Griffiths finally contrived to corner Cramer after pursuing him like a worried sheep-dog quartering an errant sheep.

'John,' he hissed into Cramer's ear, 'I would be deeply obliged if you would circulate. These people have come here to meet you, not to be introduced to actors they've never heard of.'

'That's their problem,' Cramer said. 'You wanted to put me on show. O.K., I'm here. They can have a good look, if they're so stupid that gives them a kick. I didn't promise to make polite conversation. 'Maurice, just a minute,' he called, making good his escape. 'When's the first read through?'

'Tomorrow morning, ten o'clock,' Maurice said.

'Sorry, I forgot the time,' Cramer said. 'Like we can forget this wake at the first possible moment,' he added in an undertone.

'Amen to that,' Maurice said.

Something would have to be done about this, Professor Griffiths thought. There was a distinct air of restless impatience among his distinguished guests. The titles who were being bored rigid by Marcia Hambridge were showing irritation and rebelliousness to Professor Griffiths' practised eye. There was, fortunately, a way which would effectively soothe them. The Professor patted his breast pocket and took comfort from the notes of his speech, which rested there reassuringly.

Nicola had thankfully exchanged her last smiling inanity with Mr and Mrs Geraint Rees. She found Cramer beside her, speaking into her ear in an undertone.

'I'm going to get out of this. If you want to join me, you can have a lift.'

Somewhere a spoon tinkled on a glass. Heads turned and looked at Professor Griffiths. Conversation died.

'I think he's going to make a speech,' Nicola whispered.

'Exactly. Pretend we're going to the loo.'

'I don't have to pretend,' Nicola said. 'I'm bursting.'

They slid conspiratorially through the door into the large, square, panelled hall. The Professor had begun to speak.

'I'll wait for you,' Cramer said. 'But don't be long.'

'. . . and while we rightly pride ourselves on the excellence of our productions here at Treganwy,' the Professor was saying, 'due in no small measure to the splendid actors who have appeared here, I regard it as a triumph that our reputation can attract such a famous star as John Cramer. I choose my words carefully. It is a triumph. An event which does honour to the very name of Treganwy.' Those who lived in or near Treganwy applauded enthusiastically, the remainder politely. 'I well remember the first time I met John,' the Professor reminisced. 'He was a shy undergraduate, awed I fancy by the noble and ancient traditions of Cambridge. . .'

Nicola hurried across the hall towards Cramer.

'Made it,' Cramer said. 'Come on. Before he starts sending out search parties.'

'. . . and I know you will wish to join with me in offering a warm and sincere welcome to John Cramer,' Professor Griffiths said. Applause. 'And I also know,' the Professor resumed, 'that John will wish to say a few words on this, the occasion of his most auspicious welcome to Treganwy.' More applause. 'John,' the Professor said expectantly. Silence. 'John?' More silence, broken by a few murmurs.

The Professor exchanged his reading glasses for the other pair, which he needed to see more than ten feet. Sick apprehension took hold of him as his eyes swept the gathering. People were looking at each other. Eyebrows were rising. Ben Stamford had a handkerchief pressed to his mouth and appeared to be weeping for some reason. The Professor glared at a hapless servant.

'Kindly find Mr Cramer at once,' he said coldly.

Cramer swung the wheel of the Cortina as he followed Nicola's directions, and the headlights picked out the small cottage.

'That one?' he asked.

'That's it,' Nicola said. The car completed its U-turn and came to a stop. Nicola fumbled in her handbag for the front door key. 'Well, thanks for the lift,' she said.

'No trouble,' Cramer said. 'You can share the blame.'

'They won't even notice I've gone,' Nicola said. She looked sideways at Cramer. He was staring at the hedgerows ahead illuminated by the headlights. His fingers lightly tapped the steering wheel. The engine idled peacefully. She smiled, thinking of the Professor's faintly heard words as they had pulled the massive front door of The Hall quietly to behind them. 'I almost wish I'd stayed to see what happened.'

'I came here to act in a play,' Cramer said. 'I see no reason why I have to be doing with all that shit.'

'It was pretty ghastly,' Nicola said. 'I'm beginning to think I prefer working in television. I'm sure there are just as many phonies around, but you don't seem to meet them as often as you do in the theatre.'

'Then why are you here?'

'I like to keep working, if I can,' Nicola said.

'You must have had plenty of offers after *Darien Point.*'

'Not one,' Nicola said. 'At least, not in television. I don't think it was really as good as the critics made out. They all raved about it, but they always do about classics, they're basically snobs. Just the same, it was very popular, I know I was good in it, and I felt sure something would come out of it. I turned down offers to appear at the Belgrade and York, and sat at home waiting for five months. After that I gave up hoping and took the first tour I could get. An Agatha Christie play, and not one of her best, if there's any such thing. Still, that's the way it goes.' The engine was still murmuring quietly, the headlights still on. 'I could make some coffee, if you like, unless you want to get back to the hotel.'

'No coffee for me, thanks,' Cramer said. 'Make it a drink, and you've got a willing customer.'

'There's white wine,' Nicola said. 'Or whisky.

'Fine,' Cramer said. The engine died and he flicked the headlights off.

Nicola fetched the whisky from a cupboard. It was a half-bottle. She did not drink the stuff, but Ben Stamford and Robin Haslem did.

'How do you like it?' she asked.

'With ice and water,' Cramer said. 'Do you mind if I look round?'

'Go ahead,' Nicola said. 'There's not much to see.' She made his drink, carried it into the living room. Cramer was coming out of the bedroom.

'That's it,' Nicola said. 'Except for the bathroom.'

Cramer followed her back into the kitchen and sipped his drink while she made coffee for herself.

'It's a nice little place,' Cramer said. 'Perhaps I should have done this. You wouldn't like to swap, I suppose?'

'I couldn't afford a suite at the Palace Hotel,' Nicola said. The ice clinked in his glass as he put it down on the table. 'Help yourself,' Nicola said. 'I don't like it, so I never know how much to pour.'

'Thanks.' Cramer filled his glass.

'More ice?'

'No, thanks.'

Nicola took her coffee into the living room. Cramer followed her, carrying the bottle. She knelt to light the fire which she had laid that morning. The paper flared, the dry wood crackled. Soon the coals were turning red and flames licked up the chimney. Cramer sat in an armchair, watching.

'A real fire,' he said. 'Now I know I should have taken a place like this.'

'It wouldn't have been worth it for a few weeks,' Nicola said. 'I'm here for six months. I must say, I like it though. When I close that front door as I come in I feel safe and secure. My very own home, provided I don't look too far ahead.' She smiled slightly. 'I suppose I'm indulging in one of my fantasies, but I enjoy it.'

'Do you share with anyone?'

'No,' Nicola said. She half expected him to pursue it – there was still that same light in his eye when he looked at her – but he did not. He smiled at her as he leaned back comfortably, cradling his glass, and watched the glowing fire, the occasional small hissing spurts of gas from the coals.

'I suppose you'd looked us all up,' Nicola said. 'Or had someone do it for you.' Cramer swivelled his head and looked at her. 'When we first met,' Nicola said, 'you knew something about everybody. Either you'd been briefed, or you have a very good memory.'

'Quite good,' Cramer said. 'But not that good.'

'Do you smoke?' Nicola offered him a cigarette.

Cramer shook his head. 'I used to, but I gave it up. Everyone should have one vice they can do without. That's mine.' He eyed her thoughtfully. 'What's yours?'

'Gluttony,' Nicola said.

He laughed. 'That's perfectly apparent,' he said. 'You're as thin as a bean pole.'

'You may not intend that as a compliment,' Nicola said, 'but it is one, to me.'

'It is a compliment,' Cramer said.

Nicola blew cigarette smoke towards the fire, and watched as it curled and was sucked up the chimney.

'So you didn't really see me in *Darien Point,*' she said.

'As a matter of fact, I did,' Cramer said lazily. 'Only two episodes, it's true, but I do remember you. I thought the farewell scene with your soldier lover was very well played. I know you can act.' He reached out and topped up his glass. 'Can Marcia Hambridge?'

'Well, she's the old school,' Nicola said. 'She certainly plays the leading lady all the time, which I find boring. I suppose she's making the most of it, having been out of the business for five years. She took time out to have a baby.'

'So I was told,' Cramer said.

'To be fair,' Nicola said, 'she's done some good things. I saw her Lady Macbeth at Bristol. It wasn't the way I'd have played it, but yes, she's a good actress. In her own way.'

'Can she play Paula, though?' Cramer asked. His eyes were almost closed.

'I think she can *play* Paula,' Nicola said. 'Whether she can *be* Paula is another matter. She might, if Maurice keeps her down, and she uses enough Leichner. I suppose that sounds bitchy.'

'It sounds direct, which is why I asked you,' Cramer said. 'I hardly know you, as yet, but you seem like someone who speaks her mind.' He yawned. 'Let's face it, it'll take considerable ability for Miss Hambridge to persuade us that she's a woman who drives men mad with desire, although presumably she has that effect on her husband from time to time.' He considered that idea, and shook his head. 'Can't imagine it though. He must spend his time chasing young female ASMs.'

'He doesn't,' Nicola said. 'He adores her. I've worked with him.'

'Well, they say there's a man for every woman, somewhere. Marcia must have struck lucky.'

'She's not that bad,' Nicola protested. She did not like Marcia Hambridge, but she always developed a strong streak of loyalty towards people she was working with. 'Anyway, you'll *have* to imagine she's desirable, since you're playing Stephen.'

'That's what concerns me,' Cramer said. 'Among other things.'

'What other things? The play?'

'Plays exist to please audiences,' Cramer said. 'I think this one will. At Treganwy, anyway, which is all that matters to me.'

'They'll come to see you,' Nicola said. 'They'd come to see you in anything. *Murder in the Red Barn*. Or *Uncle Vanya*, come to that. Why wouldn't you do *Uncle Vanya*? Why did you insist on doing *Paula*?'

'I'm sure that's been explained to you,' Cramer said.

'Yes, it has,' Nicola said, 'but I don't think I buy what I was told. In fact, I don't know why you're here at all.'

'I asked Maurice to make that plain to everybody,' Cramer said. 'Hasn't he done so?'

'A favour to Professor Griffiths because you're so fond of him,' Nicola said. 'If you're fond of him, I'd hate to be someone you don't like.'

'He's incredibly persistent,' Cramer said. 'In the end he wore me down.'

'You don't strike me as the kind of man who'd ever do anything he didn't want to.'

'Even I have my weak moments,' Cramer said.

Nicola studied his face carefully, and even though his smile was pleasant and genuine he looked tired and drawn around the eyes and mouth.

'You don't look too bright,' she said. 'Have you got a headache? If so, I've got some Panadol.'

'I'm O.K.,' Cramer said. 'Ready for bed, mostly.' He

stroked his forehead with his fingertips. 'I have been feeling a bit off lately though. Some sort of bug, I expect. I've been thinking I should perhaps have a 'flu jab, just in case. I wonder if there's a decent quack in this place.'

'There's a company doctor,' Nicola said. 'Dr Morgan. Apparently he's done it every season since the year dot. He's a stage buff. Crazy about the theatre.'

'I suppose you wouldn't know if he's any good?'

'He seemed fine to me,' Nicola said. 'I went to see him last week.'

'Why? Have you been ill?'

'No, not really,' Nicola said. 'Female trouble, that's all. He put me on a different pill. Said I shouldn't have been given the one I was using in the first place. I can give you his phone number if you like.'

Cramer waved his hand. 'No, it's all right. The hotel can fix it if I decide to see him. Dr Morgan. Is there only the one, or half a dozen?'

'Only the one in Treganwy,' Nicola said. 'Believe it or not.'

'Well, I suppose I'd better go.' Cramer looked at his watch and stood up. 'Thanks for the drink. I've enjoyed the last hour of the evening a damn sight more than the first part.'

'So have I,' Nicola said. She saw him to the door.

'Good night,' Cramer said. 'See you in the morning, bright and early.'

'Ten o'clock isn't all that bright and early,' Nicola said.

She closed the door and, in the silence, heard his feet crunch steadily on the gravel as he walked along the path. It took a while for him to start the car. The starter motor whined and growled for what seemed a long time, and when the engine fired he raced it in several loud bursts before driving off, which was no bad thing, Nicola supposed wryly. It would soothe the apprehensions of the neighbours who, she was pretty certain, would have been briefed by her landlords to keep an eye on her doings.

She sat on the carpet in front of the fire, smoked a last cigarette before going to bed, and thought about John Cramer. Her prejudices about him were fading. She admired the way he had pointedly refused to be treated as someone different at that dreary, stuffed shirt function. She knew that he found her attractive even though, she strongly suspected, he was the sort of man who found most presentable women attractive, and that his present wife was safely in the South of France. Nevertheless he had made no suggestions, neither overt nor implied, and he had not touched her at any point, even in that 'accidental' way which she found so tedious in men. He had not so much as given her that automatic kiss on the cheek which actors were prone to. Nor had he called her 'darling' once.

Yes, John Cramer had style, she thought. So far, she approved of him. She threw her cigarette in the fire and stood up. She noticed that the half-bottle of whisky was empty, picked it up, and threw it into the waste bin on her way to the bathroom.

She would have to replace that in case Ben and Robin came for a drink one day.

Professor Griffiths was taking it out on Maurice. His face was still white with anger, his cheek bones stood out sharply in his thin face, and his pebble eyes glittered dangerously. He was reaching what was intended to be a threatening coda.

'. . . the kind of fiasco to which I am not accustomed,' he said, his voice brittle with the worst kind of fury, that born of humiliation. 'For which I hold you entirely responsible. You knew perfectly well what my plans were for the evening.'

'I'm not John Cramer's keeper,' Maurice said.

'I would remind you that you are supposed to be Director of Productions,' Professor Griffiths snapped. 'As such, I expect you to remember your responsibility to the theatre. This evening was intended to serve a very important purpose. That purpose was not fulfilled. My guests expected to meet John Cramer. Not to stand by and watch him gossiping to you and a bunch of actors they have no interest in whatever. Least of all did they expect him to walk out without so much as a by your leave to anyone.'

'I thought you told them that he was feeling unwell, and sent his personal apologies to each one of them individually,' Maurice said tiredly. 'I'm sure that flattered them sufficiently to salvage your social reputation.'

'My social reputation, as you put it, does not depend on any actor, no matter how distinguished,' Professor Griffiths said tartly. 'My guests were carefully selected. Directly or indirectly, they all support the theatre, either as generous patrons, or by influencing the size of our various grants. Treganwy can only exist so long as it is heavily subsidised. It is not, and can never be, a commercial proposition. I'm concerned with the theatre, first, last and all the time, not any personal slight I may appear to have suffered. That's not important. The theatre is. And your sloppiness, your indifference, could have jeopardised it tonight.'

'Rattling the old tin can is your business, not mine,' Maurice said. 'You're good at it.'

'You appear to be a remarkably short-sighted man, Mr Gardiner,' Professor Griffiths said. 'You well know that under the terms of the contract, Treganwy has acquired an interest in this play. I shall be inviting some influential people to see it, including some reputable theatre managements. If you can contrive to make it look good enough there will almost certainly be a tour. The play may even reach the West End. The income which would then accrue to Treganwy would be invaluable in future seasons. We could raise our standards even higher, afford to be even more adventurous. To achieve these desirable ends, the production must be polished, stylish, and smack of success. That is your job, and it is not asking much of you, I feel, since you have John Cramer in the cast, thanks to me.'

'I know my job,' Maurice said sourly. 'I don't see your problem.' This fathead suffers from verbal diarrhoea, he thought.

'The problem is not mine, Mr Gardiner,' the Professor said softly, 'it is yours. Should the play excite sufficient interest to justify a tour, and a possible transfer to the West End, it will of course have to be recast. John Cramer leaves for America. We all know that Marcia Hambridge won't do, once we've lost Cramer, and in any case, she isn't enough of a name to support the play elsewhere. The others will probably have to be replaced as well. I am particularly unhappy about Nicola Feary.' He paused, studied Maurice, and then said significantly, 'All this means that, should the play tour in the autumn, or even go straight into the West End, it would have to be completely re-directed.'

'I know all that,' Maurice said. 'We've discussed it enough times.' He was feeling exhausted. He wanted to go to bed.

'In the normal course of events,' Professor Griffiths said, 'you would be invited to re-direct the play. But contractually your contribution does not extend beyond Treganwy. Should it appear desirable, it would be perfectly feasible to invite some other director to take the play on, in which case you would have no financial interest in its success. My opinion will be sought when the time comes to make that decision, and it will carry considerable weight, I assure you. Do I make myself clear?'

Maurice was silent. His every impulse screamed at him to tell this verbose, patronising pillar of his own mini-establishment what to do with his 'opinion', to instruct him that he could not keep creative people deferentially waiting for hand-outs at the metaphorical tradesmen's entrance, to turn his back contemptuously, walk out, and slam the door in his face.

But Maurice had developed a hunch that the play was a commercial possibility. He thought audiences would like it. Properly recast, even without John Cramer, they would probably go on liking it. Certainly enough for a decent tour, and it might even skid into the West End, the way shows had been folding in London lately.

Once in the West End, what happened then was anyone's guess. You could never tell. No one could. Really bad plays had made money there before now.

Conversely, good plays had closed in three weeks. It was a lottery. But the man who directed the play at least held a lottery ticket. He was in the game.

Maurice needed to be in that game. Apart from six months' work, that was why he was at Treganwy at all. The National belonged to the past. Maurice did not know what, but something had gone wrong there. If his career were not to wilt and remorselessly decline in one underpaid provincial theatre after another, Maurice needed a play in the West End.

A director could earn a lot of money from his royalties in a successful play. Maurice needed that money. Only if he could consistently make at least as much as Anna, and preferably more, he had come to believe, would their relationship stand a chance. And in the end, come the final choice, he loved Anna. He also hated her a good part of the time, but that was irrelevant. There was no one else for him. That mixture of hate and love was all he had. Given a play in the West End, able to pick and choose, not scrabble hopefully for the next job, she would look at him differently, he was sure of that. He would not have changed. He would still be the same man, and recognition of talent did not mean that a man had acquired any more talent, but that was beside the point. Anna was not a rational being, and if what was between them was not giving and receiving, but conflict which would never achieve equilibrium until they were on equal terms in her eyes, then so be it. That was the reality. That was what they had, for good or ill. There were no divine, objective scales in which two people together could weigh each other, or if there were, the hand which held them adopted a measurement incomprehensible to mortal men.

Professor Griffiths could not know any of this. But that learned, wealthy, former academic possessed all the refined instincts of a successful blackmailer.

Maurice sighed. After all, a few months making the right servile noises at intermittent intervals, while getting on with the job he loved, was not too much of a price to pay.

'I shall produce the play to the best of my ability,' he

said with as much dignity as he could muster. 'Naturally, I would hope to be asked to re-direct it for a subsequent tour, or whatever.'

'For my part, I hope that I shall be pressing your claims to do so,' Professor Griffiths said agreeably. Maurice found the man's condescension harder to take than his covert threats. 'And I trust that we are in agreement about your responsibility to the theatre on any future occasion, when it will assist us if John Cramer is not only there, but making himself pleasant to the people who will then be considering the future of the play?'

'Yes,' Maurice said, 'Good night.'

Cramer's eyelids snapped open as though a trigger had been released. He was drenched in sweat, and his heart was pounding so hard that it appeared to threaten to burst through his rib cage. It was four o'clock in the morning. He threw the bedclothes aside and waited for his body to cool, for his heart beat to slow down. He had been asleep for slightly under three hours.

He had thought it was going to be all right. Once back at the hotel, he had given himself half a tumbler of whisky – not too much – and sat quietly sipping it, deliberately thinking about nothing. Not the play, not his children, not his wife. Nothing. Drowsily, at exactly the right moment, he had slipped into bed, perfectly relaxed, and drifted calmly towards welcoming sleep.

Now, not three hours later, he was wide awake. There was a sour taste in his mouth, but at least the nightmare, terrifying in its obscenity, its utter, degrading humiliation, was receding. He would not sleep again tonight, he knew that. He lay quite still, consciously ordering his muscles to relax. Simply lying in bed and resting was just as good as a night's sleep. He had read that somewhere. Experience, however, had taught him that it did not work.

Breakfast arrived four endless hours later, brought by a cheerful maid. Cramer swallowed the orange juice at one gulp and drank half a cup of tea. He forced himself to eat some of the toast, and a little of the egg, but then his stomach revolted and he left the bacon untouched.

Cramer sat on the edge of the bed and rubbed the stubble on his face, blearily. He felt terrible. He could not go on like this. What was the man's name? Morgan. That was it. Dr Morgan.

He walked into the bathroom, ran the shower until it was icy cold, stepped underneath, and gasped involuntarily. He forced himself to stay there until he was shivering all over, and then rubbed himself dry with a coarse towel.

He shaved himself carefully, brushed his still wet hair, and only then did he study his face critically in the mirror. As usual, he was taken aback. He looked all right. The same as ever. The trouble was, he did not feel all right.

Cramer hesitated for a long time, standing motionless in front of the mirror. There was a remedy, but he had promised himself that he would avoid it. Yes, but this was different. He must be able to function properly during rehearsals. It was only for today, after all. This evening, or tomorrow, he could send for Dr Morgan. He considered that course of action doubtfully. He had vowed to avoid that too. It was only a question of will-power, and he had enough of that, God only knew. Yes, but in that case . . .

Cramer decided.

He went into the living room, poured a glass of neat scotch, drank it in one steady swallow, put the glass down, and waited.

Soon the fuzziness began to recede. He felt better. The tenseness left his body. He was steadier and calmer. The nausea left him as the glow reached his stomach.

He went back into the bathroom and cleaned his teeth, taking extra care, rinsed his mouth out, and then cleaned them again. Afterwards he used a mouth wash.

Cramer decided to go through the script again. There was time. He sat down with it and started work. He had been worrying himself about nothing. He was alert now, as his pen hovered over the lines in the script, a little edgy perhaps, hypercritical, but that was all to the good. He needed to concentrate all his faculties to succeed in his self-imposed task.

It was, he decided, only the tension which always arrived when starting something new, and it served a highly useful purpose. It sharpened his perceptions, set the adrenalin running, made him the perfectionist which he was. There was no need for Dr Morgan, nor need he take anything with him.

Once the hard work of rehearsals got under way, he would be O.K. He could handle it on his own.

Maurice was at the rehearsal room early. So were Linda and Alan, the two young ASMs. Nicola left her cottage in good time, and she enjoyed the walk downhill into Treganwy. It was a pleasantly sunny day, although a patch of white cloud lurked over Snowdon, and the gentle wind was warm on her cheeks. If spring had not definitely come for good it was at least forecasting its imminent arrival.

Ben Stamford, who would take over from John Cramer after Cramer left, was already there, joking with Leonard Sherwen. So was the bulky, balding figure of Bernard Fyfield. He was talking to Alan Cakin, gazing into the young man's eyes, his face serious. Alan was listening attentively, nodding now and then. Linda was making coffee.

Marcia Hambridge made an entrance at ten o'clock precisely. She had evidently decided that jeans and a sweater were no longer appropriate for an occasion such as this. She wore a dress which flattered by not revealing her shape too much, and high-heeled shoes. Perfume floated in the air around her. Her eye make-up might well have looked good from the sixth row of the stalls, but was less than appropriate from a few feet. She was presumably unaware of the precise reason for the startled glances she received. An apology for almost being late died on her lips when she saw that John Cramer was not there. She seemed rather put out.

Cramer arrived just after ten-twenty. He told Maurice that he had been obliged to talk to his London agent on the phone concerning the play he would be doing on Broadway. It was an announcement, not an apology.

'Don't worry,' Maurice said, choosing to treat it as an apology anyway. 'We can always break for lunch a bit later.'

He produced a model of the set, with a certain modest pride, and proceeded to explain it.

'All the action takes places on the patio, marble floor, Corinthian columns, all that jazz. Through the columns, the exit to the beach. Stage right, open French windows, leading into the house. We just see a hint through the windows of what we presume is an elegant drawing room. Stage left, the path leading to the helicopter pad. Upstage from there, the bar, in ostentatious, deliberate bad taste. We're hiring the beach furniture, and it'll look good, no expense spared. We'll be using disco speakers, so that we can really blast the auditorium with the noise of the helicopter arriving and departing. There'll also be wind machines for when it passes overhead, powerful enough to blow papers about, ruffle hair, and so on. During the dusk arrival of the helicopter, we're assuming it will have landing lights on, and we've fixed it so that the lights will travel overhead, across the stage . . .'

Everyone made little noises of delight and approval, which was what Maurice wanted, since the set up was basically his idea anyway, and the designer had worked to his brief. The only exception was Cramer, who stood by indifferently and seemed not to be listening.

Nicola caught his eye. His lips twitched in a small, neutral smile, but his eyes were blank. Nicola thought that the small scar on his cheek was more prominent than she had previously thought. There was an air of taut impatience about him.

Maurice put the model of the set away and looked at his watch.

'O.K.,' he said. 'Let's read it through, allowing for

moves and pauses as accurately as possible so that we get a good idea of the likely length of the play. And then, after lunch, we'll start blocking.'

They all sat round the table and opened their scripts. Linda and Alan sat at the far end.

'Everyone ready?' Maurice enquired rhetorically. 'Right, Alan.' Alan Cakin started the watch.

'The stage lights go up,' Maurice said, 'and we find Stephen, apparently asleep on a beach bed, stage centre, with a big hat covering his face. A brilliantly sunny day. The murmur of the sea, as from a distance. The sound of typing from inside the house. The typing stops and Mary enters, carrying a manuscript . . .'

Nicola and Cramer read their duologue.

'Meanwhile,' Maurice said, 'unnoticed by them, Paula has arrived from the beach.' He nodded to Marcia.

'Stop squabbling, you two,' Marcia read. 'What's a Freudian slip between friends.'

'I did cherish a fleeting hope that you might have drowned,' Cramer read.

The read went on. A slight frown appeared on Maurice's face. Nicola wondered if she had lost her place.

'Just a minute,' Maurice said. 'Stop the watch, Alan.' Maurice turned to Cramer. 'Have you got the wrong script, John?'

'That's one of the lines I've cut,' Cramer said.

'Not according to my script,' Maurice said.

'I made some more cuts this morning,' Cramer said. He pitched his script across to Maurice. 'Here. You can see what I've done.'

Maurice bent over the script, swiftly turning one page after another. Finally he raised his head and gazed at Cramer, puzzled.

'Don't you think it rather changes the play?' he asked.

'That's the idea,' Cramer said shortly.

'I want to bring out all the humour I can,' Maurice said. 'It'll leaven all the heavy stuff about Paula, I think the play needs that, and parts of it are genuinely funny anyway.

'But you seem to have taken out all your laugh lines. I don't quite see the point.'

'The point is, that I am not going to play a queer,' Cramer said flatly.

'We find out eventually that Stephen isn't queer anyway,' Maurice reminded him.

'Then the lines I've removed won't matter,' Cramer said.

'It seems to me they matter a great deal,' Maurice said patiently. 'It makes nonsense of Paula's assumption that you're queer, if you don't play up to it. And later on, Bernard has that line where he says to you, "You are obviously a homosexual. I can always tell."'

'That's the biggest laugh in the play,' Cramer remarked. Bernard Fyfield eyed him expressionlessly.

'But the main point is that we'd lose all the comedy,' Maurice said.

'You'll have to find your comedy elsewhere,' Cramer said. His voice rasped like a file on rough metal. 'There's one raving poufter in this cast already, and that's enough. I decline to play another one.' He stared contemptuously at Bernard Fyfield.

The ageing actor's lips tightened, and he looked away. Alan Cakin's face flushed scarlet.

There was a brief, shocked silence. Everyone knew that Bernard was an old queen. He did not flaunt it, but it was no secret. To them, the fact was totally irrelevant. The man was an actor. In his time, he had played husbands, fathers, passionate lovers of adorable women – all the things which he himself would never be, and never had been. None of that mattered. Even those who disliked him recognised his right to be what he was without criticism.

Nicola was sitting next to Cramer. Subconsciously, in the brief, awkward silence, she shifted her chair away from him slightly. The legs scraped lightly on the floor. The easy, relaxed, pleasant man, whose company she had enjoyed the night before, had vanished. She could not reconcile him with the one next to her now, who was capable of such pointless cruelty.

'Well, we'll carry on, and see how it reads,' Maurice

said evenly. 'Then perhaps you and I can have a chat about it over lunch, John. Right, Alan, start the watch, if you please. We'll go straight on.'

The read through continued. But all the fun and excitement had gone, Nicola thought, and been replaced by something else. No one gave so much as a hint of playing a part. Voices were flat and neutral. There were no small chuckles as speeches were read, as there had been during the first few pages. It was as if Cramer had activated a time bomb, which was silently ticking away, and they were all waiting for it to go off.

For the first time it occurred to Nicola, uneasily, that she might unwittingly be involved in something which could easily became a gruesome disaster.

# CHAPTER SEVEN

The collection of egos twisted and turned, revolved, spun in aberrant orbits, skidded and collided, like the atoms of a molecule gone mad. Somehow, the ever-threatened nuclear explosion never quite took place.

Marcia Hambridge lost whatever modicum of modesty with which nature and the disappointments of fate had endowed her, and changed as effortlessly into the complete leading lady as some female Frankenstein's monster, more than fulfilling all Nicola's predictions.

She became obsessed with her billing and rehearsed her grievance to whoever would listen to her when Cramer was not around.

'I mean, after all,' Marcia said, 'the play's about me. I'm never off-stage. It's not about Stephen, no matter how big a draw the actor concerned may be. Obviously John Cramer must have top billing, I concede that gladly, but it misrepresents the play if all the publicity says "John Cramer in *Paula*". It sounds absurd, as if he was playing Paula, which is ridiculous. We should be true to the playwright's intentions, no matter what,' Marcia went on. Now that the theatre publicity people had started to beat the drum in earnest about this 'best new play for years', Marcia had acquired instant belief in all the puffed up hand-outs designed to persuade bums on to seats. She had already worked out that the earliest the play could open in the West End was late October, and saw herself taking Shaftesbury Avenue by storm. 'Besides,' she said, triumphantly adding her ultimate, clinching argument, 'at the end of the play, Stephen's gone. It's me who's left alone on stage. It's my predicament the audience care about.'

Bernard Fyfield grunted whole-hearted agreement. He would never forgive Cramer for that scene at the read through, and his contempt and loathing for the man were absolute and unqualified. He became prone to address remarks into empty space, without warning, about 'self-inflated egomaniacs who treat professionals as though they were slum dwellers'. Everyone pretended not to hear his rumblings.

In fact, the incident had done Bernard no harm in the personal sense. Alan Cakin, shocked by the pointless insult of the older man, had crossed an invisible yet tangible line in his subsequent efforts to show that he took no notice of Cramer's abuse, and Bernard accepted the young ASM's sympathy gladly, and with sincere gratitude, if with suitable dignity. In return Bernard sympathised with Alan's dislike for the lack of privacy involved in sharing a caravan. The possibility that Alan might be more comfortable if he were to move into Bernard's flat was being tentatively explored.

Nicola, and most of the others, listened with strained patience to Marcia's repeated grumbles about her billing, and changed the subject at the first opportunity. It was easier to nod and keep quiet, rather than say 'Come on, Marcia, don't be silly.' Marcia possessed a relentless insistence about any real or fancied slight, and was about as easily deterred as a runaway bulldozer. Life was too short to argue with her. Besides, they all had their own worries. The first night was inexorably approaching.

Fortified by what she mistakenly supposed was unanimous agreement, Marcia issued her oft-rehearsed complaint to Maurice in one long torrent, ending with a veiled threat to get on to her agent about it if the matter were not rectified to her complete satisfaction.

Maurice laughed at her, and told her not to be a fool. There was a shouting match in the course of which Maurice assured her that there were dozens of actresses who would do anything short of, and possibly including, murder to play opposite John Cramer at Treganwy with no argument about billing, and if she did not believe him, he was prepared to prove his assertion at once, even at this late stage, if she felt so strongly about it that she would prefer to step down here and now.

It ended with Marcia stalking off, her face crimson with fury. Maurice sighed. The whole thing, including his threat, had been an empty, ritual performance, with no substance. Nothing short of her own sudden death would detach Marcia from this part. At least one stand-up quarrel with her was par for the course. That was the way she showed her nerves. The next thing, he supposed, would be her bloody dressing room.

Maurice took his time over blocking the play, and his methods clearly irritated Cramer, who chafed impatiently, wanting all the actors' moves cut and dried, and the business laid down, as early as possible. Maurice preferred to work in an apparently random fashion, allowing his actors to offer their first, instinctive preferences, the moves which seemed natural to them, suggesting modifications if they did not work, but always ready to listen to suggestions and to spend endless time patiently discussing why this move felt right, and that move felt wrong.

Cramer's scarcely-curbed annoyance appeared excessive to Maurice, but he thought it politic to explain to Cramer over a private drink what he was trying to achieve. The notion was some way short of successful.

'Thank you for the potted dissertation on technique,' Cramer said, making no attempt to conceal his sarcastic disdain. 'I have directed one or two things myself, you know.'

Maurice did not need reminding of the delicacy of his position. He was well aware that among those 'one or two things' was a full-length feature film with a multi-million pound budget, an assignment which might be one of Maurice's most cherished, if unlikely ambitions, but which he had not yet come within a thousand miles of achieving.

'We all tackle things in our own different ways,' Maurice said soothingly. 'I have my version of the play worked out, of course, and I'll nudge my actors towards that if they don't come up with anything better. But sometimes they can, and I believe they should have the chance to do so. As I see it, my job is to extract every ounce of talent they possess, not confine it in any way.'

'Talent? What talent?' Cramer enquired. 'Marcia Hambridge and Bernard Fyfield? A silly bitch and a pompous old poufter only too glad to work for peanuts. What the hell have they ever done?'

'They're both good actors, or they wouldn't be here,' Maurice said stubbornly.

'Come on,' Cramer growled. 'They're either all you could get, or it makes you feel good to throw them a job and have them lick your hand like a couple of grateful Labradors.'

'Listen,' Maurice said tightly, 'I know you didn't choose me as your director, but I didn't choose you either. All we can both do is make the best of it. Give it a chance, that's all I ask. I want this play to be a success as much as you do, and probably a damn sight more.'

'You started this conversation, not me,' Cramer said. 'As far as I am concerned, your methods are time-wasting amateurish crap.'

Maurice was shaking as he walked from the pub to his car. He sat behind the steering wheel until his fingers had stopped trembling. What a destructive bastard Cramer was. Where was the decent, thoughtful man with the engaging sense of humour he had first met? Where had that one gone?

Maurice had supposed that, during his career, he had met all kinds and shapes of actors. But John Cramer was something else.

And yet, somehow, by the second week in that drab rehearsal room belonging to the town council, the play was taking shape. Nicola was the first to discard her book. She was a perfectionist about her lines and had to be word-perfect before her performance could begin to emerge. She spent most of her evenings alone in front of the fire, going over and over her script, or sometimes with Leonard Sherwen, working on the one scene they had together.

'This part is a real bloody pill,' Leonard said. 'I'm sure I shall corpse on the first night, when I have to say to Marcia, "Hullo, mother." The look on her face gives me the giggles every time.'

'Yes, well, watch it,' Nicola said. 'Maurice has ceased to find it amusing. He's getting pissed off.'

'I can't help it,' Leonard sighed. 'Try as she might, Marcia always acquires this expression of outrage at the very idea I could be her son, even in a play.' A sudden hoot of laughter overtook him.

'Oh shut up,' Nicola said. She pushed her script at him. 'You haven't got much to learn. Will you read Stephen so that I can go over my scenes with him?'

'Why don't you ask John Cramer to do it with you?' Leonard asked. 'He fancies you, anyway.'

'He's hardly said a word to me since we started rehearsing,' Nicola said. 'I don't know what's the matter with him. A sore-headed bear'd be politeness itself compared with him.'

Bernard Fyfield was the next to become word-perfect, and began to enjoy visibly the one long scene in which he dominated the proceedings.

Marcia developed an attack of the anxieties about this, and took Maurice aside again.

'I feel Paula should fight back more,' she complained. 'As it stands, he walks all over me. There's one place where I feel that if I had a few extra lines . . .'

'Darling, forget it,' Maurice said firmly. 'You've got quite enough to learn as it is. Just concentrate on that. It's Bernard's scene from beginning to end. Let him put you through the wringer. That's what the scene's all about.'

Marcia's part was indeed an enormous one; Nicola recognised her courage, and approved of it, when, earlier than anyone had a right to expect, she abandoned her book and struggled along without it. She took a lot of prompts, and paraphrased all over the place, but she soldiered on, and day by day the prompts and paraphrases grew fewer in number. She's got guts anyway, Nicola thought. I'll say that for her.

Finally Cramer was the only one walking around with a script in his hand while they were rehearsing. He used it, it seemed, not for security or to remind himself of the lines, but as a handy notebook on which to record his amendments. Unlike the others, he did not work towards the script as written. He frequently decided to cut lines, or add some, or alter the ones he had. This all involved stopping on each occasion and examining whether his changes made sense in the light of the story. Maurice seethed inwardly but tried not to show it. It seemed to him that, if Cramer wished to avoid wasting time, he could stop holding everyone up while piffling changes were discussed.

But the day came when, at five o'clock, Maurice was heartened and encouraged by the way things were going.

'Thank you all very much,' he announced. 'That was a good day's work, and we're really getting somewhere. I think we're ready to try a run-through. Tomorrow morning, ten o'clock, and we'll go straight through.'

Harry Belmont had received one letter from Nicola, giving him a thumbnail sketch of Treganwy and telling him about her cottage. Her handwriting was large and sprawling, but even so, it only covered three quarters of a page. Nicola had never been a great letter writer. 'Dear Harry,' it began, and ended 'as ever, Nicola.'

Harry read what there was of it several times, but failed to discern the slightest indication that she was missing him in any way. Nor was there any repetition of her half-invitation to come and see the new play she was in. He supposed that she now regretted her impulse, and probably she was right. Since the break had taken place it might as well be final and complete.

No looking back. Quite right. Very sensible. The trouble was that Harry spent too much time looking back for comfort. Something fresh to take his mind off Nicola, that was the answer.

A new girl started work at the office. She had dark hair, a full bosom, and a demure mouth. Harry took her out to dinner. She talked throughout the meal, brightly and amusingly. Harry smiled at her well-told anecdotes, responded with half-complete answers to her casual questions about himself and only occasionally thought of Nicola.

After dinner he drove her home and was invited in for coffee. She continued to be amusing, and Harry was at a loss to understand why incipient yawns were invading the back of his throat. He supposed it must be because it was getting late, thanked her for a lovely evening, and took his car keys from his pocket.

'I've enjoyed it too,' the girl said. She looked up at him as he stood in front of her. 'Kiss me goodnight, before you go.'

Harry bent down and kissed her politely. Her lips, he found, were open, and reminded him agreeably of what he was missing. He became aware that his posture, leaning forward as he was, was awkward and insecure. He sat down beside her, which rectified that. After a few moments he absent-mindedly returned his car keys to his pocket.

Waking up in the morning with someone he hardly knew was, he found, somewhat embarrassing. No line of conversation immediately occurred to him. There seemed to be only one thing to do to bridge the awkward moment, and he did it, which was pleasant enough while it lasted as it had been a few hours previously.

That completed, a glance at his watch told him that he only had slightly over an hour to make himself presentable and get to work.

The girl watched him, with a serious expression on her face, as he scrambled into his clothes.

'Harry,' she said. He looked at her enquiringly as he tucked his shirt into his trousers and pulled up his zip. 'I'm not really promiscuous,' the girl said. 'I'd like you to know that.'

Harry drove to his flat, where he threw on a clean shirt, shaved hurriedly and swallowed two aspirins. He had a headache, he was tired, and he felt wretchedly depressed. He wished that Nicola were nudging him aside in the cramped bathroom, starting to clean her teeth before he had finished shaving.

The girl smiled knowingly whenever they met in the office, and Harry smiled knowingly back. He took her out on two further occasions and she continued to be brightly amusing, although her personal questions became more probing and direct. Harry told her something about

Nicola, and the girl listened intently, nodding sympathetically.

The bed part was fine, two bodies in active harmony, but otherwise Harry always felt at a distance from the girl, although he sensed that quite the reverse was so in her case. Perhaps that was why he was always so depressed afterwards. There was, on his part, a certain dishonesty about the whole thing. Besides, he knew that lust did not last long. As a pastime it had built-in limitations.

On the final occasion they went out together the evening did not end in bed but in the restaurant. Harry not only told her the full truth about Nicola, he embroidered it, and considerably exceeded the facts as they stood. The girl was disconcertingly upset.

'You gave me to understand that it was all over,' she said. Her eyes were bright, but not, Harry feared, from anticipation of renewed pleasure in an hour's time. Not on this occasion. More probably from gathering tears. He felt like a shit.

'Perhaps it is,' Harry said, 'but that's not what I want.'

'Then why pretend with me?' the girl demanded.

'I wasn't pretending,' Harry said uncomfortably. 'You're very desirable, very attractive . . .'

'You might have told me that you intend to go chasing off to Wales after her. God, how do you think that makes me feel? She walks out on you, she obviously couldn't care less, but you mean to go begging. I'd have thought you had more pride. Christ, she must be really something, this actress of yours.'

'I didn't say I was going to beg for anything,' Harry said. He marvelled at the disparity between what one person said and that which another person chose to hear. 'But when I go and see the play, if I get the chance, if I think it's at all possible, I'm going to see if we can't work something out after all.'

'I thought,' the girl said, 'that between us, something more was developing every time. That it was leading somewhere.'

'I'm sorry,' Harry said helplessly. 'But it seemed only

fair to tell you how I feel about her. That whatever's happened, I want to have another try.'

'Well, good luck,' the girl said. 'But I don't fancy your chances. If it went wrong once it'll go wrong again, and for the same reasons.'

She pushed her plate away abruptly. She had eaten nothing.

'Don't you like it?' Harry asked. 'Can I get you something else?'

'I'm not hungry,' the girl said. 'I'm going to the loo.'

She got up and went. Harry waited, but she did not come back. However, a waiter approached the table a few minutes later, and, straight-faced, informed Harry that madam had taken a taxi.

There were no more knowing glances in the office; in fact their eyes hardly ever met, and if they were obliged to speak to each other it was with fragile, artificial politeness. Whether by accident or design the girl was transferred, shortly afterwards, to the New Issues Department, and they rarely saw each other, except occasionally by accident in the lift, which was a great relief to Harry, even if admitting that fact gave rise to a certain obscure sense of shame.

The whole pointless episode filled him, whenever he thought about it, with anger, mostly at himself. It was not her fault. She was a nice girl, good to look at, pleasant to be with for any man with an open mind. But that was the trouble. His mind was not open, even though Nicola was far away and his flat was stripped of all her belongings.

He had in truth, because he wanted to disentangle himself from a relationship which threatened to put down roots, considerably exaggerated his intentions about trying to recover and regain that time with Nicola about which he now felt such nostalgia and yearning.

Her brief letter had given no indication that she shared his feelings in the slightest degree. To descend on Treganwy and say . . . say what? Easy enough to make generalisations across a dinner table to someone else, but when it came to the point, what was there left to say to Nicola? She had said it all by her actions.

That being the case, surely it was up to Nicola to make

the first move, to give even the tiniest hint, otherwise all these regrets and longings were completely unrealistic, pure fantasy. And even the wildest optimist would be unable to detect any such hint in that single, briefly chatty letter.

Her cottage appeared not to be on the telephone. He did call in at a travel agent's, however, and obtain the particulars of the Treganwy Festival. Deep in the small print was the stage door number of the theatre, and he called that one day. Miss Feary, they told him, was rehearsing elsewhere. Would he like the number of the rehearsal room? Harry changed his mind. No, it wasn't important. He hung up.

He looked at the brochure, at the booking form, the enclosed blurb announcing John Cramer's appearance and urging early booking to avoid disappointment, since the pressure on seats would undoubtedly be enormous.

Forget it, Harry Belmont told himself. Forget the whole damn thing.

The phone rang. Immediately, as it did every time that bell started to shrill, his heart leapt and began to pound with excitement. Perhaps, this time, it was Nicola. He lifted the receiver.

'Oh, hullo mother,' he said.

The tap on the door of the hotel suite came when Cramer was on the phone.

'Sorry, I've got to go,' he said. 'Anyway, it's time you were in bed . . . tell Graham good night from me, will you? . . . what? . . . no, I can't talk to Mummy, not now . . . call you again soon, probably at the weekend . . . yes . . . 'bye, young fellow.'

Cramer hung up, crossed to the door, and opened it.

'Sorry,' he apologised. 'I was on the phone to my five-year-old son in France. You're very prompt.'

'I always try to be,' Dr Morgan said. He was a stout middle-aged man with receding black hair and horn-rimmed spectacles. He carried a medical bag which appeared to be larger than the usual variety.

'Can I offer you a drink? Scotch? Sherry?'

'A sherry would be most acceptable,' Dr Morgan said.

Cramer poured a sherry and topped up his own glass of whisky.

'It's good of you to turn out in the evening like this,' he said. 'I appreciate it.'

'First of all, it's my job,' Dr Morgan said. 'Secondly, in this case, it's a pleasure. The theatre is a passion of mine.'

'Yes, so I was told,' Cramer said.

'I saw you many times at Stratford, years ago,' Dr Morgan said. 'Always with admiration I may say. Since then I've seen most of your films. So it's not good of me to turn out. On the contrary, I'm delighted.'

Cramer smiled, and handed the doctor his sherry. 'Your very good health.'

'And yours,' Dr Morgan said. He sipped his sherry. The reflected light of the nearby table lamp glinted on the lenses of his spectacles. 'Although, to outward appearances at least, you appear to be in pretty good health anyway.'

'Yes, I'm fine,' Cramer said. 'This won't be a very interesting visit from your professional point of view, I'm afraid. I only want a couple of prescriptions, that's all.' He handed the doctor a slip of paper.

Dr Morgan glanced at it. Cramer had printed the trade names of the drugs he required, TUINAL and HEMINEVRIN.

Tuinal was a barbiturate sleeping tablet which contained Quinalbarbitone Sodium and Amylobarbitone Sodium in equal parts. Patients could develop psychological and some physical dependence, and experience great difficulty in sleeping after its withdrawal.

Heminevrin contained Chloromethiazole. It was a fairly powerful tranquilliser, used for the treatment of stress and anxiety, and it could cause psychological dependence.

'I see,' Dr Morgan said.

'I live in France, so I've been seeing a chap there,' Cramer explained. 'Well, hardly "seeing" in that sense.

He's my wife's doctor, so it was convenient for him to dish out the odd prescription now and then.'

'And presumably, you've run out,' Dr Morgan said.

'Exactly, so if you wouldn't mind . . .'

'I assume he knew you'd be in England for several weeks,' Dr Morgan said. 'Didn't he give you enough to last you?'

'Stupidly, I forgot to ask him,' Cramer said. 'I had rather a lot on my mind at the time.'

'Quite so,' Dr Morgan said. 'Well, if you'd like to go into the bedroom and strip off, I'll examine you.'

'Come on,' Cramer protested. 'I only want you to give me a few pills, that's all.'

Dr Morgan smiled with benign patience. 'Mr Cramer,' he said, 'in my life, you are a well-known personality. As a patient, I have never seen you before. I would not prescribe drugs of this description for any stranger without first forming an opinion of my own, and I'm afraid you are no exception.' He gestured with self-deprecating amusement. 'Unlike you, I can only enjoy my performance in private, since I can never boast to anyone else about my patients, even – or perhaps especially – such a distinguished one as yourself. The ethics of the medical profession forbid it. But like you, I'm sure, I do take a certain pride in my performance. You must allow me to go through the motions at least.'

Cramer laughed. 'O.K., doctor,' he said. 'You shall have an attentive audience of one.'

'Splendid,' Dr Morgan said. 'Perhaps you'd pause at the bathroom on the way and provide a specimen.' He opened his capacious bag and came up with a plastic-wrapped glass container.

The examination was meticulous, lengthy and careful. Dr Morgan's fingers prodded, probed and explored, while he asked a lot of seemingly casual and irrelevant questions, including how Cramer had got the scar on his cheek, and finally, after asking Cramer to follow him, he disappeared into the bathroom with the specimen and his medical bag.

Cramer pulled on a towelling dressing gown and joined

him. The medical bag was open, displaying a surprising amount of paraphernalia which meant nothing to Cramer. Dr Morgan was dipping small, tipped plastic sticks into the contents of the glass container and peering at them intently.

'I thought you needed to send that to a laboratory,' Cramer said.

'If necessary, I do,' Dr Morgan said, carrying out more mysterious operations, like some mediaeval alchemist hoping to come up with the substance which would transmute base metal into gold. 'But you must remember that I'm just a country GP with rather a far-flung practice. A lot of my patients live in pretty remote places. In Treganwy itself we only have a cottage hospital, and that's really only used for convalescence. The nearest path. lab is twenty-five miles away. I often need to get some sort of rough idea on the spot. I can't be like your city doctor – if in doubt, write a note, and send the chap down the road to a well-equipped hospital with specialists on call. Don't always have time for that.' He indicated his medical bag with a crooked elbow. 'That's why I carry all this junk around with me. You could say I'm a do-it-yourself kind of quack, I suppose.'

'Thirsty work, I imagine,' Cramer said. 'Can I interest you in another sherry?'

'You can indeed,' Dr Morgan said. 'It will provide an edge to an already keen appetite. But before you go, I'll just take a blood sample.'

'You will not,' Cramer said. 'Your performance is over.'

'Not quite,' Dr Morgan said, smiling. 'Until I've done so, my examination is not complete.'

'Hard luck,' Cramer said. 'I'm allergic to needles being stuck in me for no reason.'

'You won't even feel it,' Dr Morgan said. 'I do beg you to . . .'

'Get lost,' Cramer said.

He went into the living room, poured another sherry for the doctor and refilled his own glass of whisky. Dr Morgan came in, sat down and picked up his sherry.

'Thank you,' he said.

'If I've kept you from your dinner,' Cramer said, being conciliatory, 'I can easily send for something. I nearly always eat up here anyway. I don't get much peace if I go down to the dining room.'

'I'd rather not, if you don't mind,' Dr Morgan said. 'My wife has something in the oven. Do you eat regular meals?'

'Yes, of course,' Cramer said. 'Well, as far as I can. Actors work peculiar hours by most people's standards. I may miss a meal now and then, but I'm hardly undernourished.' He smiled.

Dr Morgan nodded. 'But you do have trouble sleeping, or you wouldn't require Tuinal.'

'Sometimes,' Cramer said. 'My mind is over-active, I suppose. Usually that doesn't matter much, but when I'm working on something, as I am now, I need to be sure of a night's rest.'

'Quite so,' Dr Morgan said. 'And the other drug you'd like me to prescribe, Heminevrin, why would you say you need that?'

Cramer stared at him. There were icy glints in his pale blue eyes. 'I'm not your patient, doctor,' he said. The faint rasp sawed across his voice. 'But even if I were, would you expect me to diagnose myself?'

'I get more help from some patients than from others,' Dr Morgan said equably. 'You are not only a very clever man, you are extremely intelligent as well. Contrary to general belief, the two things do not always go together, I may say. Given that, I would expect you to be more aware than most people I am called upon to treat.'

'I don't remember asking you to treat anything,' Cramer said. 'I asked you to call because I thought it would save time, that's all. If you find some difficulty in prescribing, there's a man in London I used to see some years ago. I'm sure he'd oblige.'

'I'm sure he would,' Dr Morgan agreed. 'And if you wish you can show me the door. Until then you are, temporarily at least, my patient. I never prescribe powerful drugs without fully satisfying myself as to the patient's need for them. They exact a price which may not be worth paying. I like to think that my opinion may be worth something, Mr Cramer,' he said, with conscious, mocking, self-modesty. 'But my signature, as such, is not for sale.'

'What the hell do you want to know?' Cramer rasped.

'I can't help wondering,' Dr Morgan said, 'whether you really ran out of these drugs by accident, as it were. It is true that all too many people nowadays accept reliance on drugs to make them sleep, calm them down, give them a lift, or relieve depression – in short, restore them to what is laughingly called normal – quite happily, without question, and as a kind of God-given right in this modern world of ours, to the great benefit of the drug companies, if not to themselves. Now you don't strike me as that kind at all. I think you might resent any dependence on artificial substances, and fight against it. I could be mistaken, in which case you will correct me. But if I may hazard a guess I would say that you sent for me with considerable reluctance. That possibly that action represented something of a personal defeat.'

Cramer's bark of a laugh was sharp and mirthless.

'You fancy yourself as the perceptive country doctor, do you?' he enquired. 'Peddling wisdom instead of pills? If so, you're on quite an ego trip yourself, you know.'

'Quite likely,' Dr Morgan said gently. 'But I did admit that I could be quite wrong.'

'You know bloody well you're not wrong,' Cramer said. 'That's what makes you so thoroughly annoying.'

'Sorry,' Dr Morgan said. 'We all have our weaknesses. Some doctors go along with patients' cover stories. I don't, for which I claim no great merit. I'm not in medicine for the money, so I don't have to. You're not the first to find me annoying. I sometimes lose patients who feel their privacy is being invaded.' He smiled. 'Quite often, they come back again,' he added.

'O.K.,' Cramer said. He knew it was a surrender, but this fellow was only an obscure GP no one had ever heard of. What the hell did it matter? Morgan wanted to feel important before he made out the prescriptions and sent in his bill. Let him. 'Brief self-diagnosis coming up. I lead an erratic, irregular life, full of the kind of pressures which most people couldn't imagine, let alone comprehend. The physical stress of making pictures is exhausting. Sometimes I seem to spend weeks getting on and off bloody airliners. Lunch in one continent, arriving in time for breakfast in another, with a full day of conferences in front of me and a première that night, followed by some goddamned reception, and another plane to catch early the next morning. Who the hell can go on sleeping naturally? Not me. Then there's stress. All kinds. Responsibility, for one. Films cost a fortune to make. These days, they hang on me personally. Not only my future is at stake, but everyone else's working on the movie. There's emotional stress. My private life. But don't ask me questions about that, or yes, you will go out the door, and fast. That's my affair. So when it gets too bad I take pills to keep me functioning. In my business, I know very few people who don't. It's not a big deal, it's a fact of life. Does that give you the picture?'

'It confirms an impression,' Dr Morgan said. 'But does not quite answer my original question. You're not jetting round the world at the moment, or getting up before dawn to be on some location a hundred miles away. You're in Treganwy, which is a peaceful enough place, heaven knows. Some would say dead. You're rehearsing a play. To my knowledge, rehearsal hours are neither irregular nor erratic. Have you found pressures here which you didn't anticipate?'

'Quite the Sherlock Holmes, aren't you?' Cramer said.

'Hardly. At best, a bumbling Welsh Dr Watson, I fear,' Dr Morgan said.

'You were right,' Cramer said. 'I feel I should be able to cope without pills. I don't like the damn things, even when I need them. I thought Treganwy would be a rest cure, the chance to do without them, to knock them off entirely. That's why I didn't bring many to the UK. I thought, O.K., when they've gone, that's it. Well, I put off calling you as long as I could, but it hasn't worked out the way I thought it would.'

'Why not?' Dr Morgan asked.

'I could tell you, but I'm not going to,' Cramer said. 'That really is something I have to sort out for myself, and no one can help me. I just have to face it and beat it. I'd say the fact that I know is good enough. But I need a bit of help. That's where you come in. And not with good advice,' he added. 'There's a surplus of that commodity inside my own head. With something more practical.'

Dr Morgan nodded. 'Don't fly off the handle,' he said, 'if I say one more thing before removing the cap of my fountain pen. You're clearly quite as aware as I assumed you were. Aware enough to know that drugs are like a crutch. They may relieve the strain, but just as a fracture may require an operation, so problems which drugs may alleviate for the time being should sometimes be treated in another way.'

'Somehow, I didn't think you'd have any time for shrinks,' Cramer said.

Dr Morgan smiled faintly. 'It depends,' he said. 'I think there are dangers in rushing every so-called hyper-active child off to a child psychiatrist for example. But where problems appear to be of psychiatric origin, it would be foolish to deny that a psychiatrist will probably be of more help than me. Or my prescription pad.'

'In my business,' Cramer said, 'every other person you meet is having analysis and bores the arse off you by telling you about it. I know what my problems are. There's no mystery about them. That being so, it's up to me to tackle them on my own. I'm in the middle of a private battle. I know what I'm doing. I could manage without your prescription pad, but the discomfort would be greater. A crutch? Yes, if you like. But figuratively speaking, it's for a mental sprained ankle, not a compound fracture.'

Dr Morgan took out his fountain pen, balanced his pad on his knee with practised ease, and wrote busily. He tore off the slip and handed it to Cramer.

'Thank you,' Cramer said.

'You understand,' Dr Morgan said, 'that you shouldn't drink while you're taking these. It potentiates the effect.'

'Yes, I know,' Cramer said.

Dr Morgan put his fountain pen away and finished his glass of sherry with evident appreciation.

'I'm not a fanatic about alcohol, as will be patently obvious,' he said. 'When I get home, I intend to enjoy half a bottle of wine with my dinner. I speak as a man who likes a drink. So do you, I gather. Since I've been here you've consumed half a bottle of whisky, although it's had no apparent effect on you.'

Cramer shrugged. 'My system can cope with it, that's all.'

'Alcohol is like any other drug,' Dr Morgan said. 'Given constant use, it takes more and more to achieve the desired effect.'

'You do have a knack of putting things,' Cramer said, 'which could easily be regarded as offensive.'

'Taking offence is often a defence mechanism,' Dr Morgan said. 'I think you're more than a social drinker, Mr Cramer. I'd be surprised, given the self-perception which I believe you possess, if the possibility of being alcohol-dependent had not been of concern to you from time to time.'

'It's not a problem,' Cramer said. 'I can handle it.' He stood up pointedly. 'Thank you for coming, Dr Morgan.'

Dr Morgan stood up also, but he did not pick up his medical bag.

'Heavy drinking can cause physical damage,' he said. 'You don't have to be an alcoholic.'

Cramer laughed. 'I'm as strong as a bull,' he said. 'I'm in better shape than most men in their twenties.'

'I'm sure you are capable of great physical exertion,' Dr Morgan said. 'And I have to admit that I can't be positive, but I do urge you to allow me to take a blood sample before I leave.'

'For Christ's sake!' Cramer snapped. 'I told you no. Don't you listen?'

'I can only say to you what I would say to any other patient,' Dr Morgan said steadily. 'During my examination I thought I detected slight liver enlargement, which leads me to suspect liver damage. That suspicion should be confirmed or denied as soon as possible. That is why I need a blood sample – so that it may be sent to a laboratory at once for liver function tests.'

Cramer stared at him. 'And you, if I may say so,' he said, 'seem to be suffering from a disease called self-importance.'

'I am obliged to respect your opinion,' Dr Morgan said, 'since my wife most certainly shares it. Nevertheless, that does not change my professional opinion.'

'I was told you were potty about the theatre,' Cramer said. 'But I didn't realise that meant you saw yourself working up to the big dramatic scene before you made your exit.'

'Liver damage is not reversible,' Dr Morgan said. 'But it can be halted. I may well be wrong, but if I'm right it would be quite a good idea to do so, before it's too late.'

'You're a lousy actor, doc,' Cramer told him. 'Bad soap opera's full of hams like you.'

'At least talk to your own doctor, as soon as you get the chance,' Dr Morgan said. 'Will you do that much, please?'

'Sure,' Cramer said. 'I'll give him a word-for-word impersonation of you. He's fond of a good laugh.'

'Think about it,' Dr Morgan said. 'It might not be terribly funny. Good night, Mr Cramer.'

Cramer waved his hand at the closing door and sighed. Time-wasting windbag. He discovered that, automatically, the whisky bottle was in his hand, tilted over his glass. He hesitated, but only for a moment. His hand, he noted, was rock-steady as he poured the golden liquid.

He smiled to himself. No one in their right mind would take any notice of an idiot like that, some garrulous Welsh wizard with his magic bag of tricks. The man was a joke.

Cramer sipped his whisky. First thing in the morning, he would send a porter to the nearest chemist's which could fill the prescription. By the time he got to the difficult part of the run through he would be all right, relaxed, with nothing between him and the words.

After tonight, he would be able to cut out the scotch . . . or at least cut it down.

Cramer picked up his script and skimmed through it.

Then he leaned back, closed his eyes, and watched himself play the part inside his head. He opened his eyes, grinned, and gave himself a last measure of whisky. He was word-perfect. He knew the damn thing backwards!

It occurred to him as he slid comfortably into bed that he had forgotten to send down for any food. He considered lifting the phone now. Room service were ever-willing, accustomed to his irregular eating habits, but he decided against it. He was agreeably tired and anyway he did not feel hungry.

The major hurdle was behind him. He had beaten it, on his own. He need not have sent for the boring Welsh wizard after all. Still, he would send the porter out anyway. Just having the stuff sitting in the bathroom cabinet would probably be enough. Reassurance. He did not have to take it.

Peacefully, he went to sleep.

'I'm not saying that John Cramer isn't entitled to the number one dressing room,' Marcia Hambridge said. 'Technically, since he's a star, he is. What I'm saying is that I am, after all, the leading lady, and in any other circumstances *I* would have had number one dressing room. A gentleman wouldn't have insisted on his technical right. A gentleman would have allowed his leading lady to have number one.'

'Number two's right next door, darling,' Maurice pointed out. 'And it's just as big.'

'Yes, but number two doesn't have a private loo,' Marcia said resentfully. 'I have to go down the corridor. Which reminds me. I still don't like Paula calling Stephen a shit in Act Two. It's so vulgar.'

'There is no synonym for shit,' Maurice said firmly. 'We've wasted hours during rehearsal trying to find one, and it doesn't exist. The word is shit, and that's it.'

'When we get to the West End, I agree, it won't matter,' Marcia said. 'Four-letter words are accepted there. But I'm sure the Treganwy audiences won't like it.'

'Then they'll have to bloody lump it,' Maurice said.

'Suppose I say "bastard" in Treganwy,' Marcia suggested, 'and then when we get to the more sophisticated places on tour . . .'

'Marcia, stop being boring,' Maurice said. 'Shit fits. Nothing else does. Besides, the Professor's getting some West End managements along and bowdlerisations aren't going to impress them.'

'Oh,' Marcia said. 'Is that definite? They're really coming?'

'According to the Professor,' Maurice said. 'So kindly find something else to nag about.'

'Well, when John Cramer leaves,' Marcia said, 'and Ben Stamford takes over as Stephen, I shall insist on number one dressing room then.'

'O.K.,' Maurice said. 'Agreed. All right?'

There were three days to go until the first night. They were now working in the theatre itself. The set had been erected. The hired furniture had been delivered. Last-minute alterations were being made to costumes. The box office staff were going frantic. People who wanted seats were phoning the telephone exchange to complain that they could not get through, and there must be something wrong with the lines.

'The first week's nearly sold out,' Maurice said with satisfaction. 'If we don't break house records, I'll eat Stephen's white tuxedo.'

Naturally this happy state of affairs was due to John Cramer, and John Cramer alone. The avalanche started when the interviews with him finally appeared.

The press had respected his wish to keep a low profile for the excellent reason that he refused to talk to any of them until seven days before the first night, and then only to the local and county newspapers. That made little difference. The features were promptly syndicated over most of the country.

The reporters concerned, ambitious hopefuls in their twenties serving their time on provincials, tasted sudden glory in the shape of twenty minutes each with John Cramer. Not surprisingly the results amounted to little more than puffs for Treganwy. The theatre was swamped overnight as people woke up to the fact that the great John Cramer could actually be seen in the flesh for three weeks.

Professor Griffiths read the articles, visited the box office, and purred with contentment. His remaining chief ambition, to build a new theatre on a better site, drew noticeably closer to fulfilment.

The first dress rehearsal was ragged. Maurice sat near the back and made notes. Apprehension cramped his stomach; all the progress of the last few days seemed to have been lost. It was always like this, he told himself. During every production, at this stage, he suddenly doubted the whole thing. He had two days left to get it back on the rails, without communicating his abrupt anxiety, verging on fear, to the cast. 'It'll be all right on the night.' His mouth twisted into a bleak smile in the semi-darkness of the auditorium. Nearly always, it was too. But only nearly always.

Afterwards he vaulted up on to the stage and they sat around while he gave his notes to all of them except John Cramer. He would speak to Cramer privately. He did not consider it tactful to give notes to an actor of his stature in front of the others.

'All right, loves, that was basically fine,' he lied. 'Obviously the lack of sound effects didn't help, the tape isn't quite ready, but it will be tomorrow, without fail. Is that right, Alan?' Alan Cakin nodded. 'Good,' Maurice said heartily. 'That'll make it easier for everybody to react convincingly to the climaxes. One or two technical odds and ends first before we discuss the performances. Nicola, you didn't kneel beside Stephen when you're pleading with him.'

'I have to use the word "love" over and over again,' Nicola said. 'It suddenly seemed soppy, and I felt awkward. I decided to try standing up instead.'

'Well, you do love him,' Maurice said. 'That may not be very sensible of you, but then love usually isn't a very sensible emotion. If you convince yourself, you'll convince the audience, and I think you'll find that kneeling will come naturally. But we'll look at it again tomorrow.

Marcia, in your scene with Leonard, you suddenly went upstage of the sun bed instead of downstage.'

'Yes, because when I turned to confront him,' Marcia said, 'I thought I was going to fall over it. I think it must be in the wrong place.'

'Linda,' Maurice said, 'check that the sun bed is on its marks will you?'

'It is,' Linda said briefly.

'Then check the marks, there's a love,' Maurice said.

'But while we're talking about that scene,' Marcia Hambridge said, 'I have some very important and dramatic speeches. I wish Leonard would look at me. As it is, I'm talking to the back of his head.'

'That was because you went the wrong side of the sun bed, which took you upstage of him,' Maurice said, which was, as he well knew, a varnished version of what was actually happening. Marcia did not quite dare to try it on with Cramer, but otherwise she did her best to upstage everyone. Leonard Sherwen was too experienced to be caught that way and had no intention of playing a scene with his back to the audience. 'Leonard, if you corpse on that line "Hullo, mother," again, I'll kill you, so help me God.'

'I didn't,' Leonard said. 'Honestly. But when I came on with the suitcase, I could hardly lift it. My arm was nearly coming out of its socket.'

'There's nothing in the sodding thing,' Maurice said.

'Some joker had put a couple of stage weights in it,' Leonard said. 'I nearly ruptured myself.'

A gust of laughter hit them all. Maurice put on a polite show of shared amusement. Children, he thought. All of them.

His eyes lingered on Ben Stamford, who had attended all the rehearsals in readiness to take over from Cramer, but in fact had scarcely rehearsed at all.

'Not guilty, my lord,' Ben Stamford said promptly.

'All right,' Maurice said. 'Never mind who it was, so long as we don't have any more merry japes like that. Keep them for when you're on tour in Kirkaldy.'

'Never heard of it,' Leonard said.

'A kind of Siberia, twenty-five miles from Edinburgh,' Ben Stamford said. 'Like playing the salt mines.'

'Has the tour been definitely arranged?' Marcia asked.

'If so, my agent doesn't know anything about it,' Bernard Fyfield said.

'Forget the tour. I'm trying to give notes,' Maurice said plaintively. 'Marcia, when you throw the glass at Nicola, please try and chuck it through the open door. If it bounces back off the wall we'll get a laugh we don't want.'

'I did aim at the door,' Marcia said, 'but it's too light. It just goes anywhere.'

'Alan,' Maurice said, 'can we drill out the stem of that plastic glass and fill it with mercury or something to weight it, so that it can be thrown properly?'

'Will do,' Alan said.

'By tomorrow,' Maurice said. 'Bernard, do you have a problem with your exit after the confrontation with Marcia?'

'I've been threatening to go for so long,' Bernard Fyfield said, 'that it seemed anti-climactic.'

'It certainly looked it,' Maurice said. 'You sort of sidled off, and you were half-way through the door to start off with. From the left-hand side of the auditorium, I doubt if people could see you. Your last speech before you go, after Marcia's said "You ugly old goat. I'll see you in hell first" . . .'

'I rather expect to arrive before you, my dear, but I'm quite sure you'll join me there later,' Bernard Fyfield said.

'Yes,' Maurice said. 'Well, I shall be very surprised if you don't get a round after that, so make sure you're four-square in the doorway where we can all see you, and give it a definite pause after that speech, and then turn and go very deliberately – you've beaten her all ends up, right to the end.'

'Yes, I see,' Bernard Fyfield said. 'In that case . . . right.'

There would be no trouble there, Maurice thought. Bernard loved the prospect of a spontaneous round of applause even more than most actors. He turned the page of his notebook. 'Nicola, the final scene, where you're picking up the pages of the manuscript . . .'

Maurice tapped on the door of Cramer's dressing room and went in. Cramer was combing his hair.

'Just a couple of tiny points,' Maurice said.

'Feel like a drink?' Cramer asked.

'A small one,' Maurice said. 'Thank you.'

Cramer gave him a whisky and topped up his own glass. He seemed more relaxed recently, Maurice thought. Certainly not as spiky and difficult as he had been during the first part of the rehearsal period. Maurice reflected that, now, *he* was the one who was feeling like that.

'O.K.,' Cramer said. 'All yours.' He sat down and nursed his drink. 'It was pretty ragged, wasn't it?'

'Oh, it's always the same,' Maurice said lightly. 'The first time on the stage itself, all the business for real, silly things going wrong . . . there's plenty of time to sort all that out.'

'I hope you're right,' Cramer said.

'You were paraphrasing quite a bit today,' Maurice said.

'Yes, I know,' Cramer said.

'Was it intentional? The last week or so you've been spot on the script as is. It's not too late to make a few changes, if you like, but frankly, the fewer the better.'

'One or two things threw me,' Cramer said. 'It seemed better to press on rather than keep taking prompts.'

'Yes,' Maurice said. 'The problem is that quite often you were changing your cue line, so the others weren't sure if they were supposed to come in or not.'

'My fault,' Cramer said apologetically. 'I'm always like this at the last minute, I don't know why. It may be I have a sort of sideways approach to a part, but it always comes right in the end, I promise you.'

'Fine,' Maurice said. 'No worries in that case.' Cramer had become as co-operative and gentle as a lamb, during the last week or so. It was amazing. 'The other thing is this. Do you think you could give a bit more projection?'

'How do you mean?' Cramer asked.

'I was sitting near the back, and much of the time I had difficulty hearing you.'

'You would, in an empty theatre,' Cramer said. His expression was considerably less lamb-like.

'Well, I haven't worked here before,' Maurice said. 'I have to rely on Professor Griffiths, but he should know. He tells me that the acoustics are peculiar. An audience tends to mop up sound, for some reason. So if you *could* try a little more voice . . .'

'Just now, I'm concerned with my performance,' Cramer said. 'I can judge the projection needed when the time comes.'

'Again,' Maurice said, 'according to the Professor, the actors find it hard here to tell whether they're being heard or not.'

'Fuck the Professor,' Cramer said. 'I've played in more theatres than he's ever set foot in.' Or you, chummy, was the unspoken implication.

'You have to remember that we've got an open set, not an enclosed one,' Maurice said. 'Quite a bit of sound'll be lost that way. It's not much use you giving a great performance, if you can't be heard.'

'Jesus Christ,' Cramer said, 'when I think of the barns I've played in my time . . . don't talk to me as though I'd just come out of drama school.'

'I'm sorry,' Maurice said. He had never known any man who could change as rapidly as John Cramer. 'I've obviously put it badly. I didn't mean to seem critical. It's really quite a small thing . . .'

'If you think I'm going to boom and bellow like Bernard Fyfield, you can think again,' Cramer said.

'I know you're aiming at something far more subtle than Bernard,' Maurice said placatingly. 'What you're doing would be fine on film, but without a microphone you have to give it that little bit more.'

Cramer's frozen stare told Maurice that he had said the wrong thing with a vengeance. God, what a cock-up he was making of this.

'You're an expert on the making of films as well, are

you?' Cramer enquired dangerously. 'As a matter of interest, how many have you made, exactly?'

'Look, forget I said that,' Maurice said hastily. 'I don't know the first thing about films. But I think I know when I'm right in the theatre, and it's not my job to climb down every time you disagree with me. I'm ready to respect your views, but if it's not a two-way process I don't know what the hell I'm doing here. I might as well sit with my feet up, watching the telly.'

'When I'm asked to shout, I don't regard that as a suggestion worthy of respect,' Cramer said.

'If you were on stage now,' Maurice said, 'you could be heard in the back row of the circle by a deaf old age pensioner. And you're not raising your voice. You're not shouting. Perhaps I chose my words badly. I suppose what I'm asking for is a sort of projection of vitality, rather than voice.'

Cramer looked at him in silence for what seemed a long time.

'Let me think about that,' he said at last.

Maurice made his escape with relief. Both of them, he knew, had accepted a compromise form of words to evade a clash of wills which neither of them, including Cramer for some reason, wanted to take place at that moment – although why Cramer should care was a mystery. He had nothing to gain and nothing to lose, unlike Maurice.

Maurice went out through the stage door to his car and started the engine. Prickly bastards he was accustomed to, but Cramer, who behaved rather like a walking booby trap, liable to explode in the most harmless circumstances triggered by some perfectly ordinary action or word – that was a new experience. Maurice fantasised wistfully about the big confrontation in which he treated Cramer as he treated Marcia, and the man cracked, fell to pieces and grovelled, while Maurice stared at him with scornful contempt.

It lasted until Maurice parked his car outside the tradesman's entrance of The Hall. Then he laughed at himself and switched off his fantasy with his engine. Such satisfying day-dreams might serve as a useful emotional safety valve, but real life, he had discovered long ago, obstinately failed to stick to the script. Otherwise he would not be here at Treganwy. He would be Artistic Director of the National Theatre, paying off a few old scores – or perhaps magnanimously deciding not to.

Or he would be the man with the commercial golden touch, the one with three West End successes running simultaneously, and Pinter, Stoppard and Gray would rarely be off the phone begging him to consider their latest offerings.

Or, Brando having insisted that only Maurice Gardiner could direct the epic of all time, he would have demanded ten per cent of the box office takings and would now be living in Hollywood, a multi-millionaire, patronising the film moguls who courted him beside his opulent swimming pool, while Anna, eclipsed by his success, clung demurely to his arm as he brushed the photographers impatiently aside . . .

For Christ's sake stop it, Maurice ordered his errant subconscious as he gained his apartment in The Hall. Outside was Wales, not California; the only swimming pool for miles was the open-air municipal one which Treganwy boasted for the benefit of its hardier visitors, and Anna's career flourished. She was coming for the first night, and would stay a few days, but after that she was off to Tokyo.

Still, she would be here for the first night triumph. That still had to be achieved though.

Maurice turned his mind to the forthcoming technical rehearsal. Technical rehearsals, in his experience, demanded a degree of stoicism which he did not possess.

His forebodings were only too justified. It was a shambles. Crickets chirruped in the wrong place and the murmur of the distant sea sounded more like Hurricane Betsy at its fiercest. The telephone rang too early, the cork refused to come out of the stage champagne bottle, and the motor car arriving was a departing helicopter. Conversely, the arriving helicopter was the busy sound of a typewriter – an effect which they had abandoned two days before, having decided that Nicola should tap away on the typewriter herself, off-stage. The cast were left gazing skywards, saying things like 'Is that a helicopter?' 'Can you see it?' 'There it is!' while hair and clothes were ruffled by the wind machine, which did, amazingly, come in on cue, while the tape gave forth with the clacking of an Olympia portable, borrowed from the theatre office, at full volume.

Nicola corpsed and went into a fit of hysterical giggles as the curtain descended on this dramatic moment. Cramer did not find it amusing. He turned and strode off-stage in disgust before the curtain came down. Marcia could be heard saying, 'Oh, for Christ's sake . . .'

Maurice sat in his seat, clutching for detachment, and feeling that he wanted to weep. Desperately, he told himself that this was what technical rehearsals were for. This was when everything went wrong, and all the bugs were ironed out.

It would be all right on the night, God willing.

Maurice wondered if God cared very much about the agony of a first night at Treganwy. The odds, he supposed, were against it.

# CHAPTER EIGHT

Professor Griffiths adored first nights at his beloved Treganwy. They were truly feudal occasions and he lorded it in the bar long before curtain up, greeting the worthies from miles around who always came, entertaining them to free drinks with a nod and a gesture to the bar staff. The expense did not, of course, fall upon Professor Griffiths, but came out of theatre funds or, indirectly, the taxpayer. Even when playing to ninety per cent houses box office receipts covered rather less than half of Treganwy's running costs. The balance came from grants and subsidies. Most of the expenditure went in fixed overheads, part of which, Professor Griffiths decreed, was hospitality, at least when dispensed by himself, either at the theatre or to pay for the functions he held at The Hall. Actors, directors and stage management were not conspicuously well-paid, which was a source of regret to the Professor. Unfortunately the money simply was not there, but he was tireless in his efforts to secure larger grants and was modestly pleased with his success. The trouble was that most of any extra income was immediately swallowed up in inexorably rising costs, and there was, of course, the new theatre which the Professor was determined to see built, and which had to be provided for.

In the meantime, as the Professor would point out to grasping agents, actors were always paid above Equity minimum, and if that was far below what any self-respecting postman would work for, the position merely reflected the realities which a sensible union had to take into account. Theatres could not pay actors money which they did not have: unfortunate, but a fact. In any case, he would assert, defying contradiction, actors *liked* playing at Tregawny. It was a happy place, they all felt part of one big caring family, and there was prestige. That was the main thing. The prestige. The Professor would have another shot in his locker from now on. If John Cramer was content to appear for no more than the top going rate, why should your client expect more?

Professor Griffiths nodded slightly to one of the ladies behind the bar and she opened another bottle of champagne for a couple of the Professor's newly arrived important guests.

He chatted to them amicably while studying the crowded throng in the bar without seeming to. Two West End managements had promised to come along, or at least to send representatives, but they had not appeared yet. The Professor was not unduly worried. On first nights the bar opened early. It was a social occasion. There was plenty of time.

Harry Belmont looked briefly at the tall man holding court, whose glance skimmed across him, and sipped his glass of wine. He was lucky to be here. He had only made up his mind at the last moment, and without his diligent and tireless secretary he would never have made it. She spent most of several hours on the phone, first of all beating the engaged signal, only to be told there were no seats left for the first night, and then persistently ringing back until she happened to be on the line when a single cancellation came in. Harry applauded her feat and set her to arranging a hotel room for him. The way things were he could hardly expect to stay with Nicola who, in any case, did not know he was coming.

When he arrived to pick up his ticket there was a stationary queue at the box office, patiently waiting in the hope of last-minute cancellations. Harry was much impressed. He had seen Nicola perform many times, in many different theatres. It had never been standing room only before. There was a sense of occasion, even here in this bar. He could feel the excitement.

He wondered if he should go backstage and see Nicola in her dressing room, but he immediately rejected the idea. She had talked to him about first nights in the past, about what an ordeal it always was, and that, shaking with nerves, no actor wanted to see anybody on a first night until the play was over. He would go round afterwards.

He looked at his watch. It was coming up to the 'half'. When he had first begun, through Nicola, to learn something about the theatre, he had made the logical assumption that the 'half' meant half an hour before curtain up. It did not. It meant thirty-five minutes before curtain up. He had never quite fathomed out why, except that the theatre was not renowned for logic anyway.

His attention was attracted by a stunningly beautiful long-legged girl in her middle twenties, bone thin, who had just come into the bar. Her high cheek-boned face seemed vaguely familiar. He wondered who she was. She was accompanied, he then noticed, by a man with a somewhat cat-like smile, who was not quite as tall as she was. Instinctively, Harry Belmont turned away and lost himself in the crowd. He did not feel like making conversation with anyone.

Maurice introduced Anna to Professor Griffiths.

'Delighted,' Professor Griffiths beamed. 'Delighted.'

He gazed at her benevolently in what he imagined was a fatherly manner. Dirty old man, Anna thought.

There had been a time when Professor Griffiths had something of a reputation as a ladies' man and, in earlier days, when he interviewed aspirants for the Tregawny Festival himself, wise actresses kept the desk or some other substantial article of furniture between themselves and the Professor if they wished to avoid some embarrassing moments.

Advancing years and a number of extremely unpleasant scenes between the Professor and his wife meant that the Professor now confined himself to wistful recollections of better days, but an exceptional young beauty could still bring a glint of vicarious lust into his eyes.

Maurice murmured that he ought to go backstage, so if . . .

'Of course,' the Professor said with hearty gallantry. 'I shall be only too pleased to look after Anna. My pleasure. I expect she'd enjoy a glass of champagne, wouldn't you, my dear.'

His discreet signal was unnecessary. The cork was already popping out of another bottle. Front of house staff at Tregawny were well-trained and efficient, none more so than the bar staff.

Marcia had arrived in her dressing room two hours before the curtain was due to rise. The very fact that she was there, physically present in the theatre, provided some small vestige of a security which she badly needed.

She undressed, suddenly anxious to be rid of the clothes which she might have worn to go shopping, or to collect her small son from play school when she was at home, the accoutrements of her ordinary life which had nothing to do with the purgatory she would suffer until the show was over, the essential but painful prelude to the success she craved. She put on her theatre dressing gown. That simple act provided a warm moment of comfort. She was no longer Marcia Hambridge, wife and mother. She was Miss Hambridge, leading lady, with no thought in her head but her performance, the moment when she made her first entrance on to that stage.

She had already washed her hair meticulously before she left for the theatre. She plugged in her heated rollers before walking the few paces along the corridor to the shower room.

Her hair pinned up, covered by a plastic cap, she stepped under the shower and soaped herself all over unhurriedly, her mind a blank for the time being, enjoying the warm flow of water, the delicate fragrance of the expensive soap specially purchased for the occasion.

Satisfied that her body was absolutely clean she stood under the shower, eyes closed, for several minutes while the soothing spray rinsed every vestige of the gentle suds refreshingly away. No need to worry about the time. That was another reason why she was there long before it was necessary. The panic would be bad enough when the stage staff began the series of calls. At least approach that awful period in a leisurely fashion, with plenty of time in hand.

Back in her dressing room Marcia pottered about, seemingly aimlessly, arranging and rearranging. Her dressing room was as pretty as she could make it. Good luck cards and telegrams adorned the huge mirror. There were dozens of them, from nearly every friend and acquaintance she had in the business. The Post Office must make a bomb out of this theatrical convention. Everyone did it. Marcia religiously sent them herself. It was more superstition than anything, an act of kindly voodoo.

She was glad to receive them, she would have resented it and been upset if she had received fewer than she had expected – her attitude in this respect closly resembled that of ordinary people to Christmas cards – but only one of them really meant anything to her, in the personal sense.

That was the one from her husband. 'GOOD LUCK, DARLING. WILL BE THINKING OF YOU EVERY SECOND. WISH I COULD BE THERE. ALL LOVE . . .'

Marcia re-read it tenderly for about the twentieth time. She was not sure if she was glad or sorry that he had unexpectedly landed a part in a television play for the BBC, and could not get away from the rehearsal rooms in London, known as the Acton Hilton, presumably because nothing could less resemble that plush hotel than the barrack-like building with its self-service canteen which made the average Wimpy Bar an immediate candidate for the *Good Food Guide*.

If the play went well it would have been wonderful to know that he was out there as she stepped forward to receive the applause, turning into spontaneous cheers. But if things went wrong . . . she pushed that thought firmly away from her. It was too soon for that. The hands of the silent electric clock on the wall were already moving faster than any clock ever did on any normal day. Soon enough, she would begin to die inside. But not yet . . . not yet . . .

She opened a few newly arrived telegrams, glanced at them without really taking in their contents and found places for them around the mirror.

Below that mirror, bottles lined up as precisely as soldiers on parade, was her make-up. Not quite time for that yet. There was far more than she would need, but the fact that every contingency, every conceivable permutation was covered gave her confidence, and in some curious way made the dressing room feel more like home, which indeed it would be for the duration of the play.

Still able to ignore the clock, she lovingly rearranged the huge bouquet of flowers which her husband had sent her. There was a smaller bunch from Maurice, and a single rose from Professor Griffiths. She fiddled with those as well, stepped back, and admired her handiwork. The room was pleasant, warm and cosy, like a womb. She had given birth to her own little boy with no pain, and no fuss, thanks to an epidural. When she left this haven tonight, though, there would be no epidural available.

Marcia lay on the sofa and carried out her relaxation and deep breathing exercises. She was a great believer in yoga, after earlier flirtations with spiritualism and hypnosis. That done, she picked up her script and began to go through the difficult bits, the long speeches especially, and the final scene with Cramer with its swift changes of mood, which still bothered her.

After a few minutes she threw the script down in annoyance. If she did not know it now, she never bloody well would.

In fact she knew her part backwards, huge and demanding though it was. More, she knew every other actor's part almost as well as her own. Just the same, the responsibility she would carry lay as heavy in her stomach as a sack of potatoes. It was beginning, that mixture of depression and panic so intense as to be close to hysteria which was known as first night nerves – a misleading phrase, as though it were anything so trivial as mere nervousness.

Yoga had failed her. It always did, but she kept on hoping. She wondered if she should try doing her exercises again, but when she endeavoured to achieve the necessary complete muscular relaxation her body refused to obey her mind. She was stiff and tense. The comfortable sofa felt like a wooden board with golf balls scattered on it. She sat up, miserably. Many, she knew, gained solace at times like this from Valium, or alcohol, or both. She wishd she was one of them. It would be good to take something – anything. But such was against her beliefs. She would have to see this through on her own.

Her yoga teacher always made it sound so simple, so eminently possible, no matter what the circumstances. She lay back and tried again.

Cramer, too, was going over his script. His part was not nearly as big as Marcia's, and he could look forward to that half-hour when he was off-stage, when he could take stock and gird himself for the remainder of the play. On the other hand those people out there, tonight and every night for the next three weeks, would be coming to see him, not Marcia Hambridge.

Not that Cramer gave a damn about the audiences here in Treganwy. For them, it was a unique chance to see a genuine film star in the flesh, proving that he was a living, breathing human being, and they would regard it as an occasion to remember and relate for many years to come, the night when they saw the real John Cramer, not photographed on celluloid for distribution throughout the entire Western world and a considerable chunk of the East as well, but appearing for them, personally.

To hell with them. They would applaud until their hands were sore no matter what he said or did, or how he did it. Tonight was not for them. It was for Cramer.

Using his tooth glass he poured himself a measure of scotch, and sipped it as his eyes scanned the script, running down each page, pausing at each point where he had underlined the name STEPHEN.

Oh Christ, he could not conceivably want to pee again. With all his years of experience, Stratford, film premières, making speeches after receiving awards . . . it was pure imagination. Knock it off, he told his bladder.

His mind went back many years. He had been a good cricketer in those days, although not outstanding enough by the fiercely critical standards which Cramer applied to everything he did. Good enough though, to play – unusually – for Cambridge in his first and only year there, before he quit and went to RADA.

He had opened the innings in the Varsity match against Oxford on a rain-affected wicket. By sheer determination he had survived until one of the Oxford bowlers who was genuinely fast made a ball, which was only just short of a good length, stand up sharply: it hit Cramer in the face. He was solicitously led off the field with blood pouring from his cheek. Cramer J., retired hurt, 21, the score book read at that stage. In the dressing room Cramer refused to be taken to hospital, and a doubtful doctor stitched the cut, which healed satisfactorily later though it left a slight scar. This done, disregarding the pleas of the doctor, Cramer insisted on going out to bat again when the next wicket fell.

The warm, sympathetic applause as he walked out, his face plastered, instilled a glow in him which he had not experienced before. On that difficult and dangerous wicket Cramer stayed there, more by sheer doggedness and guts than skill, and an unwillingness ever to be beaten. When the last wicket fell Cramer was 48 not out, the highest scorer out of a total of 124.

As he walked back to the pavilion the spectators stood as one man, clapped, and roared their approval.

Perhaps they thought they were applauding a fine sportsman, but Cramer knew differently. The whole incident was theatrical. Curiously, as he walked up the pavilion steps and ageing men jostled to pat him on the back, the cheering rang in his ears, and the unconscious smiles on all their faces told of their admiration and an affection momentarily close to love, Cramer knew that he had played an heroic role and they had enjoyed the spectacle. At that moment he knew what he wanted out of life – to be an actor.

He remembered how he had felt before that innings started. How his fingers were shaking as he buckled on his pads. How, as the opposing side took the field, the umpires walked out, and there were only moments to go before he should follow, he had been forced to go into the urinal and take off the box which would protect his genitals, although he had made the same trip several times in the previous thirty minutes.

Shit, Cramer said out loud. He pushed his script aside, went into his private WC and unzipped his trousers. But little more than a dribble came out.

But at least Cramer had a private loo at his disposal. Nicola sat on the seat in the Ladies, wishing her stomach would stop churning.

One thing about first nights, she thought, there was no danger of constipation. It affected different people in different ways. Some were physically sick, vomiting helplessly in that last hour before the curtain went up. Some walked up and down their dressing rooms, shaking uncontrollably until, unable to hold out, gasping, they swallowed Valium, and then took another one for luck. Nicola got the runs. That has definitely got to be it, she thought. There's nothing else left.

Marcia sat at her dressing table and wound her hair round the hot rollers, staring at her naked face, ruthlessly illuminated by the brilliant lights. It was the face of a stranger, some worried, harassed middle-aged mother in a supermarket early in the morning, not that of Marcia Hambridge, still less Paula. Paula would emerge.

Carefully, she chose a foundation. The part, that of a rich, wilful woman, called for her to be sun-tanned. For the past week she had been covering her body with instant tan. Her facial make-up had to match that.

She used two sticks of Leichner, a mixture of light copper and rosy blush, which would do the trick. She peered into the mirror, squinting slightly – the result was pleasing. The make-up had seeped into the nooks and crannies of that naked, middle-aged face, and knocked off at least ten years. Well, from a distance anyway. A touch more highlight on the cheeks perhaps, and an amber colour to add a little more sun-tan. Good. Coming on.

She highlighted under her eyebrows and below her eyes with a stick of concealer, a whitish silvery cream, which would help to block out lines, and bring her eyes into clearer focus – the standby of every actress over the age of thirty-five.

Marcia smiled at herself, not displeased. Her confidence was growing. 'I'll show the bastards,' she thought. Right. Mouth.

Again, she highlighted above her top lip, working slowly, no need to hurry, still time in hand, to dispel the tiny vertical lines which she could do nothing about at her age, and had sadly come to terms with. Next, she outlined her lips with a brush full of vermilion red, and filled in with a bright coral colour. Not bad. Not bad at all. That face in the mirror was coming to life. She smiled again at the young woman in the mirror.

'There is not another actress in the world who can play this part better than me,' she announced out loud, nodding, and the young face in the mirror nodded agreement. Lightly, she powdered her face with a translucent substance which allowed the colour to show through.

She was so absorbed that she started in her seat when the soft, calm voice spoke from the loudspeaker above her head.

'Half an hour, ladies and gentlemen,' Linda's voice said, from the tannoy which was connected to every dressing room. 'This is your half hour call. Thank you.' There was a tiny click and silence was resumed. Except that Marcia could hear her own breathing, which had suddenly become very fast.

Deliberately, she took several deep breaths. Marcia was a seasoned actress, and no stranger to first nights, but it was more than five years since she had appeared on a stage, considerably longer since she had premièred a new play. For the first time that evening she allowed herself to travel the chart she had drawn up in her mind of the next few months. The fantastic reviews at Treganwy, the tour before packed houses, the transfer to the West End. Right. That meant an even more fearsome first night at the Cambridge, or the Globe, or the Fortune. That was where she was heading. And if she could handle that, which she could, then she could bloody well handle this. Compared with a first night in the West End, this was nothing. Nothing at all.

There was a discreet knock at the door and her dresser came in, wearing a cheerful smile, and carrying Marcia's freshly ironed costumes, which she carefully hung on the rail.

'Good evening, Miss Hambridge,' the dresser said brightly. 'We're going to be packed out tonight. I've never known anything like it.'

'M'm . . . marvellous . . .' Marcia said absently. 'Shan't be a minute, Barbara.'

'Ready when you are, Miss Hambridge,' the dresser said. Her name was, in fact, Eileen, but she did not dream of correcting Marcia. She had dressed Marcia, and been correctly called Eileen, all through the dress rehearsals, but she knew what a state the ladies got into on first nights.

Eileen was a middle-aged woman, the wife of a small shopkeeper, and, during the winter months, a pillar of the amateur dramatic society. During the season she earned a little pin money, and enjoyed becoming at least a small part of the 'real' theatre, by working as a dresser. She had done it through many summers now, and was experienced and well liked. She knew that by being efficient, but self-effacing, calm and considerate, and offering help in small ways while taking care never to upset one of her ladies, she could play a not unimportant role in enabling an actress to progress, with as little pain as possible, from dressing room on to stage.

'Can I fetch you anything, Miss Hambridge?' Eileen enquired solicitously. 'Tea or coffee, perhaps?'

'No, thank you, Barbara,' Marcia said. She did not like tea and coffee was a diuretic. Come to that, any liquid was a diuretic at times like this. And once on stage Marcia was never off. Even during the interval she had a difficult costume and hair style change which would tax them both to the limit. Better not to take any chances. 'I'm not sure,' Marcia said, 'but I think I might be getting a headache.'

'Well, here's some aspirin, just in case, Miss Hambridge,' Eileen said. She took a bottle from one of the capacious pockets in her overall, tapped out a couple of tablets, laid them carefully on the dressing table on top of a fresh tissue, and filled Marcia's tooth glass from the wash basin.

'Thank you, Barbara,' Marcia said. 'I'll see how I feel in a minute.'

Eileen carried a number of other potentially useful objects in those pockets of hers, such as hair grips, decongestant inhalant, and Tampax. She liked to be ready for anything her ladies might need.

Like all the others Nicola had been over her lines yet again, and come to the same conculsion. Sod it. If all the rehearsing, all the evenings spent going through the script time and again had not imprinted the part in her mind, it was too late now. She discarded the script and stared at herself in the mirror.

'Christ, why do I do it?' she wondered out loud. But the answer was in her still-churning guts, that mixture of panic and excitement which she shared with Marcia. It was agonising and hateful, and yet it was necessary. It was her form of fix. She was an addict. Just as withdrawal symptons heightened the relief as the needle slid, deliciously, into the vein, so this form of hell was the obligatory prelude to the glorious moment when it was all over, and she had won. When she had defeated her own fear, imposed her talent on the audience, compelled them to believe, to laugh, or to be moved, and successfully concealed from them the state of terror which she was obliged to conquer, and which only finally left her when the curtain fell at the conclusion of the play.

The ordeal she was now going through was familiar, she knew it well, like an old enemy, one which inspired fear and must be treated with respect, but one which was not invincible. Over the years Nicola had learned to make her nerves work for her rather than against her.

Like Marcia, cards and telegrams festooned her mirror. There was the bunch of flowers from Maurice, and the single rose from Professor Griffiths. She had also received a small bouquet of spring flowers from Harry Belmont. The card read HOPE IT GOES WELL. HARRY.

The message somewhat piqued Nicola. It might, she felt, have been more affectionate. True, she had left him, but she had every right to do so, the guilt-ridden bastard, with his bloody phone calls, looking at his watch and clearing his throat until she could have screamed.

She had hesitated for a long time after writing him that friendly note, and had practically decided to send him a ticket for the first night – she was entitled to one complimentary ticket – but in the mounting pressures of rehearsals she had never quite got around to it.

Now, she was glad that she had not. If that was all he could say, 'Hope it goes well', without adding 'love', or even 'affectionately', or something like that, then to hell with him. It was time she rid herself of the last vestige of Harry Belmont, and there would be opportunities some time, she knew that.

Nicola needed to use very little make-up compared with Marcia. Also, her hair was no problem; for this part she was wearing it short and straight. A shampoo, a vigorous brush, and that was it.

Nicola used a damp sponge to apply a natural colour foundation. She touched up her cheeks with some blusher and outlined her eyes with a Mary Quant pencil, highlighting a little above and below.

'A quarter of an hour, please, ladies and gentlemen,' Linda's voice said from the tannoy. 'This is your quarter of an hour call. Thank you.'

Nicola was dressed, made up and ready, but this was no misjudgement. She was meticulous in her approach to a part, always doing her best to anticipate and forestall any problems.

She left her dressing room and walked towards the stage, passing Ben Stamford on the way. Ben gave her a wink and the thumbs-up sign, but he did not speak. For those appearing the remaining minutes were private, and Ben knew better than anyone that Nicola would not want him to say anything.

Although he would not be playing the role until John Cramer left Ben Stamford was as nervous as any of them, suffering their ordeal by proxy. There was no way he could have sat still out front watching the play. His method of getting through it would be to wander about backstage, being careful not to get in the way. In some respects it was worse for Ben. When he took over from Cramer he would have his own first night, by which time the rest would be used to it, taking the play in their stride. He had to go through it twice.

Nicola made sure that the portable typewriter was in the correct position, sitting on a small table, behind a flat, and that the sheaves of paper which she would have to carry when she made her first entrance were also in place, safely tucked under the typewriter.

That done, she crossed the empty, half-lit stage to the bar. Most of the way through the play, and especially in the first scene, her part called for her to fix drinks at frequent intervals. She made certain that the correct bottles were in place, the plastic cubes of stage ice were in the refrigerator, and the right number and types of glasses were where they should be. It was not exactly that she did not trust the stage management team but anyone could make mistakes, and it was no use blaming them afterwards if, when it was crucial to the plot that she be seen mixing a dry Martini, she found there was no Martini bottle on the bar, and nothing to stir it with.

However all the props were in place, and Nicola returned to her dressing room, satisfied. It was two minutes well spent.

Marcia had donned her first costume, an elegant one-piece swimsuit, and a beach robe. She stood and looked at herself in the full length mirror. Not bad. Not bloody bad at all. The diet she had been on for the past four weeks had done its job, and she was slimmer now than she had been for years.

The cleavage which the boned costume gave her was damned sexy, she thought. She toyed with the notion of making her entrance as originally written in the script, wearing only the swimsuit, and putting on the beach robe later. She was tempted. Could she get away with it? She gazed at her reflection critically.

But she had never been blessed with long legs, and despite her rigorous slimming the tops of her thighs were thick. Nothing would change that now, short of actual starvation. Also, since giving birth to her son, her hips were broader than they had been. There was a credit side to that, of course, after the slimming regime, which had taken inches off her waist. With her full bosom rising from the swimsuit, her figure looked positively voluptuous. On the other hand . . . Marcia half turned and peered over her shoulder at her behind in the mirror. No, she decided reluctantly. Better not risk it.

She pulled her beach robe together and yanked the belt tight. Yes, that was better. That was fine. And the final touch would add that little something extra. Marcia's hair was her best feature, dark brown, thick and lustrous.

She took out the heated rollers and her hair cascaded about her shoulders in long sausages. Vigorously, yet with precision, she pulled her hairbrush through until she was happy with the way it fell. 'I'll knock their bloody eyes out,' she thought.

Maurice made his rounds just after the quarter had been called. He rapped briskly on Marcia's door, walked in, and kissed her on both cheeks.

'You look fantastic, darling,' he said. 'All the luck in the world.'

Marcia responded with a genuinely affectionate hug, although she avoided pressing her carefully made-up cheeks against his. For this brief moment all their antagonisms, all those bitter flare-ups and recriminations were forgotten. Like two soldiers on the eve of battle, past dislikes, private resentments, fell away, became unimportant, in the face of the life-and-death trial to come. They had not really vanished, they would no doubt re-emerge later, but for the time being they did not matter.

Maurice used the same formula of words with Nicola,

and then moved on to Cramer's dressing room. Cramer was brushing his teeth, the foam spilling from his lips. He rinsed his mouth into the wash basin and straightened up. Maurice did not use the conventional words with Cramer. He doubted if the man would appreciate them.

'Marcia thinks this play is hers,' Maurice said. 'I wish it were mine, but I know that for those people out there, it's yours. We're all riding on your bandwagon, but I expect you're used to that.'

Cramer grinned. He seemed as relaxed as a world champion boxer before an unimportant fight, confident in the knowledge that his opponent was no match for him.

'I suppose I've given you a bad time,' he said.

'Forget it,' Maurice said. 'The play's the thing, as some scribbler once wrote.'

Cramer had used a little pancake make-up to give himself the kind of sun-tan which a jet set hanger-on might have. His own tan had faded since last summer's filming in Spain. The South of France was not as warm and sunny during the winter as legend made out.

'You know the Professor always has one of his shindigs at The Hall after every first night,' Maurice said tentatively.

'And you'd like me to behave myself,' Cramer supposed, 'and make all the nobodies feel important.'

'The Prof doesn't have a dog,' Maurice said. 'So he kicks me afterwards, if he's bad-tempered. Which is boring, but doesn't matter all that much, because I'm quite capable of upsetting the pompous old ass at frequent intervals myself. However . . .'

'You could do without any unearned kicks,' Cramer suggested. 'O.K. For one hour, I'll be sociable sweetness and light. But I can't promise to hold out any longer than that.'

'Fine,' Maurice said. 'His dog would be grateful, if he had one.'

Cramer laughed. An armistice, Maurice thought, with relief. With any luck, peace. He made his way to Bernard Fyfield's dressing room, where he phrased his good wishes so as to flatter the older man, and completed his odyssey by sticking his head round Leonard Sherwen's door and exchanging good-natured insults which, he knew from experience, was the form from which Leonard drew reassurance.

His duty completed, Maurice hurried back to the bar, rescued Anna from Professor Griffiths, and showed her to her seat.

'Just in time,' Anna said. 'That one's a groper manqué. His wife was getting annoyed.'

'Five minutes, ladies and gentlemen, please,' Linda's voice said through the tannoy. 'This is your five-minute call. Thank you.'

Cramer picked up his script and carefully re-read the first scene in its entirety. It was simple stuff. Nothing to it. Not for a man who had held the most critical audiences in the world spellbound with his rendering of Hamlet's soliloquies.

Maurice had an aisle seat, next to Anna, but she knew that he would hardly use it, if at all. During first nights Maurice was always on the move, silently circling the auditorium, cat-like, going backstage, returning to pad round the back of the circle, every faculty alert, assessing what was happening there on stage.

The warning bell had not yet rung in the bar but already nearly every seat was occupied. The buzz of conversation was much louder than usual, signalling the way all those people were anticipating the coming event.

Programmes were being rustled. Fragments of earnest chatter drifted in the air. Maurice wondered why it was that so many people, as soon as they entered a theatre, became convinced that their spouses were unable to read.

'The action takes place on the patio and terrace adjoining a large private house, on a private island, in the sun,' a deep voice was methodically reading aloud from behind them.

'It doesn't say where it's meant to be though, does it,' a

woman replied, giving no clue as to whether or not she had mastered the art of reading in her younger days.

Part of the stage apron protruded in front of the curtain. Sitting in view of the audience were two cane chairs.

'Why have you put some of the furniture in front of the curtain?' Anna asked.

'The play was written for a conventional proscenium stage,' Maurice said. 'We've had to compromise a bit.' He looked at his watch. 'Must go, love. May see you later, during the interval. If not, after the show.'

'Good luck,' Anna said automatically.

'Beginners on stage, please. Miss Feary and Mr Cramer,' Linda's voice said on the tannoy. 'Beginners on stage. Miss Feary and Mr Cramer. Thank you.'

There were five minutes to go before curtain up.

A chill invaded Nicola and she shivered. Goose flesh prickled all over her body. The palms of her hands were wet. She could feel her heart pounding in time with her rapid, shallow breathing.

She took a deep breath and practised the warm smile into the mirror which she would give Cramer in the opening, silent moments of the play. The effect was ghastly. The bared teeth looked more like a twisted grimace of hate.

Suddenly Nicola laughed out loud. Her mind had become calm, clear, analytical, and totally in charge of her body. She took a final look at herself in the mirror and turned away.

'You silly cow,' she said out loud, and closed the dressing room door behind her.

The zither music, which Maurice had composed himself, began to play softly in the auditorium. The house lights dimmed. Conversation faded and died. The audience fell silent. The curtain rose.

Nicola stood at the typewriter, just off-stage, ready to tap on it for a few seconds before she made her entrance.

Cramer was alone on stage. He was lying on a sun bed, apparently asleep. One hand dangled limply near the floor. A large straw sun hat completely covered his face.

There was a soft, almost inaudible sigh of pleasure from the audience, and they began to clap the set. This was an infuriating habit of modern audiences, and Nicola, expecting it, had made no move to tap the keys the moment the curtain rose. It was just as well.

The clapping had almost died away when it collectively dawned on the audience that, concealed under that sun hat, was John Cramer.

The applause grew again, increased in volume until it reached thunderous proportions. The more uninhibited began to cheer.

Nicola waited until the silly buggers felt inclined to stop. The overwhelming enthusiasm remained unabated. To Nicola, it seemed to go on for hours.

'For Christ's sake, shut up,' Nicola murmured angrily.

The delay was upsetting her carefully, if subconsciously, planned pacing of herself through those last terrible few seconds before she walked out on the stage before that audience.

What the fuck did they expect Cramer to do? Stand up, wave his hat in the air, take a bow, and blow kisses at them? If so, they were disappointed. Cramer did not move a muscle. He could have been dead.

Nicola stared blindly at the keys of the typewriter. Her damp fingers were poised over them, ready, but she experienced a sudden, insane fear that when the time came she would find that she was paralysed. She would just stand there, unable to move a muscle, while Linda hissed at her, Cramer waited for her to appear as she remained rooted to the floor, and nothing happened on that brilliantly lit stage until the audience broke into surprised murmurs, and puzzled, uncomprehending laughs could be heard.

Finally, after what seemed to be an eternity, and more from sheer exhaustion than anything, the applause faltered, became ragged, subsided to a few sporadic claps, and came to a merciful end.

Nicola took one deep breath, steadied herself, and began to type. She counted up to ten slowly, stopped typing, pulled the sheet of paper from the platen, and added it to the sheaf at her left hand.

She paused for one last fraction of a second, raised her head high, curved her back, and thought 'Please . . . God . . .' She was ready. Here we go.

She walked on to the stage. The play was under way.

# CHAPTER NINE

It was not long before Nicola needed all her self-possession, every atom of the control she fought so desperately to retain.

Cramer dominated the stage by his sheer presence, there was no doubt about that. He was playing with a mesmerising, masterful authority which was leagues beyond anything he had displayed during rehearsal. The trouble was that Nicola was hearing a good many lines from him which she had never heard before.

'I thought you were asleep,' Nicola said light-heartedly, as per script, as she mixed the first drink.

'You're a peasant at heart, that's your trouble,' Cramer said. 'I'm working.'

He had run two speeches together, and missed out 'No. I'm lying here . . .' which made nonsense of Nicola's next line, but she said it anyway.

'I think you're just lying there,' Nicola said.

'It happens up here, my girl,' Cramer said, tapping his head, reversing the correct order of the speech. 'You're a peasant at heart, that's your trouble,' he went on, repeating himself. The rest of the speech came out O.K., but he missed out his final question, Nicola's cue.

It took Nicola but a fraction of a second to realise that he was not going to say it.

'You've only done fifteen pages,' Nicola said, which covered it nicely.

Unfortunately, at the same moment, Alan Cakin chose to give a prompt which, Nicola thought frantically, could have been heard in the back row of the stalls.

'How many?' Alan Cakin hissed loudly.

'How many?' Cramer repeated.

'I've just told you. Fifteen pages,' Nicola said gaily, improvising.

They battled on, and the scene seemed to be settling down until the point where Cramer had to look at one of the pages of typescript and demand: 'What the hell is that?'

'What?' Nicola asked. At least she was now getting her correct cue lines.

'Getting it right is your job,' Cramer said.

Nicola experienced a moment of utter blankness, complete disorientation. There was no such line anywhere in the play. What the hell was she supposed to say to that? Desperately, Nicola flogged her memory. There was a roughly similar line somewhere, when Cramer was supposed to say 'That's your job.' But it was not at this point. She knew it wasn't.

Then it came to her. Jesus Christ Almighty, she thought, he's cut a complete page. The whole moment of eternity had in fact occupied but a fraction of a second. No one in the paying audience would have noticed.

'I don't know what you're talking about,' Nicola invented, trying to lead Cramer back to the page of dialogue which he had missed out. The other possibility, that of carrying straight on, had flashed through her mind, and been discarded as quickly. The missing page was too important to the story. 'What do you mean, "what the hell is that?" What's wrong with it?'

'Oh, I put your glass on top,' came an agonised prompt from Alan Cakin's corner off-stage. Which *would* have been Nicola's line had all been going well.

Oh shut up, you silly little cunt, Nicola screamed inside her own head. Prompt him, not me.

Fortunately Cramer had realised what she was doing.

'This,' he said, pointing to the page of typescript. 'That's what's wrong with it. This damp, disgusting soggy circle, piddling its way round the beginning of the second paragraph.'

Which was part improvisation, but ended correctly, and got them back to where they should be.

'Oh, I put your glass on top,' Nicola said. 'It must have been wet. Sorry.'

'You stupid cow,' Cramer said.

They battled on until Marcia made her entrance, after which the agony was at least spread around a bit. The main trouble now was that Alan Cakin had evidently subsided into a state of perpetual panic, and was prompting like a lunatic, without allowing the actors a chance, often during a rehearsed pause, and usually prompting the wrong person.

The time came when Cramer said, 'No, don't do that. I'll deal with it,' which was reasonably close to the line in the script, and ran off-stage.

Nicola and Marcia began their long duologue. Marcia had obviously been badly affected. As Nicola rubbed suntan lotion into the older woman's back she could feel her body trembling, and her skin was ice cold, despite the heat from the stage lights, but Marcia's voice remained firm and clear, and she kept her gestures under control. The old cow's a trouper, Nicola thought, you've got to give her that.

Eventually the telephone rang on cue. Nicola spoke into the receiver and retired from the chamber of torment with gratitude, leaving it to Marcia and Cramer, who was due to reappear at that point.

Maurice was waiting in the wings.

'Bless you, darling,' he whispered. 'Well done. Smashing.'

'What in God's name is going on?' Nicola hissed. 'It's all over the place out there. Cramer's cocking up all his lines, we keep getting prompts in the wrong places . . .'

'It's all my fault,' Maurice whispered. 'It's Alan's first time on the book, and I didn't realise. He just went to pieces. I've pulled him off the book, and Stan's taken over. It'll be all right now, I promise you.'

'I hope so,' Nicola whispered. 'Another twenty minutes like that'd send me round the twist.' But she was heartened. Stan was the experienced stage manager, a calm, self-possessed man, who knew the score. There would be no more trouble from the corner, at least.

Nicola only had one more line in this scene, and that was off-stage, towards the end. She went to her dressing room. On the way she passed Alan Cakin and Bernard Fyfield. Alan's head was bowed. Tears were running down his cheeks. Bernard's arm was round his shoulders, hugging him close. 'It's all right,' Bernard was murmuring. 'Don't worry about it. It's all right, love.' He caressed Alan's cheek.

Nicola changed into the smart little black dress she would be wearing when the curtain rose on her and Leonard Sherwen at the beginning of Scene Two.

Out in the auditorium the audience, blissfully unaware of all this, watched the play with rapt, and mostly silent, attention. There were a few tentative titters, but hardly any laughs. Just the same they obviously enjoyed their evening, and thought their money well spent.

They clapped at the end of every scene and when the final curtain came down they nearly raised the roof. The cast took their curtain calls as the audience stood, and clapped, and cheered. The curtain rose and fell, time after time, but they obstinately refused to stop applauding.

The cast, holding hands, bowed, and smiled their acknowledgements, but it was only too transparently clear who the applause was for.

After the seventh curtain call Cramer, with a gallantry which was possibly hypocritical, guided Marcia forward. The audience responded in the spirit they supposed the gesture was meant, and Marcia curtsied deeply, her face alive with happiness.

But only one thing was going to stop them, and finally Cramer stepped forward to take his last bow. The noise could well have been heard on top of Snowdon. Cramer smiled, gestured right and left to the remainder of the cast, held up his arms in a final gesture, and the curtain fell for the last time.

They kept on applauding hopefully but the curtain remained down. Behind it, Cramer had walked off.

'They've had their pound of flesh,' he said to Maurice. 'I want a drink.'

Finally they gave up clapping and began to move out of the theatre. They were light-hearted and smiling. They had been present on a wonderful occasion. They had seen the great John Cramer in person.

Maurice made his rounds again. Marcia was creaming her face, stripping it of stage make-up. Maurice gave her a big hug.

'You were marvellous, darling,' he said. 'Absolutely marvellous.'

That was all any actor wanted to hear after the torture of a first night. The audience had applauded itself silly. It was, therefore, a wonderful audience. The actor/audience relationship was always uncertain, and rather resembled a stormy love affair liberally laced with resentment and suspicion. But tonight it had been all love, and the affair beautifully consummated.

Post-coital depression had not yet set in. Marcia was on a terrific 'high', which might last all of twenty-four hours. This was not the moment for analysis and post mortems. Tonight, everything was marvellous.

'There did seem to be rather a lot of fluffs and things,' Marcia said, inviting Maurice to tell her that it did not matter.

'No one even noticed,' Maurice said heartily. 'It didn't matter a bit. They loved it.'

'Yes, I think they must have enjoyed it,' Marcia said. 'I don't think I've ever taken more curtain calls in my life.'

Maurice forbore to remind her that she happened to be standing next to John Cramer at the time.

'Never known anything like it,' he said. 'Marvellous.'

'Someone said some of the London critics were here,' Marcia said. 'The man from the *Guardian*, and someone from the *Sunday Times*, or it may have been the *Telegraph*. Is that true? Were they invited?'

'I honestly don't know,' Maurice said, which was indeed the case. Professor Griffiths was prone to do things without telling him. They would find out soon enough, he thought, and there was no point in worrying about that now. Reviews were a lottery at the best of times. You could never predict what critics were going to say. 'Must go and have a word with the others,' Maurice said. 'And don't forget, it's everyone up to The Hall as soon as possible. I'll give you a lift, O.K.?'

'Shan't be long,' Marçia said happily.

Harry Belmont turned the wrong way when he came out of the foyer and it took him quite a while to find the stage door. When he did there were twenty or thirty people clustered round, waiting.

Harry had intended to go inside, and ask for Nicola's dressing room, but the bunch of people was closely packed round the door, and in any event, the stage door-keeper seemed to be barring the way to all and sundry. He decided to wait there for her, and hung back on the fringe where the shadows were deepest.

Ben Stamford and Leonard Sherwen came out first. No one took any notice of Ben, and none of them showed any interest in Leonard, except a slim girl with long blonde hair who shyly offered him her autograph book.

They moved to one side, Leonard signed her book and said something which made her laugh. They talked for a while, Leonard looked at his watch, and they walked off together.

'Hey. What about the Prof?' Ben called.

'He won't miss me,' Leonard said.

'Some people have all the luck,' Ben Stamford said.

Bernard Fyfield and Maurice emerged, escorting Marcia. Marcia was graciously prepared to sign every autograph book in sight, but only half a dozen on the outskirts came her way. The remainder were obviously determined not to lose their hard-won places in pursuit of lesser fry like Marcia and Bernard.

Maurice took her arm before any such suspicion crossed her mind.

'Come on, Marcia,' he urged. 'The Prof's waiting. You can't stand here signing your name all night.' He pulled her towards his car, protesting mildly, but with her ego undamaged.

The autograph hunters bunched closer to the door, determined not to miss their real prey. As it happened, they were wasting their time.

Cramer came out like a runaway bull. Gripping Nicola's arm he shouldered his way ruthlessly through them, and before they had quite realised what was happening Cramer and Nicola had run to his car. They followed like sheep, bleating plaintively, but Cramer ignored the imploring hands, slammed the door, and drove off.

They were disappointed, as they drifted away, but not unduly put out. Cramer had behaved the way a star might be expected to behave.

Harry Belmont walked slowly to his own car. He supposed, from the half references he had heard, that the cast had left to attend some function. He wished he could have told Nicola how good he thought her performance had been. He supposed he could write a note, ask the way to this cottage of hers, and push it through the letter-box. But would she not think that odd? He would have to speak to her. Perhaps he could call on her tomorrow morning? But he knew Nicola after first nights. She would sleep until noon, and he must leave for London early. Oh hell, it was all too complicated. . . .

Nicola thought that the Professor's gathering was much livelier than the first one, but that was probably because, like Marcia, she was on a 'high'. Also she felt the need of a few drinks to wind down, and she had them more quickly than she usually would, after which it seemed a good idea to have a few more.

On this occasion, Ben Stamford noted with approval, there was a wide selection of other drinks along with the champagne, and Ben got stuck into the whisky with enthusiasm.

'Where's Leonard?' Nicola asked.

'Kidnapped by some leggy blonde bird,' Ben said. 'Why couldn't it happen to me? There's no justice.'

Nicola knew that was all bullshit. Ben always missed his wife when they were apart, and from the front end of a six-month season the enforced separation seemed endless. That was why he drank like a fish. Scotch was his chosen companion.

Maurice became steadily more depressed as the minutes passed. Despite his cheery congratulations to the cast there was no 'high' for him, and the brief conversation in undertones with Professor Griffiths did nothing to improve his mood.

'Did any of your West End managements turn up?' he asked. He was really only making conversation. Important though it might be, it was something he would learn in due course anyway.

'John Aberson was there,' Professor Griffiths said, 'but he left immediately afterwards without saying anything.'

'He was probably driving back to London tonight,' Maurice said. Aberson would be good, he thought. He had a shrewd eye for a commercial play.

'I have no doubt that he will telephone me, but it may have been an error to allow him to see it so soon,' Professor Griffiths said, as though that decision had been anything to do with Maurice. 'There's still a great deal to be done to this production.'

'No play looks its best on a first night,' Maurice said, 'but the audience liked it, just the same. It'll be fine by the end of the week.'

'You've had ample time,' Professor Griffiths said ominously. 'John Cramer deserved something better than the production we saw tonight.'

He turned away, intercepted Anna, and launched into a lengthy monologue which, Maurice had no doubt, would contain a large number of dropped names, reflect credit on the Professor's acumen and capacity for brilliant, stinging repartee, and concern some event in the distant past. The Professor's anecdotes all tended to have those factors in common.

But it was Anna who was the principal cause for Maurice's growing depression. She stood beside the Professor, giving her impersonation of an attentive, amused listener – one of her many practised and skilful talents – but her eyes were never on the Professor's face. Every nod, every little laugh, every toss of her head was so contrived as to send her gaze past one or the other of the Professor's ears.

Professor Griffiths, beguiled by her charms, failed to notice this, but Maurice did.

He also knew the reason for the dancing lights in her eyes, and the target for all those apparently casual glances. He knew his Anna. The recipient was John Cramer, and Cramer was very well aware of it too.

Cramer was keeping his promise to Maurice. His behaviour was impeccable. He circulated with the utmost friendliness, chatted to all the Professor's guests, accepted their admiring congratulations with becoming modesty, gently flattered the women, smiled at the men's jokes, and convulsed them with remarks of his own. His masculine charm was turning this into the most successful ever of the Professor's little soirées, never to be surpassed. He was a wow.

Maurice could hear the fragments of awed remarks all around him, after the lucky guests had received their ration of Cramer's attention.

'Jolly nice chap . . . not at all what I expected . . .'

'Such a great actor . . . I mean, you only have to think of his performance tonight . . . and yet he's so modest . . .'

'Such a *nice* man . . . it's amazing . . .'

But what Maurice was sickeningly aware of was that small smile on Cramer's lips whenever his head turned Anna's way, and his eyes caught hers for a second, the tiny acknowledgement that he knew she was on offer.

Maurice had his own social chores to perform, the frequent use of the word 'marvellous' and its synonyms to his cast – once was never enough, it had to be repeated many times – the necessity to cheer up Alan Cakin, although the young man was in better spirits than might have been expected, and the obligation to talk to the Professor's guests, although all they wanted to hear were anecdotes about John Cramer. During all this he missed the moment when Anna must have escaped from Professor Griffiths. She was now with Cramer on the opposite side of the room.

They were talking, confidentially it seemed, Anna

seriously, Cramer with that small smile flitting across his lips now and then. Cramer was leaning casually on one corner of the Adam fireplace, a glass of whisky in one hand. Anna was not so much beside him as pressed up against him. It was true that the room was crowded, but they could not have been closer together, Maurice thought bitterly, had they been standing in a packed Underground train during rush hour.

He should have foreseen this, but somehow he had not. Anna had affairs. They were both free to have affairs. That was the arrangement, civilised, modern, tolerant of each others' needs. The snag was that Maurice did not want to have affairs so the arrangement, in practice, was somewhat one-sided. But one day, some time, Maurice liked to imagine, Anna would lose the desire for the sudden passionate encounters which speckled her life. Then they would settle down, really settle down together, and whether they married or not was unimportant, but each, from then on, would be sufficient for the other.

However although Maurice cherished occasional hopes which were promptly shattered he knew in his heart that that desirable day had not yet dawned. He really should have seen this coming. He knew his Anna only too well, certainly well enough to know that Cramer was the kind of virile hunk who would appeal to her even if his name were not John Cramer. But he was John Cramer. And, for Anna, success was sexy, and success plus fame was even sexier. Cramer was exactly her kind of scalp, a trophy she could never resist. Why had not all this occurred to him before? He supposed that he had been too engrossed in the play. Bugger the lousy play. Given the intelligence and insight of a two-year-old, he would have kept her away from Treganwy until Cramer had gone, used any excuse . . . he sighed helplessly. He was whistling in the wind. Anna, he recalled far too late, had, unusually, been actively keen to come and see the first night of his production of this new play. And, fool that he was, he had taken that as a good sign, an indication that she was acquiring more interest in his career, a signal that she was beginning to respect his achievements.

Lost in his wretched thoughts, he failed to notice that Cramer had left his position by the Adam fireplace until firm, strong fingers gripped his elbow.

'I promised you an hour,' Cramer said. 'It's nearer two. I reckon I've done my stuff. In fact, I think I deserve a good conduct badge.'

Maurice's gaze hunted round the room. There was no sign of Anna.

'So I'll just slip away quietly,' Cramer said.

'Thanks very much,' Maurice said. 'Enjoy the rest of the night.'

Cramer gave him an odd look. 'It's not important,' he said. 'It won't affect anything.'

'That's nice,' Maurice said. 'I'll be giving notes at six-thirty tomorrow, before the show.'

'See you then' Cramer said.

Maurice joined Ben Stamford and decided to switch to whisky. The only solution on these occasions was to get sloshed out of his mind. The glass was almost to his lips when his hand froze in mid-air. He stared over the rim, jolted, momentarily at a loss.

Anna had come in from the hall. She turned towards the Adam fireplace, a tiny tantalising smile on her lips, and stopped dead. As her eyes searched the room, ignoring Maurice, the tiny smile vanished. A local businessman, a generous patron of the theatre, engaged her in conversation. She did not bother to show any interest.

Maurice threaded his way through the throng and reached Anna's side as the businessman took Anna's glass and gestured at a waitress.

'I forgot to mention,' Maurice said, 'but if you want the Ladies . . .'

'I've just been,' Anna said. Her face was bleak and cold.

'Fine,' Maurice said.

Harry Belmont had changed his mind a dozen times before finally mentioning Nicola's address to the night porter. He followed the man's directions but missed the turning in the darkness, reversed, and finally found the group of cottages, clustered round a triangle of grass. He circled the triangle and found the right one.

He had decided to knock on her door if any lights were on, but the cottage was in darkness. Either she was not back yet, or she was in bed. He sat for a few moments and then backed in behind a van which was parked on the grass. He switched off his engine. He would wait for a few minutes, just in case.

Once his engine had died the silence was absolute. There were no street lights. Clouds obscured the moon. He could dimly pick out a few shapes, but that was all.

Once the residual heat in the car had evaporated he realised that the April night was cool verging on cold. His discomfort grew and with it the parallel feeling that all this was rather silly. For all he knew, the party could go on half the night. Even if she did come back soon, she would almost certainly have had a little, or more than a little, too much to drink. After first nights, she always did. In the past she had tried to explain the reasons to him, the tensions she had undergone, the state of nerves, the urgent need to relax afterwards. He could not genuinely identify, the experience was one he had never been through himself, but he accepted it.

He also knew the stages which she went through, and it would depend which one she had reached. She might be laughing and gay, for the time being loving the whole world and everything in it, in which case she would be glad to see him. Or, if she had gone past that, she might be unutterably weary, the strain of the last few days hitting her like a sledgehammer, her eyelids drooping, her only overpowering desire to stumble into bed and collapse into sleep. In which case, she would look at him as though he were an unwelcome stranger, resenting him for his intrusion, for separating her for a few moments, even if she could summon up enough energy to be polite, from the longed-for comfort of the bed.

She would probably regard him as an unwelcome intruder anyway, Harry reflected. After all, she had not invited him to come. What the hell was he doing here in this lonely, deathly silent place? Nothing. Except making a fool of himself. Also, it was no longer merely chilly. It was damned cold. He reached for the key, but as his fingers were about to turn the engine into life he stopped, listening.

For the first time since he had been sitting here, however long that might be, there was a sound, quiet at first, steadily growing louder. A car.

Hard to tell from which direction it was coming. And then he caught sight of the headlights. They swivelled, flashed across the triangle of grass, and came to a stop outside Nicola's cottage a few yards from where he was sitting.

Car doors slammed. Two shapes. Voices. He could not hear them distinctly. Quietly, he wound his window down. Now the voices were clear. Immediately apparent which stage Nicola had reached. Her voice was gay and happy and she was laughing. The other voice was deep, almost approaching a growl, and Harry had heard it recently. John Cramer.

With his window down Harry could see marginally more clearly. They were walking towards Nicola's front door. Her left shoulder dipped as if she had stumbled. She laughed, and Cramer put an arm round her waist.

A light went on inside the cottage. From his angle, Harry could not tell which room it was. He sat still, his heart beating uncomfortably hard. He told himself the good reasons why he did not drive off there and then. He had seen Nicola get into Cramer's car at the theatre. He had given her a lift to wherever they had been going. Now, he had driven her home. All that was obvious and reasonable. Quite soon, he would say good night and go, when Harry would knock on her door and surprise her.

Such was what Harry Belmont told himself. Even at the time, a part of him knew it was hopeless self-deception.

Another light went on inside the cottage. It was also on the ground floor, in an adjoining room. Seconds later, the first light went out.

Harry did what no human being should ever do, but does. Moving like an automaton, his mind blank, he eased the handle, swung his door on its hinges, and got out. He left the door open.

Slowly, walking carefully, he moved a few yards until he was square on to that room. It was Nicola's bedroom. A single light was burning. One glance should have been enough. But Harry Belmont stood there like some transfixed sleepwalker until Nicola raised herself from the bed, crossed the room, and drew the curtains. Then he returned to his car, eased out from behind the van, and drove off.

The night porter was yawning and unco-operative.

'I can't make out bills,' he protested. 'You'll have to wait until the receptionist comes on duty in the morning.'

'I'm leaving in ten minutes,' Harry said. 'Please yourself.'

He went up to his room to throw his things into his case; when he came down again the night porter resentfully handed him a scrawled bill. Harry paid it, went outside, and left Treganwy. He had enough petrol to reach the service station on the nearest motorway.

The sun was rising when he reached London. It was going to be a beautiful day.

When the last guest had gone, and the Professor's wife was beginning to wear the beginnings of a warning frown, Maurice and Anna had gone up to his apartment.

Maurice lay in bed and watched her as she sat at the dressing table. God, she was beautiful.

'I'm free until six thirty tomorrow,' he said. 'Shall we drive somewhere and have lunch?'

'Can't,' Anna said, smoothing moisturising cream into her face. 'I'll have to go after breakfast.'

'Go where?'

'London,' Anna said.

'I thought you were staying for a few days,' Maurice said. 'You don't leave for Tokyo until Saturday.'

'Things to do,' Anna said. 'Photo calls.'

'I wish you'd told me that before,' Maurice said. 'I've been looking forward to these few days.'

'I'm telling you now,' Anna said. She switched out the light and got into bed beside him.

'We've hardly had time to talk to each other,' Maurice said mournfully. Anna shifted beside him.

'This bed's bloody hard,' she said.

'What did you think of the play?' Maurice tried.

'It was all right,' Anna said.

'How about John Cramer?'

'O.K.,' Anna said.

'Did you think it was well directed though?'

'Does it matter?' Anna enquired. 'In a dump like this.'

'It does to me,' Maurice said.

Anna wriggled about a bit more, and finally seemed to get comfortable. Maurice's right hand explored her shape, defining her luscious body. He raised himself, leaned over, caressed her cheek, and kissed her. Her lips were cold and unresponsive.

'I've missed you,' Maurice said, into the darkness. 'God, how I've missed you.' Gently, his fingers circled the flaccid nipple on one of her small, firm breasts.

'Look,' Anna said, 'I just want to get some sleep. I'm exhausted, and I've got a long drive tomorrow.'

Maurice lay awake, his eyes wide open, long after Anna's breathing told him that she had gone to sleep.

It would have been all right, he thought, but for that bastard Cramer.

Maurice gave his notes to the assembled cast, ending on a note of encouragement as he always did.

'. . . on the whole, though, nothing to worry about, loves,' he said. 'After all, last night was only the first public performance. Just after another dress rehearsal, really. I know we're all concentrating on the two and a half weeks until John leaves us, but after all, that's only the beginning. We shall be performing the play, at intervals, throughout the season, so we really have got all the time in the world to achieve that extra bit of polish.

Never mind those little hiccups we had last night. I'm sure they won't happen again, and in any case, they weren't important. The main thing to remember is that the audience had a good time, and the box office are certain we shall be playing to capacity houses, or very close to it. O.K., John's the magnet, we all know that.' He paused and smiled warmly at Cramer. Cramer's only reaction was to smother a yawn. 'But since he's dragging them in for us,' Maurice went on, 'it's up to us to take advantage, and make the most of it. We've made a good beginning, and we're going to get better and better as the days go by. Well, I think that's all, so off you go, and good luck for tonight.' Maurice pocketed his notebook and stood up. As usual, he intended to speak to Cramer in private.

'Have there been any reviews yet?' Marcia asked. 'I bought all the papers, but I couldn't find anything.'

'Not as far as I know,' Maurice said. 'But they'll be put up on the board as they come in.'

Maurice tapped on the door of number one dressing room and went in. Cramer was lying on his sofa, nursing a whisky. He looked tired. He waved at a chair, but did not speak or offer Maurice a drink. Maurice sat down. He did not take out his notebook; he did not need to. He looked at Cramer for a long time, considering just what he should say. Cramer waited impassively.

'I suppose the only thing to do is to dive in at the deep end,' Maurice said at last. 'If you were an ordinary actor, I'd approach this in a different way. But you're not. I feel rather like an assistant pro on some municipal golf course, who suddenly finds not only that he's got a world class golfer playing eighteen holes, but he's supposed to talk to him about his game as well.'

'I'm not much interested in golf,' Cramer said.

'Well, bear with the analogy for a minute,' Maurice said. 'The champion can take on the best, at any time, but he's playing a strange course, which that assistant pro knows better than he does, and he may come up with one or two points which that world class golfer might find it worth considering.'

'Just get on with it,' Cramer said wearily.

'What did you think of last night?' Maurice ventured.

'You're supposed to tell me that,' Cramer said.

'I'm asking,' Maurice said.

'I think you've got problems,' Cramer said.

'Suppose you were directing this play,' Maurice said. 'What would you do about them?'

'If I were directing,' Cramer said, 'it wouldn't be here, and it wouldn't be with this cast.'

Maurice sighed inwardly. Cramer was not going to make it easy for him.

'All right,' he said. 'What I missed last night was the humour, most of which can only come from Stephen.'

'We've had this discussion,' Cramer said.

'I know,' Maurice said. 'And you're also entitled to point out that the audience cheered themselves hoarse. But that wasn't because they'd been present at a theatrical occasion. It bore no relation to the kind of reaction you used to get at Stratford all those years ago. That wasn't a knowing audience last night, not the vast majority of them anyway. They didn't care if they were watching good theatre or bad theatre. They were as happy as ticks because, for a few quid, they were actually there in the presence of John Cramer, big film star. They weren't interested in what you were doing, or how you were doing it. If you'd read the local telephone directory out loud, while suffering from a bad cold, they'd have gone for that just as much. For them, it was a glorified peep show. They were there for the same reason that people flock to the local Palais to see pop stars in the flesh. Without all the electronic gadgetry of a recording studio they're nothing, but the audience don't care if the live show is bloody awful. They've seen their heroes belting it out, right there in front of them.'

Maurice paused, hoping that Cramer would say something. If only he could tempt the man into a discussion they might get somewhere. But Cramer lay on his back, his glass resting negligently on his chest, staring at the ceiling. His face gave no indication that he was even listening. The bastard probably wasn't, Maurice thought.

'Well, that's O.K. up to a point,' Maurice ploughed on eventually. 'We'll get full houses, the theatre'll make money, and that's fine. But it's my job to think about rather more than that. I've got to be concerned with the play as a whole. Having seen it performed, and watched the audience, and listened to them, I'm more than ever convinced that I'm right. The play doesn't hold without that injection of humour from Stephen. Played dead seriously, as you're doing, the audience really wouldn't know what they were watching if they stopped and thought about it. Your name's enough for them, true, yes, but for the play, no. I'm not asking you to go for cheap laughs. God forbid. But if you could follow the intention of the script, instead of going against it, I'm positive the play would really come to life.' Cramer closed his eyes. Otherwise, not a muscle in his body showed any sign of movement. 'I'm not trying to lay down the law,' Maurice continued. There were beads of sweat on his top lip. 'I couldn't anyway, not with you, I know that. But will you at least consider what I've said? Just look at it again, with an open mind, and see if there isn't at least a little merit in my opinion, because I'm only thinking about what's best for the play.'

'Anything else?' Cramer enquired, his eyes still closed. It would take something of a super-optimist to take that as a positive reply, Maurice thought.

'Yes,' Maurice said. It would have been easier to say 'no', but in the end Maurice cared too much about his work to take the easy way out. Just the same, this was earning his money the hard way, with a vengeance. 'A lot of the raggedness came when you were paraphrasing, or missing out lines. I'm not talking about when you cut a page and Nicola took you back. That can happen to anyone. Nor am I saying the script can't be changed if we see any place where it can be improved, but I thought we'd agreed all the alterations you wanted during rehearsals. For the sake of the rest of the cast, as well as the play, I feel we should stick to the script, and that any further changes ought to be discussed first and then rehearsed in.' Maurice took a deep breath. 'On the other hand,' he said carefully, 'while

I doubt if a first night at Treganwy is a big event in your life, it may have been enough to show that you weren't quite word-perfect. You certainly seemed to be during the later rehearsals, but performing on stage is a different ball game. Besides, it's a long time since you've appeared in the live theatre, and learning a part is as much a matter of practice as application. If that's the problem, then of course I'll be only too glad to help in any way possible. All you have to do is name it. It might be a good idea, for instance, to hold some extra rehearsals for your scenes during the afternoons. Naturally, I'd make it clear that it was for the benefit of the others. I can give you as much time as you like, in any way you need. I'm entirely at your disposal. I'd like you to know that.'

Maurice wiped the drops of perspiration from his upper lip with his fingers.

'Is that the lot?' Cramer asked.

'Yes. That's it,' Maurice said, defeated.

Cramer opened his eyes, swung his legs off the sofa, put his glass down, got to his feet, and moved towards Maurice.

Maurice stood up and retreated instinctively. He had never seen anything like the cold mask which was Cramer's face. He expected to feel a bunched fist smashed into his face at any second. Cramer spoke. He did not raise his voice, but Maurice shook with fear of the man's potential, awful violence.

'You contemptible little nobody,' Cramer said, in flat, deadly tones. 'What makes you imagine, you failed no-hoper, that you can come in here and patronise me?'

'Honestly,' Maurice began, 'I wasn't trying to . . .'

'Shut up,' Cramer told him. 'You've had your boring, self-opinionated say. Now I'm going to tell you something. You're a talentless shit. You're not even a second-rater. No wonder the National got shot of you as fast as they could. You haven't an ounce of inventiveness or creativity in your empty head. Well, vanity and a puffed-up ego, my friend, are no substitute for ability. Yours isn't even zero. It's minus. You're not just a bad director. You're the most incompetent, the most time-wasting, the worst, I've ever come across. Take my advice. Find some other way to stay off the breadline. Your future in this profession is non-existent. I can predict that with absolute certainty.'

Cramer opened his dressing room door and gripped Maurice's shoulder. Maurice winced, and almost cried out. The man's fingers were a steel vice, crushing into his flesh.

A few feet away Marcia, Leonard, and Bernard Fyfield were receiving mail from the stage door-keeper.

'One last word,' Cramer said.

The little group looked towards him.

'You may have your own problems,' Cramer rasped, every syllable carrying clearly along the corridor. 'But they're not my concern. Just don't try and take it out on me because your woman's a whore.'

The second night was much like the first although Maurice was not there to see it, Professor Griffiths noted grimly. Where was the man? Maurice was in a bar, staring blankly at nothing in particular. Some time he would have to face his cast again, but he did not know how.

The reviews came in the following day. The *Treganwy Herald* was predictably obsequious in its praise. 'Treganwy Theatre celebrated its new season with another triumph . . . a resounding success for Professor Griffiths, and his devoted band . . . John Cramer electrified an appreciative audience . . . an elegant study from Marcia Hambridge . . . Bernard Fyfield was a powerful Willem . . . Nicola Feary touching . . . Leonard Sherwen's well-acted son . . . Maurice Gardiner's subtle direction . . .'

Something for everybody, which would all look good in the scrapbooks. The remaining reviews would not.

The county newspaper, which received most of its theatrical advertising revenue from another theatre, was more dubious.

'. . . although John Cramer delighted the audience . . . glaring faults in this scrappy production . . . hardly likely to be a credit to the respected Treganwy Festival once John Cramer has left the cast . . .'

That could be shrugged off. Everyone at the theatre knew that the county rag had it in for the Treganwy Festival because the editor believed he had once been slighted by Professor Griffiths.

But what Marcia had heard turned out to be partially correct. The *Guardian* had not been present, but two of the other nationals were. Both critics took the same amused, Olympian line.

'. . . held together, in so far as it was held together, only by a brilliant performance by John Cramer, who deserved better support . . .'

'. . . under rehearsed . . . flabbily directed . . . the man who worked hardest, apart from the admirable John Cramer, was off-stage – the prompter! . . .'

'. . . Nicola Feary appeared not to know what the first scene was about, although John Cramer persuaded us that he did . . .'

'. . . Bernard Fyfield confuses booming at the top of his voice with authority . . . contrasting oddly with the way John Cramer, demonstrating the magical ability of a truly great actor, brought depth and breadth and subtlety . . .'

'. . . Marcia Hambridge . . . unconvincing . . . playing a character not so much at her fingertips as beyond her reach . . . exercising a certain decent compassion, one might gently suggest that Miss Hambridge is miscast . . .'

'. . . Maurice Gardiner does not so much direct as abdicate . . .'

'. . . Leonard Sherwen, understandably surprised, perhaps, to find himself on the same stage as John Cramer . . . failed to make anything of what could have been an amusing exchange . . .'

'. . . a drab and humourless production, which only came to life by virtue of John Cramer's magnificent talent . . .'

'. . . a fiasco without John Cramer . . .'

'. . . John Cramer . . . moving . . . hypnotic presence . . . towering head and shoulders . . .'

'. . . John Cramer . . . a giant among pygmies . . .'

The reviews were of no interest to Cramer. What a couple of second string London critics thought of his fleeting excursion to Treganwy was of truly monumental unimportance in his life. This remote, parochial little place was a far cry from Sardi's after a Broadway first night, with everyone waiting into the small hours to find out whether Clive Barnes had given the play the kiss of life or the kiss of death.

The remainder of the cast, temporarily drawn together by being savaged to a greater or lesser degree, did their best to console each other. Audiences mattered, not reviews, and the audiences continued to love it. Who cared what the critics thought?

But they did care. They had offered themselves, stepped out into that dangerous cockpit, and done their best, given all of which they were each capable. They were wounded, and in no superficial way. The hurt was deep, festering inside. Moreover, everyone in the business would have read those reviews. Damaging comments on their ability could well be remembered the next time they were put up to some producer or director for a part.

Professor Griffiths received some bad news, and pressed Cramer to join him for a tête à tête lunch at The Hall so urgently that Cramer agreed. For this occasion, the Professor sacrificed one of his bottles of Mouton Rothschild, Premier Cru, and served a cherished bottle of Napoleon brandy with the coffee.

'I didn't hear from him, so I called John Aberson,' Professor Griffiths said. 'He's not interested.'

'Did you expect him to be?' Cramer asked. He drained his brandy glass. Professor Griffiths refilled it.

'I felt I had good reason to suppose that he might be,' the Professor said. 'I must confess, I'm disappointed. He didn't exactly turn me down flat. He said that, with you, he would of course gladly take the play into the West End.' Cramer laughed. 'I reminded him,' Professor Griffiths went on, 'that you were due to open on Broadway in *Last Rites for Beresford*, and I had no reason to assume such was still not the case.' He peered at Cramer hopefully. Things could change. There was always a chance, remote perhaps, but a chance.

'That's the position,' Cramer said.

'Should there be the slightest possibility that your plans might change,' Professor Griffiths said, 'Aberson would make a very substantial offer indeed.'

'*Beresford*'s tied in with the movie version,' Cramer said.

'Yes, quite,' the Professor said. He sighed wistfully. It had been a long shot, a million to one, but even Professor Griffiths was not above fantasising about the impossible. 'Failing that,' he said, 'Aberson would only consider it if we could show him a highly successful tour, with someone like Diana Rigg playing Marcia Hambridge's part.'

'Rigg wouldn't tour,' Cramer said.

'I know,' Professor Griffiths said. 'It's Catch-22. Would you like a cigar?'

'I gave them up when I cut out cigarettes,' Cramer said.

The Professor lit one for himself. He needed an aid to thought, as well as some degree of consolation. Cramer sipped his brandy. It was pleasant enough, but he really preferred whisky.

'I'll be frank,' Professor Griffiths said. 'The money you're pulling into the box office is more than welcome. I mean for the theatre, of course, which as you know is a non-profit-making trust. I have no personal interest. But after you've left us, I'm a little concerned, especially after those reviews. The Treganwy Trust has a share in the play, and if we could only exploit it, even if it never reaches the West End, a successful tour could generate much-needed funds for us. I would very much appreciate your advice.'

Cramer shrugged. 'All you can do is tour it, and hope for the best.'

'With a completely different cast,' Professor Griffiths suggested. 'Would you agree?'

'If you want to make money,' Cramer said. 'This lot's not going to pull in audiences. They remind me of the worst days of weekly rep.'

'Yes,' Professor Griffiths said. 'In fairness to myself, Im must say, they were not my choice. Maurice Gardiner persistently ignored my advice. I have to say that I find him extremely difficult. He's been a great disappointment. Not only obstinate and self-willed, but with a lack of respect which comes dangerously close to outright impertinence.'

'Get rid of him,' Cramer said.

'Yes. I had already come to the conclusion that it might be best if the play were re-directed by someone else when it goes on tour,' Professor Griffiths said.

'Now,' Cramer said. 'If you want to salvage the rest of the season. He's worse than useless.'

Professor Griffiths pulled on his cigar and studied the glowing end worriedly. 'He has a contract until the end of August,' he said.

'Pay him off,' Cramer said.

'I must take note of your professional judgement,' Professor Griffiths said. 'You've worked closely with him. You will have formed a very clear notion of his abilities as a director.'

'Which are nil,' Cramer said.

'The trouble is,' Professor Griffiths said, 'if I were to terminate his contract now, it would be rather expensive.'

'You asked for my advice,' Cramer said. 'That's it.'

Ben Stamford waited until the show was over and the theatre had ceased to resound to frenzied applause. He rattled Cramer's dressing room door and walked in.

'Feel like a noggin, John?' he asked. Drinking with Cramer was not exactly a habit, but the two men had sat in bars matching scotch for scotch several times, and Ben felt that the easy, inconsequential male talk signified, if not friendship, then something pretty close to it.

Ben knew, of course, about that awkward moment when Cramer had told Maurice that Anna was a whore. Everyone in the company knew within less than twenty-four hours and most, who had good reason to be loyal to

Maurice, thought it loutish and disagreeable, and had promptly adopted an anti-Cramer stance.

Ben Stamford, however, had his own motives for not joining the pack on this issue. Maurice, he argued to himself, might have asked for it, for all he or anyone else knew. Maurice could be pretty bitchy himself when he was in a bad mood.

'O.K.,' Cramer said. 'But back at my hotel, if you don't mind.'

Cramer had given up going into bars. Since the play opened autograph hunters had become a nuisance he had no wish to tolerate.

Leonard Sherwen was handing in his dressing room key as they came along the corridor.

'Any chance of a lift?' he asked.

'We're going to John's hotel for a nightcap,' Ben said.

'I'll join you for a quick one, if you don't mind,' Leonard said.

They went through the stage door, elbowed their way through the small crowd which still assembled nightly, broke into a trot, and made it to Cramer's car. Ben fancied that he caught a glimpse of large eyes gazing through long hair as the headlights snapped on and they drove off.

'Isn't that your blonde bird?' he asked.

'Quite likely,' Leonard said. 'I daren't look.' He shrank down in his seat.

'She can't be in the club already,' Ben protested.

'Oh, God . . .' Leonard said. 'Tell you about it later.'

There was a message at the hotel for Mr Cramer to telephone Miss Foster urgently. Cramer read it, threw it away indifferently, and took the others up to his suite.

They sat drinking scotch, warmed inside, warm for the time being in each other's company. Leonard Sherwen was explaining how fate had tripped him when he was not looking, yet again.

'I mean, hell's bells,' he said, 'she's as tall as I am, she's got all the right shapes in exactly the right places, she's a stunner, and she thought I was the best thing in the play. Sorry, John.'

'Feel free,' Cramer said amicably.

'All right, I admit it,' Leonard said. 'I was flattered. I thought, right, Sherwen, your luck's in. How the hell was I to know she was only just sixteen years old?'

'I trust this revelation came in the nick of time,' Ben said. 'Or had you already had your wicked way with her?'

'That's not all,' Leonard said glumly. 'It turns out that her father's a Methodist minister, and about as broad-minded as a knife edge.'

'One thing about you, Leonard, my boy,' Ben spluttered, 'you can always be relied upon to shed a little light of cheer into our dark days.'

'Pagliacci, let me remind you,' Leonard said, 'did not find life all that amusing.'

'What does Papa propose to do?' Ben asked. 'Publicly denounce you in chapel for fornication? Turn a blind eye while a few sturdy, outraged parishioners put the boot in one dark night? Or is it to be the fate worse than death – the shotgun wedding?'

'I wish you'd stop trying to be funny, and come up with a sensible suggestion,' Leonard said.

'Tell him you've got the clap,' Ben suggested.

The phone rang. Cramer reached out one hand and lifted the receiver. He listened for a moment.

'Can't it wait?' he asked, sipping his drink. '. . . yes, I am busy . . . oh, all right . . . hold on.'

He replaced the receiver, said 'Help yourselves, I shan't be long,' walked into the bedroom, closed the door, and lifted the bedside extension.

'Make it quick,' he said. 'I'm tired.'

'If I leave a message saying it's urgent, I mean it,' Valerie Foster's voice said tartly.

'Change the tone of voice, sweetheart,' Cramer said, 'or this conversation's coming to a sudden end. I'm still paying your salary, just remember that, please.'

'If you weren't, I wouldn't have phoned you,' Valerie said. 'I'm doing my job, that's all, and the sooner it's over the better. You can't hurt me any more, John.'

'Apart from a brief bout of self-pity,' Cramer said, 'do you have anything to say or not?'

'Two things,' Valerie said flatly. 'First, there's an interview which I think you should do. I had a call this afternoon from . . .'

'I've told you already,' Cramer cut in. 'I've done my duty by Treganwy and the great British public. No.'

'This man's a serious journalist,' Valerie said. 'He's not interested in Treganwy or your private life. What he wants to do is a feature on your return to the theatre, and your approach to the part of Beresford. He's a great admirer of yours, he carries weight in the USA, and I think it would be a useful preliminary. How John Cramer will bring greatness back to Broadway, that kind of thing. But it's up to you.'

'All right,' Cramer said with some reluctance. But she was right, and he knew it.

'I'll ring him back and give him the O.K.,' Valerie said. 'He'll want to do it within a day or two to meet his press date. The other thing is that Wendy's been on the phone to me several times.'

'Oh, for Christ's sake,' Cramer said.

'I was a bit surprised to be honest,' Valerie said. 'I'm not exactly her favourite female. But she seems to know that things are not as they were. I don't know if you've told her . . .'

'Of course I haven't,' Cramer said. 'It's nothing to do with her.'

'No, I didn't really think you would have done,' Valerie said drily. 'Her woman's instinct at work, I suppose. Anyway, it doesn't matter. But she assumes that since I'm not with you someone else must be, and she may be right for all I know. She kept asking me who it was . . .'

'God almighty,' Cramer said. 'Can't she understand that I just want to be on my own?'

'She seems pretty screwed up,' Valerie said. 'She says that you call the children, but you won't talk to her.'

'I became sick and tired of trying to explain why I didn't want her here,' Cramer said.

'Well, she assumes that's because you've got some new

bed mate,' Valerie said. 'Which after all, knowing you, isn't really a terribly unreasonable assumption. So she said, would I please have a word with you. . . .'

'Bloody marvellous,' Cramer said. 'Wife begs ex-mistress to intercede on her behalf. She should write a book. It'd be a best-seller.'

'She sounds in a bit of a state,' Valerie said. 'She was crying down the phone at one point. I think she'd been drinking. I don't mean that she was drunk, she wasn't, but. . . .'

'No, she's just having a wonderful time,' Cramer said. 'Playing out her own little drama to you, since I decline to act as her audience.'

'All she wants is to come over for a few days,' Valerie said. 'It's not much to ask. Why won't you let her?'

'Because I don't want her here,' Cramer said. 'God damn it, that's not an insult to her. I don't want anyone here.'

'I don't really know why she's making such a fuss about it,' Valerie admitted. 'She's perfectly capable of catching a plane. If it was me, I'd simply turn up.'

'That shows she knows me better than you do,' Cramer said grimly. 'When I say no, I mean no. She knows that. If she chose to arrive, uninvited, that would be it. Finish.'

'Well, I promised I'd talk to you and call her back,' Valerie said. 'God knows why I should, except that she was so miserable and unhappy I felt sorry for her.'

'She enjoys it,' Cramer said. 'It gives her a kick.'

'If I were your wife and you talked like that about me,' Valerie said, 'I'd kill you.'

'Fortunately for both of us, you never will be,' Cramer said.

'Well, I've tried,' Valerie said. 'It wouldn't cost you much to give her a bit of reassurance. Why not bring her over for a couple of days? Or at least give her a call, and talk to her nicely, or send her some roses or something.'

'She can have all that when I've finished here,' Cramer said. 'In the meantime, there isn't the space in my head for her, or you, or anyone else. You'd think the silly bitch was talking about years, for Christ's sake. We shan't have been apart for more than two months, start to finish. Tell her to keep off my back.'

'Good night,' Valerie Foster said.

Cramer hung up and returned to the living room. Ben and Leonard were talking about the prospects of work after the Treganwy Festival was over and agreeing that they would both probably be on the dole, unless the much-touted tour really did materialise.

Cramer's mood had utterly changed. The blackness had invaded him, as it sometimes did, as instantly as the flick of a switch darkened a room. Neither of the other two men noticed any change in him.

'Talking of the future,' Ben Stamford said, 'I happened to notice my screenplay lying on your desk. I don't suppose you've had time to read it yet, though.'

'Last night,' Cramer said. He poured whisky into his glass. 'I didn't feel sleepy. It was something to read.'

'And it sent you to bye-byes in no time flat, eh?' Ben supposed cheerfully.

'No. I finished it,' Cramer said. 'Read every word.'

'Really? You mean it might have something?' Ben's eyes were alive with hope and excitement.

'I couldn't put it down,' Cramer said.

'Oh, come on,' Ben said. 'You're having me on.'

'I'm perfectly serious,' Cramer said. 'The first ten pages were so genuinely awful I couldn't believe that anyone could write anything so uniformly abysmal. I thought that it must improve as it went along.' He downed a mouthful of whisky. 'It didn't,' he said.

Ben swallowed unhappily. 'Well, of course, it is only a first draft,' he said pleadingly. 'It's my first shot at a film script. I knew there'd be a lot to do to it.'

'There's only one thing you can do to that,' Cramer said. 'Forget it. I don't know if you can act, but you certainly can't write. It's rubbish. Pure crap from beginning to end.'

'Well, that's straight from the shoulder, anyway,' Ben

said. He was wearing a fixed smile on his face which did not belong there.

'You asked for my opinion,' Cramer said. 'And what you've written is shit. If the novel's ten times as good as that, I can't understand why anyone should be idiot enough to publish it. I have never, ever, read anything so bad, and I've seen some appalling stuff in my time. There's no insight, no style, no idea of construction, no tension, nothing.'

'But apart from that, you think it's pretty good,' Ben said, like a battered fighter, smashed and bleeding against the ropes, pushing out a feeble, ineffectual left.

'It's nicely bound,' Cramer said, 'which was a waste of money. That script is the kind of crap that makes afternoon soap opera look like Shakespeare.'

Ben Stamford stood up, blinking. 'Excuse me,' he said vaguely. He cleared his throat. 'Nature calls.'

He wandered off to the bathroom. The door clicked shut and remained closed for what seemed a long time.

Leonard Sherwen said, 'Ben's pinning everything on that script.'

'Then he's a fool,' Cramer said contemptuously.

'You didn't have to say things like that,' Leonard said angrily. 'You could have let him down lightly. You're not God Almighty sitting in judgement on someone's sins. He wrote a script, that's all, and even if you didn't think it was very good that's no reason to tear it to pieces, especially in front of me.'

'He had it coming to him,' Cramer said. 'Do you think I don't know why he asked me to read it? Inside his silly head he was hoping not only that I'd think it was good but that I'd pass it on to a director, promote it for him. Well, it's not good. My five-year-old son can write better than that. Like most people, Ben hasn't got the guts to face the truth. The fact is that he's completely untalented. If he can't take that, bad luck.'

'You're a real brave man with people who can't fight back, aren't you,' Leonard said. 'Bernard Fyfield, Maurice, now Ben. . . .'

'If little people want comfort, let them drivel to someone else,' Cramer said. 'We all live in the same world, we all have the same chances. The pretensions of nobodies bore the arse off me. Why they imagine they deserve some special dispensation I've never understood.'

'I don't follow you at all,' Leonard said. 'Half the evening as nice as pie, and suddenly. . . .' He snapped his fingers. '. . . for no reason, you have to hurt somebody more vulnerable than you are. What's the truth about you, I wonder? I'm beginning to think there's something wrong with you. You act like a schizo.'

Cramer laughed. 'Coming from someone who likes to grope schoolgirls, that's pretty good,' he said.

The bathroom door opened. There was the sound of water flushing. Ben came back. The smile was attached to his face again. He picked up his script.

'Well,' he said, 'it's getting pretty late, so I think I'll remove this load of old rubbish, say thank you for the scotch, and bid you good night.'

Ben and Leonard walked along the corridor. Leonard pressed the button and they waited for the lift. Ben was holding his script tucked neatly under his arm. His artificial smile had gone. He watched the indicator lights fixedly, as though it were important to memorise the illuminated numbers as the lift rose towards their floor.

'I think there's a touch of insanity about that man,' Leonard said.

'Naturally,' Ben said. 'Anyone who doesn't like my script has got to be raving mad.'

'I mean it,' Leonard said.

The lift arrived and they stepped inside.

# CHAPTER TEN

Harry Belmont was cooking a chop when the telephone began to ring. He turned the grill down and walked into the living room. He knew who it would be. His mother possessed some perverse instinct which prompted her to telephone him, with unerring accuracy, whenever he was in the middle of doing something.

'Hullo,' he said into the receiver.

'Just a "quickie",' Nicola's voice said. 'They'll be calling the half any minute. How are you?'

'Fine,' Harry said. 'And you?' He was so astounded that he could only reproduce the automatic, meaningless words.

'Oh, fine,' Nicola said. 'Listen, I don't know if you want to see the play or not, and in any case we're pretty well booked solid, but I've managed to wheedle one ticket from the box office for next Monday, and I've put it in the post.'

'I'll be working,' Harry said. It was all he could think of to say.

'Well, I didn't know if you might be able to take a couple of days off,' Nicola said. 'Anyway, I thought I'd let you know, just in case. If you can make it, I'll see you then, and if not . . . there's the half. Must go. 'Bye.'

''Bye Nicola,' Harry said, and hung up. He stood staring at the telephone, hardly able to believe that it had actually happened, the sick anger rising, bringing bile to his throat, too late to formulate into words, to tell her what he thought of her.

The bitch. The hypocritical bitch. Telephoning him out of the blue as though nothing had happened, when he had seen her writhing in the passionate preliminaries with which he was so familiar, while he watched, frozen to the spot, until she had remembered, risen from the bed, and drawn the curtains.

He went back into the kitchen, turned up the grill, and stared at the chop as the juice dripped and sizzled, and the meat turned brown, and finally black.

How could she do such a thing? Where did she find the gall to invite him to come and see the play, when she would be on stage with *him,* the one whom he had stood and watched as. . . .

Without taking his eyes from the spitting grill tray, he groped in his pocket for a cigarette and lit it. It was true, of course, that Nicola did not know he had been there. It was also true that it was all over between them, that she did not owe him her loyalty any more, and that she was free to do whatever she liked. And after all, he had himself found temporary pleasure in similar activities with someone else.

Yes, but all that was rational, and sweet reason had nothing to do with it. Nicola had not been forced to watch him at it. And now to behave as though nothing had changed, that was the ultimate cruelty.

Yes, but just a minute, some part of him tried to intervene. She didn't force you to watch. If you'd driven away as soon as they arrived you'd never have known. But I had to find out, another part of him cried out in anguish, I had to know.

Well, that's your look out, the first part said. It's nothing to do with her. She had said, 'Please don't let us be bad friends.' She's just being nice, that's all.

Nice! After doing that!

Harry suddenly noticed that the chop was now in flames. He turned the grill off and dumped the disgusting object in the sink,

Later that evening, when he had cooled down a bit, it crossed his mind that there might be something more behind Nicola's invitation.

She was not exactly a scheming girl: in fact in most ways she was more honest than anyone else he had ever known. But whether consciously or not, there was nearly always some very good motive for everything Nicola did.

He wondered if something had happened after he had driven away that night which he did not know about. If, although he could not imagine why it should, it had all gone wrong with Cramer, in which case her phone call might be more than it seemed. If Nicola was feeling down, and wanted something, for example the comfort of his company for a couple of days, Nicola would do something about it. Like first putting a ticket in the post for next Monday and then casually telephoning him.

Harry Belmont pondered that one thoughtfully for quite a long time. He had not used up all his leave entitlement and there would be no problem about taking Monday and Tuesday off. With nothing much else to do, he had been working extra hard of late and was quite the blue-eyed boy at the bank just now.

He was tempted. He imagined, with pleasure, the words he would use, the most hurtful and vindictive he could think of, the pain on her face, until she burst into tears and begged him to forgive her. And then he would walk out on *her* this time. For good. She deserved it.

Sweet reason? Sod sweet reason. After what she had done to him, he loathed her.

Nicola was pottering about in her dressing gown and a pair of fluffy slippers when there was a sharp knock on the front door. She opened the door, mildly annoyed at having her pleasant solitude disturbed, and stared, taken aback.

'Good morning,' Cramer said. He was wearing a flat cap, and a short tweed overcoat over a brown roll-neck sweater and fawn trousers. He walked in. 'You look surprisingly good with no make-up on.'

'Thank you very much,' Nicola said. 'Come in.' She closed the door with a bang.

'Do you have any plans for today?' Cramer asked.

'Yes,' Nicola said. 'I'm going to get dressed, walk into Treganwy, buy the Sunday papers, since they don't deliver them out here, walk back, and do nothing except flop around and read them.'

'Let's go and take a look at Snowdon instead,' Cramer suggested. 'You can buy the papers on the way.'

'Why?' Nicola enquired. 'Do you fancy a spot of rape on top of a mountain?'

Cramer eyed her. 'Not especially,' he said. 'Given the choice, I prefer a warm bed.'

'You don't have a choice,' Nicola said. 'I thought I'd already made myself clear, but in case I haven't, I was a bit pissed after the first night and I got carried away. As it happens, I find the exploits of sexual athletes about as monotonous as marathon runners. They bore me. Especially when they play the caveman as well.'

'You loved it,' Cramer stated.

'My body experienced an orgasm,' Nicola said. 'I can give myself one of those, if I want one, thank you very much. O.K., I've been screwed by John Cramer. Big deal. Give me a signed certificate and I'll hang it on the wall.'

Unexpectedly, Cramer laughed out loud with genuine amusement.

'Nicola,' he said, 'you're the only one in this God-forsaken dump who's worth anything. All right. Let's start again. I don't feel like being on my own all through an interminable Welsh Sunday. Put some warm clothes on, and sensible shoes, and we'll go up Snowdon. You keep saying that's what you want to do. O.K., let's do it. When we get back I'll drop you off, and that's it. Word of honour. Have we got a deal?'

'You really are the most unpredictable bastard,' Nicola said.

Cramer took a circuitous route which amounted to a leisurely dawdle along the minor roads which wound vaguely towards Snowdon. His manner was relaxed and easy, and Nicola thought that, when he was himself, he could be a very pleasant companion. Or perhaps this was not the 'real' Cramer, perhaps that was one of the others she had seen, but it did not matter. Slowly she relaxed too and began to enjoy herself.

They had the roads more or less to themselves.

Although it was nearly May the thin sunshine was fitful, there was a chill in the air, and lowering clouds darkened the sky to the west. It was not a Sunday which would tempt day-trippers into their cars.

She was not surprised when Cramer pulled up in Conwy and suggested a drink before their assault on Snowdon but she wondered if he wanted to risk being recognised.

'I'll give you ten to one no one takes a blind bit of notice,' Cramer said.

And he was right. Film stars did not drive around in Cortinas, soberly dressed like Liverpool business men who had misjudged the weather, and wander into quiet, unobtrusive hotels. It was not the behaviour which was expected of them, and he did not attract a second glance.

Nicola went to the porter's desk and bought her Sunday papers while Cramer bought drinks, and arranged for future supplies.

'My God,' Cramer said, when she came back and joined him at the table. 'You don't read all of them, do you?'

'Yes,' Nicola said. 'I develop withdrawal symptoms if I don't.'

Nicola sipped her glass of white wine while she skimmed through the tabloids and temporarily discarded them.

'You must be a speed reader,' Cramer said.

'At this stage, I'm only looking for dirt, or gossip about people I know,' Nicola said. 'I'll go back to them later.'

She accepted a second glass of white wine, but declined a third. Cramer sipped his large scotch on his own.

'Don't you ever worry about being breathalysed?' Nicola asked.

'No,' Cramer said.

'Because you can always admit who you are,' Nicola guessed, 'and they start calling you "sir", and asking for autographs.'

Cramer grinned. 'That worked when I was pulled up for speeding near Malibu once,' he said. 'Anyway, don't worry. No one's going to stop us.'

'I'm not worried,' Nicola said. 'It's not my licence.'

She decided that the heavy Sunday papers could wait. They began to chat idly about the remainder of the Treganwy Festival, and Cramer asked about her future plans with apparently genuine interest. It was quiet and warm and comfortable, and the time slid by, almost unnoticed. Nicola did not comment again when Cramer signalled from time to time to have his glass replenished. It was none of her business, and anyway the man might as well have been drinking coloured water. The talk meandered towards the rest of the cast, about whom Cramer was biting. Nicola did her best to defend them but there was no antagonism in the conversation. Cramer's manner was light and amused. They were like two good friends gossiping about mutual acquaintances.

'Come on,' Cramer said. 'Marcia's acting away like crazy, trying to be the leading lady, when she ought to be settling for character parts. Bernard's style went out with Wolfit, and all he's really concerned about is seducing young Alan. Leonard's not really bad, but you could replace him with any one of a hundred young actors and no one would notice the difference. Ben's knocking middle age, knows in his bones he'll never make it as an actor, desperately day-dreaming about making money as a writer, which he won't, because he's useless. And Maurice is a neurotic phoney, frantic to achieve a big reputation so that his model girlfriend will give him some respect, which she never will. He always gets found out. He's on his way down, running out of people who'll employ him. They're all pathetic in their different ways. If you've nothing else to do you can feel sorry for them, if you like, but I haven't the time to waste on people like that.'

There was a degree of truth wrapped up in these sweeping generalisations, Nicola recognised, but she did not believe that it was the whole truth.

'You're being too facile,' she argued. 'Contemptuous cartoon sketches like that, they're just slick – bitchy cocktail party stuff. You can't write off human beings in one sentence each, boom boom, just like that. Someone who's written the kind of books you have should be able to see deeper. And you're completely wrong about Maurice. One day he'll get the recognition he deserves. Yes, he's screwed up about Anna, but perhaps that's all a part of his talent. Anyway, who the hell isn't screwed up about something? I think he's the best director I've ever worked for.'

Cramer said, 'I suspect you only believe he's the best because he thinks you're a good actress. And that's the only opinion of his which I agree with. You are.'

Nicola looked at him across the table. 'Do you mean that?' she asked. 'Or are you just saying it to be polite?'

'I never say things I don't mean,' Cramer said. He smiled faintly. 'Least of all to be polite. Anyone who knows the business can see how you stand out from the rest of them. You're not just a good actress. You have your own unique quality, a personal style of your own, which is truthful and real.'

'High praise indeed,' Nicola said. She liked praise, she needed praise, she knew of no actor who did not. On the other hand she usually treated it with some private reserve, testing its quality against the circumstances, glad to hear 'marvellous' after a first night but not taking it at face value. But there was no reason why this man should not say exactly what he thought. A lot of the anguish which others had suffered in the last few weeks had come about because he did exactly that. And if Cramer, who had played opposite the best in the world, found her a good actress with a unique quality . . . her heart lifted. She glowed with happiness. 'So you think I'll make it then,' she said.

'It depends what you mean by "make it",' Cramer said.

'The name in lights, parts in films, all that,' Nicola said.

'No,' Cramer said. 'I don't. Sorry.'

Nicola stared at him. Somewhere inside she was suddenly numb. There was an unusual expression on his face, something akin to gentleness and regret, a look she had not seen before. He finished his whisky and gestured apologetically.

'You've asked me,' he said. 'I told you.'

'Why not?' Nicola asked. 'Is there a reason?'

'Because you won't is the main reason,' Cramer said. 'Simple but true I'm afraid. Olivier once said something like "Star acting is really a question of hypnosis, of yourself, and the audience." Personally I think that begs a few questions, but it'll do to be going on with. You haven't got it, whatever it is. As an actress you're a damn sight better than the lady who'll probably be playing opposite me in *Last Rites for Beresford,* whose name I'd better not mention. But what Olivier called hypnosis, and some people call magnetism, the ability to induce a trance-like state when the audience not only think you're great at the time, but also afterwards, whenever they see your name, a kind of imposed conditioned reflex, she's got that. You haven't. You'll do good work, and people will say "great", but somehow your name won't occur to them the next time they're casting. They'll think of someone else. Someone not as good as you, but someone they've remembered. It's unjust, and it's cruel, and I can't really tell you why it is. I can only tell you that it is so. I've known one or two others just like you, and they should be household names, and they should be playing the great roles, but they're not and they never will. Nor will you.'

'Well, that's it then,' Nicola said.

'If it hurts, I'm sorry,' Cramer said, 'and I don't often say I'm sorry about anything. But it's the truth. Whether you want the truth is another matter. That's up to you.'

'Let's go, shall we,' Nicola said.

Yes, of course it hurt. It hurt where she was most vulnerable. Her talent was all she had. Given time she would recover, as she always had done in the past, although the process was becoming slower as the years went by.

The trouble was that Cramer's prediction of her future bore an uncannily accurate resemblance to her past. At the National she had done good work in supporting roles, but despite the fleeting compliments she had never been offered a lead. *Darien Point* had been a *succès d'estime,* repeated several times in the UK, shown all over the world. And her Sonia had been good. No, it had been an outstanding performance, she knew it, down to every tingling nerve end in her body. And what she got out of that? Nothing. Not a single bloody thing.

The weather had changed dramatically for the worse. By the time they reached the Pass of Llanberis banks of thick mist were descending gloomily.

'I think we'd better give it a miss,' Cramer said.

'Not now I'm here,' Nicola said obstinately. 'Anyway, it may clear up.'

Automatically she picked up a couple of the papers she had not yet glanced at. The Swiss steam locomotive seemed like an overgrown toy, with its odd-looking rack and pinion drive, as it propelled its single coach. Cramer and Nicola were almost the only occupants. The little mountain train had scarcely begun its long, slow climb to the three and a half thousand feet summit when thick mist blanketed the coach.

'We shan't be able to see a damn thing,' Cramer said edgily.

'At least I can say I've been to the top,' Nicola said.

It took nearly an hour. The peak of Snowdon was in dense cloud. They could have been anywhere. There was no indication that they were on the summit of a mountain. More people were waiting to get on the little train than got off.

Inside the small café it was at least warm. Nicola was shivering, despite her leather coat.

Cramer left her to buy coffee, and went to the Men's. He felt bad. As bad as he had first thing in the morning when the day yawned, intolerably empty, before him. He had thought that, with Nicola, he could stave it off, but soon after they left Conwy he knew that it was coming back. His edginess had had nothing to do with Nicola's silence. He had dismissed the conversation in the hotel. It was not important. No, it was because he had to be alone for a few minutes, and her insistence on riding up the mountain had meant that the moment was postponed for what seemed an eternity.

A young man wearing an anorak was standing at the urinal. Cramer banged into a WC, locked the door, and took out his flask. He unscrewed the top, took a deep swallow, and breathed out, a long slow breath. He leaned back against the door. Soggy lavatory paper littered the floor in pools of water. Cramer lifted the flask to his lips again.

When he returned to the café he stumbled against a chair as he crossed towards the table, but Nicola did not notice. She was engrossed in one of the newspapers. Two cups of coffee stood on the table. Cramer sat down. He did not want coffee.

'There's no point in staying here,' he said. 'Finish your coffee and we'll go.'

Nicola did not lift her head, or give any sign that she had heard him.

'I said let's go,' Cramer rasped. The flask was now three-quarters empty. He wanted to get back to the car, where there was a bottle.

Nicola looked at him. Her face was pale. Her large eyes glittered. She spoke as if she could hardly contain herself.

'You miserable creep,' she said.

'What the hell's the matter with you?' Cramer growled.

'Oh, fuck off,' Nicola said. She held up the newspaper. 'Great actor,' she said. 'Great liar more like it.'

She got up and walked out. Cramer shook his head, and looked at the page she had been reading. The words blurred for a few seconds. Then they cleared.

He had forgotten that it was today the feature would be appearing. Come to that, he had more than half forgotten what he had said to the intense journalist, with the air of a quiet academic, who had probed so disturbingly without realising how close he was to a fatal insight.

Cramer's eye ran down the page swiftly. At the top a large photograph of himself, which Valerie Foster would have provided. The thick, black headline, 'A Great Actor Returns to the Theatre.' It began to come back to him.

The journalist had done his homework meticulously, which included taking the trouble to see the play at Treganwy before interviewing Cramer. He had been equally unmoved by the audience's reaction and the critics' lavishly bestowed admiration.

Certain questions, he had said, in a deceptively tentative manner, had formed in his mind. Stephen had not seemed to be an unduly demanding role, and yet, how could he put it, despite the hypnotic bravura one always expected from Cramer, there did seem to be a trace of uncertainty here and there. Almost as if – he had smiled apologetically – Cramer himself found it an exhausting ordeal after his long sojourn in films. And *Last Rites for Beresford*, if not a great play, did by general consent contain one of the great male leads of the last few decades, one of the most taxing roles of the modern theatre. One which demanded a sustained intensity, a command of the stage, such as, of course, Cramer himself had shown in his days at Stratford . . .

Cramer had then, for that journalist, played one of the great scenes of his life. Metaphorically cornered, fighting with his back to the wall, he had sat, calm and relaxed, cool and casual, his voice warm with regret as he had explained.

The direct quotes were there in the feature, accurately reported for once. There were a multitude of reasons, each one delicately inching that journalist away from the conclusion which he was within an ace of drawing.

'. . . I was assured that the script I read was merely a draft, and a great deal of work would be done . . . when I arrived at Treganwy, I found that nothing had been done . . . much too little rehearsal time . . . did my best to make the necessary changes . . . the director and myself not on the same wavelength, I'm afraid . . . had agreed to play a supporting role at Treganwy in good faith . . . found myself trying to carry the play in difficult circumstances . . . with all respect to the remainder of the cast, who were no doubt doing their best . . . the art of acting lies in giving and receiving . . . from the beginning of the first scene, I did not seem to be receiving what I had hoped for . . . one cannot act with conviction in a vacuum . . . I would have to admit that in retrospect, agreeing to appear at Treganwy was a mistake . . . can only say . . . had no personal knowledge of the cast . . . accepted the director's word that, if not especially well known, they were at least competent . . . no blame attached to anyone but myself . . . I should have made certain . . . insisted on auditioning the remaining players first, and choosing them myself . . .'

Cramer put the crumpled page down. His eyes had skipped to the last paragraph and confirmed that it had worked, as he had expected. The journalist had been diverted and won over. He ended with words to the effect that even a great actor like John Cramer shone brightest with a strong supporting cast, and *Last Rites for Beresford*, which would give him that, would no doubt adorn Broadway, giving a new generation which had never seen John Cramer on the stage the chance to witness for themselves that great actor's explosive power.

Cramer stood up and went outside into the chill, dim cloud. He supposed that some of the words he had been obliged to use must have annoyed Nicola. She had no idea of the sheer necessities which faced someone in his position. How could she? Living as she did in a world which was an unimportant little cocoon.

The mountain train was returning, emerging through the gloom on the final stages of its steep ascent again, but Nicola was not there waiting for it. He looked around, puzzled, and then realised that she must have started down the path by means of which it was possible to walk, in looping turns, down the side of the mountain. That was a crazy thing to do in this weather.

He started walking down the path himself, unable to see more than a few yards ahead.

He began to call 'Nicola! Nicola!' There was no reply. From above and to one side, he heard the little train start on its downward journey. Damn the girl. He broke into a trot, down the winding path, a few trees and bushes looming through the dingy whiteness, but found that he was reeling and losing his balance. The path was safe enough for walkers in good weather, but it was no macadamed road. Besides . . . He slowed down, and his head stopped spinning. His eyes did not seem to be focusing properly. Perhaps that was due to the all-embracing cloud in which he was enveloped. He tried to remember how much he had had to drink since he got up that morning, beginning when he emerged from the shower, and could not.

Sour anger with Nicola began to bubble inside him. She could hardly be running all this time, but she must have been striding out with those long legs of hers like a woman possessed.

It was impossible to locate his position on the mountainside, but he must have come some distance down by now. It would be a long climb back up to the train. To hell with her. Let her break her bloody neck if she wanted to.

He stopped, and was about to turn back up the steep path when he fancied he heard something below. He peered down through the gloom. There seemed to be a shape moving there.

Again he broke into a trot. The shape grew nearer. When he was within a few yards, it materialised into the figure of a woman.

'Nicola,' he bellowed. But she did not pause or hesitate, much less stop.

Angered still further, he caught up with her and gripped her arm.

'Let go of me,' Nicola said, trying to wrench her arm free. In vain. He was many times stronger than she.

'You stupid bitch. It'll take half an hour to climb back up again.'

'Then go,' Nicola said. 'And leave me alone.'

'I will,' Cramer said. 'As soon as you stop behaving like an hysterical schoolgirl.'

Nicola stopped struggling. 'I'm not hysterical,' she said calmly. Cramer released her arm.

'Right then, come on,' he said. 'Let's get off this bloody mountain.'

'You make me sick,' Nicola said. 'You think you've conned everybody, but you haven't, not quite, *dear*.' The word was not used affectionately. It was loaded with contempt. Cramer winced. No one had spoken to him like that for as long as he could remember and, in an instant, he hated her.

'That's enough,' he said dangerously.

'The critics, yes. They came to see the Emperor's

wonderful clothes, and that's what they saw. They couldn't believe you were naked. Well, that's the way critics are,' Nicola said. 'They feed off other people's talents, they run with the pack, and the leaders of the pack haven't yet turned on you. So far, they haven't caught on.'

'Damn the critics,' Cramer said belligerently. He had been about to add something else, but he found that it had gone from his mind. He screwed up his eyes. Nicola's form seemed to be swaying in the still-thickening mist.

'They didn't know why you came to Treganwy, and nor did I at first. But now I do,' Nicola said. She gazed at the unsteady Cramer. Her voice was as level and controlled as that of a judge passing sentence. Only the tautness around her mouth betrayed her anger. 'You'd agreed to do *Beresford* on Broadway, and then you got shit-scared. You weren't sure if you could do it any more. Treganwy was a dummy run. You wanted to prove to yourself that you could. Well, that hasn't worked, has it? You know now that you can't.'

'Shut up, damn you,' Cramer muttered. His hands were clenched tight.

'It's fifteen years since you had to learn a part,' Nicola said in a detached, analytical fashion. 'You've made too many films. Just a few words at a time for each take, which you could do a dozen times anyway. You can't commit a part to memory any more. In rehearsal, where it doesn't matter, yes, but on stage, when the heat's on, you go to pieces, even at Treganwy. You take a few drinks to steady yourself and that only makes it worse. You top up in your dressing room every time you go off-stage. I could always tell, from that kiss in the last act, the whisky on your breath. Oh, sure, you'd always cleaned your teeth every time, but by then nothing could mask it. I got toothpaste and booze in my face while you were trying to remember what the hell the next line was – and then you tell the papers that you had to carry us! You? No, *dear*. Marcia's better on stage than you are, now. Stick to films, John Cramer. Be a big star there, where you can get away with it. If you try and play Beresford in New York they'll tear you to pieces. Read your scrapbooks about what a great Hamlet you were, because that's all over. As a stage actor, you're finished. You're just a piss-artist who can't remember his lines, and there are few things more pathetic than that.'

Cramer's brain was not functioning properly. It had slowed down. It refused to bring the right words to his lips. But he could hear, and what she was saying was unbearable, the ultimate obscenity, which he could not listen to.

He moved towards her, his hand raised, his face contorted.

'You bitch,' he screamed. 'You bitch!'

Nicola flinched, instinctively took a step backwards, and cried out once. Then there was silence.

Cramer blinked stupidly. There was no Nicola in front of him. She had vanished. Slowly he lowered his arm. Perhaps he would not, in fact, have hit her, back-handed, across the face. He would never know.

He moved to the edge of the path and stared down. He could see nothing except the gently swirling cloud.

'Nicola!' he called. 'Nicola!'

It was like shouting into cotton wool. His voice was not carrying.

He had no idea how deep the drop was below; it could be ten feet, it could be a hundred. He could not tell.

He moved to a point where he could see the single branch of a tree groping upwards through the mist, slid over the edge, lunged at the branch, missed and fell.

Cramer sat up. His chest was bruised. It hurt when he breathed. He pulled himself to his feet. He seemed to have rolled over and over on his way down, but he did not know how far he had fallen. He scrambled about on the steeply shelving mountainside, calling 'Nicola!' over and over again, but there was no answer.

Able to see little more than ten or twelve feet, he lost his bearings. He was no longer sure if he was moving towards the point where Nicola had fallen or away from it. Once off the path the ground was wet and sticky, and he slid further down, finding it hard to keep his feet.

There was the sound of water, and he came across a

small mountain stream bubbling and rushing busily on its swift descent.

He turned back, confused, and tried to pull his senses together. This was useless. He was achieving nothing. Also, he was now hopelessly lost himself. Apprehension gripped him in the dirty white cotton wool silence, and as it grew he tried to control it, to steady it at mere fear, and not tip over the edge into panic.

Snowdon was a mountain of several facets. You could ride up and down it in the train. The path provided a safe, and relatively easy, if stiff, walk. But away from that path it was yet a mountain where skilled climbers could come to grief in the wrong conditions. Cramer's shoes, if stout, were not climbing boots, and would be dangerous indeed if he stumbled across some sheer face – and Cramer did not know where he was. The only sensible course was, somehow, to find that path again.

Cramer had no idea how long it was before, with a leap of relief close to joy, he came across the path. He stood upright for the first time in what seemed like hours, took out his flask, and drained it thankfully. Half running, half walking, he made his way down the safe, clearly marked path. He met no one. By the time he regained his car he was close to exhaustion.

The mist had drifted even lower, now embracing his car as well. A thin, cold drizzle was falling. There were no other cars in sight. The few others who had braved it had long since given up and gone home.

Cramer opened the boot and took out a weekend bag. Long ago, a millennium, that morning, he had packed the bag before driving to Nicola's cottage. He had done so in case they decided to stay at some hotel for the night rather than return to her cottage. The casual act belonged to another man whom he could hardly remember. But inside the bag was an emergency bottle.

He climbed into the car, started the engine, turned the heater up to maximum, and drank deeply while the car became warmer.

It occurred to him that his appearance was dishevelled. For some reason, that seemed important. He got out of the car and used a clothes brush from the overnight bag. Soon his overcoat and trousers were free of leaves. He wiped the mud from his shoes with a handkerchief which he afterwards threw away. He remembered his cap, which he had folded and stuffed into his overcoat pocket. He put it on. Somehow it changed his appearance considerably. With that cap on, few people would recognise him as John Cramer.

Cramer got back in and drove away. He regained the road and turned at random, not knowing where he was going. Peering through the windscreen intensely, he followed the verge. It was like driving in fog. He had just enough self-perception left to realise that a considerable proportion of that fog was inside his own head.

Vaguely, he had intended to find a telephone box. He did not see one, or did not perceive one through the inner and outer fog, and a different worry overtook him. His hands felt loose and numb on the steering wheel. The car was weaving, occasionally bumping against the verge; there was no doubt now, even in his mind, that he should not be driving at all.

Supppose he did telephone, and someone came? He did not know where Nicola had fallen, or how long ago. They would ask, and he would not be able to tell them. He would be obliged to identify himself. And he was pissed, he knew that, pissed out of his mind, worse than he could ever remember. It would be news. A story. And it would look bad. The last kind of news he needed at any time, let alone now.

It was all too complicated. But he must do something – he could not simply leave Nicola there where she had fallen. She could be hurt. It suddenly crossed his drink-slowed mind that she could be dead. Oh, Christ . . . oh, God, help me . . .

A sign at the side of the road announced an AA/RAC-approved hotel two hundred yards ahead. It was set back from the road and he almost missed it, but he wrenched the steering wheel at the last moment, stabbed at the brakes, and came to a stop in the nearly empty car park.

Cramer switched the engine off. He returned the bottle

to the weekend bag and climbed out. The air outside struck cold, making him shiver momentarily. He used every ounce of concentration he possessed to see him through the short walk into the hotel, the brief, monosyllabic conversation with the receptionist.

He registered as J. Cramer, but the girl did not look at him twice. The middle-aged, haggard, weary-looking man in front of her bore no resemblance to any film star.

In his room Cramer placed a phone call to Miss Valerie Foster at the River Park Hotel, London. When he was connected she sounded tense and angry.

'Where the devil have you been? I've been trying to reach you all day.'

'Never mind that,' Cramer said, his voice slurring. 'You've got to do something for me.'

There was a pause at the other end. Then Valerie said, gently, 'What's happened, John?'

Cramer told her, missing out bits, repeating himself, but she rapidly grasped what he was saying.

'. . . I can't report it,' Cramer ended. 'It looks bad. You'll have to think of something . . . some way . . .'

'Yes, all right,' Valerie said. 'Stay where you are, and I'll be with you as soon as I possibly can.'

'What do you mean?' Cramer queried, confused. 'She's got to be found . . . you can handle it from there . . . phone now . . . or . . .'

'No, I can't, John,' Valerie said. 'There could be problems. It's worse than you think. Try and get some rest, and don't have any more to drink. Do you hear me?'

Cramer was asleep on the bed when Valerie arrived. She looked at him, removed the half-empty bottle and the glass from the bedside table, went into the bathroom, came back with a towel soaked in cold water and shook him awake.

He rubbed his eyes. 'Thank God you're here.' His hand reached out automatically.

'I did tell you not to have any more,' Valerie said. 'Here.'

She gave him the wet towel, helped him as he rubbed his face and neck, and dried him with another towel.

'Are you all right now?' Valerie asked. Cramer nodded. 'Well, listen,' Valerie said. 'And try to take it in. The reason I've been trying to reach you . . . there's some bad news. Wendy's dead.'

Cramer blinked at her uncomprehendingly. 'What?'

'She was found this morning,' Valerie said. 'Apart from trying to find you, I've spent most of the day on the phone. The children are all right, their nanny's looking after them. So far I've managed to stall the press, but . . .'

'Dead?' Cramer said vaguely. 'Why? How?'

'I've talked to the doctor,' Valerie said. 'She took an overdose. Thank God she didn't leave a note. We're saying that she's been under treatment for depression, she had a bit too much to drink last night, and it was an accident. Which it may have been for all anyone knows. But I've had to tell reporters that you didn't know yet. That I was trying to find you.'

Cramer buried his face in his hands. 'Oh, God, what a mess,' he said brokenly. 'She had to do it now, today of all days.'

'Very inconsiderate of her,' Valerie said. 'What time did this girl Nicola fall, exactly?'

'I don't know,' Cramer groaned. 'After two o'clock anyway . . . three . . . perhaps four . . . I just don't know.'

Valerie looked at her watch. It was dark outside, Cramer realised.

'It's not going to look too good,' Valerie said. 'Your wife's dead, you're out with a girl, she has an accident, and you don't report it . . .'

'They'll crucify me,' Cramer said, agonised. He gazed up at her, his eyes pleading. He was utterly shattered and beaten. 'Can you get me out of this, Val?'

'I don't know,' Valerie said. 'But if I do, you know what I'll want.' Cramer nodded dumbly. 'I believe you,' Valerie went on. 'Since you'll have no choice.'

Cramer stood up unsteadily. His eyes had located the bottle.

'No,' Valerie said sharply.

'Please,' Cramer pleaded.

'You'll have black coffee,' Valerie said. 'Then you're going to make yourself sick until there's nothing left in your guts. One of the first things I shall arrange is for a private ambulance to take you to a London clinic. And you're supposed to have collapsed from grief, not from boozing all day.'

Valerie lifted the telephone.

Valerie was in charge, unquestionably and completely in charge.

Harry Belmont liked to drive in silence when he was alone, but when he unexpectedly ran into patches of thick mist as he neared Treganwy he switched on the car radio to hear the weather report. That was when he heard about Cramer's bereavement, which was, somehow, not altogether unconnected with the search being conducted for an actress, Nicola Feary, who was still missing. Harry's foot stabbed the accelerator. He made the rest of the journey fast.

Inside the theatre he found Maurice talking to Ben Stamford and Linda.

'You'll take over John Cramer's part, Ben,' Maurice was saying. 'Linda, please God they'll find Nicola soon, and she's all right, but you'll almost certainly have to go on tonight, at least . . .'

'The show must go on,' Harry said with angry sarcasm.

'We're all worried sick,' Maurice said apologetically. 'But there's nothing we can do . . .

'How did it happen?' Harry demanded.

'I don't know, honestly,' Maurice said. 'No one seems to know anything.'

Harry went back to his car and drove to Snowdon. As he neared the mountain he could no longer hurry. Visibility was down to a few yards. Someone directed him to the Mountain Rescue Team mobile control centre.

Men were talking into radios at intermittent intervals. Nicola had not yet been found.

'It's this freak weather,' one of them explained to Harry. 'Bad it is for this time of year, and that's a fact. The bloody birds can't fly in this, let alone the helicopters. But don't you worry. We know this mountain. We'll find her soon.'

'She'll have been up there all night,' Harry said steadily. 'What are the chances?'

'Oh, not bad,' the man said. 'Not too bad at all. It's true it was a cold night, damn near freezing it was, but if she's managed to find a bit of shelter somewhere . . . usually, we know pretty well where to look,' he said, 'but in this case we don't, you see.'

Harry hung about for a while until he could bear the inactivity no longer. He set out along the path. An easy climb it might be, but after a while the muscles in his legs began to ache as he slogged upwards.

Two men from one of the teams crossed the path, heading downwards, tough, weathered, wiry men, moving effortlessly on legs of steel. Harry hailed them, grateful for the excuse to stop for a minute, explained that he was a friend of Nicola's and asked if there was anything he could do.

'There is,' one of them said. 'Don't get bloody lost, man.' He lifted his head, his nose raised high, like a dog sniffing the air. 'This lot'll begin to clear soon. Then we'll stand a better chance.'

The basis for this forecast was not clear to Harry. The damp cloud in which he was climbing was as dense as ever, and showed no signs of thinning to his eye.

Doggedly, he plodded on until he reached the summit, still shrouded in cloud. By expending a considerable amount of effort he had achieved nothing. It suddenly occurred to him what a stupid thing he had done. In the meantime, they might have found Nicola. Without thinking, he turned and began to run back down the path. It was easier going downhill, but he was tired now, and he soon slowed to a walk. Then he heard voices and the crackle of a walkie-talkie somewhere in the mist below, and he knew that she had not been discovered yet.

It was uncanny, as though she had disappeared from

the face of the earth. But she must be here somewhere. She must be. And, most tantalising and frustrating of all, not far away – although whether alive or dead, he forced himself to recognise, was another matter.

He had been descending for about fifteen or twenty minutes when the prophet's prediction began to materialise. For no apparent reason the cloud began to swirl and lift, and although it was still above and below, encasing him in a kind of cocoon of mist, Harry found that he could see twenty or thirty yards.

Nicola must have been walking along this path . . . although she might not have got this far. He stopped, considering whether to go back, but remembered the voices and the bark of walkie-talkies. They were further up, and the lifting cloud would have reached them by this time. The search would gather pace now.

Harry continued down, walking slowly, his eyes searching the steep slopes below as far as he could see.

His gaze was not focused close to the path and he almost missed it. The realisation came when he had passed, and he turned back. He swallowed in sudden nervous excitement. It might be nothing . . . probably just a small stone . . . but he slid carefully over the edge, and inched down until he could reach it. He picked it up and looked at it.

'Here!' he bellowed. 'Here!' shouting over and over again.

It seemed like an hour, but was probably no more than thirty seconds, before he heard the running boots coming down the path. They saw him, and came down as rapidly and sure-footedly as mountain goats.

'I gave her an amber necklace last Christmas,' Harry explained. He showed them the small amber bead. 'It was lying just here. I happened to see it.'

At once they were gone. Harry followed, slipping and sliding. Even so, knowing she must be nearby, it was minutes before they found her. She was in a small gully and it was almost impossible to see her body, except from directly above. Her head was wedged between two jagged rocks. Dried blood caked her face and matted her hair.

They handled her with gentle care, speaking urgently into their walkie-talkies, receiving squawks in reply which were incomprehensible to Harry.

Harry stared helplessly at her inert form.

'She can't be dead,' he said. 'She's not dead, is she?'

# CHAPTER ELEVEN

'Concussion and exposure,' the doctor said. 'She's a lucky girl. The fact that she fell into that gully protected her, to some extent, from the worst effects of exposure. But she's young and strong. She'll soon recover. Apart from that, quite severe facial contusions, fractured cheek-bone, broken nose, but nothing that won't mend.'

'She's an actress,' Harry told him.

The doctor said, 'In that case, I expect she may like to consider a little surgery later on, if her face is her fortune, as you might say.' He smiled whimsically, in a friendly way, and glanced abstractedly at his watch.

'Can I see her?' Harry asked.

'Not today,' the doctor said, and hurried off.

Harry walked back into Casualty and found a telephone. He put through a call to his office telling his secretary that he would not be back for a few days.

Professor Griffiths was on his nightly patrol from the box office to his own office, where he intended to pore over the pleasing details of the takings, when his attention was captured by an unusual noise from the auditorium which took him aback – a deep-throated roar of laughter. The Professor frowned, eased his way carefully through the nearest door, and stood at the back of the stalls where he watched with growing concern and displeasure.

All the media coverage concerning Cramer had done the Treganwy Festival no harm at all. In fact there had been an additional flood of advance bookings, proving perhaps the accuracy of the old adage that there is no such thing as bad publicity. There had been no cancellations, and the theatre was packed, which was excellent of course. But the whole atmosphere had changed. The audience might have been watching a different play. The respectful silence, broken only by the occasional half-hearted titter, with which they had received John Cramer, had gone. Tonight the play was punctuated by delighted belly laughs.

Ben Stamford's interpretation was totally different to Cramer's. The Stephen on stage tonight was no bitter, tormented, if virile man, savaged by self-knowledge of his betrayal of his own talents. Ben's Stephen was ambivalent and mocking, using sarcastic wit as a defence, only allowing his anguish to peep through, poignantly, in the final scene.

Professor Griffiths could see that, within the performance, Ben Stamford relished the enjoyment he was generating, and was milking every possible laugh line to the limit.

The Professor's distaste grew by the minute. He had never found anything especially funny in this play, and the surly bravura of Cramer's interpretation had amply confirmed his opinion. Besides, as a great actor, Cramer's must be the definitive version, which should be treated with respect, not stood on its head and cheapened by all this rollicking laughter.

The Professor determined to have some very sharp words indeed with Maurice Gardiner and instruct him to restore the play to its original form. Then he remembered that, after his talk with Cramer, he had decided to terminate Maurice's contract. That would mean his assistant taking over, who would certainly be pliable, but was inexperienced . . . and after tonight, Ben Stamford would have the bit between his teeth. It would take a strong hand to curb him. Someone of repute could be imported, of course, but a strong director at short notice would come expensive, Professor Griffiths thought gloomily.

As he sipped a worried brandy in the bar after the show he found Dr Morgan at his elbow. The Professor summoned up a warm and friendly greeting. Morgan was a staunch supporter of the Festival, and his services as company doctor were deeply valued by Professor

Griffiths, since they mostly came free. Dr Morgan had attended the first night and the ensuing soirée, but had come again, he explained, to escort his elderly aunt, who was at present ensconced in the Ladies.

'Glad I did, now, I must say,' Dr Morgan said. 'Interesting, the comparison, I thought.'

'Very interesting,' Professor Griffiths said with feeling.

'Enjoyed it much more as a play, to tell you the truth,' Dr Morgan said. 'John Cramer was riveting, of course, the way he played Stephen – like a man suffering from acute emotional stress and anxiety.' Dr Morgan felt that he could safely go that far without betraying any professional confidences. He was rather curious about the events on Snowdon, the reports of which seemed to him to be surprisingly sketchy. He had the feeling there was a good deal that someone was not saying, although he supposed he would never know if such was the case or not. 'But somehow,' Dr Morgan went on, 'Cramer didn't seem to relate to the other actors. He wasn't talking *to* them. He was just talking. Whereas Ben Stamford belonged in that set-up, and because he made me laugh in the end there was more pathos. I felt closer to him. I cared about him.'

'Really,' Professor Griffiths said.

'A very shrewd piece of re-thinking, if I may say so,' Dr Morgan said. 'It makes it another play, of course, but a more commercial one, I'd say.'

'Do you think so?' Professor Griffiths enquired.

'Definitely,' Dr Morgan said. 'The audience had a good time tonight, they were enjoying the play – even without a star name. Nicola Feary's a great loss, mind you. A highly accomplished actress, that lady. But once she's back, I think you'll have a production that will be popular, and could make a lot of money.'

The phrase was one which Professor Griffiths always found irresistibly musical. 'Let me get you another drink,' he suggested cordially.

'Thank you,' Dr Morgan said. 'Ah, here's my aunt now. . .'

Professor Griffiths sat up late that night, thinking hard.

Dr Morgan, it was true, for all his love of the theatre, was no more than an enthusiastic amateur. On the other hand he was a fairly typical member of any theatre audience, the all-important people who handed over their cash at the box office. Besides, bearing in mind the reaction of tonight's audience. . .

Suppose . . . just suppose . . . Morgan was right. It would cost nothing to ask a reputable touring management to look at the play as it stood. A successful tour, say thirteen weeks around the provinces, could generate a lot of cash. Professor Griffiths was a realist. If a play could make money for the Festival, it mattered not if he disliked it personally. And if a tour could be negotiated . . . he pondered . . . it would certainly be more economic to retain Maurice Gardiner than to replace him . . . the Professor had been swayed by Cramer, but the cost of a clean sweep had always bothered him . . . well-known television actors who would be a draw were prone to demand a percentage of the box office before agreeing to do a tour, an attitude which Professor Griffiths found highly offensive . . . the present cast on the other hand could all be held to the previously agreed and comparatively modest touring fees . . . Linda would have to be replaced, she was too inexperienced to play Mary on tour . . . but presumably Nicola Feary would have recovered by then . . . Professor Griffiths still could not imagine what other people saw in the girl, but they seemed to think she was good . . . and she would certainly be cheap . . .

When Professor Griffiths went to bed, he slept peacefully and well. It seemed more than possible that things might be working out to the distinct advantage of the Treganwy Festival Theatre after all.

Valerie Foster did a nearly perfect job, fortuitously aided by the fact that the last thing Nicola could remember was riding in the train up Snowdon. By the time she had recalled what had actually happened in detail it was months later, and no one cared any more.

With a clear field, Valerie dextrously transposed one or

two times and events. John Cramer, she said at the press conference she had called, was naturally prostrate with grief, due to his wife's tragic and accidental death, and was unable to speak to anyone. Moreover, he would be flying to France for his wife's funeral and to be with his small children. However, she had managed to ascertain from him what had taken place . . .

They listened attentively and took notes, and asked a few questions, but not too many. Valerie laid more stress on Cramer's deep shock at the death of the wife he had adored than on the events on Snowdon.

The public learned that Cramer, with a fellow member of the cast, was descending the mountain when she accidentally slipped and fell in conditions of appalling visibility. Cramer spent hours, at considerable risk to his own safety, in searching for her. Realising that he must get help, he returned to his car and drove to the hotel, where he had telephoned at once.

Why had he phoned Valerie, instead of the emergency number? He was not *positive,* Valerie pointed out, that Miss Feary was hurt. She might have regained the path without Cramer knowing it, become tired of waiting, and made her way home – where she was not on the telephone. Cramer had intended to ask Valerie to make certain she was missing, but had then received the news of his wife's death.

Stunned, he rang off in a state of collapse, believing that a search for Nicola would be under way. But Valerie had misunderstood him. It was not until she reached the hotel that she realised . . . it was all her fault . . . which accounted for the delay.

It came out as a tragic episode in which Cramer had satisfyingly played the expected heroic role, and in any case Nicola was not seriously hurt, whereas Cramer's wife was dead. That was by far the bigger news, and the public responded with warm sympathy for Cramer in his heart-breaking loss.

Not quite everyone was satisfied. Dr Morgan raised a sceptical eyebrow over his morning newspaper, but then his special knowledge could never be shared.

In Fleet Street Vincent Consel said to his editor, 'I detect the faint aroma of stinking fish.' His editor told him that he had a thing about John Cramer, and to forget it. Besides, Consel was leaving on one of his agreeably expense-laden trips, to Hawaii this time, where a star-studded movie was being made. Vincent Consel forgot it.

Nicola put on a brave front, but Harry Belmont was shocked, although he did his best to conceal it, when he was allowed to see her – or at least as much of her as her bandaged face would allow. A nurse had placed the flowers he had brought into a vase.

'I always did fancy a nose job,' Nicola said. 'Perhaps it's a blessing in disguise.'

'A pretty heavy disguise,' Harry said. 'There was nothing wrong with your nose the way it was before.'

'A friend of mine had one done, and it was marvellous,' Nicola said. 'I'll find out who did it and go to him. I must have it done as soon as possible, though. Maurice rang. He thinks there'll be a tour, starting in September, finishing the week before Christmas. They're hoping to get the author to do some re-writes so that the part will fit Marcia better. Maurice said Ben Stamford's bringing the house down every night. With any luck, I should look all right again by September.'

'I'm sure you will,' Harry said. 'So then you'll be off again, living out of suitcases.'

'The money's lousy, but at least it's work,' Nicola said. 'I could probably get out of it, if something better came up in the meantime.'

'Well, let's hope it does,' Harry said.

'Harry,' Nicola said thoughtfully. 'Do you think I shall ever make it as an actress? Really make it I mean? The name in lights in the West End, all that bit?'

'Of course you will,' Harry said. 'Why?'

'Someone told me I wouldn't,' Nicola said.

'Take no notice,' Harry said. 'You're better than any of them.'

Nicola said, 'The trouble is, you don't know good acting from bad.'

'Oh, God, let's not start that again,' Harry said. 'Listen,

the doctor thinks you'll be discharged early next week. I may as well hang on, and then I could drive you back to London.'

'What about your work?' Nicola protested. 'The bank'd raise hell.'

'At the moment they think the sun shines from the appropriate portion of my anatomy, so I may as well take advantage,' Harry said. 'They've given me a rise and a fat bonus. So we'll do that. O.K.?'

'What shall I do about my lovely cottage? I signed an agreement.'

'I'll arrange something with the owners,' Harry said. 'Don't worry about that. Anyway, you'll have to get back to London if you want your nose done quickly. You could stay with me,' he said carelessly. 'At least, until you've had the operation, and sorted yourself out.'

'Perhaps we both need sorting out,' Nicola said. 'Harry, you can't go through life always looking backwards. Or perhaps you can, but if so, I don't want to know.'

'In the end, it's always you,' Harry said quietly.

Nicola stared at him. There might have been a small smile on her lips, but it was hard to tell. 'I don't remember anything about it,' she said, 'but they told me it was you who found me.'

'Not really,' Harry said. 'I was there, that's all.'

'You were there,' Nicola said. 'That's what matters. I could have died. I know about the amber beads. They told me all of it. To think, if I hadn't decided to wear that necklace you gave me. . .'

Wishing for a period of seclusion after his terrible bereavement, John Cramer withdrew from the Broadway production of *Last Rites for Beresford,* although he did allow himself to be prevailed upon to sign a contract to star in the film version later. Everyone sympathised.

Much of his period of seclusion was spent at a luxurious establishment south of Paris, a clinic, where he was dried out. Valerie Foster visited him frequently. She was relieved by his ready acceptance when she suggested that this discreet clinic would be a sensible idea. She had been prepared to be very firm indeed, but it was not necessary. She was slightly surprised by his docility. But she did not mind. She had always known that Cramer would have to be tamed. She had no intention of becoming another Wendy or, even worse, another Denise.

On sunny days Cramer sat in the grounds, sipping a glass of fresh orange juice. He had lost just enough weight to flatten his stomach, and while his face was a little leaner, it suited him, as Valerie told him. Cramer nodded without much interest. He answered her questions, but otherwise sat in a self-enclosed silence.

Valerie brought the revised screenplay of *Last Rites for Beresford*. Cramer read it. She expected him to produce a sheaf of notes, but he had none.

'Shall I say you approve it?' she asked.

'It'll do,' Cramer said. He yawned, stretched, and studied his orange juice.

'It won't be for much longer,' Valerie said. 'I expect you're getting bored.'

'Not really,' Cramer said.

'What do you do with yourself when I'm not here?'

'Not much,' Cramer said. 'Think, mostly, I suppose.'

'Planning your next novel? You could start writing it.'

Cramer shook his head. 'I've abandoned that,' he said. 'It was going to be about a woman who was always threatening to commit suicide, and never did it. Events have rather decapitated that idea.'

'You'll think of another one,' Valerie said.

Cramer's head turned in her direction. He was wearing sunglasses. She could not see his eyes. 'I sometimes wonder what you'd have done,' he said, 'if Wendy hadn't made one hysterical gesture too many, and miscalculated. You couldn't have anticipated that.'

'I always tried to make you treat her decently,' Valerie said with a trace of asperity.

'You wouldn't have given up, though,' Cramer said, from behind the blank sunglasses. 'I've realised that. So I occasionally reflect, just out of interest, about what other possibilities you might have had in mind.' He yawned again. 'Not that it matters much.'

'You don't have to go through with it,' Valerie said. 'All you have to do is to ring the newspapers and tell them the truth.'

'Yes, that's true,' Cramer said. He laughed, directing his amusement at the clear blue sky above. 'That's all I have to do.'

The following spring, in Los Angeles, USA, John Cramer was married to Miss Valerie Foster, his former secretary, who had been a close friend of his wife, Wendy Cramer, before her untimely death.

It was an especially happy occasion for everybody. With the exception of his daughter all Cramer's children were present, including his two teenage sons by his first wife, who would be making their home with their father from now on. Cramer had bought and furnished a big family house for all of them in Beverly Hills. The new Mrs Cramer was delighted. She loved each one of Cramer's children, although, she shyly revealed, she expected to bear him some herself.

By common consent, *Last Rites for Beresford* was not only a smash hit, but the outstanding movie of the year. It attracted nominations for several Academy Awards. John Cramer received an Oscar as Best Actor.

His acceptance speech was moving in its simple, almost stumbling brevity, and Valerie shed tears of unashamed pride and happiness. Her husband had finally received the artistic recognition he so richly deserved, and she floated through the ceremony on a cloud of joy.

That night Cramer disappeared. When he was finally found in an anonymous motel room in New Mexico he was unshaven, unwashed, and had been drinking for a week.

Valerie stared at the dirty, haggard, middle-aged man with the red-rimmed eyes lying on the bed. 'What in God's name has got into you?' she demanded. She tried to keep her anger under control. 'Why do this? You've got everything. You're one of the best actors in the world. You've proved it. What more do you want?'

'Nothing,' Cramer said. 'Not a thing.' He pointed unsteadily at his Oscar, which was standing on the dressing table. 'Give me a first-class director, an outstanding cameraman, dozens of takes when I get the words wrong, and a slick editor who knows just what to leave on the cutting-room floor, and I'm a star, by God, and not only that, a great actor, and there's the proof.' He sat up, hugged his knees, and began to rock to and fro, shaking with helpless laughter. 'John Cramer, great actor, that's me. The best Hamlet for decades, they all said so. Mind you, put me on my own these days, and I can't do it any more, I'm not even good, even in some shitty little dump in the heart of nowhere. But that's no problem. Just spend enough millions of dollars, and I'm great. That's me. Great.' His laughter died away, and he fell silent.

He was not just drunk, Valerie thought, he was raving. Her mouth tight, she lifted the telephone. Cramer, staring absently into space, ignored her. She ordered a private ambulance and arranged for his admission into a clinic. Then she busied herself in concocting a suitable story which could be released to the press.

It occurred to Valerie Cramer, née Foster, that she had done this before.

**EYE OF THE NEEDLE**

**Ken Follett**

'Top notch thriller, as gripping and persuasive as THE DAY OF THE JACKAL'
Ira Levin, author of THE BOYS FROM BRAZIL

His weapon is the stiletto, his codename, THE NEEDLE. He is Henry Faber, coldly professional, a killer, Germany's most feared deep-cover agent in Britain. His task: to discover the Allies' plans for D-Day, and get them to Germany at all costs. A task he ruthlessly carries through until Storm Island and the woman called Lucy.

'An absolutely terrific thriller, so pulse-pounding, so ingenious in its plotting and so frighteningly realistic that you simply cannot stop reading'
*Publishers Weekly*

'A tense, marvellously detailed suspense thriller built on a solid foundation of fact'
*Sunday Times*

**THE SPIKE**

**Arnaud de Borchgrave and Robert Moss**

The sensational novel by two top investigative reporters that exposes the sinister truth of KGB manipulation of the Western media. A story so explosive it can only be told as fiction.

'The first thing to say about this book is that it is a tour de force. An unexpected bonus is that they tell their tale so grippingly, with such verve and with – what is rare in this kind of thriller – such humanity.'
*Daily Telegraph*

'de Borchgrave and Moss have concocted a thriller that is several steps ahead of the headlines. These men have scouted the real underworld of espionage and counter espionage, have listened to real spies and defectors. You sense their expertise on every page.'
*John Barkman*

**FIRST STRIKE**

**Douglas Terman**

Douglas Terman joins the ranks of the world's most exciting thriller writers with this adventure novel of an ex-fighter pilor caught up in a Soviet scheme to paralyse America's defences before launching an all out nuclear attack.

In a plot packed with twists and surprises FIRST STRIKE combines a nightmarish scenario of the future with some of the most enthralling flying sequences ever put on paper.

'Agonisingly intense'
*Wall Street Journal*

'Enough to scare the eyeballs out of any reader . . . a winner'
*Ernest K Gann*

All Futura Books are available at your bookshop or newsagent, or can be ordered from the following address:
Futura Books, Cash Sales Department,
P.O. Box 11, Falmouth, Cornwall.

Please send cheque or postal order (no currency), and allow 45p for postage and packing for the first book plus 20p for the second book and 14p for each additional book ordered up to a maximum charge of £1.63 in U.K.

Customers in Eire and B.F.P.O. please allow 45p for the first book, 20p for the second book plus 14p per copy for the next 7 books, thereafter 8p per book.

Overseas customers please allow 75p for postage and packing for the first book and 21p per copy for each additional book.